THE SPIRIT PATH

ALSO BY KATHERINE GENET

The Wilde Grove Series

The Gathering

The Belonging

The Rising

The Singing

The North Star

Wilde Grove Series 2

Follow The Wind

The Otherworld

Golden Heart

Wilde Grove Prayer Books

Prayers Of The Wildwood

Prayers Of The Beacons

Wilde Grove Bonus Stories

Becoming Morghan

The Threading

Non-Fiction

Ground & Centre

The Spirit Path

KATHERINE GENET

Wych Elm Books

Wych Elm Books

Otago, NZ

www.wychelmbooks.com

contact@wychelmbooks.com

ISBN: 978-1- 7386247-1-3

For Sheena, who introduced me to the Great Queen.

1

SOME SAY IT IS THE JOURNEY THAT MATTERS, NOT THE destination. That you must live your life fast and furious, accumulating experiences and possessions, so that you arrive at your own graveside howling with laughter, spitting in the face of death.

I, Ravenna, Priestess of the Ancient Way, am here to tell you that the journey determines the destination, and that where you end up when your flesh has spent its time and fallen away, is of the utmost importance.

We have stood here before, on the cliff of the Summer Isle, staring out over the stretch of water between the eternal land and our own. Do you remember? We are the Ladies and Lords of Life and Death, of the Wilderness, and we hold in our cupped hands the eggs of our own souls.

Morghan looks at me, then lowers her gaze to the shore, where the boats are still bringing the dead from your land, just as they were a turn of the sun ago, a hundred turns of the sun.

With a light touch on my arm, she takes us there, to coarse sand under our feet, and she steps forward to help the souls, lost, now found, from their small round boats, holding them tenderly as they find their footing, then watching with reverence - as I watch her - as each of our new refugees are handed an egg.

An egg for the soul.

When I look at Morghan again, there are tears coursing down her cheeks, and when she sees me, her face sets, becomes stubborn, and with another touch, we are elsewhere once more, standing atop her tor, and I, Ravenna, am once more at her side, while Catrin takes the other.

Morghan stands between us, staring out over the darkening view, eyes fixed on the pinpricks of gold, and her chest heaves with emotion. A swift movement, and she is stepping forward, bringing out her arms, letting her light shine, a beacon to you all.

And how she shines, bright and fierce with all the love for the world that lives inside her. She burns with it as we watch, brighter and fiercer.

Bright and fierce.

2

———

CLARICE SLIPPED HER SUNGLASSES BACK ON AND SHOOK HER head at Krista. 'You don't really want one of these, do you?' she whispered.

Krista's mouth twitched but she tamped down the smile that wanted to come. 'One of what?' she asked instead, feigning innocence.

Clarice narrowed her eyes behind the sunglasses and scanned the small faces looking up at them at Ladybird Lane Daycare Centre. 'You know,' she said. 'One of these mini-mes. Except it would be a mini-you, of course.' She sniffed and watched as one child concentrated intently to pull on bear paw mittens to match the ears he already wore.

Okay, she thought. So that was kinda cute.

'Ah,' Krista said and now she did let herself smile. 'Are they so bad?'

'Possibly not,' Clarice agreed grudgingly. 'But they're very small.'

Clarice's appalled tone made Krista laugh, rocking back on her heels.

'What's so funny?' Erin said, coming with Clover to join them.

'Clarice is discombobulated by the size of the children.'

Erin was confused, looked around at the gaggle of kids being herded onto the patio ready for the blessing ceremony. They'd done several of these sorts of ceremonies in the last five months since the world had discovered Wilde Grove, thanks to the Trafalgar Square videos.

'What's odd about that?' she asked. 'They're kids.'

'I like kids,' Clover said. 'They still have faith in the world.'

'Krista wants to have a baby,' Clarice said, her lips comically puckered as though she'd sucked on a piece of sour candy and was unable to decide if she liked it or not.

Erin's eyes widened. 'A baby?' She glanced around. 'You tell me this now? How am I supposed to concentrate now?' She grinned suddenly. 'Wow. A baby.' She poked Krista on the arm. 'You're going to tell us all about this after we're done here.'

They turned as Ginger, the daycare owner, came towards them, and they let her manoeuvre them into position. Clarice put aside all question of babies and the unnatural smallness of children as she stood in a loose semi-circle with Erin, Clover, and Krista. She paid attention to her breathing as she listened to Ginger Lowry talking about the garden, how good and necessary it was that the children, even as young as these were, be able to learn about growing food. Children needed once more to learn the cycles of life that grew from the soil and how to tend to those, and afterwards, to enjoy the bounty of food that came from that tending.

Clarice smiled. Here was a woman with her head on straight, she thought.

She tried to ignore the chanting from outside on the street.

Ginger nodded to the assembled group of parents and children. They'd had quite the turnout, despite the wet and cold weather. Not just the mums, but plenty of dads too.

She blew out a breath. More kids stayed enrolled than were removed because of this blessing. That was good. Unfortunate that some had left. Good that more had stayed.

And she, Ginger, proud owner of Ladybird Lane Daycare, had to do things the way she thought was right.

Trouble was - everyone thought they were right, didn't they?

Her gaze flicked over two-year-old Robbie in his bear paws and ears, and his mum Rowan, and stuttered a moment. Those two, she thought suddenly to herself even while she continued with her prepared speech.

Those two needed help.

She paused, then smiled and gestured to the Wilde Grove priestesses come to give their humble garden a blessing.

Erin took a small step forward. 'We are so glad to be here with you today,' she said, and beamed at the small crowd, most of whom were gazing at them with astonishment - and that included the parents

Television, she thought. The internet. This was what came from going viral.

Everything had changed since then. She caught the sound of the crowd outside on the street.

And not all for the better.

'There is almost nothing we like better than a garden,' she continued, making sure her voice carried the way that Morghan had taught her. 'Because gardens are all about flourishing, and here you all are, set to flourish, as families and as community.' She took a breath and inclined her head to address the children specifically now. 'We are here to help you say thank you to the land that your garden is on, that your garden is made of. To sing a prayer to it, letting it know that you will be looking after it, so that it might look after you in return, as is the proper way of things.'

She glanced at Clarice, and then at Krista, nodding at them, and they moved to stand relaxed and glad beside the newly dug beds that would become the children's garden. Then she moved back a step again so that Clover could work her unseen magic.

Unseen by most, that was, but Erin, taking that sideways step that broadened her sight, watching as Clover lifted her arms and the web of the world brightened around her.

She had said the chant *world to world to world* often now, but Clover's presence in her life had made Erin wonder if perhaps the chant was not quite right, because when Clover worked her magic, all the worlds were one, very deep and very wide, and vibrant with life.

Erin's mouth twitched into a smile, even while her heart stuttered a moment, as she saw a small gnome sitting on one of the rocks, looking most interestedly at the goings-on.

Of course, she thought. Of course there would be gnomes in a children's garden. She wondered how many of the children, after this was done, would be telling their parents they'd seen a gnome. More than one, she'd bet.

But it was rude to stare at the fellow, and she had a task to perform, so she turned her gaze away, and began the prayer of blessing.

This is the land on which we live,
The land that we love and share.
This is our promise to the spirits of this place,
That we will tend this earth with love and grace.
We give, that we might receive.
We receive, that we might give again.

AFTERWARDS, EACH CHILD, WITH THEIR PARENTS, PLANTED something in the garden. Cabbages, carrots, broccoli, the children's hands growing sticky and dark with soil.

Erin, along with the others, helped, smiling over the tiny seedlings, telling the children not to forget to talk to the plants, tell them how well they were growing, how mighty they were.

Fortunately, the garden and play area were at the back of the building. The chanting from the crowd on the street - Erin wondered how big it was now - could barely be heard from back where they were.

She was glad that Ginger had not allowed the TV cameras in. It was bad enough the parents were videoing everything on their phones.

She and Clover washed their hands and accepted the cup of tea on offer once the planting was done.

'I hope it stops raining long enough for something to

actually grow,' Ginger said. 'We're thinking we'll have to put a shelter up over the garden if it keeps up like this.'

'Do you have rain tanks, to collect the water?' Clover asked. She'd been helping Stephan organise setting up just such tanks at the community gardens.

Ginger nodded. 'Not that we need them right now, but at least the frosts have stopped. Perhaps the weather will turn soon enough.' She grimaced. 'Then we'll probably have a heat wave.' She blew out a breath between pursed lips, and turned to look over the children, most of whom had returned to their regular play, their knees damp with dirt their parents had tried in vain to brush off.

'What sort of world are they going to grow up in?' she asked, then grimaced. 'I'm sorry. I didn't mean to think those words out loud.'

'It's all right,' Clover said and nodded. 'They're going to grow up into a world we're doing our very best to improve.' She paused, but only for the briefest moment. 'Thank you for this,' she said. 'For inviting us here to do this today. It makes such a big difference.'

Erin agreed.

Ginger looked at them. 'Does it?' she asked. 'I mean, does it really make a difference?'

Clover and Erin glanced at each other. They were getting used to this. Being asked more and more to come and spread their blessings over land, over buildings, over gatherings of people, at least in Banwell, but oftentimes farther away too.

Usually those ones were turned down, but more people all over the place were doing the new Wilde Grove training to become Beacons and Well-Keepers, so eventually, Clover hoped, there would always be someone local to do the blessings.

Not that the establishment – the churches – were very pleased about that. Clover tried to ignore the shouting from outside, on the street.

She and the others always got questions, though. Being asked to reassure that it really was something they were doing, and that it was helpful. That it was real.

That it made a difference.

Clover wished everyone could see what she did, the way the world responded to their care and acknowledgment.

Although perhaps not quite to the same extent that she could. Not everyone needed that.

'Yes,' she said now to Ginger. 'It does, really.'

Ginger gazed at her, then nodded. 'I believe that,' she said. She laughed without much humour. 'I mean, I have to believe that, or it would be too easy to give up, to say, why bother, we've ruined things, gone too far, there's nothing we can do about it.'

But she looked around at where she was, at the children playing, giggling together. She shook her head. 'But I can't think like that, because of the children. They deserve all our efforts. I want them to grow up into a world that welcomes them, not a husk of a thing that we ruined with our greed.'

She flushed. 'Sorry,' she said, and heaved a breath. 'It's easy to get upset. I just want it to not be hopeless.'

'It isn't hopeless,' Erin said, and touched Ginger's sleeve. 'There's everything we can do about it.' She'd noticed this was what more people were saying now. A trend toward not denying climate change anymore, but saying there was nothing that they could do about it.

There was always something that could be done.

'Well, I know that we can't quit,' Ginger said, interrupting her thoughts. 'Or we're giving up on them.' She swept a hand around at the children who rushed to and fro, their laughter drowning out the sudden spring rain that began hammering down once more on the roof.

That in turn drowned out the protesting crowd outside.

3

'I'M SORRY THERE ISN'T A WAY TO AVOID THEM,' GINGER SAID.

'Did you lose many enrolments?' Krista asked.

Ginger's frown deepened. 'A few,' she admitted. 'But you saw the turnout today - most of the parents are curious, figure at the very least it's not doing any harm.'

Krista nodded, looked out the window at the crowd that jostled each other, mouths angry slashes in faces shining with righteousness, despite the rain.

When they'd first started these public blessings for smaller events, only two priestesses used to go along. Now, Morghan insisted all four went.

Safety in numbers.

'Well,' Clarice said. 'I guess we'd better do this.'

'I'm so sorry,' Ginger repeated.

Krista touched her on the shoulder. Lightly, just for a moment. 'Don't be,' she said. 'Thank you for inviting us along. We're glad you did.'

Ginger nodded, stepped back to open the door. 'Thank you,' she said. 'It was really brilliant having you here.'

Erin stepped first out of the door. She resisted the urge to duck and run, and instead simply paused on the stoop, gazing out at the crowd, keeping her features serene, holding her energy still and contained around her, so that the ugliness of the crowd didn't touch her.

She was getting used to this.

What did that say about things?

The others stepped out beside her and paused. The crowd went quiet, as though they were all suddenly engaged in a stand-off.

Erin made herself look at the faces staring back at her. They were the same crowd as always.

Maybe even a few less of them. Maybe.

Or maybe, since this was a weekday morning, that didn't mean anything.

A woman screamed suddenly at her, stretching her arms out, making the sign of the cross with her index fingers.

'Daughters of Satan!'

THEY LOCKED THE CAR DOORS AFTER GETTING IN, NONE OF them mentioning the action but doing it anyway. Erin got the Mini moving, forcing the clustering protesters to part around them.

Clover spied one of the Banwell police officers standing watching them. 'They don't do anything,' she said.

'Who?' Krista asked.

'The police.'

They were silent then, waiting until they were on the road back to Wellsford before moving and talking.

'Well,' Erin said, then glanced in the rear vision mirror at Clarice and Krista. She forced a smile that turned real a moment later. 'A baby?'

Krista laughed. 'You sound as bewildered as Clarice.'

Erin shook her head. 'No,' she said. 'Of course not. I think it's an incredible idea.' She looked at Clarice, her face for once not hidden behind dark sunglasses. But Clarice was gazing out the window.

The window wipers swished away the rain.

'What about you?' Krista asked. 'Stephan would make a doting dad.'

'Oh, wouldn't he though?' Erin smiled as she thought about it. 'We're not even close to being ready for that. There's too much to do.'

Everyone was silent for another minute and the rain sluiced down onto the car.

'I'm in my 30s,' Krista said at last. 'I guess the maternal drive has kicked into gear, because I can't stop thinking about it.' She looked out the side window, saw nothing except rain against the glass. 'Even with everything going on, I still want it.'

CLOVER OPTED TO WALK FROM THE VILLAGE UP THROUGH THE woods to Hawthorn House. The trees would give her a measure of shelter, but she didn't care if she got wet; she just needed to walk the ancient paths, feel the steadiness of the trees around her.

She was doing okay with the public events, even

managing to have coherent conversations with people, despite the noise and images that clamoured against her. She'd been working with Morghan on turning the dial down, so that she could function just a tiny bit easier. It seemed to be working.

But it was hard, like holding a cork in a bottle while the pressure built up.

And the protesters outside every event didn't help.

She stepped into the woods and touched the nearest tree, leaning her forehead against its damp bark.

'You're lucky to be a tree,' she whispered. 'So deeply rooted, only the wind to sway you.' She closed her eyes and imagined the tree's roots spread all around in the earth. Woven in and out with all the other trees in a network. A community.

She had community. She was deeply rooted, growing stronger all the time. She had work to do. Important work to do.

'Clover?'

There was a touch on her arm.

'Are you all right?'

Clover lifted her head. 'I didn't hear you coming.' She hesitated. 'Or feel you.'

Morghan smiled. 'Only because you were occupied in talking to the tree.'

The comment made Clover smile. 'I was feeling sorry for myself. That I wasn't born with bark and branch and leaf.'

Morghan put an arm around Clover's shoulders, turned her back towards the path. 'Well,' she said. 'We must bear our burdens with grace. Being a tree would have its pleasures, but alas, it was not our fate.'

Clover laughed, let her feet carry her freely along the path that led up the hill towards the house.

'How did it go today?' Morghan asked.

'At the daycare centre?' Clover hunched her shoulders for a moment then made herself relax. 'There was a surprising turnout, actually. A lot of the parents made the effort to come for it.'

Morghan nodded, pulled her hood up tighter as the rain chilled.

'And the atmosphere?' she asked.

Clover took her time answering, giving the question her consideration. She and Morghan had been having these little talks after events. Clover had come to think of them as their debriefs.

'A lot of curiosity, I think,' she said. 'As usual, hoping to see us doing something weird and spectacular. More than half of them had their phones out recording it.' Clover wrinkled her nose. 'But the curiosity is good, right? And there were a few who actually seemed to be really into it.'

Morghan nodded. A few were better than none.

'But once the ceremony was done, I could feel that the majority of the parents went back to their usual train of thoughts – houses, jobs, cars, worrying about money or if they didn't have to worry about it, then thinking about how to spend it.' Clover shook her head. 'We've got a hard road ahead of us,' she said. 'It's like people's attention spans don't have the bandwidth.'

She paused. 'That's not fair, really. The problem is what you and I just keep coming back to, isn't it? People don't really believe in the soul anymore. Not as something they absolutely need to consider the well-being of.' She sighed. 'I keep thinking of my vision of the future,' she said. 'I can't stop thinking about it. That it's what we're heading to.' She glanced over at Morghan. 'How do we keep going, when that's where we're heading?'

'The future is fluid,' Morghan said. 'What you saw may not be what comes.' She paused. 'And the protesters?'

'All the usual were there,' Clover said, pressed her lips together.

She frowned. 'Morghan?'

Morghan turned and looked at her. Saw the serious expression on her face. 'What is it?'

'I don't think I'm doing the right thing,' Clover answered.

'What do you mean?'

Clover shook her head. 'I mean, going and doing the public stuff with the others. In some ways, I love it, and I love how we're working together doing something that's really important...'

'But?'

'But it doesn't feel right. I don't think it's a good fit, even with all the work we've been doing, trying to get me able to turn the, you know, the volume down.' Clover frowned down at her feet as they trod the same paths that priestesses of the Grove had been walking for thousands of years.

Finally, she looked over at Morghan. 'I think we have it all back to front – when it comes to me, at least, and why I'm still here when Rue and Selena and Ebony have gone back home.'

Morghan considered her for a moment before nodding. 'Tell me,' she said. 'I'm listening.'

'We speak about stepping onto our soul's path,' Clover began, feeling around for the right words to tell Morghan something that so far she hadn't figured out how to express to herself. 'Well, sure, my soul's path was to bring forth Rhian's knowledge into this life, right?'

'True.'

'But I've done that, so it's like, now what? All this for that? I mean, I'm only twenty years old, there are a lot of years left, if I've already done the main job, you know?'

Morghan nodded, folding her hands together under her cloak and listening for a moment to the sound of rain on the leaves.

'I do know,' she said at last, glancing at Clover's upturned and serious face. 'I've had similar thoughts about myself, but your case is even more...pronounced, being as young as you are.'

'You thought the same thing about yourself?' Clover burnt with sudden curiosity.

'I thought, after Grainne died, that my purpose was played out.'

Clover looked down at the soil under her boots again. 'I miss her,' she said. 'Grainne. It must be terrible for you.'

Morghan smiled, tipped her head up and felt the moisture on her face. 'Yes,' she said. 'It is terrible, and yet also not. I miss her, but I know the separation is only temporary.' She sighed. 'Grainne has gone on ahead, that is all.'

Clover hesitated, then asked her question. 'Do you dream about her?' She looked off into the leafy depths of the woods. 'Every so often I dream about my mother, but I

never really see her in the dreams. She's just this warm presence every now and then.'

'Sometimes,' Morghan said. 'Sometimes, I do.' She
paused, then turned the conversation around. 'So, then. If
your purpose continues, where do you think it leads you?'

Clover winced, glanced sideways at Morghan. 'Is it okay
if I think that my purpose isn't to help the others with the
public blessings?'

'Yes,' Morghan said.

Clover waited for more, but that simple yes was all she
got. She nodded, took a breath. 'Here's my thinking,' she
said, as they arrived finally at the edge of the lawn at the
rear of Hawthorn House and paused, still under the shelter
of the trees.

'Go on,' Morghan said.

'Well.' Clover flushed, glancing at Morghan's face, at her
calm eyes. 'I don't want to sound stuck up.'

'Stuck up?' Morghan's eyebrows rose and she laughed.
'Clover. If you are about to speak of your particular gifts and
talents, then I think you can own them without arrogance.'

'I just...oh what the heck.' Clover shook her head. There
was no point beating around the bush. 'I just think, if I'm
doing something that requires me to you know, stifle my,
um, gifts and talents, then it's probably the wrong thing.'

She pressed her lips together and looked at Morghan.

But Morghan was nodding, considering Clover's words
carefully. She drew her hands out from under her cloak and
looked at them.

'You might well be right, Clover,' she said. Her golden
hand gleamed dully in the dim green and grey light of the

day. She tucked it away under the fabric of her cloak again. 'What do you have in mind, then?'

Clover considered for a moment being disingenuous, asking what made Morghan think she had something in mind, but she shoved the impulse away impatiently.

Because she did have something in mind.

'I want to do something about the lost souls,' she said.

Morghan looked at her. 'Which ones?' she asked slowly.

Clover nodded. 'That day,' she said. 'Ages ago. When we went to see the Queen. And you commented how many more spirits there were in the tunnels, do you remember?'

Morghan remembered. 'There were a surprising number. Many more since I had last gone that way.' She fell silent, thinking about her recent travelling, the vision she'd had, of the boats coming to shore on the Isle of Apples, bringing the souls of those from her world, helping them to safety.

Clover was nodding. 'Yes, and I said something – I don't remember what, now – and Maxen asked something along the lines of who would be their shepherd?' She swallowed, looked earnestly at Morghan.

'I want to be their shepherd.'

She paused, took a breath.

'And when I'm not doing that, I want to come with you on your trips to the Fair Lands.'

4

———

ROWAN STOOD AT THE KITCHEN SINK, HER HANDS DANGLING IN the water as she stared out the window. There was nothing there to see though, in the struggling back yard, only her attempts at a garden, which had turned to little more than mud with the wet winter they'd had.

One of Robbie's toys, the plastic motorbike ride-on, was lying on its side in the grass.

Rowan wasn't looking at it. She wasn't watching the bird that landed hopefully on the feeder she and Robbie had hung up in the branches of their one lonely tree at the beginning of the winter.

There was a frown bent between her eyebrows. She blinked a few times, and the frown deepened. She'd been thinking about the garden blessing at Ladybird Lane the day before, but now slipped into her favourite daydream. Inside her head there was the feeling of a sunlit field, near a cliff – was it a cliff? She always thought it might be, but she was never quite sure. But the sun was shining, and there was a young woman running across the grass with a little dog bounding after her. The woman flung her arms out and spun about, hair rippling out around her. Somewhere to the woman's right, out of sight, Rowan knew there was a little cottage. She closed her eyes, trying to feel the cottage. There was the scent of the sea on the air. Maybe. Rowan squeezed her eyes shut tighter. No, maybe not. Maybe it was just that it was so sunny. The house was whitewashed. Tiny. She let out a breath in pleasure. Just the right size. The cottage was just the right size, and she loved it. It made her happy living there.

Behind her on the stove the kettle whistled, and Rowan's eyes snapped open.

The cottage disappeared. The woman spinning around and around in the sun vanished.

All that was left was longing. She pressed her lips together and turned to pick up the steaming kettle, her movements jerky, disappointed.

Paul's sudden voice made her startle. 'Can't you keep this bloody kid out of my way?'

Rowan's hand jerked and the kettle spilt boiling water over the back of her hand. She yelped, then pressed her lips together, tears hot in her eyes, and put the kettle back on the stove – awake again now, and not forgetting to check that the burner wasn't lit.

'Rowan!'

She hurried from the kitchen, holding her hurt hand behind her back. The pain was deep and sharp. 'He's just playing, Paul,' she said, speaking before she even reached the living room at the front of the house.

'He should be playing in his room.' Paul stood at the

living room windows. He'd been gnawing at his nails again. They were ragged and bleeding. He didn't look at her, just stared out the window.

They did a lot of that in this house.

Robbie was on the floor with his farmyard animals. They were small, soft, made of felt; Rowan had stitched them herself, making each face quirky and sweet. Robbie loved them. Rowan looked down at him, then knelt, scooping up the scatter of small sheep and cows and piggies, ignoring the burn's red slash against her tender skin. She dredged up a smile for Robbie, but her son just looked back at her, eyes too large for his face. Rowan wanted to cry, but she tucked the soft little animals into their quilted barnyard bag instead and nodded.

'We'll go play with these in your room, how about that?' she asked.

But Robbie shook his head with its neat cap of orange hair. He crawled forward and wormed his way into Rowan's lap, and buried his face in her neck. She stood up, bringing Robbie with her, holding the barnyard in her injured hand.

Paul turned and glared at her, his eyes beady in his puffy face. He'd been drinking too much. Brooding too much. It was showing in his pasty skin, the slightly wild, unfocused cast to his eyes. 'What are you waiting for?' he asked. 'Take him upstairs. He can stay in his room. I can't bear him always leaving his things all over the floor.' Paul sniffed, wrinkled his top lip in the way Rowan hated. 'You're useless at this, Rowan, but you could at least try.' He lifted his thumb to his mouth and tore at the skin around the nail.

Rowan stared at him, quivering slightly. She wanted to

press a hand to her stomach, which was growing rounder and fuller with the child, but Paul didn't know about the baby yet and she didn't want him to.

The sun had been shining in her imagining; she'd felt it, and the little dog barking and happy. Robbie would love a little dog. Rowan hugged him tighter.

Paul spoke around the hangnail he was worrying. 'Every time I turn around, he's there, lurking in the shadows.'

'He's just a little boy, Paul,' Rowan said, and she hated the thin, apologetic habit of her voice. She cleared her throat. Robbie burrowed deeper into her arms. Rowan swallowed and tried to sound firmer. 'He's just doing what children do – playing with his toys.'

But her husband shook his head. 'The house is too small with us all cooped up in it like this.'

Rowan looked around the living room. He was right, but she blamed the claustrophobia on him, not Robbie. The electric heater was on high, and the room was stuffy, the windows firmly closed. It was spring, but the weather had been awful, chilly and wet. Made worse with Paul always being around now, since he'd lost his job. He barely left the house anymore, and so nor did Rowan. Nothing more than walks to the park with Robbie; they were allowed, if they didn't last longer than 40 minutes. The time limit was new, since the pandemic, and Rowan missed the degree of independence she'd used to have. It would be nice to go out on longer walks, window shopping or to the charity shop. Anywhere really, other than just to the supermarket or to take Robbie to nursery school three days a week.

Rowan wished Paul would find another job.

Except, she was fairly sure he wasn't even looking.

Robbie stirred in her arms and she hefted him higher, gave him a smile and popped a little kiss on his forehead.

'We'll go for our daily walk, then, shall we? Before it starts raining again?' She was looking at Robbie as she spoke, but she said the words loud enough for Paul to hear. 'We could do with some fresh air.'

Rowan took a breath, added the question she knew Paul expected her to ask, even though she didn't want his company and he never agreed to come with them. Paul wasn't into family trips to the park or strolling in the speck of spring sunshine when it shone through the clouds.

'Would you like to come with us?' she asked, and she managed to keep her eyes on her husband's face, even arranging her lips into a smile.

Paul had never been into changing nappies or even holding Robbie either. Rowan had tried nagging him to, when Robbie had first been born, but she'd given up soon enough. Which had been a trial, as Robbie hadn't liked to be put down. He'd cried every time she'd set him down for the first four months of his life.

She thought of the child growing inside her. What would it be like with two children? Her heart swelled at the thought. She was going to find out. She loved the baby already. The baby, and Robbie.

She just wasn't sure she loved everything else.

In the deep, hidden recesses of her mind, she spun around in the sunshine on deep green grass.

Paul looked at her like she had just suggested he cut off his own head. 'To the park?' He left his position at the window and walked over to where she stood. Robbie ducked his head and pressed his face against Rowan's shoulder. Paul ignored him, reached out and stroked Rowan's face instead. His thumb rasped against her soft skin and left a smear of blood.

'You go on and play on the swings,' he said, his voice filled with the false bonhomie Rowan hated. He dropped his hand finally and stepped back, distracted again. He glanced towards the door. 'I need to spend some time on the computer, start up this new business of ours. You know I do.'

Rowan thought about the spare bedroom Paul had claimed as his a month after he'd come home with no job anymore. He'd stuck all her sewing things in the hallway and told her he was going to work from home now. When she'd asked what he was going to do, he'd told her he had ideas, and that they were good ones. He'd sort it out. She knew that so far all he'd sorted out was how to play games on the computer for hours on end and go down those conspiracy holes on the internet. But she'd never let on that she knew he did that. They were living on the government benefits, and Rowan was glad that Paul made her pay the rent with the bit that came into her account.

Paul smiled at her, and there was blood on his teeth from his torn thumb. She swallowed and smiled back, relieved when he turned and went back to the window.

'Get me some brandy,' he said. 'Just the cheap stuff will do. That one you got last time.'

Rowan nodded, pressing her lips together against the sigh threatening behind them and made herself smile again.

'Sure,' she said, and turned out of the room and went

back to the kitchen. She popped Robbie on one of the chairs at the small table and plumped his barnyard in front of him. Her burnt hand throbbed.

'You be Mummy's darling boy and play with your animals here for a minute,' she said, smoothing her good hand over his hair. It was bright orange, the same colour she had vague memories of her father's being, before it turned snow white. She gave the round-eyed boy a smile and stifled a sigh before going to the kitchen tap and running the cold water over the burn on her hand, holding it there for the count to forty. Better late than never, she thought, and wished again – for the thousandth time – that she was brighter, stronger, knew how to leave Paul.

'You made your bed,' she murmured. The old refrain.

Yes; she'd made her bed, and now she was lying in it. Boy, was she ever.

'Do you want to play on the swings?' Rowan asked, glancing down at Robbie in the pushchair. He shook his head and shrank down into his padded jacket.

'You're right,' she said. 'It's not very warm today.' She looked up at the sky and saw that the jumble of dark clouds had come nearer on whatever ill wind was bearing them. She sighed.

Rowan sighed a lot. She was barely ever aware she did it.

'Let's go look over the bridge, then,' she said, and turned the pushchair away from the small park and towards the small river that wound lazily around the edge of Banwell and only two streets over from where she and Paul and Robbie played at happy families.

Robbie at least, loved the river, and Rowan steered him close to the iron railings so that he could see over.

'It's running high, Robbie,' she said, watching the water rush away beneath them, in a hurry to get to the coast.

Robbie turned his head and looked up at her.

'It's because of all the rain, love,' she said. 'It's made the river rush, see.'

Robbie wasn't much of a talker, not yet anyway. The doctor had said that it would probably come in its own time, since there didn't seem to be anything else amiss.

Rowan leant over the rail a little way, frowning at the water beneath them. It was far up the banks, higher than she'd seen it in a good long while, if ever. It was rough too, gushing and rushing, churning up the mud and grass.

'Come on,' she said, suddenly perturbed by the river's unaccustomed roar. 'Let's go look at the shops instead, shall we?'

Robbie sat back in his chair.

They stopped at the off-licence for Paul's bottle of brandy. Rowan slipped it out of sight under the pushchair and opened the bag of crisps she'd bought for Robbie, pinched one out for herself as he watched.

'Opener's fee,' she said, smiling. Robbie grinned back at her and reached for the small bag.

Rowan checked her phone for the time. They'd been half an hour already, so she must have been walking slowly, dawdling. They'd have to hurry back, or Paul would start texting her, asking where she was, what she was doing.

Tell her she'd better hurry back.

It was probably best to anyway, she thought. The rain would be coming down any minute. But still, she dithered in front of the community noticeboard at the post office, its fliers safely behind glass. A small poster caught her eye.

It was about the priestesses in Wellsford.

They'd looked just as amazing at Ladybird Lane the day before as she'd thought they would. There'd been no ravens appearing though.

Rowan had seen that footage on the television. She imagined everyone in the country had. Maybe even farther afield. The three women in Trafalgar Square, the ravens.

She'd thought they'd all looked hauntingly beautiful. Had felt an odd sort of yearning for something she didn't have words for. Perhaps the place in her favourite daydream.

Paul had snorted beside her on the couch, shaken his head. 'Some sort of trick,' he said. 'Doing it for their five minutes of fame, of course.'

Robbie had gotten up from his seat on the floor where he'd been playing with his blocks, and stood staring at the television, mesmerised, even when Paul had shouted at him to get out of the way. Rowan had had to scoop him up to sit on her lap, and they'd both watched it together. The news programme played the footage twice.

And Rowan, from then on, always thought of her daydream when she saw the Trafalgar Square video, or any of the other things about the Wilde Grove group. She didn't know why, but somehow, for some reason, they were tied up in her head with the woman in the sunshine, spinning around, the little dog dancing in the grass.

The first thick splat of rain roused her, and she realised she'd been standing there, staring at the poster, oblivious to everything. She glanced down at Robbie, but he was okay, sitting and eating his chips, his dear little face half covered by the hood of his jacket. Rowan took a breath, lowered the pushchair's canopy to cover Robbie, then turned for home.

5

ROBBIE WAS ASLEEP BY THE TIME SHE GOT HIM THROUGH THE door, and Rowan unzipped his jacket, lifted him out of the pushchair, and held his warm weight against her for a moment, thinking about the new baby, the one who was rounding her belly already.

She'd have no choice but to tell Paul. He'd notice.

Tomorrow, perhaps. She'd tell him tomorrow.

'DID YOU REMEMBER THE BRANDY?'

Rowan held it out to him. 'Of course.' She sat down on the couch and reached for her knitting. She'd definitely have to tell Paul about the baby the next day, before it became obvious she was knitting another baby blanket with the yarn she'd found at the charity shop.

'The river was high,' she said.

Paul unscrewed the lid on the brandy bottle and poured himself a generous measure. 'Oh yeah?'

Rowan nodded. 'Will it go over the banks, do you think? If it keeps raining like this?'

Paul glanced toward the window. He wanted to get back to the computer soon, in the room he now thought of as his office. He was waiting for the replies to come in on the comment he'd written on one of the forums he'd discovered. They were good, those forums. He felt understood there, wasn't just him against the world.

Wasn't just him thinking there was something rotten under the surface of the world. There had to be people making it that way, pulling the strings, trying to get the better of normal blokes like him, who were just trying to get by. Who couldn't catch a break.

He narrowed his eyes at Rowan suddenly.

'You took longer than normal,' he said. 'Who were you talking to?'

There was a flicker of something in Rowan's expression and Paul's frown deepened to a scowl.

'I wasn't talking to anyone, Paul,' Rowan said. 'I didn't even see anyone else out – not that I remember anyway. It was starting to rain.'

'Then what took you so long?'

Rowan shook her head. 'I don't know. I was looking at one of the notices on the board outside the post office.' She blinked at him. 'It's just next to the off-licence?'

'I know that,' Paul said, though he didn't, not really. But he made a mental note to check, next time he went into town. 'What was so interesting about it?'

Now, Rowan glanced away from him, just for a moment, little more than her gaze sliding to the side then back, but Paul caught it.

She was hiding something. He knew it. Or she was planning something. He looked her over. Maybe she had been talking to someone. She was still good-looking, after all, although getting a bit thicker around the waist. He supposed motherhood would do that.

She'd been the woman of his dreams when they got married. Literally. He'd daydreamt about her constantly. Thought she was out of his league really, got a hell of a surprise – not that he'd shown it – when she'd agreed to go out with him.

Now she was his, which made his wildest dreams come true. Still, he always felt like there was a part of herself she held back from him.

He hated that. It made him feel unsure of himself, and he hated that even more.

'What was it about?' he asked again.

Rowan cleared her throat, then looked studiously at her knitting. 'There's a new Wilde Grove group starting.'

For a moment, Paul didn't know what she was talking about, then he realised. Wilde Grove. That woke bunch of weirdos from up the road in Wellsford. There'd been quite a lot said about them on the forums. It had been when the guys there started paying him more attention, when he said he lived in Banwell, just a few minutes away.

'What sort of group?'

'Ah, it's like, a personal growth course,' Rowan said, trying to put it in the most inane way she could think of.

'Personal growth?' Paul snorted. 'Is that what they're calling their rubbish?'

Rowan's cheeks flushed. She looked up at her husband and wondered why she had ever married him. They had nothing in common. She wished she was brave enough to just pack up and leave, but she never was. He said there was no way he'd ever let her keep Robbie, if she left, and that the courts these days didn't automatically favour the mother.

She hunched her shoulders and dropped her gaze, unsure why she was even bothering thinking about the Wilde Grove group. Paul never let her do anything. Except housework and childcare, and even those she never did to his standards.

'I think it would be worth going,' she said. 'I've heard they teach things like learning to manage and prune your thoughts.' She'd read about their Stations of the Heart. She looked hopefully at him, heart lifting at the thought. 'There's lots more to it as well. You could come along too. It's not just for women.'

Paul scowled. 'No,' he said after a minute. 'I prefer to keep my thoughts to myself, thank you very much.'

'Well, I'd like to go,' Rowan said.

'No,' Paul told her. 'They're all a bunch of lesbians there.'

Rowan gaped at him. 'Paul,' she said, horrified. 'What a thing to say!' She gripped her knitting. 'And what, you're afraid I'll get converted or something?'

Paul shrugged. 'The bible says marriage is between Adam and Eve, not Adam and Steve.' He swallowed a mouthful of brandy and shook his head at Rowan. 'What?'

'Why are you spouting bible stuff?' Rowan asked, truly amazed. 'You're not a Christian.'

'I was before we got married, remember?'

Rowan frowned. She'd forgotten that. 'You went to that

evangelical church down the road,' she said, feeling a dull futility sweep over her.

'That's right. Cornerstone Church,' Paul said, and he sounded suddenly excited.

Rowan looked at him again.

'What?' she said. Her turn.

'We could go there,' Paul told her. 'That way, we can do it together.' He glanced through the doorway at the stairs that led to the bedrooms. 'As a family.' The idea had him nodding. He'd find people there who thought the way he did. He'd probably even get help to make Rowan settle down. She thought he couldn't feel her restlessness, but he did; some days it felt almost like something he could grab hold of and wrestle with. Why else did he insist on knowing where she was all the time, who she talked to?

If he didn't keep a tight rein on her, she'd be off like a flash, or some other bloke would whisk her away.

'I'm pregnant.'

'What?' Paul zeroed his attention back in on her. 'What did you say?'

Rowan hadn't meant to say anything at all. But it was out now.

'I'm pregnant,' she said.

Paul looked down at his hands, at the glass half full of brandy in one hand, the almost full bottle in the other.

Now he'd really have to get the business up and running. Maybe he could network at Cornerstone. A smile spread slowly across his face and when he lifted it to Rowan, he was beaming.

'You're going to have another baby.'

'We're going to have another baby,' Rowan corrected him, but he didn't hear her.

He shook his head, feeling the relief well up inside him. Yes, he thought. Now he had a plan. Go back to church – some of the biggest names on the forums went to churches like Cornerstone. They'd congratulate him and take lots of notice of him when he told them about it.

And Rowan. She'd be pregnant again. Waddling around like a little duck, then nursing an infant. Not much trouble a woman can get up to when she was busy breeding.

This could be just the thing they needed.

Paul set down the glass and bottle and went over to where Rowan was sitting on the couch. He knelt down in front of her, moved her knitting.

'What are you doing?' Rowan asked.

But Paul didn't bother answering. He pressed a palm against her belly.

Rowan swallowed, looked down at his balding head. 'It won't be kicking for another few weeks.'

Paul lifted his head to look at her. She saw with some horror that his eyes were wet with tears.

'How far along are you?' Paul asked, and he shuffled closer so he could put his cheek nearer to her tummy. 'Have you had your first appointment yet? Are you having a boy or a girl?'

His voice was muffled, his mouth practically in her crotch and Rowan could feel his warm breath. She wanted desperately to squirm away from him. Instead, she squeezed her eyes shut. Paul would whine for days if she pushed him away. She concentrated on answering his question.

'I'm thirteen weeks,' she said, sitting as still as possible. 'You can't tell what sex the baby is until you've had a scan.'

Finally, Paul sat back, rocking on his heels to look at her face to face. She stifled her sigh of relief.

'Thirteen weeks,' he repeated.

She nodded.

'When were you going to tell me?'

'I'm telling you now.'

Paul frowned, then let his mind drift back to the new plan. Church again. A nice fuss. 'When will you be having a scan?'

'At sixteen weeks.'

Paul nodded, got to his feet, and grinned at her. 'I'm going to go tell everyone,' he said.

Rowan frowned. 'Everyone?'

Paul paused. He'd meant everyone on the forums, but he supposed they would have to tell his parents as well. 'Mum and Dad,' he said. 'We'll have to tell them.'

Rowan's shoulders drooped.

Paul perked up again. 'They'll give us some money,' he said. 'For the little one. We'll need loads of stuff, won't we?'

'We still have everything,' Rowan said. 'From when Robbie was a baby.'

Paul wrinkled his nose. 'What if it's a girl? We only have boy stuff.' He savoured a mouthful of the brandy while he reflected on the matter. Finally, he shook his head. 'Won't matter,' he said. 'They'll slip us something anyway. We'll go see them tomorrow.'

'Tomorrow's Wednesday,' Rowan said. 'Robbie has daycare.'

'Right,' Paul said, eyes lighting up. He liked the days

Robbie was in daycare. Rowan was always in the mood for a little tussle between the sheets after she'd dropped the kid off and come home to make his breakfast.

'You should have come to the groundbreaking ceremony yesterday. The Wilde Grove priestesses were there, for the kiddie's new gardens.' Rowan picked up her knitting again, carefully untangled the yarn.

Paul was confused. 'What do gardens have to do with kids?'

'They're vegetable gardens,' Rowan said, looking at him again. 'To teach the children about growing food. It's a good thing.'

'Maybe,' Paul said, and suddenly imagined them on one of those lifestyle blocks, Rowan all plump and pregnant, barefoot as she harvested from the garden and made soup or whatever for the kids. He could learn to brew his own beer. They'd be away from everyone. It'd be great.

Except they didn't have money for a bit of land, were probably behind on the rent for this place. Rowan paid that out of the family benefits that went into her account.

'Well then,' he said. 'Why did they need a ceremony? You know I don't like that Wilde Grove lot.'

Rowan opened her mouth to answer, then promptly closed it again, rethought her response, and tried again.

'Just to make it a special thing,' she said.

Paul nodded. He couldn't see the point of it, personally. 'We'll go see Mum and Dad after you pick Robbie up tomorrow. Tell them the good news. They'll be happy to see us.' He paused. 'Shame it's not Sunday already though.'

Rowan was lost. 'Sunday?'

'Yeah,' Paul answered. 'You gave me a brilliant idea, you

did. We should start going along to Cornerstone again.' He nodded. 'It'll be good for us.'

Rowan stared after him when he left the room, then sank back into the cushions.

Cornerstone Church, she thought.

She had not been expecting that.

She was pretty sure they'd been among the protesters outside Ladybird Lane.

6

ROWAN DIDN'T DRIVE. SHE DIDN'T HAVE HER LICENSE. PAUL had said it would be a waste of time getting it, as she was such a dreamer she'd only daydream while driving, then the car would drift over the centre line and then a lorry would hit them, and she would have killed his son.

It was a remarkably thorough scenario, as though he'd given it considerable thought. Maybe he had, or perhaps that had been just what popped into his head when she'd asked him.

Either way, it was ironic how Robbie was his when dead and yet they had nothing to do with each other while Robbie was perfectly alive and well.

Rowan was nervous. It was important not to show it, even though she'd been on tenterhooks all the last few days, so she turned her back as she reached for her dressing gown. Robbie was safely at daycare, and she'd come back home, made Paul his breakfast, gone to bed with him, all as usual. He would be in a good mood, since he'd just had sex

39

and the day before they'd been to his parents' place, and they'd passed him a fifty-pound bill.

This would seem usual too, if she played it right. Her hands shook as she tightened the belt around her thickening middle. Paul was already getting dressed again.

'I'm going to hop in the shower,' she said, glad her voice seemed steady. 'I've got my doctor's appointment this morning.'

Paul frowned. 'This morning? You didn't mention that.'

Rowan managed a smile, and a shrug. 'I thought it was next week. Got the dates wrong. It's not an important one, though. Not the scan or anything.'

Paul yanked his jumper on, annoyed. 'I don't want to go sit around at the doctor's office. They're always running late. We sat there in the waiting room for an hour last time – remember?' He shook his head. 'That was when Robbie was sick too. Bloody shameful how this country's going down the drain.'

'You don't have to come, Paul. Robbie's at daycare, I'll pick him up after just like usual.' Rowan wrinkled her nose in a good pretence of casualness. 'I should pop into the supermarket too. Get some more bread and milk. We're running low.'

Paul also hated the supermarket. He'd usually pick an argument when he took her to do the big grocery shopping, so that he'd have an excuse to sit in the car. Once, she remembered, he'd actually driven away, and when she'd come out of the supermarket, with Robbie, a trolley full of groceries, and the last of her money spent, there was no way to get home.

In the end, a kind stranger had driven her.

She slid a glance at Paul, saw with hope that he was nodding his head. 'All right,' he said.

Rowan's knees felt weak with relief.

'I've got some stuff to do on the computer,' Paul said, getting up and making for the door. 'We need more coffee, as well.'

Rowan nodded, blew out a careful breath between pursed lips, and pressed a hand to her heart. It was thumping madly against her chest. She closed her eyes a moment.

'Thank you, thank you, thank you,' she whispered. To whom, she didn't know. Perhaps there was a goddess with a soft spot for women trapped in lousy marriages.

Rowan hurried to the shower.

She hadn't meant to take Robbie with her, had meant to go without him – after all, she ought to be back before his daycare session ended.

And yet, her feet had taken her right to Ladybird Lane Daycare Centre, and she'd made something up, fetched Robbie away from the craft table, and brought him right along to the bus stop with her.

She felt braver when she had him with her. Can't go falling apart when you've got responsibilities like a kiddie to look after.

Now they were on the bus and Robbie was looking out the window with round eyes, pointing every now and then and tugging on her to look as well. Rowan couldn't stop checking her phone for the time, or a text message from Paul, asking where she was.

The fear of that was irrational, and she knew it. He would think she was still at the doctor's office, and he was right – the wait times there could get ridiculously long.

He wouldn't start to wonder about her until perhaps half an hour after the time that Robbie was supposed to finish at daycare.

Except, she thought, and she tried to shut the idea down before it bloomed properly in her mind. Except, didn't she remember the day that Lizzie had driven her to the benefits office to get her signed up for the solo parent payments?

She'd been going to do that, then rent the house they'd scoped out for her. Just her and Robbie in a place of their own.

Except, Paul had turned up at the office, come to stand looking at her, arms crossed over his chest. He'd taken her home, and she'd crumbled, said no, of course she wasn't planning to leave. How he'd known, she hadn't been able to understand, except that it had seemed to be some sixth sense he suddenly had.

Lizzie, her only friend, had quit on her then, and she'd moved away herself, soon after. Rowan still didn't know how Paul had cottoned on to what she was doing. It had been some sixth sense or something.

The bus wheezed to a stop, blew out a gust of air, then the doors swung open.

'Come on, Robbie,' Rowan whispered. 'This is where we get off.'

A minute later and they stood on the footpath, and Rowan gazed around, chewing nervously on her cheek.

'What we doing, Mummy?' Robbie said.

Rowan looked down at him, a round small figure still in

his winter jacket, his little hand curled around her fingers. She smiled suddenly and knelt down to his height.

'We're having a bit of an adventure, Robbie,' she said. 'That's all. Just a tiny adventure.'

He looked solemnly at her, not smiling, and she wondered if he picked up on her apprehension.

Because she was apprehensive. But she was also excited, and as soon as she thought that, the excitement grew, flooded through her.

'Come on, Robbie-Dot,' she said. 'Let's go meet some really nice people.'

THE CLASS WAS BEING HELD IN HAVEN FOR BOOKS; ROWAN knew that from the flier on the noticeboard outside the off-license. She popped Robbie in his pushchair and looked around, realised she was standing directly opposite the bookshop.

'Here we go,' she said, with a last glance at her phone. She was on time, and there were no text messages.

She crossed the street, Robbie leaning forward in his pushchair. When they entered the shop, he gazed up at the shiny things hanging from the ceiling, eyes widening.

Rowan looked around, biting at her cheek again. Then she spotted a sign pointing through a doorway, the name of the class printed neatly on it in yellow chalk.

'Hello,' Krista said, coming up to them. 'You two look familiar – haven't I seen you somewhere recently?'

Rowan managed a nervous smile. 'We were at Ladybird Lane when you came to do the blessing.'

'Oh, of course!' Krista smiled widely at them, then bent

to talk to Robbie. 'There are some toys and books over there, if you'd like to go and see. There are even a couple of new friends for you.'

'I didn't know if I should bring him,' Rowan said. 'Only I didn't have anyone to look after him if I was late getting back.'

Krista was already shaking her head. 'It's no problem at all,' she said. 'There's a play area set up, and kids are welcome, at least for this class. We'll have someone look after the kiddies when it's time to learn from Morghan.' She smiled again. 'I'm Krista,' she said. 'I don't think I caught your name the other day.'

'Oh. It's Rowan. And this is Robbie.'

'I'm glad you could come. Make yourselves comfy. We'll start shortly – I think everyone is here.'

For a moment, Rowan was mortified. 'I didn't book a place,' she said, her voice almost squeaking.

Krista paused, looked more carefully at Rowan, and this time she saw the strain lines around the woman's eyes, the hesitant mouth.

'That's not a problem either,' she said, feeling now the anxiety that radiated from Rowan. More of it, she thought, than such a simple thing ought to give rise to. 'There's plenty of room for you. I'm glad you could come.'

Rowan got Robbie unbuckled, showed him over to the play corner, then sat self-consciously on the chair nearest him. The chairs were set in a wide semi-circle, and she clasped her hands tightly in her lap, now second-guessing her decision to come along. She wished she'd stayed home, where no one would notice her.

She hoped desperately that they weren't going to go around the circle introducing themselves.

'Please don't, please don't, please don't,' she murmured, lips tight against her teeth. She kept her gaze down, riveted on her white knuckles.

She was glad when Robbie came over with a book and climbed onto her lap.

The rest of the chairs filled, people rustling, settling, smiling at each other. Rowan risked a glance around. Everyone looked comfortable, she thought. At ease. She tried to slow her breathing down. She could feel her heart again. If she had one of those smart watches, she thought, her heartbeat would probably show a hundred and fifty beats a minute.

Krista, with her American accent and wide smile, introduced herself to the circle, then another woman did the same; Winsome, she said her name was. Her voice was warm, and Rowan felt tears start at the corner of her eyes for no reason. She bent her head against Robbie's and blinked them away.

'Welcome to the First Station of the Heart,' Winsome said, smiling at them. 'This is the beginning of an ongoing course that aims to teach you how to live deeply and calmly in this world of ours.'

Deeply and calmly. Rowan wasn't sure about deeply, although it sounded good. Calmly though, she'd take that for sure. She could do with that. Calm wasn't something she ever felt for long.

She gripped Robbie tighter, and he squirmed against her a moment, then turned the page on the book he was holding and stilled again.

Winsome was still talking. 'We are going to be making space in the world for ourselves, space in which we can flex our spirits and begin to shine. Space in which we can feel secure and comfortable, laying the groundwork for all that comes next.' Her smile widened. 'Krista is going to tell us a little about what does come next, but you're probably all familiar with it to some extent from the materials we sent you.'

They'd sent out materials? Rowan's heart sank. She hadn't enrolled properly, so of course she hadn't received them.

She was stupid. She shouldn't have come. Should have known you didn't just drop in to something like this. This was a proper thing. An ongoing group. A course of sorts.

She should have taken a photo of the flier when she'd seen it. That way she would have known all the details, could have gone about it properly.

Except Rowan knew she wouldn't have gone through with it, then. She wouldn't have enrolled or anything like that. She would have become paralysed with indecision.

This way had been the only way she could do it – making it almost a spontaneous decision, telling Paul the lies, then getting on the bus. Knowing where the group was being held, and when, but nothing else.

Suddenly, everyone was standing up, and Rowan realised she'd missed everything that had been said. Had been curled up inside her own head, in a panic. Hurriedly, she put Robbie down and stood. He looked up at her, and she tried a smile, but it crumpled at the edges, then disintegrated completely.

Robbie, as though it was contagious, began to sniffle, then cry.

Rowan grabbed him up, scurried behind the line of people, snatched up Robbie's pushchair, and shook her head. Someone was saying something to her, but she couldn't make out the words; she just shook her head, dragged the pushchair out of the room and into the bookshop, aiming for the door.

Somehow, she got it open, and then it was being held for her.

'Are you all right?' Winsome asked. 'Can I help?'

Rowan shook her head. 'I'm sorry. I...I need to get this one settled. He was about to make a giant fuss.' She kept her head down, hoping the woman with the kind face wouldn't see the tears in her eyes.

Winsome was torn. She had to get back to the class. 'Perhaps you can take him for a walk around the village,' she said. 'And I would love to meet you for a cup of tea afterwards, what do you say?'

Rowan lifted her head, blinked at her. 'You would?' she asked. 'Won't you be busy?'

'No,' Winsome said. 'Not too busy.' She nodded with her head toward The Copper Kettle across the street. 'How about I meet you there in ninety minutes? Or perhaps you were planning to leave?'

Rowan shook her head. 'I came on the bus,' she said.

'Ah. Then we can have that cup of tea – I'm going to need one rather desperately after this, I can tell you. The bus only comes three times a day to Wellsford, so we'll have time.'

'I have to take the next one home,' Rowan said, but she

was nodding, something inside her shifting, as though the rock that usually sat heavy in her chest were rolling around.

Winsome smiled. 'Ninety minutes,' she said. 'Across the road. My treat.' She smiled. 'They know me there, so just say you're waiting for me.'

Winsome waited until the woman had nodded her agreement, then let the door close, and hurried back to Krista and the rest of the group.

Rowan stared at the door for a moment longer, then realised that she was still gripping Robbie around his middle, his clothes riding up so that his little tummy was bare and getting cold. She tucked him into the pushchair.

The next bus wasn't due for two hours. So, there was time, she thought. To have a cup of tea with the nice woman.

She had to stay in Wellsford that long anyway.

7

ROWAN PUSHED ROBBIE DOWN THE STREET, HER HEAD turning left and right to look at everything. There wasn't much, she thought, and felt a twinge of disappointment. It looked like almost every other village she'd ever been to. Pretty, but quite small.

There was the bookshop, of course, and she had to admit that it hadn't been quite like any she'd ever stepped foot in. Not with the strange things dangling from the ceiling. Some sort of symbols, she guessed.

There was a tiny clothing boutique, and she paused outside that one for quite a while, staring at the window display.

Okay, she thought, so things were a bit different here. She glanced at the name of the shop, The Celtic Knot, and then gazed back at the robes and dresses in the window. What might it be like to wear one of those, she wondered, her eyes going to a golden yellow dress, with Celtic style embroidery around the neckline. It was long, looked heavy and like something from the Middle Ages. Just right, Rowan supposed, for magical rituals under the moonlight.

She made herself walk on. Those weren't clothes for her, even if she couldn't help imagining what it would feel like to wear them.

There were other little shops along the way. Mostly selling handicrafts, it seemed. And a grocery shop. A bakery.

She smiled and then ducked her head when the shop bell tinkled and someone stepped out, giving her a cheery hello as they passed.

With a sigh, Rowan turned away, shivered in the cool breeze. At least the rain had cleared, for a little while anyway. She crossed the street, Robbie fallen asleep tucked in under his blanket. They'd go for a walk, she decided. It was too cold to just sit and wait, and she didn't want to go to The Copper Kettle yet, since she didn't have any money to buy a cup of tea. It would be awkward, even if she did say she was waiting for someone, with an hour to go before they turned up.

She walked past an old church and paused to read the sign. Bridget's Sanctuary. There was the faint sound of singing.

'That a nice name, isn't it, Robbie?' she murmured to the sleeping child.

In fact, she didn't think she'd ever seen a church with a better name. There were no service times on the sign, however, just an odd message which said:

Stations of the Heart: Finding Belonging.

Rowan frowned. Hadn't that been what the woman had said back in the class?

It was. She'd said *welcome to the first Station of the Heart.*

Belonging, Rowan thought wistfully, and she wished she knew what that felt like. Her hands gripped the pushchair handle tighter and she closed her eyes for a moment, imagining that old, favourite daydream of hers. She didn't know why it was always the same scene, or where it had come from. She felt as though she could remember it even from when she was a child.

A woman, a little dog. The feeling of the sun shining.

Rowan opened her eyes and took a breath, pushed on past the church, tears misting her eyes again. The daydream was such a happy one, she didn't know why it had to always make her cry, as though it was a memory of better times.

Times that were long gone.

The road back to Banwell spooled out in front of her, and she turned away from it, the pushchair wheels kicking up a small spume of water from a puddle. There was a narrow lane that branched off and, with no idea where it went, and not caring, Rowan turned down it. She wiped her eyes with the back of a hand, but the tears sprang back again.

She leant forward to check if Robbie was still asleep. He was. That was good, and she let go a small sob.

God, but she was useless, she thought. Couldn't do anything right. Here she was, come all this way, sneaking away from Paul, and she hadn't even been able to do what she'd come for.

She wiped her eyes again. Dug around in her jacket pocket for a tissue.

Kept walking, letting the cold air seep under her clothes and chill her. It would serve her right if she caught cold.

'Mummy, a cat!'

Rowan blinked. When had Robbie woken up? Had he heard her moaning and carrying on?

'Mummy, look!'

She sniffed, blotted the tissue against her eyes, and looked around.

'Where, sweetie?' she asked.

Robbie pointed and sure enough, there was a cat, a big orange tabby, sauntering towards them.

'Goodness,' Rowan said. 'Hello, puss.'

The cat came right up to them and bumped himself against Robbie's legs. Robbie reached out to touch it and a moment later – Rowan wasn't quite sure how it happened – the cat was sitting on Robbie's lap with Robbie's arms wrapped tight around it.

'Oh.' Rowan looked around, not sure what to do. The cat was purring loudly as though it did this sort of thing all the time.

'Look Mummy,' Robbie said. 'He likes me.'

'He sure does,' Rowan said, and tucked the tissue absently back into her pocket. "I guess we should find where he lives.'

Robbie continued hugging the cat with one arm and pointed with the other. 'He come from down there.'

Rowan looked down at her son, whose small face was beaming. She nodded, although he couldn't see her, then cleared her throat.

'He did, didn't he?'

She looked down the driveway, and for a moment, her daydream was back, and she was spinning in the sunshine, laughing.

Rowan cleared her throat again. Looked down at the orange cat, who looked very comfortable and showed no signs of getting off.

'What the sign say, Mummy?' Robbie asked.

Rowan blinked and looked where he was pointing, and then wondered how she'd missed it.

The Sacred Well, it said.

Then, in smaller print: Stations of the Heart: The Sacred World.

'Stations of the Heart,' Rowan said. She didn't know what it meant, but saying the words made her feel good, as though there was a container somewhere for all her feelings, all her worries and fears.

She shook her head. That didn't make any sense. Yet, she said the words again, low, under her breath.

'Stations of the Heart.'

And the *Sacred World*? Rowan puzzled over that for a moment. In her experience, the world wasn't a sacred place. It was precarious, full of pitfalls.

She started down the driveway, her eyes dazzled from the sun in her daydream.

'We takin' cat back, Mummy?' Robbie asked, twisting around to look up at Rowan, still gripping the cat. He could feel the rumble of its purring against his own small chest.

Rowan nodded. The driveway was gravel, trees crowding either side. The pushchair tyres crunched over it.

Then the trees fell away and she stopped. Robbie and the cat both looked up at her, but she didn't see them.

Rowan shook her head.

She wasn't dreaming.

Then why did it feel as though she was?

The driveway curved away to the side of the small cottage, and in front of the cottage was a wide, grassy area, and for some reason - Rowan had no idea why or how – but she was gripped suddenly with the conviction that this was the same place as in her daydream.

All it needed was the sun to come out.

She squinted up at the sky, but it stayed stubbornly grey, the clouds heavy once more with rain.

Rowan looked around again, moved forward in a daze.

There was a path that branched off to the front door of the cottage. The cat jumped down from Robbie's lap and sauntered up the path, then squeezed in through the doorway and disappeared.

Rowan's mouth was dry.

'What's say?' Robbie asked. This time he was pointing at a sign on the blue cottage door.

Rowan licked her lips. 'It says *welcome to the Well-Keeper's cottage.*'

'We go in?'

Rowan gave Robbie a trembling smile and nodded, amazed at all the sudden, full sentences from him, then with a deep breath, she pushed the door open and stepped inside, hearing immediately the murmur of voices and preparing to back straight out again.

'Oh no,' someone said to her. 'Don't go. Please come in. You're welcome here.'

Rowan froze in place, then nodded, found a smile. 'Thank you,' she said.

'We found a cat,' Robbie said.

Erin came over and smiled warmly at Rowan before

crouching down in front of Robbie. 'Was it an orange cat?' she asked. 'Quite big and fat?'

Robbie glanced at his mum then nodded. 'Berry big an' fat,' he said.

Erin laughed. 'That's Sasquatch,' she said. 'He's always bringing people here. Did he lead you here?'

Robbie shook his head, then changed his mind and nodded. 'He sat on my lap.'

'Goodness,' Erin cried. 'You must be just about squashed, then!'

Robbie shook his head. 'I okay,' he said happily.

Erin patted his knee. 'I'm glad.' She got up and smiled at Rowan. 'Welcome to the Well-Keeper's cottage,' she said. 'Feel free to have a cup of something nice and hot, and a scone – they and the drinks are free – and look around, warm up a little. Then I can take you out to the sacred well, if you'd like.'

Rowan was staring at Erin. She'd seen her at Ladybird Lane, of course, but not up close, not like this.

'I like your dress,' she said, then groaned inwardly. What a stupid thing to have said. She should have said something more intelligent. Asked about all the books or something. Anything.

'Thank you,' Erin said. 'The colour makes me happy.'

It was a rich rusty orange, Rowan thought. A shade brighter than Erin's hair. 'I saw some like it in the village.'

'That's Lynsey and Marshall's shop. They make every-thing themselves. I fell in love with their clothes when I first came here.'

Rowan nodded, made herself look around, took in the couple other people in the room, the shelves of books, the rustling fire in the grate behind the guard. 'You have a lot of books,' she said.

'This is our lending library,' Erin said. 'You're free to sign up, then you can take a book home with you to read.' She smiled gently and prodded her senses around the edges of Rowan's aura, feeling the tension and knots there. 'We have a little apothecary as well, with some tinctures and flower essences, herbal teas and so on that you might find nice.'

Rowan shook her head. 'I don't think so,' she said, and glanced behind her at the door. She'd barely come more than a few steps in, and perhaps she shouldn't have.

She didn't really know what this place was.

Or why it had felt so much like she'd recognised the outside of it. That it was the same place as in her daydream.

'Are you all right?' Erin asked. 'Won't you come in and warm up? I'll get you a cup of tea. Please let me take care of you for a minute.'

Rowan looked at her, alarmed. 'Take care of me?'

Erin smiled again. 'You look like you've had a rough morning. It certainly is a bit chilly out, isn't it?'

Rowan blinked at her. 'Who is the Well-Keeper?' she asked suddenly.

8

ERIN'S BROW ROSE AND SHE SMILED MORE WIDELY. 'WELL, YOU are, if you've come here,' she said.

Rowan looked at her. 'I don't understand,' she said.

'The Sacred Well is the symbol of the flow of spirit through our lives and the land. All of us are Well-Keepers, if we want to live a deep and rich life.'

Erin decided it was time to move away, let this woman and her child come farther into the room. 'I'll make you some tea – you can try one of our special blends.' She glanced at the little boy in the pushchair. 'Would you like a yummy cup of hot chocolate?' she asked. 'With a marshmallow on the top?'

Robbie nodded, his hands going to the buckles strapping him in.

'I hoped you would,' Erin said. 'A pink marshmallow or a white one?'

'Pink one,' Robbie said, then twisted around to Rowan. 'I get out?'

Rowan didn't know. 'Can I let him out?'

'Of course,' Erin said. 'Why don't you make yourselves at home, and I'll bring you your drinks.'

ERIN SCANNED THE JARS OF STEPHAN'S BLENDS, THEN plucked one down. It was a soothing blend, designed by Stephan to calm and warm the mind. She had a feeling that the woman who had just come in with the little boy could do with a bit of soothing and pampering. She scooped out a measure into one of the little teapots, stilling her own mind as she did so, and whispering a short prayer.

'May you be blessed and soothed, warmed and loved.'

Erin nodded, then made the hot chocolate, with a pink marshmallow in it and one on the side for good measure, and she carried everything over to the small table where the pair had seated themselves, the woman still with the look of a deer caught in headlights.

'I'm Erin, by the way,' Erin said, setting the things down. 'Would you mind some company for a minute?'

Rowan nodded mutely, then found her voice. 'I saw you,' she said.

Erin nodded. 'On the TV, right? Or online?'

Rowan touched her fingers to the little teapot, then withdrew them to tuck them into a knot in her lap. 'Yes, but you were at our daycare the other day too.'

'Oh!' Erin turned to the little boy. 'Did we see each other at Ladybird Lane?'

Robbie, on his knees on the chair, one hand gripping the handle of the kiddie cup Erin had given him and the other clutching the pink marshmallow, nodded and gave her a shy smile.

'You're going to have a wonderful garden, I think,' Erin said to the little boy, then smiled at Rowan. 'Hopefully the sun will come out and we'll get some good growing time.'

Rowan nodded. 'I saw you on the television too,' she said. 'My husband said it was a trick, what you were doing. What happened.'

Erin was unperturbed. 'I imagine lots of people said the same thing.'

Rowan cleared her throat. Thought of the strange sensation of recognition she'd had outside, and felt her cheeks burn. 'Was it?' she asked.

'A trick?' Erin looked at her, shook her head, then let her gaze rest on the flames in the open fireplace for a moment as her brow wrinkled. 'It wasn't a trick.' She looked back at the woman across the tiny table, whose name she didn't know yet. 'I think it was a calling.'

Rowan was confused. Whatever she'd expected Erin Faith's answer to be, it wasn't that.

'What do you mean, a calling?'

But Erin was shaking her head. 'A calling to all of us, is what I've come to think. You must understand,' she said. 'That it wasn't planned, or choreographed, or any of those things people have been saying. I shifted, and it happened.'

'Shifted?'

Erin laughed a little, shook her head. 'I'm sorry. Sometimes I forget that people don't know all my words for things.' She sobered, picked up the teapot and poured the brewed liquid into the cup. 'Please,' she said. 'Try that.'

Rowan lifted the cup, sniffed at the herbal brew and

closed her eyes for a moment. 'What's in it?' she asked. 'It smells wonderful.' It did too; it smelt like herbs and fresh air. It smelt like a sunny day and spinning in a warm breeze, a little white dog at her ankles.

Rowan shivered.

'What is it?' Erin asked, leaning forward to catch Rowan's elbow. 'Are you all right?'

Rowan shook her head, then opened her eyes, glanced at Robbie, who was absorbed in taking tiny bites out of his marshmallow, alternating it with sips of his drink.

'I'm fine,' she said, despite the fact that she'd just shaken her head. She looked down at the cup. 'What's in this?'

'This one has lemon balm, chamomile, rose, and oat in it,' Erin answered, watching her closely.

Rowan nodded, took another sip. It tasted good. Ordinarily, she wasn't much for herbal teas, but this one was good. It made her feel a little better.

'What is shifting?' she asked, then remembered her manners. 'I'm sorry, I shouldn't be barging in with questions.'

Erin shook her head. 'I don't mind your questions at all,' she said. 'Although I would like to know your name.'

Rowan's cheeks turned pink. 'Rowan,' she said. 'I'm Rowan, and this is Robbie.'

'That's better, now,' Erin said. 'I'm pleased to meet you, Rowan and Robbie.' She smiled. 'The rowan is a lovely tree.'

Rowan felt a flush of pleasure. 'I'm named after my Gran.'

'Rowan and Robbie,' Erin repeated. 'Perfect!'

Robbie looked up from his drink and grinned at her.

'Gosh,' Rowan said. 'He's usually a lot more shy than this. He barely talks, usually.'

'Children are good at picking up on the atmosphere here,' Erin said, and wondered why the little boy didn't talk much.

'The atmosphere?' Rowan asked.

Erin nodded. 'You're in Wellsford,' she said. 'Wilde Grove, really, here at the cottage. It's a special place.'

Rowan nodded, chewed on the inside of her cheek, the way she was always trying to get herself to stop doing.

'It's a lovely village,' she said, but she was frowning. 'I came here to do the Stations of the Heart course.'

'Ah,' Erin said. 'With Winsome and Krista. Yes, they're starting another group on it today.' She flicked a glance at Rowan. 'Isn't that on right now?'

'I walked out.'

Erin waited for more.

Rowan took another sip of her tea, heaved a sigh. 'I got scared.'

Erin nodded. 'Why?' she asked.

The question made Rowan freeze. She should have expected it, she supposed. But it was very direct.

'I...I didn't have the materials. I hadn't enrolled properly. I would have just dragged everyone else there down, if I'd stayed.'

'You were afraid of letting everyone else down?'

Rowan frowned, looked down at the cup she was holding. It was ceramic, but as though it had been hand-thrown. She'd been interested in pottery once, had been learning how to do it. But Paul had made her feel silly for wanting to play with clay, and she'd given it up.

'Yes,' she said. 'Maybe.'

'Winsome would have been glad to give you the materials so you could catch up.'

Rowan managed a nod, even with her chin tipped down. 'I just…got scared.'

Erin nodded. 'New things can feel a little overwhelming.'

But Rowan was shaking her head. She wanted to say more, to confide, perhaps. The woman at the table opposite her, Erin Faith – Rowan knew her name from the TV coverage – was young. In her early twenties, Rowan thought, a good ten years younger than herself, and yet, she wanted to tell her, to say something to this young woman with the kind face and the expression that said she'd seen things most people wouldn't believe.

But then, Rowan thought, she always wanted to tell someone. Always was trying to reach out and ask for advice, help.

But she could never find the words, really, and people were always busy, and rightly so. Why should they listen to her? Most people barely knew her to speak to except to comment on the weather.

Rowan pressed her lips together, then spoke anyway. 'It's not that, or not just that.' To her alarm, a knot formed in her throat, and she shook her head, helpless.

'My husband,' she said. 'Paul. He doesn't know I'm here.'

Erin nodded, felt suddenly out of her depth, then remembered what Winsome had been teaching her, about listening to people, being there for them. That most of the time, they didn't need someone to come up with solutions, they just needed someone present for them, listening with a kind and open heart.

'Would he mind?' Erin asked, and she pushed her shoulders back slightly, so that her body was more open, looser. On a quiet exhale, she let her energy expand outwards, to touch just lightly and gently Rowan's tightly furled aura.

A word popped into her mind – shrinking – and she realised that was how Rowan felt. As though she were shrinking away to nothing. Erin took another breath and let it out slowly.

Rowan was looking down at her hands, clasped around the small, ceramic mug. It had a lovely blue and green glaze and she rubbed a thumb over it.

'I used to do pottery,' she said.

Erin accepted the sudden shift in direction, because it wasn't one really, she knew. So, she waited.

'That was before Paul and I got married.' Rowan felt the thick dribbles of glaze down the side of the mug where it had been allowed to run in rivulets. It felt good under her thumbs.

She gave a self-deprecating smile, not looking at Erin's face. 'Once we were married, he talked me out of continuing with it.' She sighed, barely aware of it. 'I let him talk me out of it.'

'Would you like to try it again?' Erin asked. 'Stacy and Andrew have set up a little pottery studio here in Wellsford. It's open for anyone to come along and have a go. It was Stacy who made these cups.'

Rowan was shaking her head. 'No,' she said, and she put the cup back on the table and looked over at Robbie, coming back to her senses. This woman wouldn't want to hear her list of woes either. 'Look at you, Robbie darling,' she said. 'Let's get your face washed, and then I think it's time for the bus.'

She shot Erin a smile without looking at her, and got up, bustling about Robbie, picking him up and putting him back in his pushchair, getting a wet wipe out of her bag and rubbing off the chocolate and marshmallow before finally straightening.

'Thank you for the tea,' she said, looking down at the floor. 'It's been very nice meeting you.'

She wheeled Robbie around, glancing at the other people sitting drinking tea and flipping through books, then made for the door, her eyes feeling as hard as glass. She wrestled with the door a moment, then Erin held it open for them.

'Thank you again,' Rowan said.

'Fank you for mushmellow,' Robbie said and waved.

Rowan got them through the door and down the path, her legs wooden and stiff in her hurry.

'We've got to get back, Robbie,' she said as soon as they were out of earshot and the lovely little cottage with its grass lawn was behind them. Rowan kept her eyes resolutely ahead. She didn't look back, not even to feel in her mind the way she, or someone else who felt like her, spun across the grass in the sunshine.

'There is no sunshine,' she muttered, and they reached the driveway.

In fact, it was starting to rain, she realised, once they were back on the lane and walking towards the village again. She stopped and pulled the pushchair's rain cover from the parcel tray under the seat.

'Keep you dry while we wait for the bus,' she told Robbie without meeting his eyes. She tied it in place.

'You goin' to get wet, Mummy,' Robbie said.

But Rowan shook her head. 'I'll be all right. We'll be on the bus in a minute, and then home, won't we?'

She wheeled Robbie back up the lane to the village, got to the main street, and looked down the length of it, past the lovely old church to the cafe. The Copper Kettle. She'd said she'd meet that woman there, have a cup of tea with her. Winsome.

Rowan checked the time on her phone. It was just a cheapie from the supermarket, her phone, good for telling the time and getting text messages and phone calls, but that was all. Still, there were five minutes before they were supposed to meet. And forty minutes until the bus was due.

There was the bus stop right in front of the cafe, and Rowan continued looking that way for a minute longer, before turning the pushchair in the opposite direction.

There would be another bus stop down this end, she thought. She'd wait there. With a bit of luck, it would be well out of sight of the shops.

9

Erin watched Rowan and Robbie until she couldn't see them anymore, then went reluctantly back into the cottage, reviewing what she'd said, and wrinkling her nose in displeasure.

She'd done exactly what she'd told herself not to do only a minute beforehand. She'd pushed Rowan instead of just listening. She should have just sat there and held the space for the woman to talk, to say whatever was on her mind.

Erin shook her head and picked up another log, moved the guard, and tipped it onto the fire.

It was taking her too long to learn how to do the things she needed to, she decided. Winsome's lessons just weren't getting through to her.

Erin tipped her chin back and stifled a groan, mindful that there were still people in the little cottage's library room with her. She smiled at them, then made her way outside through the back door, standing for a moment in

66

the little garden, the way she always did, admiring the work everyone had done to bring it to life. It was a lovely space now, with outside tables, just in case the weather ever improved, and hanging baskets of flowers to match the ones in the tubs.

But she lingered only for a moment, before walking down the path to the small gate into the orchard. Erin paused at the gate, making the effort to draw herself taller, to become present and calm, then swung the gate open and stepped through, walking the short distance to the wellspring.

The ancient spring welcomed her, with its great rocks placed centuries before like a protective wall behind it, and smaller ones in front so that the water pooled in shallow basin.

Erin crouched before it, hitching her skirts to keep them from the wet grass. A raindrop hit her bare head, then another. She'd best not tarry too long, or she'd be soaked. She reached out and dipped a finger in the small pool of water, then touched its dampness to her forehead.

'Water is life,' she murmured. 'I am the Well-Keeper and the world flourishes.' She closed her eyes and tried not to believe that the last thing the world was doing at that moment was flourishing.

'As my spirit blooms, so does the world,' she said, and felt marginally better. That bit she could at least believe whole-heartedly. If everyone were to bloom in that way, the world really would flourish. Erin rocked back on her heels.

It was hard though, learning new ways of being, of seeing things, of acting upon them. Or perhaps it was easy enough to learn them, just far more difficult to always remember to do them. She shook her head and made herself be quiet.

The rain made splashes and ripples on the scooped pool of water and Erin stood up, looking up at the sky, which was grey from horizon to horizon. She looked back at the sacred spring and closed her eyes briefly.

'I am a Well-Keeper,' she repeated. 'The flow of my spirit is strong. I am a Beacon, whose light shines brightly, world to world to world.'

The spring was in a field of orchard trees, and Erin spent a moment gazing at the nearest, whose branches were tied with small pieces of cloth. These were prayers, she knew, the cloth dipped in the waters of the wellspring and then tied loosely to the tree, so that as the narrow strip of fabric flapped in the wind and sun and rain and disintegrated, the prayers would be dispersed to the elements and a cure for whatever ailed the person would be given.

It was an ancient custom, and Erin gazed at the hundred or so ribbons of cloth – only the biodegradable ones they provided at the cottage were allowed to be hung from the apple trees – and knew this was only a fraction of the prayers and healing that people were desperate for.

There was a vibration in her pocket, and Erin pulled her phone out, gaze still on the trees. She answered the call, realised the rain was coming down properly now and she was getting wet, and she ducked her head as she hurried back to the warmth and shelter of the cottage.

'Erin? It's Winsome. You haven't had a woman and her little boy visit, have you?'

Erin slipped in the door and gave herself a shake, wiped her boots on the mat.

'Yes,' she said. 'They left not long ago.'

There was a pause before Winsome spoke again. 'I was going to meet her at The Copper Kettle, but she hasn't shown up.'

Erin stepped into the cottage's main room, which was now their small lending library, and saw that it was empty. She warmed herself before the fire.

'I've a feeling that she'll be waiting for the bus,' Erin said, stretching one hand then the other towards the flames. 'She was like a cat on hot stones, and just when I thought she was going to confide in me, I said the wrong thing, and she gathered up her boy and left.' Erin sighed. 'I'm sorry,' she said. 'It's hard, just listening, instead of making suggestions. I guess I'm still learning that bit.'

There was a pause before Winsome spoke, and Erin held the phone more tightly.

'She's not waiting for the bus at this end of the village,' Winsome said. 'She must be at the farther stop. At least there's a bit of shelter there.' This time the sigh was Winsome's. 'Well, nothing to be done right now, only to send our prayers with her. You're about to get an influx, I think. Several people are braving the rain to visit the well.'

Erin heard voices outside the door and nodded. 'They're here,' she said. 'I'll see you tomorrow.'

She pressed end, slipped the phone back into her pocket and turned to greet the new arrivals.

It was late afternoon and still raining when Lucy had come to take over the shift at the cottage and Erin let herself into Ash Cottage and stood in front of the closed doors, a smile on her lips.

'What,' she asked, 'is that delicious smell?'

Stephan grinned at her. 'Me, of course,' he said, coming over to scoop her into his arms and kiss her. 'Freshly washed and powdered.'

Burdock gave a low woof and pushed his nose into Erin's dangling hand.

'Yeah,' Stephan said. 'Burdock is also freshly washed and brushed and looking fine.'

Erin laughed, extricated herself, patted Burdock and smiled at Stephan. 'You are both definitely fine and very clean.' She grinned. 'But I was talking about the delicious smells from the kitchen.'

Stephan rolled his eyes and shook his head. 'Burdock,' he said. 'She only loves us for our cooking.'

Burdock chuffed good-naturedly. He loved it when his people goofed about.

'She loves you for a great many reasons,' Erin said, laughing some more. 'But yes, high up on that list is your cooking.' She looked hopefully over at the pots and pans. 'Is it ready?'

Stephan trailed behind her into to kitchen and shook his head. 'It's a casserole,' he said. 'Won't be ready for a while, yet. I can make you a toasted sandwich?'

'That,' Erin agreed, 'would be amazing.' She stepped back into the circle of his arms and rested her head on his shoulder. 'I wish everyone were as lucky as me.'

'I don't think there's enough of me to go around for that,' Stephan said.

Erin smiled, but it was more sadly this time. 'I met a

woman today, bit older than me, in her thirties, perhaps?' She straightened, kissed Stephan on the cheek and reached for the tea kettle. 'She had her little boy with her, but she was so sad it almost hurt just to look at her.'

Erin filled the kettle and set it back on the cooker. When she turned back around, there was a frown marring her forehead. Burdock wrinkled his own head and sat himself down beside her, leaning his weight against her in comfort. She stroked his head.

'I said the wrong thing to her, just as she was about to open up, and then she left. I've never seen someone scramble away so quickly.'

Stephan shook his head. 'I'm sure it wasn't something you said.'

'Oh, it was.' Erin pursed her lips. 'I just wanted to make her comfortable, you know? She was talking about how she'd done pottery once, and I got excited, I suppose, told her we had a pottery studio here in Wellsford that she could come along and use.'

'What was wrong with saying that?' Stephan asked, getting two mugs down from the shelf, and turning to grab the loaf of bread. 'I would have said the same.'

Erin scanned the tea selections and picked one. 'Except she'd just finished telling me that she'd let her husband talk her out of doing pottery after they'd married.'

Stephan paused, bread knife in hand. 'Oh,' he said.

'Yeah. So, you know, I don't think the conversation she wanted to have was about playing with clay. And I screwed it up.'

Shaking his head, Stephan put down the knife and looked at her. 'Maybe,' he said. 'But you won't next time.'

'I don't think she'll be back,' Erin said, glum, frowning as she patted Burdock. 'She'd been going to meet Winsome after coming to the Well-Keeper's cottage, but she didn't.' She lifted her gaze to meet Stephan's. 'Which is also on me. I don't know how to make that one right.'

'You probably can't,' Stephan said promptly. 'Unless you run into her again.'

Erin pursed her lips. 'Her boy goes to Ladybird Lane Daycare. That's where we were the other day for the garden blessing.'

'Well, she's pretty local, then. She might come back.'

That got a nod from Erin, but she wasn't convinced. 'How was your day?'

Stephan fetched the cheese from the fridge and began expertly slicing it. 'Good,' he said. 'Although I wish to all the Gods that it would stop raining for more than five minutes. The fields are turning into swamps. The seedlings are taking ages to sprout because it's not warm enough.' He shook his head. 'The weather just seems totally unpredictable now. The forecast is hardly ever right.'

'Things are changing quicker than I expected,' Erin said, and zipped her thoughts away from the Fae she'd met at the quarry, who would happily have watched her die. One less human to destroy things. Erin breathed out. Poured the hot water into the teapot and watched the steam rise.

Stephan slid the sandwich into the pan to toast. 'I met the new doctor today,' he said, changing the subject.

'Oh,' Erin perked up. 'I'd forgotten he was arriving this week. What's he like?'

Stephan flipped the sandwich over. 'He's fantastic,' he said. 'I liked him straight away. Tall fella, great accent, wears a Thor's Hammer.' Stephan slid the toasted sandwich onto a plate and cut it in half. 'I can't wait until I'm qualified as an herbalist. It's going to be brilliant to work beside this guy.' He wrinkled his nose. 'Of course, I've two more years to go, yet.'

Erin leant against him for a moment. 'You're doing fine,' she said. 'And you're really busy working all the time, so be kind to yourself.'

'Yeah.' Stephan took the plate over to the table and sat down, watching Erin bringing the teapot and mugs. She was dressed in a deep orange, and it looked great on her.

'What are you looking at?' Erin asked, catching his gaze.

'You,' Stephan said frankly. 'Krista wants a baby. She said Clarice had told you all.'

Startled at the change in topic, Erin sat down and nodded. 'I don't know if Clarice is convinced.'

'She is. Krista said that too. Have you thought about it?'

'About it?'

Stephan nodded. 'About having a baby.'

Erin's eyes widened. 'What?' she asked. 'With you?'

'Well.' Stephan laughed, took half the sandwich and pushed the plate towards Erin. 'I'd be hoping it were with me.'

'Of course it would be with you,' Erin said, then frowned at him. 'You're not...wanting one, are you?'

Stephan shook his head. 'I don't think so – or not yet anyway. Maybe one day.'

'One day,' Erin echoed. 'What will the world be like, though? I mean, would it be even fair to bring a child into this world when we're on the brink of so much upheaval?'

Stephan chewed his bite of toasted sandwich and

thought about it. 'I think so, yes. I don't think we can put off living like that, bringing life and joy into the world, because of things.'

Erin considered his words. She shook her head. 'I don't know. I keep thinking about Clover's visions of the future. It was pretty bleak. Food shortages, suicide plagues.' She put her sandwich down and looked at it, appetite disappearing.

Burdock pricked up his ears from his bed by the fireplace and whined.

'I wouldn't want to put a child through that.' She shuddered. 'I don't want to go through it myself. And pandemics – I bet we'll have more of those.'

Stephan put his sandwich down, leant across the table and put his hand on Erin's. 'Which is why what we're doing here, and helping people to do elsewhere, is so important. And Clover's vision – you've heard Morghan talk about it. It's only a possibility. Not set in stone.'

Erin nodded, closed her eyes a moment, then opened them and looked at Stephan. 'I'm not ready for a baby, Stephan Reed, but I think I'd like to marry you.'

Stephan's eyes widened. 'Are you proposing to me?'

'That's not how it's supposed to be done, is it?' Erin said.

Stephan shook his head, felt suddenly an echo of Finn inside him. A smile spread slowly across his face.

'On the contrary,' he said, and his voice was hoarse, his skin prickling. 'I think when there's a priestess of the Grove involved – a Lady of the Grove – this is exactly how it's supposed to be done.'

He got up and scooted around the table, then knelt in front of Erin.

Burdock sat up.

'My Lady,' Stephan said. 'I am always in your service.'

Tears wet Erin's eyes and she too felt the flicker of the past all around them. 'Will you be always at my side?'

'I will,' Stephan said.

'Will you always give me your wise counsel, the strength of your embrace?'

'I will,' Stephan said.

'Will you be my partner for as long as we are together in this lifetime?' Erin let her tears fall and brushed the curl from Stephan's forehead as he nodded, her hand smoothing against the warm skin.

'How I love you,' she whispered. 'Will you marry me?'

Stephan clasped her hands in his. 'I will,' he said.

10

Erin stepped through the woods, following Morghan's well-worn path to the river, where it was still shallow and slow enough to step into. The sun was rising in the east, streaking the clouds with red and purple bruises. It was beautiful, even as it spoke of more rain.

She walked over to the river's edge, glad to see that she'd been right in thinking Morghan would be there at this time of the day. Morghan stood still and tall, her hair loose down her back, silver in the dim light of the dawning. She had her eyes closed, and Erin simply took her place beside her, and let her breathing calm.

They stood in silence next to each other for a minute, before Morghan opened her eyes and turned to smile at Erin.

'Your energy is bright this morning,' she said.

'I've news,' Erin told her.

'Good news.'

It wasn't a question.

'I thought I should tell you first,' Erin said. 'It seems right to tell you first.'

Morghan's brows arched. 'I will be honoured to hear,' she said.

Erin nodded. Took a breath that tasted of soil and water and life. 'Stephan and I are getting married.'

She felt suddenly shy. 'I mean, we're living together, and we will be together anyway to the day we die, just like Macha and Finn, and maybe even beyond that, who knows?' Her voice trailed off and she lifted her gaze to Morghan's. 'So, it just seems right.'

Morghan's smile was wide. 'My congratulations. I'm delighted for you both.'

Erin took another breath. 'We wondered...if you would marry us? Perform the handfasting?'

'Now, that would be a privilege,' Morghan said, turning fully to Erin and looking at her, delighted. Erin's aura was wide, floating in the morning light, full of vitality and excitement. 'It will not be legal, however. I am not a celebrant.'

'You're the Lady of the Grove,' Erin said, and bowed her head. 'It will be binding, if not legal.' She looked at Morghan. 'Perhaps Winsome will help? And then it could be legal as well.'

Morghan smiled again. 'That's an excellent idea. You must ask her.'

'I will,' Erin said. 'I'm heading there after this. I need to tell Mum too, of course. And we'll have to tell his parents.'

There was everyone to tell, really. Wayne – she wanted to be the one to tell him, too.

Erin nodded, looked seriously at Morghan. 'May I have your blessing, first, though?'

Morghan took her hands in her own. 'My dearest Erin, of course you have my blessing.' A shiver passed through her, and for a moment, it was as though she could see the weaving of Erin's lifetimes. Macha, Kria, many more. And often they stood with Stephan, whoever he had been in those lifetimes. Loved ones, she knew, travelled through lives with each other. They were the soul family. Stephan and Erin were family.

'I am overjoyed for you both,' she said. 'Erin, you are a precious soul, as are each of us, but I am so proud of you, of the work you have done over the last eighteen months, over the many lifetimes you've had. We've hard times ahead, but you will have Stephan by your side, and myself also.'

Morghan paused. 'Shall we once more step into the flow of this water, as we have done before, and ask blessing of the world for you also?'

Erin nodded mutely and bent down to unlace her boots and slip them off. Barefoot, she returned Morghan's smile, then drew up to her full height, took Morghan's hand, and stepped into the water, letting it clasp her around the calves, higher than usual from the rain, cold and sharp. She breathed into the shock.

Morghan spoke, and Erin let her words flow into and around her, inhaling them in, nodding.

'We step into the flow of this gracious river,' Morghan said. 'We step into it in a conscious reflection of our desire to step into the flow of our lives and purpose in this world. As water greets us and holds our story, remembering us, so too do we remember our tasks and gain strength for them.'

She bowed her head, feeling the river at her feet, the trees at her back, the birds, animals, Wolf waiting on the bank for her, the whole world spreading out around them, everything connected.

She felt too, the pockets of darkness, disruption, the fractures they'd brought the worlds, and turned her mind away from them. This day was for blessing. This day was for joy, for without these joys, what would be the use of it all?

Erin's hand was clasped in her golden fingers, and Morghan raised them in the air between them.

'My Goddess,' she said. 'My kin, my allies, my friends, my fellow travellers. We present you with our joy today, our continued dedication, and ask in return your blessing upon Erin, for she has returned to walk with us, and with Stephan, in commitment to you all.'

Morghan felt the world shift slightly around them, and from a branch, a bird sang out, a song thrush, high and clear in the stillness.

Erin heard the song and smiled, knowing it was part of the blessing she'd asked for, and she nodded, let go of Morghan's hands and bent over to cup running water in her palms. She held it for a moment, then lifted her hands, letting the water fall and pressing her wet hands to her forehead.

'Hail to you, blessed water,' she said. 'Air, earth, fire, and spirit, hail to you all.'

She straightened, glanced at Morghan, saw her standing there, her silvery green aura surrounding her, the golden hand gleaming. Erin closed her eyes, tilted her head towards the sky, took a deep, satisfied breath, then smiled.

'From sky to root,' she said. 'From each birth to each death.'

She'd learnt the prayer soon after coming to Wellsford, from hearing Morghan say it, but now, after all this time, she was finally claiming it as her own too. She spoke the last lines into the early morning, and watched them spread out, become part of the sacred weaving of the world.

'My life dedicated. My service freely given.'

Hopefully, Veronica would be out of bed already. Erin tried the side door to the vicarage, and it opened under her fingers. A good sign. She knew that Winsome was at Blackthorn House as Morghan had said she was heading there herself.

Which was a good thing, Erin told herself. Speaking alone to Veronica was the right thing to do, with news such as she had.

'Erin,' Veronica said, bending over hand on chest to catch her breath. 'You about scared me out of my skin.'

'Sorry, Mum,' Erin said wincing.

'Haven't you ever heard of knocking?'

'It's impossible to hear anyone knocking on the door in this house.'

Veronica blew out a big breath and straightened. 'Cup of tea, then?' She smiled. 'Or shall we be decadent and go to The Copper Kettle for coffee and cake?'

'It's not even nine in the morning, Mum. I don't think I can do cake at this time of the day.' Erin grinned at her mother, shook her head, then went to put the kettle on. 'Tea will be fine. I've got something to tell you.'

'Wait!' Veronica held up her hand. 'I've got something too. I dreamt about you last night – we were all out in the woods somewhere...' She paused to roll her eyes. 'Of course, because here there's nothing but woods. Anyway, everyone was there, and you were getting married.'

Erin turned around, kettle in hand, eyes wide. 'But Mum, that's what I came to tell you.'

Veronica looked blank a moment, then shook her head. 'No,' she said. 'No, really?'

'Your dream was right.' Erin set the kettle down. 'I asked Stephan last night.'

'You asked him?'

'Well, we kind of asked each other, I guess. But it was me who brought up the subject.'

'Brought up the subject?' Veronica pulled out a chair from the kitchen table and sat down on it. She was flummoxed that she'd dreamt this. 'This isn't sounding romantic at all.'

Her comment made Erin laugh. 'Mum, it was plenty romantic, don't you worry.'

'Are you sure you're ready, though?' Veronica asked, looking Erin over. She'd had her hair trimmed recently and it was a thick red cloud over her shoulders. 'Why's the hem of your dress all wet?'

Erin looked down at her skirts. 'Oh,' she said. 'I greeted the day with Morghan at the river.'

'You stepped in it? I'm surprised you can still feel your feet.'

'Mum?' Erin walked around the table and knelt beside Veronica. 'Aren't you happy for me?'

Veronica looked down at Erin, reached out a hand and

stroked her hair. 'I remember when you were a little girl,' she said. 'I used to have to chase you around the house to get your hair brushed.'

'And then you got it cut because the baby curls tangled all the time.'

'Because you howled when I tried to brush them out, you mean.'

'I love you, Mum.'

'Oh Erin.' Veronica pressed a kiss to her daughter's forehead. 'Of course I'm happy for you.' She paused a moment. 'If you're sure. You're still awfully young.'

'Not as young as I was when Jeremy and I got engaged.'

Veronica's mouth flattened. Then she laughed. 'Look at us,' she said. 'Who would have expected things would turn out this way?' Her smile wobbled slightly. 'My grandparents would be proud.'

Erin got up from her knees and shifted another chair closer so she could sit with her mother, knees touching.

'They would,' she said. 'I'm sad I never got to meet them.'

Veronica nodded, then changed the subject. 'So, I had one of those whatsitcalled dreams.'

'Precognitive,' Erin said.

Veronica nodded. 'It's this place, isn't it? Opens you up. You can't help it.'

'It's this way of living,' Erin said. 'It makes us whole.'

Another nod from Veronica, and she linked her hands in Erin's, then sat up straighter. 'Who's going to give you away?'

Erin had already thought of this. She and Stephan had

lain in bed, stretched out against each other, hands warm against bare skin, and made plans.

'No one,' she said, then grinned. 'I'm a sovereign being.'

Veronica frowned. 'What does that mean?'

But Erin shook her head. 'It doesn't matter. But we're not going to have that sort of wedding. It will be a handfasting.' She smiled. 'In the woods.'

Veronica held her tongue on that one. 'Will your father be there?'

'I think so, don't you?'

The answer made Veronica sigh, but she nodded anyway. 'He does love you.'

'And that's what it's all about, isn't it?' Erin straightened, but there was a crease between her brows. 'Mum?'

'Mmm?' Veronica was already thinking about what appropriate attire for a handfasting in the woods might be.

Erin cleared her throat. 'Do you...do you know who my birth father is?'

Veronica's mind went blank, and she stared at Erin, then remembered to blink. 'You've taken me by surprise.' She looked around the familiar and rather shabby room, then back to Erin's face. 'You've never asked that before.'

'No,' Erin agreed. 'Nobody's ever known, so there wasn't anything to say about it.' She smiled slightly. 'But if it's something you've just never told me, I promise I won't be mad.'

Veronica frowned, shook her head. 'Becca never said. Never gave a name at least. When we asked, she just said he was a guy she'd slept with once.'

'Once as in just the once, or once as in once upon a time?'

Veronica searched her daughter's face. 'You're the spitting image of Teresa Lovelace,' she said. 'I've looked at all the photos of her. There's no clue in your face as to anyone else, not that I've seen on the faces around here, at least.' She reached out and stroked Erin's hair again. 'I don't know which she meant, love. Could have been either.'

Erin nodded, grasped Veronica's hands and squeezed them. She hadn't been expecting anything else.

Perhaps though, she'd ask Wayne. She'd never done that before, and he'd not ever said.

11

———————

'THE WELL-KEEPER'S COTTAGE IS SUCH A SUCCESS,' WINSOME said and looked over the table to Morghan. 'I'm so glad you thought of using it this way.'

Morghan shook her head. 'Of course it must be part of the Stations of the Heart.' She paused. 'It was Selena's really, her little retreat, but she was glad for it to be of use again.'

Ambrose brought the fresh pot of tea to the table and sat down. 'How are Selena and the others? Have you spoken to them recently?' He turned to the fourth member of their small group, the new doctor. Kurt Lundquist had moved his chair out from under the table so he could more comfortably fit his 6'4" foot frame into the space.

'Selena was Lady of the Grove before Morghan, and Rue is Clover's sister.'

'I wish I had been in time to meet them,' Kurt said.

Morghan nodded. 'It's taking Rue some time to become used to the separation from Clover, I think, especially as it wasn't by her choice. But they have moved ahead with their

85

plans for the shop and so on.' She too turned to Kurt with a smile. 'Rue and Clover's friend Ebony, who came here to Wilde Grove with them this last time, has an esoterica shop called Beacon. They're extending it to offer the Stations of the Heart teachings.'

Winsome nodded. 'I saw a picture of them online the other day,' she said. 'Rue and Ebony looked rather wonderful, I thought,' Winsome said. 'Clover showed it to me.' Her brow wrinkled. 'Clover is doing all right without them, isn't she? It's her first time without her sister too.'

'She is the tiny one?' Kurt asked for confirmation, wondering if he'd ever get straight the history of the place. 'Who glows almost too brightly?'

Winsome smiled. 'Yes, that's Clover.'

Morghan nodded and turned her chair slightly and stretched her own legs out while she considered Winsome's question. 'I think she has been homesick and misses Rue terribly. I also think she made the right decision to stay here a little longer.' She looked over at Ambrose. 'I'm going to start taking her with me on my visits to the other courts.'

Ambrose paused in pouring the tea. These impromptu meetings were becoming a regular thing as the three of them came together and shared their various plans and visions.

He corrected himself. Four of them now, with Kurt's arrival. He fit in as though he'd always belonged.

'How many have you visited already?' he asked for Kurt's benefit.

'Only four,' Morghan replied. 'They've taken Queen Alastrina quite some time to organise.'

'And you've been made to prove yourself in each place?'

Morghan glanced at Ambrose, then looked back at the flames in the fireplace. They danced about the wood, and she thought how cosy it was to sit in a kitchen with the people she loved best, while the rain beat upon the window.

Except it was too much rain. The whole winter had been terribly wet, and the spring had just given them more of the same.

But Morghan pushed the thought away and turned back to the conversation at hand, straightening in her chair and accepting the cup of tea with a nod of thanks.

'You know I have, yes,' she answered at last.

'It seems dangerous,' Winsome said.

'It is.' Morghan shrugged. 'Or could be, I suppose.'

'Of course it is,' Ambrose said. 'We don't want a repeat of what happened with you when you went back to Blythe.' Ambrose was not pleased with his own thought.

Morghan smiled. 'But that is why you drum me there and back,' she said.

'Ha. If only you paid me mind every time. My drumming you back only works if you wish to hear it.' Ambrose scowled down into his tea, then felt Winsome's hand gentle upon his arm, and he forced himself to relax, take a breath.

'It can't be a good idea to take Clover with you,' he said, attempting to sound reasonable instead of madly concerned. Since the Trafalgar Square incident, Morghan had been running herself ragged. They all had, really. But Morghan particularly. It was a wonder she hadn't become ill. A miracle that she hadn't. The TV appearances for one – there'd been a terrible fly going around that winter. Ambrose had done several appearances with her, and not enjoyed any of them.

Still, they'd been important, those appearances, and Morghan, for someone who never even watched the television as far as Ambrose could tell, had done devastatingly well. She looked good on camera – she and Erin were a pair to reckon with, and he supposed he didn't fare too badly, either.

They'd put Wellsford and Wilde Grove well and truly on the map.

Kurt held up his hands. 'Wait,' he said, his Swedish accent curling around the word. 'What is this business that it is dangerous? And dangerous in which way?'

'To her health,' Ambrose said.

Morghan looked steadily at him for a moment, then turned to Kurt. She had taken to the tall Swede with his silver Mjolnir – Thor's Hammer – hanging from a cord around his neck. He was a welcome addition to their community, and the timing of his arrival couldn't have been better, when everything was being reshuffled and resettled.

'The priestesses here have been allied with the local Fae tribe for thousands of years,' she explained. 'We recently had some trouble with a group of Fae who are, shall we say, feeling less than patient with humans.' Morghan put her feet back under her and swung around to rest her elbows on the table. 'The local Queen, Alastrina, and I have been visiting the courts of the other tribes to sound out their views and willingness to create alliances.' She rubbed at her face. 'It's a very delicate business. The Fae do not take a great deal of pleasure in dealing with humans.'

Kurt was frowning. 'And how do you go about these meetings and dealings?' He shrugged his shoulders. 'I mean, what sort of state are you in, for it must be somewhat altered, yes?'

'Yes,' Ambrose answered, before Morghan could play it down. 'A shamanic trance state. A deep one. She did one last year she was lucky to come back from in one piece.'

'How is that?' Kurt leant forward, his empty cup dangling from a finger. This was, he thought, a fascinating place in which he'd ended up, and he'd only been here a week so far. He'd barely unpacked. He looked carefully at Morghan, who fascinated him with the quiet power she radiated. It must have taken years of training and discipline to be the way she was.

'She was so deep in the trance and for so long, that her blood pressure dropped,' Ambrose supplied.

Morghan resisted the urge to roll her eyes. 'I was fine,' she said. 'Everything ended well.' She smiled at Winsome. 'Didn't it?'

'Well, erm, yes,' Winsome said. 'But you did only just squeak through in the end.'

'Thanks to you and Erin.' Morghan looked back at their new doctor. 'Erin also accompanies me, since, as she will be the next Lady of the Grove, it is necessary that the Fae courts meet her also.'

Kurt followed the conversation. 'But I did not realise that this could be the case,' he said. 'That a trance state could affect like this.' He would research it once he got back to his new home. Or he would ask Ambrose when they were on their own. Ambrose looked as though he'd done plenty of research of the phenomenon, from the expression on his face.

Morghan reached for more tea. 'That was a slightly

different set of circumstances than the ones we're facing now.'

Kurt let that one go – he would definitely be asking Ambrose later. 'The girl, with the plant name...'

'Clover,' Winsome said with a smile. 'You'll learn who everyone is, soon enough.'

Kurt nodded. 'It is safe for her to go with you on these...'

'Travellings,' Morghan said. 'I call them travellings. I prefer it to the term journeying, although it is, of course, the same thing.'

'Okay.' Kurt nodded. 'It is safe for her to go on these travellings, with you?'

Morghan bowed her head. 'Safer for her than for perhaps anyone,' she said. 'Rhian, a past life aspect of Clover's soul, was once raised by the Fae. Clover retains the second sight and talents they gave Rhian.'

ERIN POKED HER HEAD AROUND THE DOOR AND GRINNED AT Wayne. 'There you are,' she said.

'Here I am,' Wayne said, beaming. 'And still surprised about it myself.'

Going into his room, Erin leant over to kiss his leathery cheek, then stood up. 'Don't be silly,' she said. 'Now, let me plump your pillow,' she said. 'You know it's the most essential part of my work here, especially now when I'm not coming in every day.'

Wayne lifted his head, grinning as Erin swiped at his pillow, then lay back down. 'You look positively glowing,' he said. He cast around the room. 'Where's Burdock?'

'He's out with Stephan,' Erin said. 'I'll be going to the

hospital later, so they're hanging out together.' She nodded and dragged over the chair and sat beside him. She wished she could say that Wayne was also glowing, but his skin was sallow and gaunt upon his cheeks. 'I wish I still worked here every day,' she said. 'So I could keep a better eye on you.'

'You do see me every day,' Wayne said, reaching for one of Erin's hands and giving it a squeeze. 'Practically, anyway.'

'Hmm. It's not the same,' Erin said.

'How's the new job treating you?' Wayne asked. He missed Erin working at the care home full-time, especially since his health had gone downhill again. But even he could see that her new work at the hospital was treating her well.

And then, he thought. There was all the other stuff. The appearances on the telly – he'd watched every one of those, in the lounge with old Mrs Sharp, their eyes practically glued to the screen. Erin had got him a tablet too, that had YouTube on it, and he liked that. There were a surprising number of videos of her on it.

'It's hard,' Erin said, answering his question frankly. She sighed, rested her elbows on the bed. 'There's a lot of suffering in hospitals.' She frowned. 'I mean, of course there is, but trying to make it just a little bit better and knowing you can't really, that's hard.'

'A little bit better?' Wayne said. 'I can promise that you make it that.' He poked her shoulder. 'Anyway, that's not what put that glow on your face, I know that for a fact, so 'fess up. What's happened?'

Erin broke into a wide smile. 'You know me pretty well, now, don't you?'

'I do at that,' Wayne said. 'And a privilege it is, too.'

'Stephan and I are getting married,' Erin said.

Wayne's eyes widened and he struggled to sit up straighter in the bed, leaning forward to envelop Erin in a hug. 'Congratulations!' he said. 'Oh, I am pleased about that.'

Erin squeezed him and felt joy spread through her, prickling pleasantly at her skin. 'It's wonderful, right?'

'It certainly is. There's no denying you two are made for each other.'

Erin nodded. 'You'll come, of course,' she said.

'Couldn't keep me away, if you do it in time,' Wayne told her.

Immediately, Erin's face fell. 'You have to come,' she said.

'When will it be?' He patted her arm. 'You know I'll do my best.'

'We haven't set a date yet,' Erin said, grasping his hand and holding it tightly. 'We want it to be outside, in the woods, perhaps at the stone circle.' She glanced toward the window. 'Or perhaps on the village green. I don't know.' Frowning, she turned back to Wayne and looked at him. 'Wayne?'

'What is it?'

'Can I ask you a question?'

Wayne would have laughed, except for the look on Erin's face. The smile had evaporated, replaced by a frown Wayne knew by now to recognise. She was working away at some puzzle or another.

'Ask away, love,' he said. 'If I know the answer, I'll give it to you.'

Erin nodded, looked down at her hands, the furrow between her brows deepening. Finally, she sighed and looked directly at Wayne. 'Do you know who my birth father is?'

There was a pause before Wayne answered. She'd taken him by surprise.

'It's not me,' he said, wishing it was. 'But you knew that.'

Erin nodded.

It was Wayne's turn to frown as he searched his memory. 'She never gave me a name,' he said, shaking his head, then looked at Erin, shoulders hunching. 'I wasn't curious about it either, I have to say. She was giving the baby away, and that was that.'

'She must have said something, though?' Erin said. 'Anything at all?'

Wayne searched his memory again. The trouble, he thought, with that though, was that it was full of holes. There was more from that time that he couldn't remember than that he could.

'I'm sorry, Erin,' he said. 'I feel like she said it was just from a one-night stand, but I don't know if I'm just imagining that, or what.'

Erin nodded. 'I knew it was a long shot.' She found a smile. 'I just thought I'd ask, since I've just told Mum, and we're tackling Stephan's parents later.'

Wayne found her hand and held it in his. 'I wish I could help you.' he said helplessly. 'I wish it were bloody well me.'

Erin grinned at him and kissed his pale cheek. 'I do too,' she said. 'Now, get some rest, and I'll pop back in before I leave.'

12

Ambrose met Maxen on the way to the cave, the faerie man stepping out of the folds of the worlds with an ease that had ceased to surprise Ambrose many years before.

'We are well met,' he said, with a slight bow.

'My greetings to you, my friend,' Maxen replied. 'The Queen is ready.'

Ambrose shook his head. 'I don't know how I feel about this.' He glanced at Maxen. 'I know Morghan and the Queen have made such trips already, but I can't help but be nervous about it.'

'As you should. Not everyone is as open to these diplomatic visits as we should like.' Maxen walked along the old pathways of the Grove at Ambrose's side.

'But they are necessary,' Ambrose muttered on a sigh.

'I wish I could say that they are not.'

Ambrose nodded, shook his head. 'With each visit, however, I am expecting it to be to the tribe to which those at the quarry belong.'

There. He'd spoken aloud his fear. Of course, he'd voiced it to Morghan as well, as much use as that had been. She'd rested a hand on his arm, and smiled with that faraway look she had, and told him – that she hoped to meet with them, and see what could be negotiated.

But he wasn't convinced that would prove any use. In fact, it alarmed him greatly.

'You know my concerns,' he said aloud now, and ducked under a branch that hung lower than usual, leaves drenched with rain.

Maxen smiled. 'I am no mind reader, Ambrose,' he said. 'But yes, you have expressed them previously to today.' It was beginning to rain once more, but Maxen paid the water no mind, for he did not walk in this world in solid form, and the rain did not touch him.

'Do you have more or different fears?'

Ambrose, his drum in its carry bag on his back, shook his head. 'My previous fears are plenty,' he said, and returned to the nugget that took up a great deal of space inside him these days. 'What is the likelihood, do you think, of them coming true?'

'Of a meeting with those from the quarry?'

Ambrose nodded. They stepped around the stone circle and Ambrose paused a brief second to nod his greetings to Grandmother Oak and the stone keepers before continuing.

'I fear there would be no convincing them of our mission and sincerity,' he said. 'I see it all the time on our internet – opinions are fixed and there is no persuading otherwise.'

Maxen tipped his head in agreement. 'I do not think you have to worry about a meeting with those folk from the quarry. They will never agree to a meeting in the first place.'

'I would like to believe that,' Ambrose said on another sigh, and he pulled up his hood to keep the rain off, and brooded the rest of the walk to the cave.

CLOVER LOOKED UP AT AMBROSE'S ENTRANCE. 'I KNOW,' SHE said. 'I'm early.' She saw movement behind Ambrose. 'Maxen! You're here too.'

Maxen bowed. 'I will be escorting you. I am part of the Queen's delegation.' A smile played around his lips. 'It was my request to be so,' he said, then sobered. 'But you are coming also?'

'Morghan said you wanted to,' Ambrose said, setting his drum down and looking to the fire. It was cold along with the rain, but once he had the fire going, the smoke curling up and out of the cave through an ingenious and ancient chimney, the womb-like room would warm up swiftly.

'I do,' Clover said, and gave Maxen a sidelong glance. 'Do you think the Queen will mind?' She hadn't seen the Faerie man for some weeks and was flushed with pleasure at his presence. Morghan had not mentioned that Maxen was part of the delegation party.

'I do not presume to know Queen Alastrina's mind,' Maxen said, lowering his head in another slight bow to take any sting out of his words. 'That position is for others than myself. I am not Her Majesty's close counsel.'

'But you come back and forth between our worlds all the time,' Clover cried. 'You know everything that is going on.'

Maxen smiled affectionately at her. 'I have heard that you have been doing good work.'

Clover turned and held her hands out to the growing fire that Ambrose had set. She'd meant to do that herself but had only arrived moments before Ambrose and Maxen.

'I don't know if it is work that I need be doing,' she said after a moment.

Maxen lowered himself to the ground. Here, in this ancient cave, a pocket of sacred space in all the worlds, he was more visible – especially to Clover. He suspected he was always visible to her sight.

'Why is that?' he asked her, and felt his friend Ambrose pause and still to hear the answer.

Clover glanced over at Ambrose, but she did not mind him hearing her reply.

'When we go out to do our blessings and so on,' she said. 'I lift the veil from the land we must bless.'

Ambrose and Maxen nodded their understanding.

'Because I learnt from Rhian how to do that,' Clover continued. 'But then, as soon as the blessing is sung, I let it lower again.'

'And what is wrong with that?' Maxen asked, genuinely curious.

'Well.' Clover frowned, sorting out how to put her thoughts into words. 'Isn't the whole point to not have the separation of the veil? I mean, it's going to be removed anyway, isn't it? I mean, haven't the Fae already decided to remove it – so that the worlds are merged again?'

Maxen nodded. 'That is so,' he said. 'But it is not something that we intend will happen overnight. Perhaps hundreds of years, so that humankind may get used once more to living in a spirit-filled world.'

Ambrose nodded. 'As it stands, most people don't believe they even have a soul, such are the times.'

Clover nodded, but she was glum. 'What if we don't have hundreds of years?' she asked, and looked over at Ambrose, her face beseeching. 'What if we need to realise this sooner?'

But it was Maxen who answered her. 'Perhaps you are right,' he said. 'Which is why you are here, why all of you are stepping up your efforts. Because your people must be prepared as much as is possible.' He shifted slightly. 'Because...'

There was movement at the entrance to the cave, and the murmuring of prayers, then Morghan entered, Erin beside her.

Morghan bowed a greeting at the three, and Erin, giving Clover a quick grin, did the same.

'What were you saying, Maxen?' Morghan asked, sitting down gratefully at the fireside. It was cold outside, the wind coming up as they'd walked there.

'Clover was asking about the need for the disintegration of the veil to be a gradual process, and then, pertinently, whether there is time for it to be so.'

Morghan listened, nodded, looked at Clover. Erin had sat down next to her and Morghan could feel the quickening of her interest. There were always questions around this, she thought. It was a hard concept to grasp.

'And you were explaining it?' she asked now, unwilling to interrupt Maxen's reply more than their arrival already had.

'I was,' Maxen said. 'I had said that the beacons must be given time to become bright, to shine the way, and the well-keepers to become deep, to hold back the wasteland.' He looked kindly at Clover, reached out and stroked her hand lightly, knowing she would feel his touch. 'Because once the veil is completely removed, not everyone will be able to survive it.'

Clover looked at him, her face blank with shock. 'I don't understand,' she said. She looked at Erin, whose expression mirrored her own. When she looked at Ambrose and Morghan, she saw that they already knew this.

'What do you mean, not everyone will be able to survive it?'

'You have long turned away from the state of being necessary to comprehend the world as it really is,' Maxen said. 'It has happened, after all, over thousands of years.'

'And we don't have thousands of years in which to reverse it,' Clover said, and her voice shook.

'Yes,' Maxen said. 'You would, but you must face the crisis you have put the world into. That, coupled with the dark ones who take advantage of confusion and fear and corruption. It will be a difficult time.'

'There are some,' Morghan said, her voice as calm as she could make it, 'among the Fae who wish the veil between the worlds to be destroyed at once. We have come up against them already.' She gave Erin a kind look. 'But that would spell disaster for us. And war, which is what humans always turn to when they are afraid.' She looked over at Maxen, then continued. 'A war the likes of which has not been seen before, as the human population is so large, and we have weapons previously unheard of.' She straightened. 'Which is why our mission here is so important.'

She smiled, somewhat sadly, and reached for Ambrose's hand, held it in her own as she looked at the younger people. 'Which is also why it is important for you, Erin, and perhaps also you, Clover, to be part of this. For I will not be around to see the end of it, and our work must carry on, from my generation to yours, and onward from that. We play a very long game here, making moves, the benefit of which we will not necessarily be around to see, or at least not in this flesh.'

But Clover shook her head. 'What about Wilde Grove and Wellsford?' she asked. 'I mean, as we discovered last year, there has been only the thinnest veil over Wellsford and none over Wilde Grove. And everyone here is all right. So, I guess I don't understand.'

Morghan squeezed Ambrose's hand and let it go. 'The difference is that Wellsford has always been this way, and the people who live and have lived here have always known and accepted the magic.' She smiled slightly. 'It is a common dare for the teenagers in Wellsford to come spy on the quarterly rites at the stones – and has been for hundreds of years, I imagine. They grow up knowing and seeing the spirits of the land, the Fae with whom we are fortunate to be allied. Most have seen them with their own eyes, even if they wouldn't tell you about it.' She paused. 'It's this knowing, this acceptance of our world's deepest realities, that makes it a special place to grow up in. I doubt you'd find many in Wellsford who would deny that the world is a deep place rich with spirit.' She smiled faintly, thinking of Mariah. 'Some, it is true, are damaged by it, but that is mostly a case of upbringing, or a weakness in their physical system. Those who move here either fit in with the strong energies, or they move away again, perhaps without quite knowing why they want to.'

There was silence in the cave, except for the crackling of the fire. Morghan let it stretch out a minute longer, then nodded.

'We need to begin,' she said, and reached into her bag for the herbs with which she would make her initial offerings.

Queen Alastrina raised one delicate, perfectly arched eyebrow at Clover's presence.

'My Lady,' Clover said, and knelt on one bent knee.

The Queen nodded and Clover rose, tried not to look around, staring at everything. It had been some time since she'd been to the Fair Lands, and she'd never got used to them. It was hard, she thought, to see leopards stretched out under a tree full of fragrant blossoms, while a peacock paraded past, tail spread like an exotic fan. She turned her head away from the sights.

She caught Erin's eye and faint smile. Erin had also had trouble getting used to the place. To the sweetly fragranced air, the constant balmy sunshine, the animals. And the people, of course. The Fae.

'You did not go back to your own land, then?' the Queen asked Clover.

Clover thought it impossible that the Queen hadn't already known this, but she answered anyway. 'No,' she said. 'I thought I had more to do and learn here. For now.'

'But the others did.'

Clover nodded assent.

The Queen appeared to contemplate this for a moment, then turned, businesslike, to Morghan. 'Come then, let us depart.'

Departing meant quite the retinue, Clover discovered. Then she frowned to herself. They were, after all, not simply going visiting, but providing a delegation, and a diplomatic one at that. Besides Morghan, Erin, and now herself, there were the Queen's people. Fae of tall and sombre statue.

And Maxen, of course.

Clover caught his eye and smiled at his wink, then her gaze was captured by another of the Fae and she frowned at the sudden, deep sense of knowing that flooded through her. The woman looked back at her, a slight smile on her face, and Clover wanted to go up to her, ask her who she was, how they knew each other.

Except she couldn't, of course, for in a moment, they would be on their way, and there would be no accepting a delay.

But Clover noted the woman, and the feeling, and held it close inside her. Here, she thought, was another piece of her personal puzzle.

For she had the distinct impression that it was through Rhian that she knew this person.

13

THEY WENT ON HORSEBACK, CLOVER SURPRISED TO FIND THAT apparently she knew how to ride a horse. She looked wide-eyed at Erin next to her and Erin leant a little toward her, her voice low when she spoke.

'I know,' Erin said. 'I bet I looked just the same my first time.'

'I've never ridden a horse before,' Clover said. 'Not in all my travellings.'

Erin smiled and stroked the horse she rode. 'Things are different here, that's for certain.'

Things were very different, Clover thought, if she knew how to ride a horse without any practice or even any thought. Her body just seemed to know what to do. She shook her head slightly and marvelled, not for the first time, or even the hundredth, that the Otherworld was full of surprises.

Such as the way Morghan looked, astride one of the

Queen's horses. She sat atop its back as though she'd been riding all her life, but that wasn't what made Clover stare.

'Does she always look like that?' she asked Erin in a whisper. They were flanked by the Fae on either side, which was one more thing Clover hadn't got to calculating yet, but first things first.

'Who?' Erin asked.

'Morghan,' Clover said, and then her horse was moving, falling effortlessly in line with the others. She felt the rolling gait under her and made herself relax.

Erin looked ahead to where Morghan rode with the Queen. Or almost with the Queen. If you looked again, Erin thought, you noticed that Morghan was always just a step behind the Queen's grey-speckled horse. She wondered if it were the horse that did that of its own accord, which did not seem impossible when her own moved with the group rather than from anything she herself was doing. Or did, perhaps, Morghan keep that one pace back because she made the decision to?

It was hard to fathom that one day Morghan would no longer be Lady of the Grove, but that she, Erin would be riding up the front there, one careful step behind the Faerie Queen. Erin, even when she tried, could not imagine it, and her constant prayer to the Goddess was that Morghan would live a long life, healthy in both body and mind.

She nodded to Clover. 'Yes,' she answered. 'She always looks like that, or something near.'

Morghan was dressed in deep forest green, the fabric fine woven cloth, but it wasn't really that which drew the eye, Erin thought. It was the feathers in the hair, the cloak tossed almost casually over her shoulders, and of course, the great dark-coated wolf walking at her side. Erin wasn't sure really if it was Morghan who rode at the Queen's side, or Ravenna.

Morghan, she decided, not for the first time. Ravenna had dark hair, and Morghan still had hers grey. Plus, there was the golden hand that glinted in the light.

Erin looked across at Clover and grinned at her. 'Look at yourself,' she said. 'Look at me – my clothes change whenever I come here.'

'You look like Macha,' Clover said, pitching her voice low, feeling the small smile of Maxen, who rode beside her. She wanted to turn in her saddle and look for the woman she felt she had recognised but didn't let herself.

What had it been like for Rhian, she wondered. Growing up here, with the Fae?

MORGHAN RODE SILENTLY ONE PACE BACK FROM THE QUEEN. She was comfortable in the saddle of her great black horse, but her mind was not entirely at ease, no matter how calm she might keep her features or her energy. Wolf turned his head and looked at her, eyes piercing, and she knew that he sensed her disquiet, if no one else did.

She would be tested, she knew, when they arrived at their destination. It had been the same at the courts they had visited previously and would be so again.

What it would be this time was what she did not know. Whatever the task would be, however, she had to pass it. There would be no negotiations if she did not.

Ambrose's concerns for her bodily health were the least of the problems they could encounter.

They skirted around the World Pool, and Morghan let her gaze fall to the great round lake at the bottom of the steep-sided valley, watching for a moment the pale shadows of the whale pod that swam in the waters. Then she turned her eyes forward and paid attention as they left the paths with which she was familiar and rode deep into the forests of the Otherworld.

'We do not gain entrance through tunnels?' she said after a while of expecting to go down into the darkness of the underground.

'Not this time,' the Queen replied. 'This tribe is... wilder than those we have visited previously, than my own.'

Morghan's eyebrows rose. 'Wilder?'

'They enjoy a very active lifestyle.'

The contours of the land had changed, and their horses walked single file now, along a path that wound around a steep gully. The forest had thickened further, become almost a jungle.

Morghan thought for a moment of her body, sitting in the cave before the fire, and Erin and Clover across from her, all of them as though asleep or dead, Ambrose watching over them, his drumbeat matching the quiet rhythm of their hearts.

Not that she needed his drum to travel, but it was wise to have him present, particularly when they were going this deep, this long.

She doubted he would let her not have his presence.

She leant forward over her horse's neck. 'Time here is still compressed?'

Alastrina turned to look at her, face smooth, barely lined

despite the Queen's great age. 'Why would it not be?' she asked.

Morghan sat back. It had been a needless question, of course. Time passed more swiftly in these lands. When she woke to her own flesh in the cave, only an hour would have passed. Perhaps two.

There was movement, a sudden flash of white, and then she was being pulled from her seat, dragged between the trees, soil and leaf kicked up under her heels, held up against the trunk of a great, unyielding tree.

This was it, she knew, struggling to keep up with the suddenness of the attack.

This was the initiation. The test. She reached out with her hand to touch Wolf's warm head.

He was not at her side.

He was always at her side.

And yet, he was not there. She stared at the two people who had pulled her from her horse and dragged her off as though she weighed nothing. They were Fae, she recognised at once, despite being shorter than herself. There was still the litheness of limb, the fineness of features.

The strength and fleet-footedness, Morghan thought also, and fought not to let her thoughts sour against them.

One of the pair, who both were dressed in a softly luminous and creamy white, bowed suddenly to her and produced a bow of beautifully finished wood, and a fletch of arrows. She held them out to Morghan, all but thrust them into her hands.

Morghan's heart sank – how good a shot would she be with these? Would she even be able to draw the bowstring back? Schooling her face not to give anything away,

Morghan accepted the proffered bow and arrows, set the sling of arrows upon her back as the faerie pair wore theirs, then held the bow and experimentally pulled the string back.

It came easier than she expected.

Still, no one had exchanged a word, and when Morghan straightened and glanced back the way they'd come, she could see no sign of their passage, and certainly no glimpse of Alastrina's retinue.

The pair in front of her turned suddenly, fell into a half crouch, and Morghan watched, holding in her astonishment as a huge white buck stepped into view, stared at them for a moment, then turned and bounded into the forest.

The Fae ran after it, and Morghan knew at once that she was required to join the chase, that it would be her arrow that must be the one to fell the great stag.

She launched herself after them, willing her body to be fast, agile, as she bounded over the uneven ground, slipping between this tree, around that one.

On the pathway, Erin looked around in consternation. 'Where has she gone?' she called. 'We've got to find her.' She glanced at Clover, whose astonishment matched her own, then looked to the Queen.

'We've got to find her,' she repeated, gathering her horse's reins, preparing to dismount.

'We do not,' Queen Alastrina said.

Erin looked around at the trees. It had happened so quickly. One moment they had been riding along, the horses picking their steps carefully over tree root and around stone, and then – a flash of white, and Morghan was snatched from her horse and gone.

The horse was still with them on the path, and to Erin's greater consternation, she saw that Morghan's wolf was also.

'But we have to find her,' she cried, dismayed to see the wolf there, staring intently into the undergrowth. Why had it not gone with Morghan? Was it not always with her?

'She is being tested,' the Queen said shortly, and turned her blue gaze back to Erin. 'As she has been with each of our visits to the other courts.'

Erin shook her head. 'But not like this,' she said. 'Not snatched from her saddle. Where have they taken her? What are they going to do with her?'

Why hadn't Wolf gone also?

Erin looked over at Clover. 'You must be able to see,' she said.

Clover shook her head. 'I don't know,' she said.

The Queen was moving again, urging her horse forward; Morghan's, the saddle empty, stirrups hanging, followed her. The Fae on his horse behind Erin and Clover made a clicking sound, and their horses started along the path again also, Erin helpless on her mount's back.

'Where are we going?' she asked. 'Shouldn't we wait?'

She had asked the questions half to herself, not expecting anyone to hear, let alone answer, but as always, she underestimated the Fae's hearing. The Queen turned her head so that Erin could see her profile.

'We go to wait at the meeting place. Then, if Morghan returns, we will have our discussions.'

Erin was appalled. 'If she returns?'

Alastrina looked to the front again. 'We must hope that she does.'

14

Rowan nodded, straightened, let Paul look her up and down, his expression assessing.

'You'll do,' he said at last, then stopped, frowning. 'How come you never wear lipstick anymore?'

Rowan frowned. 'You didn't like it.'

Paul thought for a moment. 'That was because you put it on every morning, no matter what. You don't need makeup on to cook breakfast and go to the shops.' Another assessment. 'Do you still have some?'

Rowan thought about it. She guessed there might still be a lipstick in her old makeup bag. 'It'll be out of date.'

Paul snorted, shook his head. 'Those sorts of things don't go out of date. Put some on, and some mascara too. We've got to make a good impression.'

It was important, this day. True too, that he wanted to make a good impression. Wanted to be welcomed back into the fold, him and his little family embraced, fussed over a bit. He looked back from the doorway.

'How far along are you?'

Rowan blinked at him. Robbie was playing on the floor with his barnyard. Or sitting on the floor holding it, at any rate, his big dark eyes had been following her around as she'd got ready.

'Far along?' she asked stupidly.

Paul rolled his eyes. 'The new baby,' he said. 'How far along are you?'

'Oh.' Rowan had found her old makeup bag in the bottom drawer of the bedside table. 'Um.' She swallowed. 'Fourteen weeks.'

'Huh.' Paul pursed his lips. 'We'll be able to feel it kick in a week or so, then.'

Rowan looked at him, astonished. 'How do you know that?' She couldn't fathom how he knew that, or even that he had any interest in knowing such a thing.

Paul smiled slyly at her. 'I looked it up. Now get a move on. I'll be in the car.'

He disappeared out the door and Rowan stood there, make up bag in hand, staring after him. She had a bad feeling about all this, she realised.

'Mummy?'

She looked down at Robbie, smiled automatically. 'What is it, darling?'

Robbie got to his feet, still clutching his soft barnyard full of animals. 'Where we goin'?'

Rowan took a quick breath, got the bag unzipped. 'We're going to church, love,' she said brightly, and rummaged around in the bag.

There was a lipstick in there and she pulled it out, then tugged the lid from it to see the colour.

Plum Promise had been her favourite colour. She looked down at what she was wearing. Paul had chosen the clothes for her from the wardrobe, and the skirt also, like the lipstick, predated her marriage. It was too tight around her middle, and she hadn't been able to zip it up properly, but that didn't matter because the new blouse covered it.

Paul had bought it, the blouse.

She'd almost had a heart attack the day before, when she had Robbie had walked home from the Wellsford bus and discovered that Paul was out. Where was he? She'd pulled her phone out and looked frantically for new messages, sure there would be some, maybe a missed call too, asking where she was, why she wasn't at Ladybird Lane, that there had been no doctor's appointment because he'd gone there, and the receptionist had told him that she wasn't booked in until the next week.

But there'd been no missed calls, no text messages, and when Paul finally got home, it had been with shopping bags under his arms, and not a single question about what she'd really been doing, only the triumphant presentation of the blouse she was now wearing.

It was high necked and long sleeved and covered in big blousy purple roses.

Oddly enough, the lipstick matched it, or near enough. Rowan scraped some across her lips, then dipped back into the bag for some mascara, maybe a little blusher. The mascara was old and mostly dry, and Rowan was convinced she'd get an eye infection from it, but it worked. Somewhat. She dabbed the blusher on her cheeks, a little on her eyelids, then heard the car horn blowing. When she glanced out the window, Paul was sitting in the car, exhaust blowing out in great plumes.

'Come on, sweetheart,' she said, throwing the makeup down and picking up Robbie. 'We'd better get a wiggle on.'

Robbie tucked his barnyard under his arm and Rowan debated trying to get him to leave it at home, then at another blast of the horn from the driveway, decided there wasn't time to argue with Robbie about it. She grabbed her handbag and hustled downstairs.

PAUL WADED INTO THE CROWD OUTSIDE THE CORNERSTONE Church like, Rowan thought, hanging back with Robbie on a hip, the second coming of Jesus, or Moses parting the red sea, or whatever. She wasn't up on her bible stories.

She guessed that was about to change. Paul had on his most genial smile and was soaking up the attention like a sea sponge. She saw him turn and look for her and her heart sank when he gestured expansively for her to join him.

'This is my wife, Rowan, and my little lad Robbie,' Paul said, and Rowan manufactured a smile out of nothing, and barely heard the other person's words over the commentary running in her head.

Funny, she thought, how Robbie was suddenly his little lad, when every other minute of every other day, he was hers.

But she smiled and nodded, allowed some middle-aged geezer to put his hand on her lower back to usher her inside.

This was what Paul wanted, and when Paul got what he wanted, she got what she wanted – a few days peace from him. If she had to sit in this awful warehouse of a church for two hours a week to get that, it might well be worth it. She didn't put Robbie out with the other kiddies, though, when it came time. Instead, she murmured perhaps next week, when he was more used to things.

They would be coming back next week, Rowan could see that already in Paul's face. His eyes were shining as he gazed up at the husband and wife team on the dais, a microphone held in each of their hands.

There were electric guitars. A whole band, really, Rowan supposed, with a tall weedy guy bashing away on the drums and a good looking girl with hair down almost to her waist chortling the words of some song praising Jesus.

Actually – Rowan backtracked along her thoughts and gave the girl the credit she deserved. The kid could sing. Rowan imagined she'd see her on some show before too long. Britain's Got Talent, or some such thing.

But maybe not. Rowan sighed, moved a squidge away on the bench seat from the fella with the opportune hands, and, at Paul's insistent nudge of the elbow, made herself clap along.

She couldn't go so far as to wave her hands in the air though, when the song finished and a quieter one came on. She was glad Paul didn't as well, and a little surprised by it. But he always was a good one for knowing how far to take something in order to get the best impression. Rowan expected that he'd told the folk outside that they were returning to the fold after being seduced away by the world, so it would stand to reason that they had to show a little decorum when it came to the hand waving.

Rowan closed her eyes, hoped people thought she was praying, if they noticed. She tipped her chin down for good measure and thought about her life.

This is what it's come to, she thought. I wanted to join Wilde Grove, and instead I've ended up in an evangelical, Pentecostal church. How do these things happen, she wondered?

The question repeated itself over and over in her mind for the rest of the service, and by the time she had Robbie strapped back into his car seat and she was buckling her own seatbelt after the service and the obligatory coffee and cake and so on, all she wanted to do was go home and have a nap.

'That was awful,' she said, when Paul got in the car. 'I didn't enjoy that at all, did you? The band music has given me a headache.'

Paul looked at her. 'I thought it was marvellous,' he said. 'And Pastor Eric, when he got going, was amazing. That man can preach.'

Rowan pressed her lips together. Pastor Eric could make a scene, was what she thought, but she said nothing.

'And they were so kind when we were taken to the library and introduced to the church and everything they do there.'

Rowan stared at her hands in her lap. Hard. They hadn't been herded into the church's library room to be given the grand spiel about what the church could offer them. It had been, she thought, a barely concealed opportunity to quiz them about their suitability to grace the Cornerstone Church's hallowed warehouse of the soul.

Not for the first time she wondered if Paul was a bit dim, or if she herself was just too cynical.

And their questioning had made her very uncomfortable. It was like the smarmy guy's hand pressed to the small of her back, uninvited and unwelcome.

'We don't really have to bring Robbie to daycare here, do we?'

Paul glanced at her as he started the car and backed out of the car park, entering the flow of vehicles leaving the church.

'Don't worry about it,' Paul said, and turned left towards the town centre. 'It will do our Robbie some good, to mix with the kiddies there. Let's go have some pancakes, shall we? To celebrate?'

'Pancakes?' The thought of them, sweet and sticky, made Rowan's mouth turn down. 'I'd rather not, Paul,' she said. 'I've got a headache, like I said.'

'They'll do you good,' he said. 'You've got to eat, and it can be a treat, just for today.'

Rowan sank back into the seat and said nothing. It was obvious that they were going to have pancakes. At least she wouldn't have to go home and cook lunch, she supposed. She really did have a headache.

At the pancake house, she saw exactly why they were there, when half the tables were taken by families from Cornerstone. It was, apparently, the place to take your kids for an after church treat. Paul accepted the offer to share a table with one such family, and Rowan found herself sitting opposite a woman about her own age, heavily made up to look as though she wasn't wearing makeup.

Rowan stabbed her fork at the pancake stack on her plate. The only consolation to all of this, she thought, was that Robbie, who was showing signs of a sweet tooth already, was sitting in one of the shop highchairs, happily peeling his pancake into surprisingly dainty strips before eating them like spaghetti. His hands were covered in syrup.

'Not hungry?' the woman opposite asked. Rowan hadn't caught her name.

'Not very,' Rowan said. She forked a mouthful of pancake and chewed, trying not to seem ungracious. Paul was shooting her looks from his seat beside her.

'Your boy is very handsome,' the woman said, nodding toward Robbie who had somehow gotten maple syrup in his hair making it stick up like a punk rocker's spiky gel job. 'Your husband said he goes to Ladybird Lane Daycare?'

Rowan swallowed the lump of pancake and nodded. 'He's been going there since he was just a year old. He loves it there – the caregivers are all so kind.'

But the woman was shaking her head. 'They had those Wilde Grove women there just the other day, so I heard.'

'To give a blessing for the new children's vegetable garden,' Rowan said. She glanced at Paul, but he was in a hearty conversation with the woman's husband.

'Only Jesus can give blessings,' the woman said. 'Or us, in his name.' She took out her outrage on the waffle on her plate, then looked directly across at Rowan.

'You weren't there for it, were you?'

Rowan blinked. 'Um. I was, actually. A lot of parents were.'

The woman nodded, her mouth a flat line as though this were no more than she had expected. 'The devil gets around,' she said.

'What?' Rowan almost squawked the word and Paul glanced at her. She ignored him. 'I'm sorry. What did you say?'

But the woman ignored her question. 'What were they like, these priestesses?' She spat the last word out as though merely saying it left a bad taste in her mouth.

But the woman didn't give her time to answer. Instead, she poked her fork in the air, the prongs stabbing repeatedly in Rowan's direction for emphasis.

'We're going to give them what for,' she said.

'What for?' Rowan asked and glanced again at Paul. Surely he was hearing this nonsense? Surely he'd let them get up and go home?

But Paul was lapping up whatever rubbish the woman's husband was dishing out, and Rowan had a sudden clear thought – wasn't this what Paul was like? Lapping up whatever nonsense someone coughed up, like a dog chowing down on its own upchuck.

'I'm afraid I don't know what you mean,' she said, and looked glumly at her plate, then placed her knife and fork down upon it, neatly lined up. She hadn't wanted the pancakes in the first place, and she was done trying to eat them. She was ready to go home, and if it wasn't for Robbie, quite obviously enjoying this rare pancake occurrence, she'd pluck him up and leave right then.

The woman leant forward over the table towards her, a confidential smile on her beige lips. 'We've got a man,' she said.

'A man?'

A nod, and the woman straightened, dug her fork into the syrup-laden waffle on her place.

Rowan wondered vaguely how she could eat that many and stay slim enough for the bones of her clavicle to jut out as they did.

'He's coming from America,' the woman said. 'He'll give them what they deserve.'

'What do they deserve?' Rowan asked, and she shook her head slightly. 'They talk about fairly sensible things, I thought. The need for close communities who look out for each other in all areas. The need to take responsibility for the way we think and discern things.' She closed her eyes a moment, remembering the fiasco of walking out on the Stations of the Heart class. She wished now that she hadn't.

Stations of the Heart. Even the sound of that comforted Rowan. Not like the banners she'd seen at Cornerstone, the ones that proclaimed that God had a plan for her life. If God had had a plan for her life, then why had He allowed it to get so shitty?

The world was pretty shitty, for that matter. On the whole.

They had to find a way to make it less so, really. Which, she thought, was what the Wilde Grove people were trying to do. Rowan thought of the ravens surrounding the priestesses at Trafalgar Square. She'd stopped and watched those pieces of footage every time she'd seen them playing.

There was something behind that, she thought. Something real, magical.

Hopeful.

And the three priestesses, each one different and yet,

they were united. That was what the world needed to be like.

But the woman was speaking, her high ponytail bobbing up and down. Rowan tuned back in.

'I'm sorry,' she interrupted a moment later, certain she couldn't have heard it correctly. 'What did you just say?'

The woman – Rowan really didn't know her name – seemed plenty happy with having to repeat herself, and Rowan realised that the two husbands had stopped their yapping now and were listening in, both of them nodding like a pair of bobble heads in a car on a bumpy road.

'We're getting together God's Army.'

'Oh.' That didn't make any more sense than Rowan thinking she'd heard it as Dad's Army, which probably hadn't even played on the television for twenty years at least. She shook her head. 'What does God need an army for?'

'To fight the devil, of course.' The ponytail swung. 'What isn't of God, is of Satan.'

The woman leant back in triumph.

Her husband nodded enthusiastically. 'John Stoat will be preaching next week. I'm so glad you've come back to Jesus in time.'

Rowan blinked at him, then his wife, unable to fathom what she was hearing, and then suddenly she was standing up, wiping the sticky syrup from Robbie's face and hauling him out of the highchair.

Without saying a word, she turned and walked out.

15

Rowan got Robbie upstairs and into his bed. The poor kid had conked out, overdosed on sugar and Jesus, Rowan thought sourly, kissing his soft forehead and smelling maple syrup even though she'd wiped him carefully clean before walking out to the car to wait for Paul to come spluttering and red-faced to drive them home.

She'd told him to be quiet until they got home and she got Robbie to bed.

He'd yelled anyway.

She'd ignored him, but home now, she could hear him storming around downstairs. She'd have to go and face him.

Rowan kissed Robbie once more. She'd sat in the back seat next to him all the way home, holding his hand, looking into his dear eyes even while Paul blustered and shouted. She'd felt the warm little hand in her own and concentrated on that, willing peace and love through their touch.

It must have worked, because Robbie was asleep before Paul pulled into the driveway and yanked the handbrake on. Admittedly though, the last half of the drive had been done in silence, Paul obviously deciding to wait until they were home.

Rowan had been surprised he'd managed to control himself.

'It's going to be all right, darling,' she whispered to her sleeping son, and she tucked his barnyard in beside him before turning, sighing, and going downstairs.

It was fortunate, Morghan thought, that she did not feel the full weight of her 51 years while in the Otherworld, or, even fit as she was, there would be no succeeding in this task. The land was hilly, the ground uneven, the forest thick.

She sprang up a new path, her hands sweaty where they gripped the bow, and she caught another flash of white.

The stag.

Not, she thought, the idea jouncing around in her head as she ran, the White Stag of the Wildwood, but almost as lovely. He was thick with muscle and fleet of foot. How he didn't get those great antlers of his caught on the close-growing trees, she didn't know, but he did not, and they ran on.

The two Fae who had pulled her so unceremoniously from her horse were nowhere to be seen. Not that Morghan had the time to look.

But she knew they were close by. Not only did they run as easily as the deer themselves, even on terrain such as this, they did so silently, slipping behind the trees to watch her. She could feel their attention upon her.

Her foot caught on a root, and she stumbled, hit the ground with a thud that shouldn't have been able to happen in the Otherworld, where she ran in spirit, not flesh, and yet there was a thud, and the impression of flesh, of a jolting tumble, then Morghan was on her feet again, taking a lungful of air, lifting her head to look for the stag.

It would not do, she knew, to lose the animal. He was her prize, the one she was supposed to loose an arrow at and bring back to the meeting place news of the slaying. She wished Wolf were at her side, for perhaps he would point her in the direction she needed to go.

But Wolf was not there with her, and neither had Snake made an appearance. She risked a moment to gaze upward, but saw no sign of Hawk on the wing, or perched on a branch to watch.

She was on her own. And the white stag, she realised, had gone. She'd lost him.

The meeting and the negotiations would be over before they'd begun.

That could not happen, and Morghan made herself move, up the short steep hill, to peer between the trees. Perhaps the stag had been enjoying the chase, she thought. Perhaps by some miracle, he waited, chest heaving with his breath, just behind the rise.

There was nothing, no sign of him, no sound of his heavy footfall, the crack of branches as he stood on them.

Morghan closed her eyes. She had failed, she thought, and felt the gaze of the Fae upon her from their lookouts between the trees. In a moment, they would step out and reveal themselves, lead her back to the others and send them on their way, to return empty handed, no negotiations, no promise of more time, of peace.

That could not be allowed to happen.

Morghan pushed her shoulders back, stood to her full height, made herself relax, and hoped that an answer would come to her before the two Fae did.

But it was a memory instead that came to her.

ROWAN DETOURED TO THE KITCHEN. SHE NEEDED A CUP OF tea and something to do with her hands. And Paul would hear her and follow her, she had no doubt of it, and did not try to keep her movements quiet, didn't creep around as she often found herself doing.

'Well?'

Paul stood in the doorway. Rowan looked at him.

'Well, what?' she said.

He shook his head, and there were round spots of pink high on his cheeks. 'You walked out,' he said, and the words flew out of his mouth covered in spittle. 'How could you do that? It was important!'

'What was important?' Rowan asked, putting the kettle down and turning to him, feeling her own temper rise. It came over her on a long slow tide, and she felt it like that, just like a wave.

She decided that for once, she would ride it.

'It was important to eat pancakes and waffles we couldn't afford with two people so ignorant and bigoted they wouldn't recognise a fact if it stepped up and slapped them in the face?'

For a moment, Paul stared at her as though she'd slapped him in the face, then his eyes narrowed at her.

'What would you know about facts? All you do is ponce around being crap at everything. You're a shit mother – you let that kid do whatever the fuck he pleases. You're a shit housekeeper, and you're a completely bloody useless wife.'

The wave rode up and broke over her, swamping her. She picked up the cup she'd set out for tea and the milk sloshed in it and went flying when she threw it.

She'd never been so furious, and she howled as the cup arced through the air and shattered on the wall several feet away from Paul.

Furious and full of despair, that's what she was.

'You missed,' Paul sneered. 'Can't even aim well, can you.'

Rowan's head was down, the fury leeching out as though sucked out to sea. She was left with the despair, with the knowledge that this was how it was, how it always would be.

'I didn't aim it at you,' she said, lifting her head and staring at him. 'I'm such a shitty person, I guess, that I won't even throw something at you.' Her voice rose a little. 'God, Paul, those people are going to insist that we take Robbie to their daycare – don't you even care?'

'It's a good idea!' Paul shouted.

'He likes it where he is! He's been going there since he was a baby!'

Paul put his hands over his ears the way he always did when Rowan shouted back, or even when she was just trying to say something, anything, about what she felt, what she needed.

'Shut up,' he said. 'You're hurting my ears. Your voice is hurting my ears.'

Rowan stared at him.

He looked back at her, dropped his hands. 'We're going to go back to Cornerstone. Robbie will go into their daycare. It's the answer to everything.'

Rowan frowned.

There was a new look on Paul's face. It was mottled red now, but that wasn't what was new, that made Rowan rock on her feet, not fury rising again on the next wave, but unease, anxiety. She shook her head.

'We've got to make a stand,' Paul said.

'Against what?' Rowan wrapped her arms around herself, wished she was anywhere else but there in the kitchen with Paul, his eyes gleaming like a fanatic's, rubbish spouting from his mouth.

But there wasn't anywhere else for her to be. Robbie was upstairs, asleep, hopefully, in his bed. She had no family, no friends. No money, nowhere to go.

'Against everyone who wants to keep us under control,' Paul was saying. 'The ones who want us to stay in our houses and be good little sheep. Sit down and shut up while they do whatever and trample over us.'

'What are you talking about?' Rowan stared at Paul, thinking she barely recognised him. 'Oh god,' she said. 'I knew you were in that room on the computer playing silly games instead of working, but you weren't just doing that, were you?'

She couldn't help it, her voice was rising again.

'You were reading all the stupid bloody conspiracy stuff

again, weren't you? Stupid bloody Paul, you never were good at figuring things out for yourself, were you?'

His eyes bulged at her, and she knew she'd gone too far.

But he'd pushed her, she had time to think before the next words were out of her mouth. He'd pushed her this far.

'Led like a dumb little bunny, down the rabbit hole you go!'

He lunged at her then, and she gaped at him in surprise, because despite everything he'd ever done, curtailing her outings, making her stop doing her pottery, yelling at her for every little thing, whining until she had sex with him, despite all the things, he'd never hit her.

He didn't hit her now, but grabbed her by the arms and hustled her to the door, the glass one that led from the kitchen out into the backyard, the strip of greenery where she'd dug a little garden, planting it with herbs, and where she'd put one of those plastic paddling pools, shaped like a clam, and filled it full of sand she'd bought one bag at a time from the gardening section of the hardware shop and lugged home under the pushchair.

Robbie loved that sandpit.

'Ow, what're you doing?' she cried as he slammed her into the door.

'Putting you outside!' he roared, and grappled with the doorknob, got it open, and shoved Rowan out.

She stumbled, tripped over the step – there was just the one, thank goodness, and landed painfully on her rump, sending a jolt of pain through her tailbone.

It was raining again, the water thundering down from a sky the colour of blacked iron. No one heard Rowan's scream of pain.

Everything inside her head went white with shock and hurt, and she rolled over onto her side, curling her knees up, not noticing her grazed palms even while she wrapped her arms around herself and moaned.

The rain came down and soaked her, muffling the clicking sound that was Paul locking the door.

Finally, a minute later, perhaps, maybe two - Rowan couldn't tell, wasn't thinking about the time – the white flare of pain receded, and Rowan, wincing, moaning under the thunder of the rain, got to her hands and knees.

She levered herself to her feet, stood tottering there, bent over, waiting for the pain to recede further, for the tide to go out.

It didn't, but the waves got smaller, and Rowan straightened a little, tentatively, then lifted her head. Water ran into her eyes.

Paul was looking at her. They stared at each other from opposite sides of the glass. Rowan wary, like a fox suspecting a trap, Paul, with a smile on his lips, smug, hateful.

Rowan knew, without having heard that small snick of a sound, that the door was locked. She saw it in Paul's eyes. Beyond a doubt, he'd locked her out.

She turned, gingerly, her tailbone throbbing – was it possible to break your tailbone?

To get around to the front door, she had to go out the back gate, into the alley that ran the length of the terraced houses. The bolt on the gate was stiff under her cold and slippery fingers. It didn't want to come free.

Rowan turned and looked back at the house. The kitchen light was on; she'd turned it on herself when they'd gotten home, when she'd gone in there after putting Robbie to sleep in his bed, to give her hands something to do when Paul came to yell at her.

She'd known he was going to.

She hadn't known she'd end up outside. Locked out. She looked up, at the window on the right. Robbie's room. There was no light on in there, and she hoped he was still asleep.

'Please,' she whispered. 'Stay asleep until I get back inside.'

Paul would just be playing with her. She'd go around, walk all the way around in the rain, soaked and sore, to the front door, and get back inside. The front door wouldn't be locked. He wouldn't have locked her out. Not like that.

The bolt slid open under her fingers, pinching the skin on her thumb and Rowan yelped, realised she was crying. She peeled the gate open on its rusty hinges.

Paul was just playing. He wouldn't lock her out. Robbie needed her. Paul wouldn't want to look after him, take him to the toilet, make his meals.

She'd left Robbie with him once, Paul swearing up and down that he would take care of him while she went to the doctor.

She'd had to wait an hour to see the doctor, then, when she'd got home at last, Paul had been asleep on the couch, and Robbie's nappy was wet and soiled, stuck to the red skin of his poor little bottom, and he hadn't been fed either. Paul, who demanded that she always be in the same room as Robbie when he was awake, had slept through the toddler trying to make himself some toast.

They were lucky he hadn't electrocuted himself.

So of course Paul was just playing. Rowan made her way

down the alley, taking tiny steps, holding herself as still as possible. It would take her ten minutes at this rate, to walk all the way around to the front door, let herself back in.

Her teeth chattered together, the rain bringing a sinking cold with it.

The door though, that would be unlocked when she got there.

It had to be.

16

Erin nudged forward a tiny step, leant toward Queen Alastrina. 'Should we go look for her?' she whispered.

The Queen didn't turn her head. 'She will return,' she said. Then added, 'one way or the other.'

That wasn't reassuring, and Erin regained her place beside Clover and gave her a worried look.

'Has this happened before?' Clover asked.

Erin gave a sharp shake of her head. They stood in a group, waiting, in a courtyard surrounded by trees, and Erin's anxiety rose in her chest like a great bubble. Morghan had never taken this long before.

In fact, Morghan had never been taken away like this. Were they sure it was a test? It seemed more like a kidnapping.

Clover's hand closed gently over her arm. 'You have to be calm,' she whispered.

'How?'

But Clover only nodded slightly. 'She'll be back,' she

said. 'I know she will.' She glanced toward Maxen, who turned his head and the feather-light touch of her attention and nodded.

Erin took a breath, tried to feel some of Clover's confidence. She whispered again, trying to look as though she weren't. 'Do you see it, or are you just trying to make me feel better?'

She paused a moment, had a thought that almost made her start from the place where she was standing.

'I should go to her.'

This time, she caught the Queen's attention, and she turned to look at Erin, a faint frown between her brows. Erin swallowed but held that blue gaze.

And, almost inconsequentially, realised that this Queen was aging. It was faint, the signs of it, but there was a fine cobweb of lines at Alastrina's eyes, and her chin was no longer as firm as Erin was sure it must have been.

The idea that Queen Alastrina was aging shocked Erin and mingled with the thought of Morghan never coming back.

What would happen when the Queen died, if Morghan didn't come back?

'I should go to her,' she repeated, her hands going to her skirts to lift them so that she could move swiftly into the forest. 'I am her apprentice and heir. Her wellbeing is partly my responsibility.'

'Her wellbeing is her own responsibility,' Alastrina said. 'You will remain here.'

The Queen returned her gaze to the front once more.

'Don't go against her,' Clover whispered. This was her first time on one of these trips, and she was as shocked as

Erin at Morghan's unceremonious kidnapping from the seat of her horse, but she could see the intricate weaving of the web, and knew that right now, if the wrong strand were tugged upon, things would go awry.

Badly so.

'You can see her,' Erin said.

Clover glanced at her, took in the pale face. Nodded.

'Well,' she amended from her nod. 'Not her, exactly, but the pattern of this moment.'

It was Erin's turn to frown. She wanted to say more, but the Fae next to her shifted on his feet as if in warning, and she stilled, kept herself silent.

One thought leaked through, however.

Would this be one day her job? To go through whatever it was that Morghan was being put through?

She wished she were back home at Ash Cottage, helping Stephan with his herbs, or dancing in front of the well.

She wished she was pretty much anywhere but here, waiting like this, thinking these things.

How would she ever learn enough to take Morghan's place? The idea made her waver in her trance, and for the briefest of moments, she thought she would pull out of it, to sit blinking and disoriented back in the cave.

Clover's touch again. 'Stay here,' she said. 'Breathe slowly.'

Erin did as she was bidden and slowed her breath, knowing even as she did so deep in this travelling, her body back in the cave was also steadying.

'Now focus back here,' Clover said, and she'd turned fully now, was holding both Erin's hands.

Erin fixed her gaze on Clover's.

Clover smiled. 'There,' she said. 'That's the way.'

Erin nodded. Her next breath smelt of forest and something sweeter, like one of Stephan's incenses, and she nodded again.

'I'm good,' she said. 'I'm here.'

Erin smiled at Clover's steady, serious gaze, the blue eyes and fair hair glowing in the sunlight.

Clover checked her once more and looked around quickly to see if anyone was paying them any mind. No one was, although she could feel the watchfulness in the Fae who stood either side of them. They were in a clearing of the greenest grass, trees growing around the edges of it to form graceful columns, their branches spreading out to give shade. Beyond them, Clover had seen movement, knew that there was a whole warren of people and accommodations within this forest of the Fae. She looked back at Erin, squeezed her hands, and let them go.

'Just wait,' she said.

Erin nodded, turned her attention back to Morghan. Where was she?

What were they making her do?

'It's all right, Robbie,' Rowan said. 'I'll be there in a minute. It's just a trick. Daddy's just playing a trick.'

The rain was cold, as though it weren't March, but still the deepest days of winter. Rowan, dressed for church in the blouse Paul had bought her, and her best skirt and shoes, shivered and wrapped her arms about herself, tucking her chin down to keep the driving rain from her eyes.

She rounded the corner to her street finally, her face

wet, tears mixing with rain, and somewhere in the depths of her mind she realised she was sobbing. Her tailbone screamed at her and all she wanted was to get inside and make sure Robbie wasn't scared.

A car pulled up beside her, the passenger's window scrolling down.

Rowan didn't notice it. She'd lifted her head to look down the path to where her house was. To where Robbie was, still asleep hopefully. Her mouth opened, twisted in a howl of anguish.

Then there were hands on her shoulders. A shout in her ear over the rain.

'Rowan? What's happened? You're soaked.'

Rowan shook her head. She couldn't stop. She had to get to the front door, see that it was open. Of course it would be open. Paul didn't mean it. He was just playing a trick, teaching her a lesson.

Well, she was taught. She'd learnt. Just let the door be open, just let it be open. Let Robbie still be sleeping.

The hands on her shoulders were rougher suddenly, and she spun around, crying out at the jolt of pain from her poor tailbone.

'Rowan?' The woman gripping her shook her head. 'It's me, Ginger.'

'Ginger?' Rowan shivered again, a great wrack of cold shaking her.

'My god, you're soaked through. What's going on?' Ginger was also in the process of getting soaked through, but the look on Rowan's face, she'd seen it from the car, could never have driven past that. 'You're bleeding.' Ginger looked at Rowan's hands where the blood oozed from the grazes.

'Robbie,' Rowan croaked.

'Robbie? Where is he?'

Rowan shook her head. Let her eyes close for a moment – but only a moment. She opened them and stared at Ginger.

It was Ginger. Robbie's teacher at Ladybird Lane. Robbie loved Ginger. She couldn't tell Ginger what had happened. Rowan tried to wrench herself away, but Ginger's hands just tightened their grip on the bony knobs of Rowan's shoulders.

'Tell me,' Ginger said. 'Right now.'

'He locked me out,' Rowan said, and slumped down once the words were out, as though they'd expelled all the fight with them. 'But the front door will be open. I know it will be. Paul won't want Robbie, not really.'

Ginger's lips pressed together. She did not like Paul Sutherland. Had never understood why Rowan stayed with the man. A small man, and self-important to make up for it, that's what Ginger had always thought of him.

'Where's your house?' she asked now.

Rowan pointed. It was midway down the street.

'Fuck this rain,' Ginger said. 'Get in, I'll take you there. It will be quicker and drier than walking.'

Not that being drier would make any difference, as Rowan was already drenched, her flimsy clothing clinging to the goosebumps on her skin.

But the car would be warmer. Ginger had the heater on high – and that would make a difference. She steered Rowan to the car, opened the door and all but pushed her in the way she'd seen the cops do it on all the American television shows.

She got the car turned around.

'What number is it?' All the terraced places looked the same. Except for the colours of front doors and the model of car parked in the short driveways.

Rowan strained to look through the rain-smeared window, sitting awkwardly and painfully on one buttock only. 'It's that one,' she said, pointing. 'The door's yellow. I painted it last summer; I thought it would cheer the place up. Paul hated it, he thought the landlord would kick us out. Over a door. I had to go and talk to the landlord, smooth it all over.'

Ginger shook her head. Her lips were in that thin line again. She pulled in behind the vehicle that sat in the driveway. Watched with dismay as Rowan scrambled out the car and up the steps to the front door.

It was yellow. A soft and buttery colour, sweet and optimistic.

And its promise of joy completely wasted on this household, Ginger guessed. She unbuckled her seat belt – Tiggy, her car, wouldn't let her drive without doing it up securely – and opened the car door.

'This rain,' she muttered, slammed the door closed, and went after Rowan.

The yellow front door was locked. Ginger had known it would be. Or would have bet very good odds on it. She put an arm around Rowan, feeling the woman's body shake with crying and the cold.

'Don't you worry,' she said, tugging Rowan gently from the door. 'We'll get little Robbie.'

Rowan shook her head, strings of wet hair flying. She couldn't believe the door was locked. Even when she'd slammed her fists against it, the door had stayed locked.

'He's locked me out,' she said and squirmed in Ginger's grip to go back to the door, bang on it, yell and cry and beg Paul to open it. She'd promise him anything he wanted.

'Yes,' Ginger said, and she put her hands seriously on those skinny cold shoulders again, dipping her chin to look at Rowan. 'And I'm going to take you to the police station now, and then we'll come back and go inside.'

Rowan shook her head, eyes wide, and Ginger opened her mouth to convince her of the necessity of going to the police.

'No,' Rowan said. 'You can't! Paul will have a fit!'

Ginger stared at her, debated, shook her head. 'It's the only thing to do,' she said.

Rowan shook her head. 'I can't leave here,' she said. 'What if he opens the door?'

Ginger blinked. Scowled. 'Fine,' she said. 'We'll call them.'

She shook her head at Rowan's automatic headshake. 'No argument. We're doing it. You're hurt,' she said. 'And while we wait, you'll sit in the car and warm up, or you'll catch your death of cold.'

Rowan considered this, calmed a little by Ginger's firm tone, then went down the steps, turning to look in the windows, but she couldn't see anything. She couldn't hear anything over the rain, either.

Couldn't hear Robbie calling out for her.

She doubled over at the thought, the anguish like a physical pain, and was only dimly aware of Ginger bundling her back into the car where the engine was running and the heater going.

'I'm pregnant,' she said, when Ginger had gone around to the driver's side and gotten in.

'You're pregnant?' Ginger reached for her phone.

Rowan nodded, then turned her head and fixed her gaze on the yellow door. Surely, she thought, Paul would open it now, or at the very least, she'd see him unlock it. She'd see that, wouldn't she? He'd open it an inch for her, so that she'd know.

The door didn't move. There was nothing behind the net curtains in the windows either. Not even the lights were on, and the lights would be on – should be on, it was raining, the afternoon darkening as the rain kept falling. Rowan pressed her forehead against the window, straining to look at the upstairs windows, but Robbie's room was at the back, and so there was no use trying.

'They're on their way,' Ginger said, pressing end on her phone and looking at Rowan, who dripped with water. Tiggy's front passenger seat would be very wet. For that matter, Ginger guessed, so would the driver's seat. She reached between the seats and snagged the travel throw she kept back there. It was mostly there to pick up Biscuit's dog hair, and it had been a while since she'd given it a good shake out, but it was better than nothing.

She folded it around Rowan's shoulders, wrapping it around her. She'd never realised that Robbie's mum was so thin. Barely more than skin and bone.

They waited for the police to come. The car fogged up, and Ginger turned the demister on. Tiggy would be going through the gas, she thought, and scowled. Petrol was expensive nowadays.

But she looked over at Rowan, hunched forward in her seat, and kept Tiggy's engine and heater on. The bastard Paul would just owe her, she thought. Not that she had any idea of getting anything out of him.

There was a blip of a siren and thank all the many and varied gods, Ginger thought. The police were finally there. She opened Tiggy's door and got out to meet them.

17

MORGHAN WORE THE ANTLERS ON HER HEAD AGAIN AS SHE stood in the forest. Ravenna's antlers, for they had never appeared in her costume in the Otherworld until Ravenna walked at her side.

Morghan moved her head, looking for a moment for Ravenna herself, but the woman was not there.

Or not, at least, outside of Morghan's own consciousness. Almost, she thought she could feel her within herself. An echo of a past life, a shivering of ancient strength and knowledge.

Morghan closed her eyes, smiling slightly. She knew now, what she must do to find the stag once more.

She must repeat something she had done only once before in her own memory. And that had been done long ago. Years ago, when she was just stepping into her role as Lady of the Grove.

Her smile widened for a moment, for how far she'd come since then. How long ago now it seemed. And how afraid of change she'd been back then! Now, it seemed that change was around every corner.

Except for the one thing. The truth behind all others.

Morghan heard the beating of her heart, and it sounded like hoofbeats. She felt its quickening in her breath, and lifted her head, with its weight of antlers.

The stag was close enough. She could smell him, musky and strong as she shapeshifted into her deer skin and ran transformed, her steps surefooted and fleet across the uneven ground.

Between the trees. Up the hill, down again. Across a river, the water up to her hocks, wetting her thick pelt.

She could smell him, his excitement in the chase, his love of being alive and strong and king of all the stags.

She chased him, both of them running with the fresh wind in their faces, hooves pounding, branches snapping, clods flying.

At last, the stag wearied of the fun and turned, and Morghan, chest heaving, stepped back once more into her own form, and she raised the bow, drew back the string, her nose flaring, the thrill of the chase still inside her.

She aimed, a small smile on her face, marvelling even in this moment over the majesty of the animal in her sights.

And he was marvellous. He was magnificent, snorting in the forest, gaze fixed on her, even as she held him in her sights.

The string was tight against her fingers; her arm muscles strained with the tension. Just a moment more and the arrow would loose, fly swiftly through the air, sharp, carrying death with it.

Morghan swung around, bringing the bow with her, and her fingers let go, and the arrow flew towards its target.

It hit the ground, buried itself in dirt halfway up the shaft and Morghan straightened, lowered her arms, and looked at the Fae standing behind the landed arrow.

'You will take me to your Queen, now, I think,' she said, and bowed her antlered head slightly.

Behind her, the stag stamped his hooves against the ground and stepped off between the trees.

THERE WAS A MURMURING, A FLURRY OF MOVEMENT AS SLIGHT as a summer breeze and Erin came alert, glancing quickly at Clover beside her before turning her gaze to the tree line, where two Fae, dressed in white, as everyone seemed to be here, for whatever reason, stepped into the royal clearing, Morghan right behind them.

Erin's hand flew to her mouth to stifle her gasp.

Morghan looked as though she'd never been dragged unceremoniously from her horse, as though she'd not just been through whatever testing these people had set for her.

She looked incredible, Erin thought, and her eyes stung with sudden tears. Even the thought that one day she might carry herself as Morghan did right then was both terrifying and humbling.

Morghan wore a pair of antlers on her head, her cheeks painted with their spirals, her robe down to her ankles, embroidered in gold thread with symbols that looked themselves like magic spells in the soft shine of light.

She looked as though she were about to lead them in a ritual. Or as if she'd just been through one.

Erin took a breath. Perhaps she had.

She also looked like Ravenna, Erin thought, and felt that part of her that was Macha, stirring in recognition.

She wanted to bow her head, she thought suddenly, and so she did, dipping down and holding it for a moment in recognition of Morghan and her authority – for it was obvious to Erin that whatever had happened in this strange, faraway forest, Morghan had come back from it in full authority.

Beside her, Clover bowed also.

'HE CAN STAY WITH ME?' ROWAN LOOKED FRANTICALLY AT THE nurse, her arms locked around Robbie. They'd travelled together in the ambulance.

'You don't have anyone to look after him?' the nurse, whose name tag introduced her as Susan, said.

Rowan shook her head wordlessly.

'I can call a relative for you, if you like,' Susan said, putting on a smile for the little boy, whose eyes were wide and puffy from sleep.

Rowan shook her head slightly, but even that much movement made her hurt more. Which was odd to her, because her head was quite some way from her tailbone.

Although everything up her back was hurting as well, as though the pain was wanting to share its fun generously around the rest of her body.

'I don't have any family,' she whispered.

Susan frowned and leant closer. 'I'm sorry,' she said. 'I didn't catch that.'

Rowan cleared her throat and spoke louder. 'Robbie's all the family I have,' she said.

There was another wincing pain in her belly, and she shook her head. 'Is it going to be all right?' she asked.

Susan put a hand on Rowan's blanketed hip to soothe her. 'One way or the other,' she said. 'It's going to be all right.' She smiled gently. 'Now, we need to find somewhere for this little guy while you go get your ultrasound.'

There was a small commotion outside the curtain in the ER and Ginger popped her head through.

'I can take him,' she said. 'Sorry – the car park was quite full. It took me a few minutes to get here.'

'Ginger,' Rowan said, and the tears spilled over her lashes.

Ginger stepped over to the bed, stroked Rowan's hair for a moment. It was still damp. She looked at Robbie, smiled at him.

'Come on, Robbie my lad. Mummy has to go with the doctors for a little bit. I think we need an afternoon snack, what do you think?'

Robbie looked down at his mother.

'You can go with Ginger, love,' Rowan said. 'She'll take good care of you, and I won't be long.' She looked hopefully at the nurse. 'Will I?'

'Not too long, I should think,' Susan said, and she was already pushing back the curtain and gesturing for the porter to come to get the bed rolling.

Ginger took Robbie in her arms, and he clung to her like a little monkey, looking back at his mum with those wide eyes. She patted his back, and they watched Rowan roll away, lying on her side on the bed, eyes closing under the blanket.

'Where shall we wait?' Ginger asked the nurse, still patting Robbie's back.

'She'll be brought back to here, and then likely admitted for the night, depending on the state of things. The doctor will decide.' Susan smiled again. 'Wait here, if you like. She shouldn't be too long.'

'Can you lie on your back?' The radiologist had the ultrasound wand at the ready, and the tube of gel.

Rowan swallowed, tried to let out a slow breath, but it came ragged with pain. When she moved, trying to roll onto her back, she almost screamed in shock.

'Perhaps not, then,' the radiologist said as Rowan curled into even more of a foetal position. 'Let's have you just straighten your legs as much as possible. We might get a good enough view of the little one.' She checked with Rowan, who nodded, and stretched carefully out, then drew back the blanket.

'How far along are you?' Annabelle, the radiologist, asked. She dearly hoped the baby she was about to try to find still had a nice strong heartbeat. This woman – Rowan – had taken a nasty fall, was in shock as well.

Rowan shivered as the cold gel was applied to her belly.

'Almost fifteen weeks,' she said.

'Sorry about the cold,' Annabelle told her. 'But it's good news if you're fifteen weeks. We should be able to see the little girl or guy even with you in this position.'

She pressed the ultrasound wand firmly against Rowan's abdomen.

'When was your last check-up? Who's your midwife?'

Rowan closed her eyes. The ultrasound screen wasn't turned to face her, so she couldn't see that anyway. She shook her head a little.

'At twelve weeks,' she said. 'I don't have a midwife yet.'

Annabelle nodded, then frowned and moved the wand around.

Rowan gasped. 'I'm having another one,' she said.

'A contraction?'

Rowan nodded miserably.

Annabelle could feel it, waited until it subsided, looked again for the baby.

'I've got it,' she said. 'And a nice strong heartbeat.' She paused, kept looking. 'This is good news.'

'But the contractions?'

Annabelle looked at the ultrasound picture on the screen. 'If we're lucky, those will settle and peter out.'

Rowan didn't ask about what would happen if she was unlucky. She already knew the answer to that one.

Her voice wavered a little. 'Can I see it?' she asked. 'Can you tell if it's a boy or a girl?'

She wanted to know. Especially if she was going to lose the child, she wanted to know who she would be grieving for. Perhaps even give them a name.

Fortunately, she was lying on the side where she could see the monitor. Annabelle turned the screen towards her.

'See,' she said. 'Look at those long legs – this little one's going to be runner.' She manipulated the wand, looking for the telltale sign.

'Huh. There we go. Your child's sex is female,' Annabelle said. She was careful how she phrased it now, since George, her younger brother, had come out as transgender. 'Do you have any other children?'

Rowan gazed at the screen. A little girl. Grace. She'd call her Grace.

Please, she prayed to whomever might be listening. Please let her live.

'A little boy,' she said, her face crumpling. 'He's two.'

Annabelle nodded. 'The terrible twos, people say, but I think they're so interesting at that age, don't you?' She wiped the wand clean, then mopped up the gel on Rowan's tummy.

'Robbie is wonderful,' Rowan whispered. 'He doesn't give me a moment's trouble.'

'My Poppy does,' Annabelle said. 'That is one head-strong kid.' She smiled helplessly. 'But it's all worth it.'

She tucked the blanket back around Rowan and patted her arm. 'I think the doctor's going to decide what to do about that tailbone of yours. And hopefully give you some-thing for the pain.'

'What about the baby?' Rowan looked at her with tear-stained eyes.

'It'll be something safe, don't you worry,' Annabelle said.

'But will I lose her?'

Annabelle hated that question every time she was asked it.

She gave Rowan's arm another pat, knowing what a small gesture it was.

'I hope not,' she said. 'Baby's heartbeat is still strong, so that's a good sign. Doctor will talk to you about the rest.'

18

Joyce reached for Winsome's hands.

'I can't thank you enough for coming all this way to see me,' she said.

Winsome sat down in the chair by the hospital bed, but she didn't try to take her hands back.

'It is no hardship, Joyce,' she said. 'I am glad to be here.'

The old woman stared at her through rheumy eyes. 'I wish you were still behind the pulpit, Winsome. The church should be honoured to have you.'

'I'm still serving God,' Winsome said, smiling. 'Now isn't that the main thing?'

'It is. Bless you, but it is.' Joyce tried shifting in the bed, winced, and gave up. 'My daughter will be here soon. Coming all the way to be with me, she is, taking time off work as well, and we'll have an argument about me going to live with her again.' Joyce looked glum. 'It will be harder to win it, now that I've gone and broken my damned hip.'

Winsome smiled. 'Your daughter, she lives in Bartleby, doesn't she?'

'Bartleby,' Joyce repeated. 'And doesn't that name make you want to chortle?'

Winsome laughed. Joyce had obviously been given the good stuff for the pain.

'It does, yes.'

Joyce sobered. 'But Bartleby's not Wellsford, and such marvellous things are happening in Wellsford, Vicar – as you well know.'

Winsome didn't bother correcting her. Calling her Vicar was a slip of an old tongue, influenced by pain medications.

And besides, technically, Winsome was still a vicar. Plans were underway for her formal leave-taking from the church, but they hadn't yet been completed.

She gave Joyce's hands a gentle squeeze, mindful of joints that might be tender with age.

'I do know,' she agreed. 'I'm very proud of every single one of us in the village.'

'Leaving it will be a wrench,' Joyce said. 'All my friends.' Her eyes danced suddenly. 'And just when it's getting so exciting!' She shook her head. 'The rest of the world seems to be taking a very long dump in the toilet bowl.'

Joyce giggled suddenly. 'Goodness,' she said, and let go of Winsome's hands to half cover her mouth. 'My language! What on earth was in that medicine they gave me for the pain?'

'Something very good, I think,' Winsome said. 'I wonder if they'd give me some, if I asked.'

Joyce chortled, then stilled. 'Ouch,' she said. 'The pain's still there, underneath it all.' She blinked. 'Where was I?'

'Contemplating going to your daughter's,' Winsome answered.

Joyce's wonderfully mobile face turned glum once more. 'Yes, that's right. Only, Chortleby's not Wellsford, is it?'

'It could be,' Winsome said, ignoring the slip of the tongue. 'Lots of communities are starting to pay attention to what's happening in Wellsford. And lots have been doing terrific things even before Wellsford made it onto the map.'

She smiled lightly. 'Perhaps you could be part of that, if you stay on there.'

'Margie's going to want me to,' Joyce said. 'Now that I've broken my hip.' She grimaced. 'It's such an old person thing to do, breaking a hip. And so easily too. Like snapping a twig. One moment, I'm walking to the letterbox, the next I'm on my bum on the path yelling bloody murder and drowning in the never-ending rain.'

She subsided into thought and Winsome watched her, heart filled with love for the old woman.

'I'll miss my friends,' Joyce said. 'But Margie's got a nice house, and she's on her own since Larry passed on, although she's still working some, of course. She's lonely.'

'I bet there are all sorts of things to get involved with, in Bartleby,' Winsome said.

Joyce nodded. 'Maybe Margie and I can get something started. Teach the young ladies – and men, for that matter – how to clean their places properly.'

Winsome blinked. 'Clean?'

'I'm a fiend for cleaning, I am, Winsome, and there's all sorts of tricks to it, you know, ones you don't learn anymore, now that you just go to the supermarket and buy all those bottles of chemicals.' Joyce shook her head. 'I won't have any of those chemicals in my kitchen.'

Her eyes widened in affront. 'I cook in there, for crying out loud. I don't want my counters wiped down with things that aren't things, just a bunch of formulas and numbers!'

Winsome nodded. 'That's an awfully good idea, then,' she said.

'And Margie's the same,' Joyce said, her voice filled with satisfaction. 'Not one for a dirty house, is Margie. I taught her the tricks, you see.' She groped around the bed for one of Winsome's hands again.

'I feel much better now, Vicar,' she said. 'You've such a comforting presence. And now I've a plan, I think.' She sighed, looked at Winsome.

'Margie'll be here soon. But will you pray with me a minute first? I feel the need to thank the good Lord that it was my hip and not my neck that I broke.'

Winsome smiled. 'Of course,' she said. 'Of course.' She cupped her hands around Joyce's.

'Lord of all that is bountiful and beautiful,' she said, letting her heart open in gratitude.

'We are here, dwelling in your blessings.'

ERIN SAT BESIDE MORGHAN, AND RISKED ANOTHER GLANCE AT her, then Clover. Morghan was gazing straight ahead at the Queen of this realm and her Consort, listening intently, and Clover had her head bent, eyes lowered. Erin wondered if Clover had had much to do with the Fae before.

Each time she had ridden out with Alastrina and Morghan, Erin braced herself to meet those who had taunted her at the quarry, despite assurances that the tribes they were headed to would not include them in their members.

How she could be sure of that, when they didn't know the group's alliances, Erin didn't understand.

She doubted it would have stopped them, anyway.

Erin realised she was being introduced, and squared her shoulders, then bent forward in a slight bow. She'd been given explicit lessons on etiquette before they'd begun undertaking these journeys, and absolutely didn't want to make a misstep, despite how distracted she felt.

'I am Erin,' she said. 'Daughter of this Grove, of the Antlered Goddess, in alliance with the revered Queen Alastrina, and I am also Macha of the Forest House, the original Grove, reborn with purpose upon this earth.'

She bowed again, closing her eyes fully for the three beats of her heart as instructed.

Her greeting was acknowledged with a tilt of the head from the Queen of this new court, dressed very simply in a white gown caught around her waist with a band of green fabric that reminded Erin of peridots and forests, aptly enough.

Erin felt the Queen's attention leave her and move to Clover.

'You are not of this Grove,' Queen Bessanae said, with a voice that sounded like a cool autumn breeze.

Clover too, inclined her head in a bow, before straightening.

'The land of my current birth is across a great ocean,' Clover said. 'But I am a priestess of the Lady Morghan's Grove, and was once Rhian, priestess of the Forest House.'

Queen Bessanae raised delicate eyebrows, glanced at Alastrina, then spoke once more to Clover.

'You are the one taken and changed,' she said. 'The Oracle.'

'That has not been discussed,' Alastrina said.

Bessanae's gaze returned to Alastrina. 'But is it not so?'

A pause.

'It is.'

Bessanae's interest returned to Clover, who had stilled, barely moving to breathe.

'You see what has not yet come to pass, do you not?'

'I hold the veil back,' Clover said.

'But you also have sight of the great weaving, do you not? Of the future?'

Clover wanted desperately to look to Morghan to see how to answer, but that would be a rudeness. Instead, she lowered her head as was appropriate and spoke to Queen Bessanae's feet.

'In glimpses only,' she said.

Queen Bessanae leant back upon her chair and contemplated her guests. 'So, the rumours are true, then.'

She looked at Alastrina. 'This is where your hopes lie?'

Alastrina gazed levelly at her. 'It is,' she said. 'According to our planning.'

A smile quirked at Bessanae's lips. 'According to your long planning. Even out of the way here as we are, we have not been unaware of your schemes.'

'You were part of them,' Alastrina said, her voice as lazy now as the soft light, as though what they discussed were inconsequential, the shade and colour of a fabric, perhaps. The glint of a particularly lovely gem.

'Your agreement was sought and given in the matter of the veil.' Alastrina smiled and laid her hand upon the arm of her chair, her fingers touching the warm grain of the wood. 'As was the case with each tribe.'

'We had little choice,' Bessanae said, and there was no corresponding lightness in her tone now. 'Our time was overtaken by that of men. It was depart or be killed.'

Clover wanted to look from one Queen to the other. What were they talking about? Oracle? She was the Oracle? What did that mean?

She had no idea, but finally, the compulsion she'd felt to remain behind when it was time for Rue and Selena and Ebony to go back to New Zealand made sense.

This, she needed to know.

Taken, Queen Bessanae had said. And changed. The oracle.

'Nonetheless,' Queen Bessanae said now, leaning forward to look at the three humans more keenly. 'I am interested,' she said. 'I confess I had thought your schemes sure to come to nothing, Alastrina, but perhaps I was wrong.'

She directed her next remark to Morghan, daughter of the Deer Mother, whose priestesses had used once to run like the wind.

As this one had still known how to do. A fact which the Queen allowed to astonish her.

Perhaps there was reason for optimism.

'How do you hope to succeed?' she asked. 'When it is a long game you are playing and yet your lives are short and most often sour?'

'Our lives in the one body may be short,' Morghan

replied. 'But our souls are a different matter. From one life to the next, my priestesses and I remember our task.'

Queen Bessanae leant back in her chair and the light turned her hair to a halo of fire around her head. 'An inefficient manner of doing it,' she observed, but there was a slight smile on her face.

Morghan matched the smile. 'I'm sure it was not the original intention for our species.'

'Not to remember, certainly, for that would have shadowed the quality of joy to be found during a lifetime,' Queen Bessanae agreed. 'But yours did go so greatly wrong in your ways.'

'And now must find our way back to the truth of our souls,' Morghan said. 'A long game, yes, but I see nothing else to be done.'

Queen Bessanae turned her attention to Alastrina. 'My concerns do not alter with your arguments.'

'She passed your test,' Alastrina said, and there was some acerbity in her voice.

'Yes, and I am impressed – I will admit that.' Bessanae pondered the next move, her face smooth, expression betraying nothing of her thoughts. 'You are visiting each court?'

'Yes.'

'Why?'

'To forge more alliances.' It was Morghan who answered.

Queen Bessanae regarded her. 'Even your language is violent,' she said after several moments. 'Forge, you say – does this forging not involve metals and fire and force? The creating of bondages rather than bonds?'

'Is there a better way for me to have expressed my intention?' Morghan asked. She leant forward slightly, greatly interested in the question and answer. For the Queen was correct. Language was important.

Particularly in situations such as this.

'In this land,' Bessanae said, 'we look to the trees for our example, the way their roots weave together under the soil, and the way we weave together their canopies for our shelter.' She paused and raised an eyebrow. 'Alliances, I tend to think, are strongest when purpose and need are woven together like the strongest of vines.'

Morghan closed her eyes and smiled. She nodded and bowed to the Queen.

'I acknowledge your wisdom,' she said. 'Let us twine our purpose together, then. Let us create bonds not through force or violence but woven into the very fabric of our lives.'

Bessanae laughed. 'I will consider it.' She pointed a finger at Morghan. 'You, however, will not weave us into a safety net for yourselves. If it comes to it, we will act to protect our lands and our people.'

Morghan considered this. She was unsure what this proposed action would entail, but on the surface it seemed reasonable.

Except, negotiating with the Fae was a tricky business. They did not lie, but they were agile with words, and hid meanings within them.

'What would this action look like?' Morghan asked finally. Best perhaps to be blunt on this occasion.

'That, I could not say,' Queen Bessanae replied, tapping her long fingers upon the arms of her chair, which was carved in an intricate design from a pale rose wood.

She turned her gaze to Alastrina. 'What does the Council have to say?'

Morghan turned her head. Council?

Which Council was being referred to?

Queen Alastrina pursed her lips and ignored Morghan's startled look.

'It is a delicate juggling act,' she said after a moment.

Bessanae threw her head back and laughed. 'And many strands to be woven, it is for certain.' She sobered. 'I wish them luck.'

Her gaze turned to Morghan, and she inclined her head upon her graceful neck. For a moment, she seemed to blaze and dazzle in the light.

'I am impressed with your facility with the Old Ways, and thus will let you have your wish,' she said. 'We will not move against you at this time.'

Her eyes sought out Clover and regarded her with bright speculation.

'But the Oracle,' she said. 'I had not thought that plan one likely to work.'

19

———

Winsome skirted around the bed being expertly manoeuvred down the corridor, making sure to take a quick glance to assure herself that it wasn't someone from Wellsford.

She still thought of them as her parishioners. That sort of thinking would have to come to an end, she knew. There must be a way for her to reframe it.

She'd tried to think of one and had actually come up with several. But, like old Joyce's slip of the tongue, the residents of Wellsford still came to mind as her parishioners.

Perhaps she could let herself have that. They lived in a parish, and so were parishioners.

Winsome shook her head and pushed the tiresome thoughts away and took a peek at the woman in the bed.

Not someone from Wellsford.

But she recognised her all the same.

Winsome watched the porter push the bed down the hallway and turn it expertly onto the ward. A woman holding a little boy followed, her face wearing a complicated array of frowns and lines. Winsome gave it until the porter came back out then straightened.

'Winsome,' Frank said. His was a job that suited him. A way to be kind and helpful, he enjoyed that. 'Sad one, her,' he said, jabbing a thumb over his shoulder at the door to the ward.

'I think I've met her before,' Winsome said.

Cù seemed to think so too, standing at the door to the room looking in at all the activity.

'Not from Wellsford,' Frank said. 'Not according to her records. Took a fall, anyway. On bed rest for the night, so as not to lose her baby.'

Frank's long face looked woebegone. He liked babies. Had five grandchildren himself, doted on every one of them.

Winsome patted him on the arm. 'I'll go have a chat with her, I think,' she said. Cù turned to look at her, waiting, then walked on in to make himself comfortable.

'That's a good idea,' Frank said, his face lifting in hope. 'She's got the whatsitcalled? The aura of one who's a bit lost, Winsome.' He sighed. 'Anyway, must get back. Come down to the break room and have a cup of tea if you get a minute and fancy it.'

'I'll do that if I can,' Winsome agreed, and let Frank go, then looked towards the door of the ward.

The look of one a bit lost, Frank had said. Winsome couldn't have put it better herself. She'd had the same look at Haven the week before.

And she'd not been at The Copper Kettle when class

had finished. Erin had said she'd met her at the Well-Keeper's Cottage, but that she'd run off from there as well.

Winsome's hand smoothed the stole she wore. It had been made for her by one of her...parishioners. It was a deep green, embroidered with Celtic designs, intertwined with Brigid's sacred flame.

'Help set you apart as a chaplain,' Lynsey had told her when she'd presented it to her at Bridget's Sanctuary a month ago. 'Now that, you know, you're not wearing the collar and so on. You need something, for certain, I think.'

It helped, putting it on, Winsome had found. Not the collar and so on she was used to, but the silk stole was beautiful and meaningful. She thought of Ceridwen's cauldron and nodded to herself.

She was filling it slowly, tentatively, with the ingredients for a deep and meaningful life.

Winsome ducked onto the ward and over to the new arrival's bed. She smiled at the pale woman tucked under the blankets, and marvelled, not for the first time and likely not for the last, how everyone looked so much smaller and more fragile in a hospital bed.

'Hello,' she said. 'I'm not sure if you'll remember me, but we met in Wellsford briefly last week.'

Rowan's eyes widened slightly, then took on a shuttered, ashamed look.

'I'm Winsome Clark,' Winsome said. 'An interfaith chaplain here at the hospital.' She shifted her gaze to the woman at the side of the bed, holding the little boy, whose big wide eyes in a pale face tugged at her heart.

She smiled and nodded a greeting, then looked back at Rowan.

'May I sit with you a few minutes?' she asked.

Ginger wrinkled her brow. 'Wellsford?' she asked. Recognition hit her. 'You're Winsome Clark, from Wellsford.'

'Yes.' Winsome smiled. 'That's me.'

'You run Bridget's Sanctuary.' Ginger stood and scooted away from the chair, offering it to Winsome.

'I do, yes,' Winsome said. 'You're not staying?'

Ginger glanced at Rowan in the bed and sighed. 'I need to get Robbie here home and give him some tea.' She looked at Robbie. 'You and me, we're going to keep each other company for the night while Mummy rests up here, aren't we?'

Robbie nodded solemnly.

'That's wonderful,' Winsome said.

Ginger paused. 'Can I have a word with you a minute, do you think?' She looked at Rowan, who was staring wanly at the window. 'Do you mind, Rowan?' she said. 'If I tell Winsome what happened today?'

Rowan closed her eyes. Shook her head slightly.

'Thank you,' Ginger said, relieved at the permission. She had the strongest feeling that if anyone would be able to help Rowan, it was Winsome Clark.

Ginger scrabbled a moment for her bag, then leant over and put a gentle hand on Rowan's head. 'We'll be back tomorrow, first thing. Don't worry about Robbie, I'll make sure he's okay.'

Winsome followed the pair back out into the corridor. There was a small lounge room not much farther on, and she smiled, led them there.

'Thank goodness you're here,' Ginger said, then looked

abashed. 'I'm sorry. It's just that I saw you on the telly, and I admire so much what you've been doing – that's why I had the new garden at Ladybird Lane – that's my childcare centre – blessed by the priestesses.' She wound down and blew out a breath, stroked Robbie's hair.

'That's how come Robbie's comfortable with me, you see. He comes along to Ladybird Lane three days a week.' She paused. 'I don't think Rowan has any friends, otherwise.'

'What happened to her, do you know?' Winsome asked, smiling gently at the little boy who was watching her from Ginger's arms.

'Well.' Ginger's hand cupped Robbie's ear, covering it so she could speak more freely. His other was against her soft, ample breast. 'Rowan's husband locked her out of the house. I found her absolutely soaked to the bone and limping her way around to the front of the house. They live on a terraced street, and she was distraught, because Robbie was inside, you see. And she's pregnant.' Ginger's mouth flattened to a line.

'I called the police,' she said. 'They let me gather up Robbie and a few things for the both of them. Rowan was brought here in an ambulance. I think she's bruised or broken her tailbone. We'll know that for sure in a little while, when the doctor looks in on her.'

Winsome nodded, kept her voice low. 'The husband is abusive?'

'Not physically before today, as far as I know.' Ginger frowned. 'But he's controlling. I've never taken to him. Rowan's lovely, but she's quite under his thumb, I think.'

Ginger hesitated. 'She can't go back to him. But where will she stay?'

'There's a refuge,' Winsome said. 'They'll take her in.'

Ginger smoothed her palm over Robbie's fine orange hair and shook her head. 'I've got a spare room. She can stay with me, until she gets on her feet.' She nodded. 'If she wants to.'

Shifting on her own feet, Ginger nodded with more certainty. 'Yes. They can stay with me.' She gave Winsome a piercing look. 'After all, we've all got to do our bit, don't you think?'

'Our bit?' Winsome asked.

'To build community,' Ginger said. 'To support and care for each other. Just like you and Morghan Wilde said on the television interviews. It's the only way forward. I agree with you.'

WINSOME SAT DOWN IN THE CHAIR BESIDE THE BED AND GAVE Rowan a gentle smile.

'How are you doing?' she asked.

Rowan shifted her cheek on the pillow. The cotton case was damp from tears.

'I'm sorry I didn't meet you that day,' she said, her voice rough from crying.

'Oh,' Winsome said. 'That's no matter. None at all.'

Rowan sniffed. 'I wasn't brave enough. To do any of it.'

'It sounds like you were very courageous just to come along in the first place.'

Rowan sighed. 'Paul, that's my husband, he doesn't like me going places.'

'Is he quite controlling?' Winsome asked, keeping her voice neutral.

'He doesn't like me having friends.' Rowan felt a great pressure inside, and the words tumbled from her as though carried on a tsunami. It was because of the woman sitting beside her. Something about her, about her expression perhaps.

And she didn't have anything to lose, now, did she? There wouldn't be any going back to Paul. Not now. Not now the police had come and taken her away.

Paul wouldn't get over that in a hurry.

'I don't want to go back,' she said in a whisper. 'I don't have to go back, do I?'

Winsome leant a little closer and shook her head. 'No,' she said. 'You don't have to go back.'

'I've nowhere to go to, though,' Rowan said, knowing she was skipping around, making little sense. 'I don't have any family – Mum and Dad died just before I got married – they had me late in life, you see. And I was an only child. I think I might have an aunt somewhere, but if so, I haven't seen her since I was little.'

'There's the Refuge,' Winsome said, nodding. 'They can look after you, help you get back on your feet. Ginger, when I was talking to her just then, said you'd be welcome to stay with her.'

'Ginger's got Robbie,' Rowan whispered. 'He'll be all right?'

'From what I saw, Robbie knows and trusts Ginger. They'll be fine.'

Rowan nodded. Sought out the view of the sky which

was all she could see through the window. It was grey. Grey clouds and rain smeared glass.

'I'm going to have another baby,' she said, staring at the snail streaks of rain. 'Paul said if I ever left him, that he'd make sure I couldn't keep Robbie.' Her gaze shifted to Winsome. 'But he couldn't do that now, could he? Not now I'm pregnant with Robbie's sister. No judge is going to split us up, are they?'

Winsome felt a spark of anger. How many men and women held this sort of thing over their partner's head?

'No judge will split you up,' she said. 'I can practically guarantee it.'

Rowan nodded. 'He doesn't want Robbie anyway,' she said. 'Not really. He's never even changed a nappy.'

Tears dampened her cheeks again. 'Oh god, how could I have let it get to this?' She looked at Winsome, shook her head. 'I used to be someone, you know? Not anyone important, just a normal person, but I was okay. I looked after myself. I had interests. I did things. I had friends, hobbies; I laughed at things.'

She snaked her hands out from under the blankets and pressed her palms to her face. 'I don't know how I let it come to this. How did it happen?'

'Slowly, I imagine,' Winsome said. 'Insidiously. Just one thing after another, until you were undermined and uncertain.'

'I have a checklist,' Rowan said, swiping almost angrily at the tears now. 'Do you know that? A checklist. I had to make myself one, so that I wouldn't forget all the things I need to do in a day so that he, Paul-' She spat the name out. 'So that he won't yell at me, tell me I'm useless. I'm a useless wife and mother, he says, and when I try to get him to listen to me, he tells me the sound of my voice hurts his ears.'

She shifted slightly in the bed. There was a twinge of pain from her tailbone, but none, thank goodness, from her womb.

'I should have seen it, from the start. When he told me he needed ten hugs a day. When we were in bed, and he told me all about the things his ex wouldn't let him do.'

Winsome took one of Rowan's hands and squeezed it.

'I didn't believe it, at the time, you see, that he was being manipulative,' Rowan said. 'I mean, you don't, do you? He'd ask me why I was putting makeup on, was I going out? After a while, it was easier just to not put makeup on.' Rowan's eyes were dark, liquid.

'It's just like you say. It sneaks up on you, and one day you realise you're just a wet rag, a doormat, too used to walking on eggshells to do anything else.' She closed her eyes. 'I hate myself for it.'

Winsome shook her head.

'You got through it the best you could,' she soothed.

Rowan shook her head but didn't say anything.

20

CLOVER HEARD THE BEATING OF AMBROSE'S DRUM, SMELT THE scent of the herbs that Morghan had thrown upon the fire, and she took a deep breath, coming back to her body.

She was sitting cross-legged, and her muscles felt cramped. Usually, she was never in the Otherworld for this long.

Not that she knew how long they'd been in trance. Time went at such a different speed in the Otherworld. But it had been a while, judging by how stiff her legs were. She straightened them and groaned.

'I've got pins and needles,' she said, and rubbed at her calves.

'There's no good way to sit while you do this,' Erin agreed, stretching, then almost tipping over before she caught herself.

'Eat,' Ambrose said, putting his drum down, and coming forward to press one of Elise Palmer's buns into Erin's hands. He offered one to Clover, then looked questioningly at Morghan.

She hadn't moved yet, although he saw her eyes were open and aware.

'Are you all right?' he asked her.

She breathed in, tipping her head back, and letting her breath out in a whoosh. She nodded.

'Yes,' she said. 'Although that was a particularly taxing trip.'

Ambrose passed her a currant bun, poured tea from the Thermos and gave them all cups. He took one for himself, glad that they were back. It had taken some time for them to return – one of the longest times they'd been gone. Perhaps he should start insisting that Kurt was in the cave when they were gone.

'What happened?' Erin asked Morghan, then looked at Ambrose. 'They took her right off her horse, dragged her into the forest.'

'What?' Ambrose sat straighter, looked at Morghan. 'Is this true?'

'It was a test. We were aware of the probability of being tested.'

'Dragged from your horse?'

'Yes.' Morghan stretched where she sat, rolling her shoulders about, loosening the tension. She reached for the tea, took a sip. It was good and hot.

'But what happened afterwards?' Erin asked. 'I wanted to go after you, but the Queen said no.' She paused. 'She's good at saying no, isn't she? I'm a little frightened of her, I think.'

'You'll grow used to her,' Morghan said with a slight smile and took another sip.

'What did happen?' Clover asked. She wanted to bring up the subject of being an Oracle, whatever that might mean, but there would be time for that.

She would make time for that.

And she was curious. What had been the test? Morghan had passed it, that much had been obvious, but she had also looked a little displeased when she'd met them in the clearing afterwards. Stern, and imposing, in her antlers.

Clover definitely wanted to know what had happened.

'They gave me a bow and arrow and set me after a stag, to see if I could bring it down,' Morghan said, keeping the explanation as brief as possible. There were things she wanted to think about.

The council. No, she thought to herself. It had been Council, with a capital C.

But what was it, this council? Not her own soul council, she was almost 100% sure of that.

'They wanted you to bring a stag down?' Ambrose was incredulous. 'With a bow and arrow?'

'Did you?' Erin asked. 'You must have, because just before you came back, one of the Fae came out of the woods and talked to the Queen we'd come to see, and then we got to stay.'

'I did not bring down the stag,' Morghan said. She bit into the currant bun and chewed a moment before elaborating.

'I chased him, lost him. He was magnificent and swift, and I was clumsy in pursuit.' Morghan gave a half smile. 'So, without knowing what else to do, I ran in the body of a deer to catch him again. When he tired, I stood back in my own skin and lifted the arrow.' She glanced at Ambrose who stared wordlessly at her.

'But I did not take the shot,' Morghan finished.

'Why not?' Erin asked. She was wondering if she'd been able to do what Morghan just had. Turn into a deer? How had she done that?

How had she even known to do that? By the Goddess, there was still so much to learn.

Morghan smiled. 'I've already said – he was magnificent.' She looked at Ambrose. 'Shall we go? I am stiff and sore, as though I really did run through the forest.'

They gathered their things, and Ambrose extinguished the fire. Morghan paused on the way out of the cave and put a hand to the rocky wall.

'Thank you, Mother, for the sacred space with which you provide us. We are blessed by you and honour your gift.'

There was a pause as everyone bowed their heads for a moment and added their thanks to Morghan's.

'The world is a joy,' Erin murmured. It was something she'd begun saying to herself, hoping the truth of it would sink deep inside her if she said it often enough. 'I am made for joy.'

There was the familiar lightening, lifting sensation in her chest when she finished her small utterance, and she looked up at the rain with less dismay than she might have.

'Erin,' Morghan said. 'What are your plans for the rest of the day?'

'Oh.' Erin drew up the hood of her cloak. 'I'm getting

changed and meeting Winsome at the hospital,' she said. 'Do you need me?'

'Later perhaps,' Morghan said. 'It will wait.'

Erin nodded, turned her face to the sky. 'Will it ever stop raining, do you think?'

'It had better,' Ambrose said, moving to lead them down the path into the woods where it would be a little drier. 'The stream is beginning to ride high.'

Morghan let Ambrose and Erin go ahead and fell behind to look at Clover. 'You're very quiet,' she said.

Clover nodded her head. 'You heard what the Queen said.' She paused just a moment. 'Do you know what it means?'

Morghan stepped into the shelter of the trees with relief. The rain was not only damp, but cold.

'That she called you an oracle?' She considered the question, knowing this was the part that would be sticking in Clover's mind. It had lodged in her own also.

'Not just an oracle,' Clover said, a frown deep between her brows and her hands tucked under her arms to keep the fingers warm. 'The Oracle. That's what she said. The Oracle. And she said something about not thinking the plan would work. What plan, Morghan?' She shook her head. 'I thought I'd got to the bottom of everything, you know? Or near enough to. That I'd figured out what Rhian was doing, way back when.' She shrugged helplessly. 'Now this, and I feel like I'm back at the beginning, knowing nothing.'

'I understand that feeling,' Morghan said, with more fervour than she had intended. She smiled at Clover's startled glance.

'The Council that was mentioned,' Morghan said and

spread apart her hands. 'Which Council? This is the first I have heard of this.' She let her hands drop. 'Although really, it makes sense that there are more behind these plans and schemes than just Queen Alastrina and the Lady Elen.'

'You know what I think?' Clover said, frowning mightily. 'I think politics in the Otherworld are just as complicated as they are in this one.' Her shoulders drooped. 'And that gives me the heebie jeebies.' She shook her head, then straightened and looked at Morghan.

'My wizards,' she said. 'They belong to some sort of council. Perhaps it is the same one?' She wrinkled her nose. 'After all, I seem to be mixed up in all of this in ways I don't even know about.'

Morghan considered this, a thrum of energy surging suddenly through her tired body. Clover, she decided, could very well be right.

ERIN SMILED AT THE GATHERING OF RAVENS ON THE HEDGE IN front of Ash Cottage. They'd taken over her yard for their congregation spot. She pressed her hands together in an attitude of prayer and bowed to them.

'Hail to you, my feathered allies. Be blessed this damp and chill day.'

She got a chorus of caws in response and was grinning as she ducked in the door to stand in the kitchen, face tipped up, soaking in the warmth like a sponge.

'Oh,' she sighed. 'To be warm.'

Automatically, she looked around for Burdock, but he was off with Stephan, of course. She missed him. She missed them both.

Getting married! Erin giggled, shucked off her cloak and hung it up by the fire to dry. What a ridiculously wonderful thing to do! She wondered for a moment how Burdock would look in a doggy tuxedo, then groaned. It wouldn't be that sort of wedding.

Although, they could get married in Bridget's Sanctuary. Erin narrowed her eyes as she thought about that, checking she had time to make a quick cup of tea before heading to Banwell.

The Sanctuary, she thought. Or the lawn of Hawthorn House?

Possibly.

The stone circle?

There was a rustling sensation inside her, then Macha appeared at her shoulder.

'That is where we bonded ourselves to each other,' she said in Erin's ear.

'At the stone circle?'

'Was not in ceremony though,' Macha said. 'But just between ourselves.'

Erin's eyes widened in surprise. 'Why?'

'I was a priestess, promised to the purpose of the Goddess.'

'Did that make a difference?'

'The usual trappings of marriage were not ours to have. But love – that belonged to any who found it.'

Erin's lips curved in a smile. 'And you found it with Finn.'

'For life after life.'

Erin moved her head slightly. 'Is that usual?' she asked. 'To return to the same lover over and over?'

Macha's voice was the breath of a breeze in her ear.

'It is not.'

Erin turned, but Macha was gone.

ERIN TOOK HER MUG OF TEA UPSTAIRS WITH HER. SHE NEEDED to get moving, get changed, and drive into Banwell. Winsome would be there already, but that couldn't be helped.

Morghan insisted that Erin accompany her and the Queen on their missions to the other tribes. Erin knew this was important, but she lived in a state of uneasy anticipation of the day they'd ride into the lands of those she'd met at the quarry.

Not that she was afraid of them, anymore. They couldn't harm her. Not now.

Erin ran a brush through her hair, plucked a leaf out of it, then changed her dress for one of plain blue wool. She didn't know why she always felt compelled to dress up for these trips to the Otherworld – she never turned up there in the clothes she actually wore.

But there it was. The effort was what counted, she'd decided.

Why, she wondered now, had Morghan not taken the shot at the stag, when clearly that was what she'd been supposed to do?

Erin gave a delicate shudder. She didn't know if she'd be able to shoot an arrow into a deer, either. Especially a fairy stag.

Maybe that was why Morghan had stayed her hand.

Erin imagined that you didn't go around shooting such creatures willy nilly.

Although, she'd been told to, hadn't she?

'I'll ask her,' she said out loud to her mirror, then, satisfied with her tidiness, she skipped down the stairs and out to her car.

Winsome would be waiting for her.

Then later, Stephan.

21

ERIN POKED HER HEAD INTO THE BREAK ROOM THAT THE hospital chaplains shared with everyone else. There was an office for their coordination as well, away from the main building, but that was ruled over by an Anglican so disapproving in his manner that Erin had had to resist the urge to hide behind Winsome when she'd met him.

Winsome had seemed unperturbed by the man's attitude and Erin had marvelled over how she'd managed that.

'I heard - or read, I don't remember which - some advice, you see,' Winsome had said. 'It was to imagine when doing any sort of public speaking, that your audience is naked.'

'Naked!' Erin was dumbfounded. 'Wouldn't that be rather, ah, distracting?'

'I would think so, yes.' Winsome smiled widely. 'But I do a variation of it, you see. Instead of naked, which would be frankly a disturbing and inappropriate thing to do, even in one's head, when I come across someone like Reverend Christie there, I simply imagine them as a large...' She paused and frowned. 'A large and somewhat lumpy child.'

'A child?'

'I know,' Winsome said, sighing. 'Perhaps a bizarre thing to do, and I'm not entirely sure that it's not inappropriate too, but it reminds me to be kind even in the face of petulant behaviour – because something is stopping that person from growing up, don't you think?'

'I don't know,' Erin said uncertainly. 'Most children seem better behaved than Reverend Christie.'

'True,' Winsome said and laughed. 'Perhaps I shouldn't be imagining him in nappies needing a good feed and a nap.'

Erin giggled at that unlikely picture and Winsome patted her hand. 'It's never going to be easy,' she said. 'When you're outside the mainstream. People are always going to lead with their preconceptions when interacting with you. Which is when it becomes important to remember that your behaviour is the only thing that will stand a chance of changing those preconceptions.'

'Even when they're being jerks?' Erin asked. 'He was bordering on rude to you, Winsome.'

'And thus did I serenely ignore him,' Winsome said. 'And carry on blithely as though there were no disagreements between us.'

'But what if he'd been openly rude?'

'Then I would have pointed out that and asked him to refrain from it.'

Winsome shook her head. 'Erin, dealing with people is a dance. Each person requires something different from you, but each also needs to be met with a warm heart.' She smiled and swept off down the hallway. 'A warm heart does wonders eighty percent of the time.'

'What do you need for the other twenty, then?' Erin had asked, hurrying after her.

'A very strong spine,' Winsome had replied.

NOW, THERE WAS NO SIGN OF WINSOME IN THE BREAK ROOM. Just a pair of orderlies making coffee.

'If you're looking for Winsome,' Frank said. 'She's on the maternity ward.'

'The maternity ward?' Erin had never been there.

'Past dental and up on the second floor.'

'Oh. Okay, thanks Frank.'

Erin ducked back out and straightened her shoulders. The maternity ward.

'Goddess,' she whispered. 'Please don't make me have to comfort a family who have lost their baby.'

She could barely imagine a pain that would be worse than that.

Smoothing down her blue dress, she took the lift, found the right place. She stopped a nurse.

'Excuse me,' she asked. 'Have you seen Winsome Clark?'

The nurse nodded. 'Reverend Winsome is in the third room on your left.'

Erin nodded her thanks, knowing that most of the nurses still called Winsome by reverend, and took a deep breath, and knocked briefly on the closed door, then let herself tentatively in the room.

Winsome looked up from her seat at the bed and saw Erin, smiled for her to come in.

'We're with Rowan today,' Winsome said, then turned her attention back to Rowan. 'Would you mind if my colleague Erin Faith joined us for a minute before we let you sleep?'

Rowan turned her head. She was tired. The doctor had been along, reassured her that her tailbone was only bruised not broken, and given her an injection of something meant – hopefully – to stop the premature contractions.

It seemed to have worked. But now she was tired. Talking to Winsome had been good, but exhausting.

She'd never told anyone before. What Paul was like.

'It's you,' she said now, seeing Erin.

'Hello again,' Erin said, recognising her at once and hurrying to hide her surprise beneath the sort of calm warmth Winsome, and maybe Morghan too, would be proud of her for. She imagined her energy spreading out from her heart, and that inside her head, all was serene. Difficult, but she was discovering, by no means impossible. 'I'm so sorry to see you in the hospital.' She glanced at Winsome. 'We met at the Well-Keeper's Cottage.'

Rowan's face collapsed. 'I never got to see the well,' she said, and her voice was full of tears again. She'd thought she'd cried herself out, but apparently there was a well of her own inside her, filling to the brim with fresh tears.

'Oh goodness,' Erin said, coming to stand next to Winsome, who reached up and grasped her hand for a moment, gave it a squeeze.

'You can come and see the well anytime,' Erin said. 'It's been there for thousands of years – it will still be there when you're up and about again.' She looked at Winsome, a question in her eyes.

'Erin is right,' Winsome said. 'As soon as you're back on your feet, we can take you to see the well. Perhaps you'll want to make an offering of thanks, that you and your babies are safe.'

Erin let go of the breath she was holding. There wasn't going to be a tragedy of epic proportions to deal with.

Perhaps she'd make an offering of thanks, too.

'Is that what you do there?' Rowan said. 'At the well?'

'Hmm. Part of it,' Winsome said and smiled. 'It's part of it.'

'I want to learn,' Rowan said, but her eyes were closing. She was so tired. She didn't think she could stay awake a minute longer. 'I'm sorry,' she mumbled. 'I'm tired.'

Winsome stroked her hair gently. 'That's all right, my dearest,' she said. 'You get some sleep. You've all your strength to be getting back.'

Rowan moved her head in a nod against the pillow. Winsome had turned it over to the dry side a little while before. It was cool and soft against her hot face.

'LET'S GET A CUP OF TEA,' WINSOME SAID, OUT IN THE hallway. 'I've been talking almost non-stop for the last two hours and I'm parched.'

The break room was empty, and Winsome sighed with relief. She loved almost everyone who worked in the hospital, but she needed a moment's respite from interaction.

'Actually,' she said, changing her mind as Erin was lifting the kettle to fill. 'Would you mind if I just grabbed some water and spent a minute in the chapel?'

Erin shook her head. 'Shall I come with you?'

'I'd like that,' Winsome said, nodding, and she gulped down some water.

The hospital chapel was small, but peaceful, with a stained-glass window meant, Erin thought, to represent the sea. She liked it, liked the blue green, the movement in it that somehow managed to be alive and peaceful at the same time.

There was a small altar at the front, all the chairs arranged before it. Only a white cloth covered the altar.

Winsome sat down on one of the chairs and lowered her head in prayer, then looked at Erin.

'Will you say the Lord and Lady's prayer with me?' she asked.

Erin took a breath and nodded.

'That prayer always takes me back to the day with Blythe,' she said, pitching her voice low in the quiet of the room.

'I know,' Winsome said. 'A scene like that never really leaves you, does it?'

Erin frowned, thought for a moment. 'Winsome?'

'What is it?'

'Morghan,' Erin said.

'Ah. What's she done now?' Winsome's lips twitched in amusement.

'Everything,' Erin said. 'She does everything.'

Winsome laughed out loud now. 'That she does.'

'I'm never going to be like her,' Erin said.

'Do you need to be?' Winsome asked, shifting slightly in her chair so as to face Erin more comfortably.

'Well,' Erin considered. 'Don't I need to be?'

'In which ways?'

Erin looked down at her hands and linked the fingers together. 'In every way, I suppose. I mean, there's nothing much she can't do, or won't do. Or that's how it seems.'

Winsome drew breath. 'Erin, my love,' she said. 'You are never going to be Morghan. You can't be.'

'But I have to be – I'll be Lady of the Grove someday.'

'Yes, I dare say,' Winsome said. 'And we don't know what that will look like, when the time comes, since things are changing so much. But that is almost beside the point.'

Erin looked at her.

'The real point is, that you will be the Lady of the Grove who stood in Trafalgar Square, all the ravens gathered around her. You will be the Lady of the Grove who passed the initiations set for her, who nursed the sick and dying at the hospital here, who did everything that you are doing. You can't do the things that Morghan has done, the way that she does them.'

'But some of them, won't I need to?'

'And if so, then you will have learnt from her example.'

Erin was still frowning. 'She was tested today. I mean, she always is, when we go to a new Fae court, but this time, it was much more than the other times. She passed the test, of course.' Erin shook her head. 'But Winsome, I don't know if I would have, if it had been me they were testing, because I don't understand why she didn't shoot the deer.'

Winsome looked speculatively at Erin. 'Shoot the deer?'

'She was supposed to run after this great stag and shoot him with an arrow. But when it came time to take the shot, she didn't.'

'Did she say why?'

Erin shook her head. 'Only that he was magnificent.'

She dragged her gaze to Winsome's face. 'But I think...I think I would have shot the stag. I don't think I'd have been able to stop myself.'

Winsome laughed, put an arm around Erin's shoulders, and held her there, next to her.

'Erin,' she said. 'You'll find the necessary wisdom as you go along – that's how each of us does it. Experience brings wisdom, if we teach ourselves discernment.'

'I don't know,' Erin said. 'Doesn't wisdom come with age?'

'It comes with experience,' Winsome repeated. 'And by not being rigid in your ways.'

Erin nodded, but she twisted her fingers further together. 'Rowan,' she said.

'What about her?'

'When I was speaking to her at the cottage – I messed it up.'

'Messed it up in what way?' Winsome asked, thinking that was hardly likely, or too easy, Rowan being as nervous as a cat on the proverbial hot tin roof.

'I stuck my oar in and offered a solution, instead of just listening, the way you've been trying to teach me.'

'Trying to teach you?'

Erin sighed. 'Have been teaching me.' She laughed a little. 'You're like Morghan,' she said. 'Always making me watch the way I speak.'

'Yes, well, there are many things Morghan and I are in agreement upon.' Winsome rubbed Erin's shoulder. 'It's difficult not to offer solutions,' she said.

'It is,' Erin agreed on another sigh. 'Rowan was talking about how she used to enjoy doing pottery, so I just piped up and said she should take it up again, that we have kilns and things in Wellsford.'

Erin leant forward in her chair and put her head on her hands. 'But it's not that simple for Rowan, is it?'

'Things often aren't simple for a lot of folks. Time and money and relationships. The state of those things can go a long way to dictating what we can do.' Winsome shook her head and sighed.

'Rowan,' Erin said again. 'Her husband – he's not very nice, is he?'

'No,' Winsome said. 'I don't think he is.'

'What makes someone like that, do you think?'

Winsome had wondered this a great deal herself. 'Fear, I think,' she said. 'When it comes down to it. Often brought about through a lack of care and support.'

'That doesn't seem easy to solve,' Erin said. She straightened. 'Sometimes I think the human race needs like, a reset, or something.' She smiled but there was little humour in it. 'New firmware, perhaps, like your printer at the vicarage keeps asking for.'

Winsome laughed, smiling widely.

'What?' Erin asked. 'What's funny about what I said?'

Winsome shook her head. 'Oh, Erin my dear. You are the new firmware.'

Erin stared blankly at her. 'What? What do you mean, I'm the new firmware?'

Winsome gazed back at her. 'I mean that you are a living example of what we have to become.'

Erin still wasn't sure she understood.

Winsome ticked it off on her fingers.

'Connected,' she said. 'To both the earth and to spirit. To ancestors, guiding lights, allies.'

Another finger. 'Discerning, balanced, whole.' Winsome paused a moment. 'I was going to say healed, rather than whole, but whole is the word I want. And we become whole, how?'

'Through a process of connection and healing,' Erin said.

'Indeed,' Winsome agreed. 'All the things that Morghan has been teaching you and I for the last year and a half.'

Erin gave Winsome a sideways glance. 'Teaching you?' She shook her head. 'But you already know so much.'

'Through my own experiences,' Winsome said. 'But Morghan has widened those experiences considerably.'

'She kind of does that,' Erin said, and she laughed a little.

'You did that too, for a lot of people,' Winsome said. 'That day in London, and all the times since then that those videos of it have been viewed. And all the things you've been doing in the last few months.'

Erin considered this, looking at Winsome's kind face as she did. 'You're good at this,' she said.

'Good at what?'

'Pep talks,' Erin answered. 'Making people believe in themselves.' She shook her head slightly. 'How do you do that?'

'Oh Erin,' Winsome replied. 'That part's easy. I believe in people, in everyone, just like I do you.'

'Everyone?'

Winsome leant back in her chair and looked at the stained-glass window.

'Yes,' she said at last. 'Everyone.' She turned and smiled at Erin. 'Now, let us pray together and give thanks for being born in these interesting times.'

Erin nodded.

OUR FATHER, WHO ART IN HEAVEN,
  Our Mother, whose body is the land
  Hallowed be thy name.
  Blessed be thy flesh.
  Thy Kingdom come, thy will be done,
  On earth as it is in Heaven.
  As above, so it is below,
  As it is without, so also is it within.
  Give us this day our daily bread
  And forgive us our trespasses as we forgive those who trespass against us.
  Your bounty is also our own, we are in service to your needs.
  Lead us not into temptation,
  But deliver us from evil.
  For compassion lives in our hearts and kindness moves our hands.
  For thine is the kingdom, the power, and the glory,
  Forever and ever.
  For we are eternal and connected
  And we grow in the spirit of love.
  Sot it is, so it has always been, and so it shall remain,
  World beyond time,
  World without end.

22

———

Clarice looked dubiously at Clover then turned a helpless gaze towards Krista.

With a laugh, Krista held her hands up and shook her head. 'Don't look at me,' she said. 'I think it's an awesome idea.'

Clarice blew her breath out in a huffing sigh. 'You're supposed to be on my side,' she said. 'And yet, you're always getting me in more trouble.'

Krista grinned at her and laughed again at the smile twitching around Clarice's lips.

'Okay,' Clarice said, turning back to Clover. 'I'm game. I'll help.' She rested her head on forefinger and thumb in just the way, had she realised it, that her mother had used to do. 'It'll be the nearest I've been to the Fair Lands since I was banished from them.'

'You know you're not banished anymore, don't you?' Krista said.

But Clarice just gave a shrug. 'I know.' She thought of her friends there, how much time she'd used to spend roaming to and fro, and she shook her head. 'The Queen and I spoke about it, remember? We agreed that I ought to only go there with a purpose in mind.'

'One that doesn't involve just having fun,' Krista said archly, the smile still on her lips.

'Quite,' Clarice said, and decided to change the subject. 'I'm ready whenever you are, if we fit it in around everything else.' She paused, frowned at Clover. 'What do you make of this Oracle business, though?'

Clover shook her head. 'I don't know what to make of it. I've been brooding about it since yesterday, when Queen Bessanae said it.'

'It's got something to do with getting that glimpse of the future,' Krista said, leaning over the high table in Haven's back room where they were all gathered. The shop was closed for the afternoon and Minnie was taking her turn down at the Well-Keeper's Cottage, so for once, it was blessedly quiet.

'But that only happened that once,' Clover said. 'And I don't even have those episodes anymore. They went away once, you know, Rhian showed me what her purpose was.' Clover lowered her eyes. She wasn't telling quite everything. The white mist, for example. That was still there. Clover could feel it, at the edge of everything.

But she turned away from it every time she felt it there.

She could get lost in that mist.

And she definitely didn't want to have any more visions of the future. Not the future she'd seen that time, anyway.

'Well,' she said at last. 'Now at least I maybe have a reason for the need I felt to stay on here.'

Krista nodded. 'Have you heard from Rue lately?'

'I think she's still mad at me,' Clover said. 'For staying.' Clover frowned and looked down at her fingers. 'I mean, she's always looked after me. Always.' A small smile played around her lips. 'Did you know, when I was small, I could make her hear my thoughts? If I shouted them loud enough?'

Clarice looked at her. 'That doesn't surprise me,' she said. 'When I was young, my mum could find me when no one else could.' She laughed. 'Mostly because I always thought I could hear her calling me, and so I'd come back from wherever I was, only to discover she hadn't called at all, or at least not out loud.' She reached out and laid a hand over Krista's. 'You develop bonds with people. Things become possible that you would never have thought of.'

Krista turned her hand over and threaded her fingers with Clarice's. Then looked at Clover.

'When do you want to make a start?' she asked.

Clover pursed her lips, glanced at Clarice. 'Well,' she said. 'What about now? Do you have anything on for the next hour or two?'

Clarice squeezed Krista's hands, then straightened. 'No,' she said. 'Krista has, but I'm quite free.'

Clover looked at both of them, and narrowed her eyes slightly. 'Is there something happening I don't know about?'

Krista laughed and stood up. 'Yes,' she said. 'But it's just personal stuff.'

'Ha. Speaking of personal stuff – how's Camera Guy?' Clarice asked Clover.

Krista gave her a nudge on the arm. 'Don't tease,' she said.

'Alex is good, thank you,' Clover said, and tried a prim smile before being unable to hide her grin, being teased or not.

'I bet. Another reason to stay behind, yeah?' Clarice laughed.

'Ignore her,' Krista said, shaking her head. 'I'm glad you met him. He's nice.'

'He's not too bad,' Clarice agreed, then straightened. 'Right, let's get this underway, shall we?' She glanced at Krista. 'And you're going to go see Ambrose?'

Krista nodded.

Clarice's expression was serious. 'And you're sure?'

Clover looked from one of them to the other, then her eyes widened as she caught their intentions, and quickly she ducked her head, drawing in all her energy in the equivalent of putting her hands over her ears, so that she wouldn't overhear their thoughts.

'I'm sure,' Krista said, then paused. 'Are you?'

Clarice nodded slowly. 'Yeah. I'm sure.' She grinned suddenly. 'It's crazy, but I'm sure.'

'So,' Clarice asked Clover as they walked out into the woods. 'How do you want to go about this?'

Clover shook her head and glanced over at Clarice. 'I don't know.' She thought a moment. 'Clarice?'

'Yeah?'

'You know Alex, right?'

'Camera Guy. I don't really know him.' Clarice drew her

cloak tighter around her. By some miracle, there was no rain, but it was still unseasonably cold. She thought about Krista, heading off to see Ambrose, then drew her thoughts back to the present with an effort. 'What about him?' she asked. 'Are you two getting serious?'

Clover wrapped her arms around herself, tucking her hands under her arms for warmth, wishing she'd not forgotten her gloves.

'I don't know,' she said. 'Maybe. I don't want to date anyone else.' She drew in a breath and couldn't help the smile on her lips. 'He's the first guy who doesn't crowd my head, you know?'

'Well, you taught him that, didn't you?'

'Yeah,' Clover said, but she waggled her head from side to side. 'I did, but he was pretty good at it naturally. Maybe something to do with keeping a low profile behind his camera all the time?'

Clarice considered it. 'Maybe,' she agreed.

'Anyway.' Clover glanced sideways at Clarice. She'd wanted to ask Rue this question, but Rue, she thought, wasn't ready for that. Whenever they spoke on a video call, the emotions between them were thick and complicated. Rue was having trouble moving on from the way things had been.

Which was okay. It had only been a few months since Rue and Ebony and Selena had gone home without her.

'What I want to ask, is...' Clover paused, frowning.

'Is what?' Clarice asked, slowing her pace and turning to look properly at Clover. 'I don't know if I can help,' she said, serious now. 'But you can try me.'

'Well.' Clover braced herself, asked. 'How do you, you know...'

'Okay, I correct myself. If you're asking about sex, then I definitely can't help. Didn't Rue or someone give you the birds and bees talk?'

Clover huffed out a laugh. 'It's not about sex,' she said, and felt her cheeks warm at the mention of it. 'No, it's more like this – how do you keep doing normal things, like going on dates, and making friends, and so on, when you've got all this happening?' She gestured helplessly with her hands.

'Ah.' Clarice stopped walking and gave Clover all her attention. 'I don't know,' she said after a minute. 'The rest of us paired up in house, so to speak. And I only leave Wellsford when you guys force me to.'

'Good grief, Clarice. We don't force you to.'

Clarice shook her head. 'Sorry,' she said. 'I was being flippant. Old protective habit, I'm afraid.' She sighed, looked around at the woods, damp and fragrant, the trees standing dreaming together in the greyness.

'Okay,' she said. 'What we do is important, but it's only part of life, right? Being with friends, falling in love, making love, feeling connected to other people – that's what it's all for. Having those minutes when you're with someone and you're in perfect harmony, and you get that sort of nostalgic feeling? Or you don't even have to be with someone, you might just be hanging out on the sofa with your dog or your cat, I don't know. But that sense of connection, that sense that life is precious, that breathing in and out right then and there, that's precious and good and delightful, that's why we do all the rest.' She paused, frowned, wished it were easier to put it all into words.

Finally, she shrugged. 'We don't come here to struggle, that's what I think. Or that wasn't the original purpose. We come here to seek and nurture joy. So, enjoy everything you can. The hard bits we do are so that joy is found more easily.' She paused again, then looked finally completely at Clover, letting her guard down, lowering the shields she kept around her energy just as a matter of course, knowing that as she did so, Clover would be able to feel her, feel everything that was in her heart.

'We're here to love, Clover,' she said. 'We're here to love it all.' She sighed. 'And that's what brings us hope and sustains us – all those small moments of love that we have to seek and keep on seeking. The light through these dreaming trees, the snoring of the dog on the sofa, the laugh of someone we're falling for. We have to let it all touch us, because that's what we're here for.' She shrugged. 'The rest is just fixing where we went wrong.'

'But it's going to be hard, Clarice,' Clover whispered, even while she felt the strength and clarity of Clarice's heart. 'The things we're asked to do and go through; they're going to be hard.'

Clarice nodded. 'And then we'll die. We might die during the trying to do something. And if we have love in our hearts, all will be well. We'll die and all will be well.'

Clover smiled. Nodded. 'You're right,' she said. 'You really are right.'

'Eh,' Clarice said, and they turned to walk again. 'I've been known to be right, on occasion.' She reached out and touched Clover's shoulder, felt their spirits touch for a moment. 'Now, let's go save some souls that got themselves a bit lost on the way, shall we?'

'Yes,' Clover said. 'So that all can be well for them also.'

'WHEN WAS THE LAST TIME YOU CAME DOWN HERE?' CLOVER asked, keeping her voice low as she and Clarice made their way down the spiralling steps underground into the Otherworld.

'Just after Solstice,' Clarice said. 'When my banishment came to an end. Since then, not so much. Usually, I just spend time in the Wildwood, you know – the borderlands between here and there – but I've not gone deep here because that would just make it too hard to stay away from the Fair Lands, and anyway, I'm too busy now.' She placed a palm on the dirt wall and took a deep breath of the cool air that smelled of soil and magic.

Clover was taking careful steps behind her. 'Selena said once that she thought I lived in the Wildwood. That was how I could always see so much, because there was never any veil between worlds for me, so the Wildwood was home, if we think of it as the real world without any discon-nection between spirit and, I don't know, object, I guess.'

'That would make sense.' Clarice stared down past the light she'd made, into the murk of the tunnel. 'We're almost there. Do you know how we're going to do this?'

'No clue,' Clover said. 'I figured that would come to us when we got here.'

'Good,' Clarice said, taking the last step off the winding staircase and into the tunnel. She lifted her hand and focused for a moment, and the orb of light that she'd spun glowed brighter.

The spirits glowed also, and when Clover came to stand next to her, they looked in silence at the milling crowd of spirits, all of whom glowed, although some more brightly than others.

'How did they get here?' Clover asked, whispering, dismayed. 'There are so many.'

Clarice shook her head, also disturbed at the number of spirits. They were clustered together in tight knots, all along the tunnel for as far as Clarice could see.

'I think we need some help with this one,' she murmured.

'Help?' Clover asked. 'From who?'

'I don't know, but there has to be someone around who can help with this, right?'

Clover giggled, and the sound had an edge of nervousness to it. 'I left my phone at home,' she said.

Clarice stared blankly at her. 'What?'

'Who you gonna call?' Clover said. 'You know, Ghostbusters.' She winced. 'Lame, I know. Alex and I streamed it last week.'

Clarice startled her with a wide smile. 'I get it,' she said, and laughed. 'Come on, let's find us some help.'

Clover nodded, looked around. 'We need a boatman,' she said, thinking of her mother. 'There's a river around here, right?'

'You are a genius,' Clarice said. 'That's exactly what we need. Come on, let's go to the river and see if we can find one.'

They edged gingerly past the spirits, Clover murmuring apologies every time she bumped against one. They were cold when she touched them, not because they had any form other than their light, really, but because they were lost and afraid.

She followed Clarice, who strode quickly ahead, through the warren of tunnels, finding her way with an unerring knowledge of the path.

'Right,' Clarice said when they got to the wide, vaulted tunnel through which the black river ran. 'This is it.' She stopped and stood there above the fast-flowing water.

'What is it?' Clover asked. 'What's wrong?'

'There's no one about,' Clarice said. 'This place used to be a bit like King's Cross Station.'

Clover peered up and down the waterway. 'What happened to everyone, do you think?'

'I don't know,' Clarice said. 'Things are changing.' She looked at Clover, suddenly speculative.

'What?' Clover asked, catching her gaze.

'The Oracle,' Clarice said. 'We really need to find out what that means.'

'Well, it's already on the list,' Clover said. 'Where's the boatman? That's what I want to know right now.'

'Fair enough,' Clarice said. 'One thing at a time. But tomorrow – tomorrow we find out what was meant by calling you the Oracle.'

Clover didn't answer. She didn't know what to say.

'Let's go this way,' Clarice said, picking a direction.

'But the water flows the other way,' Clover said.

Clarice stopped. 'You know what?'

'What?'

'We have no idea what we're doing.'

'That's true,' Clover said. 'We need our kin.'

'Good idea,' Clarice said, and groped in the dimness for Clover's hand. 'We'll call for them.'

They took a step back from the ledge's edge, and each brought to mind images of their kin. Clarice thought of Sigil, for her animal kin was also an owl, indistinguishable from the owl she'd been taking care of for over ten years. She thought of the rushing of wind, silent under Sigil's wings, of the feathers, light in the darkness of the tunnel.

She raised her arm, and her kin landed softly on her, long toes curling around her forearm. When she opened her eyes, she saw that a great lioness stood beside Clover.

'Wow,' she said, unable to help herself. 'I knew your kin was a lion, but...'

'It's still a shock to see her, I know,' Clover said, and rested a hand on the great cat's shoulders. 'Blackbird hasn't come, though.'

'The one who comes is the one you need,' Clarice said, quoting some long ago but not-quite-forgotten lesson of Morghan's.

The lion swung her head around to look down the tunnel, and Clarice's Owl kin launched itself from her, and flew away in that direction.

'I guess we go that way,' Clover said, stepping forward.

'Wait,' Clarice said, her voice suddenly thick. 'Someone's coming.'

Clover blinked into the dimness. Two someones, and suddenly she wanted to cry. A great wave of feeling overwhelmed her, and she all but doubled over under the unexpected strength of it.

'Mama,' she said, as the two figures drew near.

'Mum,' Clarice echoed over the rush of the river.

23

Krista knocked, then pushed the door of Blackthorn House open and stepped in.

'Hello!' she called. 'Ambrose?'

He was in the study, and she smiled at him when he called her inside. 'I feel like I haven't seen you for ages,' she said, warming her hands at the fire that grumbled away in the grate.

'It's our Stations of the Heart books,' Ambrose said, shaking his head then stretching behind his desk. 'They're taking up all my time. I've had to cut way back on my genealogy research jobs.'

Krista nodded. 'I bet. I also bet you're loving every moment of working on them.'

Ambrose laughed. 'Too true,' he said, and got up. 'Want a cup of something?' He smiled, knowing her weakness. 'I have coffee.'

Krista shook her head. Her stomach was churning too

much to pour anything into it, let alone coffee. 'Thanks, but no,' she said.

Ambrose stepped around the desk. 'What's wrong?'

'Nothing's wrong,' Krista replied, and sank down into the armchair by the fire, watching as Ambrose came and sat in the one opposite.

'You can tell me anything,' Ambrose said. 'You know that – has that niece of mine been giving you grief?'

'Clarice?' Krista shook her head. 'Clarice is her own self, as we know, but she's fantastic. We've really settled in together, in fact.'

Ambrose considered her in silence for a long minute, then nodded. 'There's something though, isn't there?'

There was. Krista grimaced. 'I'm nervous,' she confessed. 'I didn't know if I would be, but I am.'

Ambrose leant forwards and looked at her. 'What is it? How can I help? I'll help if I'm able.'

'That's just it,' Krista said, her mouth dry now. 'You can help, but I don't know if I should be asking.'

'You came here to, though?' Ambrose said, sensing in Krista's aura an odd mix of excitement and anxiety. 'To ask me something?'

Krista closed her eyes, took a couple of calming breaths, and reminded herself who she was speaking to. It was Ambrose, who had taken her under his wing from the day she'd stepped foot in Wellsford, overwhelmed and far from home. They shared interests – books, art, history. It had been he who had suggested Haven for Books. Ambrose who had convinced Morghan to lease her the building for it.

She took a breath, blew it out between pursed lips. 'Okay,' she said, then laughed. 'Wow, I'm so nervous.'

Ambrose stared at her. 'What on earth is it? Won't you just tell me?' He reached over and took one of her hands. 'It's just me,' he said. 'You know you can feel at home with me.'

Krista nodded. Made herself say the words she'd practiced all the way through the woods to Blackthorn House.

'Clarice and I want to have a baby,' she said.

Ambrose sat back and gazed at her. Whatever he'd thought she might say, it hadn't been this.

'A baby?' The thought dazed him. 'A baby,' he repeated, more softly this time.

Krista nodded. 'I know it's quite soon. She and I have only been together for six months or so.'

Ambrose smiled. 'You both pined for each other for a lot longer than that. You've known each other for years.'

'And I'm in my thirties now,' Krista said. 'Not getting any younger.' She hunched over and looked sheepishly at Ambrose. 'I guess my maternal instinct kicked in, because I can't think of anything else. Despite everything going on, this is what I want.'

'And Clarice is in agreement?'

Krista nodded.

'Complete agreement?'

Krista nodded again. 'We've talked of hardly anything else.' She examined her hands, pretended to warm them again in front of the fire. Outside, the rain started again, a damp drizzle from clouds too overloaded to hold it in a minute longer.

Ambrose tried to imagine Clarice with a baby, but what came to his mind instead was a pretty picture of Winsome with a child in her arms. Did Winsome want children, he wondered? They'd never spoken of it. Perhaps they needed to. Neither of them were getting any younger.

'Ambrose?'

He looked at Krista, nodded. 'I think it's quite wonderful,' he said. 'Congratulations.'

Krista laughed. 'Don't congratulate me just yet,' she said, and gave a wide grimace. 'There's something I need to ask you now, since I've told you.'

Ambrose's brows rose. 'Of course,' he said. 'I'll help however I can.'

'Wait until you've heard what I have to ask, first.' Krista looked frankly at Ambrose. He was Clarice's uncle, but he was also her own good friend. She swallowed.

'I was wondering, if you would father the child for us?'

There. She'd said it. The words had actually come out of her mouth.

She looked at Ambrose.

'What?' He shook his head. 'Oh. Goodness. I wasn't expecting that.' Pushed back the flop of blond hair and leant back in the chair. 'I was not expecting that.'

Krista couldn't make herself say anything more. It had taken everything she had just to get the question out of her mouth. She pressed the palm of her hand surreptitiously to her chest, where her heart hammered behind the ribs.

She forced herself to speak. To explain.

'Only,' she said. 'You see, it's going to be me who carries the child – and I want to. I'm the one that wants to.' She paused only a moment to draw breath. 'But I'd like for there to be something of Clarice in the child. In their genes.' She petered out.

Ambrose felt quite dazed. 'I can see what you mean,' he said. 'I can see that quite clearly.'

Krista nodded. Now for the other part of what she'd come to ask. 'Will you consider having a genetic test for albinism? That's if you might consider the um, proposition in the first place. Clarice is adamant that it doesn't get passed on, if at all possible. I think only because she was teased so much when she was younger.'

Ambrose shook his head.

Krista drooped. Every part of her felt suddenly boneless.

'No,' Ambrose said, seeing her dismay. 'No, you mistake me. I don't need the testing, you see.'

'No,' Krista said. 'What do you mean?'

Ambrose grinned, bemused at the sensation of gladness that rose in his chest. 'I don't have any more than the usual risk for it. Clarice's albinism came down to her from Grainne's father's side of the family.'

Krista stared at him, understanding dawning. 'And you had different fathers.'

'Exactly.'

'Wow.' Krista shook her head slowly. 'We didn't know that. Or forgot it, or didn't think about it, or something.'

'So that, at least, isn't an issue.' Ambrose got up. 'I need a cup of tea. Are you sure you won't change your mind about a coffee?'

'I'm far too wound up for more coffee,' Krista said. 'But I'll share a pot of tea with you.'

The fire was burning in the kitchen grate too, and Krista stood in front of it, watching as Ambrose made the tea. He and Clarice shared some of the same mannerisms, she realised. Subtle things, the way they held their heads, slightly tilted. The way they moved.

She wanted her baby to have some of those mannerisms too.

Ambrose parted ways with Krista at the vicarage and tapped lightly on the door before entering. It was stuffy warm inside after the chill rain, and he unwrapped his scarf from his neck and held it while looking around for Winsome.

The sound of voices came from the small room Winsome and Veronica kept for their private use. He peeked around the door.

'Ambrose,' Veronica said. 'Winsome's not here, I'm afraid – she's out doing her rounds.'

'Her rounds?'

Veronica threw a coy look at the other person in the room. 'That's what I call it when she does her house calls here in the village.' Veronica looked back at Ambrose. 'You'd know where she was, if you had a phone.'

'I have a phone,' Ambrose said.

'If you used your phone,' Veronica elaborated.

Ambrose stepped more fully into the room, and saw Kurt on the couch, his long legs crimped at the knees, a cup and saucer balanced precariously upon them.

'Kurt,' Ambrose said. 'Good to see you.'

Kurt unfolded himself from the sofa, trying to hide the look of relief on his face. 'Ambrose,' he said. 'Just the man I wanted to catch.' He turned his head to Veronica. 'Thank you for the tea, but I must go now.'

'Oh, no,' Veronica said, standing up as well. 'But you've only just got here. You've not finished your tea. Do stay. Hearing you talk about Sweden is fascinating.'

'I cannot, I am sorry,' Kurt said, and glanced wide-eyed at Ambrose. 'I have important things to discuss with Ambrose; they cannot wait.'

'Oh well,' Veronica said, gazing up at him with a beatific smile. 'Of course you do, and I expect you need to get back to work as well. I am grateful for the house call.'

Kurt nodded, held up the cup and saucer. 'Thank you for your hospitality,' he said. 'I shall rinse it in the kitchen on my way out.' He glanced again at Ambrose.

'That's all right, Doctor,' Veronica said, and plucked the crockery from him. 'I'll be glad to do it.'

A minute later, out on the street, Ambrose looked at Kurt with raised brows.

'She likes me, I think,' Kurt said, wincing at the words.

'We all like you,' Ambrose answered.

'But not all in that way, I hope, making pretty eyes at me.' Kurt shook his head. 'I do not know that house calls are a good idea.'

'That was an official visit?'

'It did not look as one, did it,' Kurt said, sticking the hand that wasn't carrying his doctor's satchel morosely in his trouser pocket and hunching his shoulders up around his ears. 'She was not ill.'

'She looked rather pink with health, actually,' Ambrose said, and laughed.

'She is old enough to be my mother,' Kurt said.

'I fear she won't be the only woman in the village to

admire you in such a way.' Ambrose shook his head, but there was a smile still on his face.

'Perhaps,' Kurt said, and sighed. 'But I will not like it if they all pretend to have a little cough.' He shook off the thought and looked at his new friend. 'Thank you for your rescue of me.'

'You're welcome,' Ambrose said, and followed Kurt in the gate to the medical centre. 'Do you have a minute, actually?'

'I do,' Kurt said. 'As long as you do not mind talking while I eat my lunch.'

The mention of food made Ambrose's stomach rumble. He'd probably forgotten to eat breakfast. Work on the next Stations of the Heart book was absorbing him, even more than his personal studies usually did.

'Not at all,' he said, and his stomach gurgled again. Kurt raised an eyebrow at him and led him to the fridge in the break room, where he retrieved his package of sandwiches.

'I will share with you,' Kurt said, and a minute later, between bites, he nodded at Ambrose. 'What is on your mind?'

'I've...well, I've been asked to be a sperm donor,' Ambrose said, and frowned at the half a sandwich in his hands.

'By someone you know well?'

'Yes,' Ambrose said, putting the sandwich down. It was good, and he'd finish it in a minute. 'For my niece and her partner – that's Clarice and Krista. You've met them, of course.'

Kurt raised his eyebrows. 'Which is your niece? I liked them both very much when I was introduced to them.'

'They're marvellous women, the two of them,' Ambrose said. 'Clarice was my sister's girl.'

'Was?'

'Grainne died some time ago. About six years now, I expect.'

'Ah.' Kurt lowered his head. 'May she have found peace in Helheim.' He touched the Thor's Hammer on his chest and nodded, then smiled at Ambrose. 'You wish my advice on the genetics of albinism?'

'Oh, no,' Ambrose said. 'I'm sorry, I think I just wanted to tell someone.'

Kurt smiled widely. 'And I was available, and in return for my rescue from the lovely but grasping clutches of Veronica, I will be glad to listen.'

Ambrose laughed, picked up his sandwich and took a bite, ruminating.

'Grainne and I had different fathers, and the albinism came from her father's side of things, so we're okay on that score, if anyone thought it to be an issue.'

'And there is no other physical impediment to the scheme?'

'No, none that I can think of.'

'You hesitate?' Kurt finished his sandwich and brushed the crumbs onto the plate. 'It would be a fine thing, to give your niece and partner a baby, if they long for one, would it not?'

'Yes, although the mechanics of it...' Ambrose trailed off, realising he had not thought of the physical aspect of it.

Kurt tipped back his head and laughed, then got up from the table and disappeared into the storage room. He was back a few seconds later.

'Here you go,' he said, presenting a sample cup with lid and a plastic syringe. 'These are the only implements you will need, and even then, only the cup is for you.'

Ambrose received them with some amusement. 'You are laughing at me,' he said, through his own.

'Perhaps, but we laugh together, and new life is a fine thing to contemplate. Even if the transmission is in this manner.'

'THIS CAN'T BE,' CLARICE SAID. 'IT CAN'T BE YOU.'

Beside her, Clover stood still, tears streaming down her face. 'Mama?' she said again.

Beatrix reached for her daughter and drew her into her arms. 'My love,' she said.

'I'm dreaming,' Clarice said.

Grainne smiled, shook her head. 'Not dreaming but travelling.'

'Yeah, sure. That explains me,' Clarice said, standing still, staring. 'You though. It doesn't explain at all.' She took a breath. 'You look just the same.'

Grainne smiled. 'A little older, a little wiser. As it seems so are you. So grown up, and how brightly you shine now, my darling.' She looked at Clover, then back to Clarice. 'My daughters,' she said. 'Daughters of the Grove, of destiny.'

Clarice glanced at Clover wrapped in the arms of the woman who was apparently her mother also. She shook her head.

'What's this about?' she asked and looked back at Grainne. 'Why are you here? How are you here?'

It was Beatrix who answered, standing back and smiling at Clover.

'We've come to help,' she said.

'But...how? How are you able to come back here?'

Grainne smiled, laid a hand on Clarice's arm. 'We asked to,' she said.

'Asked who?' Clarice could feel her mother's hand on her arm, just as though they were both there in the flesh.

'Our Soul Council,' Beatrix said.

'Soul Council?' Clover looked over at Clarice, frowning, then back at her mother. 'The same council that Queen Bessanae spoke of?'

'I do not know a Queen Bessanae, I'm sorry,' Beatrix answered, after a quick glance at Grainne who made no answer. She gave Clover a gentle smile. 'Our task is to help you with the gathered lost. We will take them to the shores of the Summer Lands.'

'The realm of the dead,' Clover said.

Grainne nodded.

'This is so weird,' Clarice muttered, but she was unable to take her eyes from her mother. She wanted suddenly to tell her mother everything, to bring her up to date on all the small details of her life.

To tell her about Krista. And the baby.

The maybe baby.

Grainne smiled at her.

When Clarice opened her mouth, however. Something completely different came from her.

'Why did you have to do it, Mum?' she asked. 'Why did

you have to go on that trip? You died out there, in the ocean, so far away from us.'

Clover's eyes widened, and Clarice was dismayed. She shook her head, bent to look at her feet.

'I'm sorry,' she said. 'I didn't mean to ask that.' She looked at her mother again, marvelling that it really was Grainne there. Just as she'd looked the last time they'd seen each other when Grainne had been whole and well.

'It was my time,' Grainne said. 'I lived a lot longer than I ever expected to.'

'But we missed you,' Clarice said, and touched her chest above her heart. 'Here, every day. Morghan misses you still.'

'She knows we will find each other again,' Grainne said. 'All will be well. She has much to do.'

'Don't you miss her at all?' Clarice all but howled.

'Hush, my daughter. We also have a task, so let us begin it.' Grainne felt a prick of regret in coming in this form. She should, she thought, perhaps have come as another aspect, so as to save Clarice some grief.

But the deed was done now.

'Please show us the way to the gathered souls,' she said.

Clarice looked at her for another moment, then shook her head.

Clover leant close. 'Are you all right? Do you want to keep going?'

Clarice, about to nod, shook her head instead. 'No,' she said. 'I don't think I can. I need to go back.'

Her answer had Clover nodding in understanding. She linked their hands together, threw an apologetic glance over her shoulder at their pair of mothers, and then the air rushed around them, and they were outside the tunnels, in the light again, making their way back through the Wildwood.

'You're extraordinary, you know that?' Clarice murmured, as they crossed the border and blinked themselves awake, back in their bodies.

Clover stared up at the roof of the cave. She'd lain down for this travelling, knowing it would likely take a while.

'Well,' Clarice said, sitting up and resting her head in her hands. 'That didn't go as expected.'

'I'm sorry,' Clover told her. 'I never expected they would turn up. I had no idea at all.'

Clarice gave her a weak smile. 'It's all right,' she said. 'I know you weren't expecting them either.' She looked toward the mouth of the cave and shook her head. 'It was just a shock. That's all. I mean, Mum's come to me in my dreams, and here once, while I was drumming, but...' She shook her head, tried again. 'But they were just so matter of fact about it.'

Clover nodded. 'It's all such a puzzle, isn't it? I feel like I'm trying to do a jigsaw puzzle with only half the pieces the right way up so I can't make out what the picture is.'

'That is exactly what it's like,' Clarice said and huffed out a breath. 'Wow, there's just so much going on.' She looked over at Clover. 'Are you going to tell Rue?'

Clover thought about it for a moment, then nodded. 'Probably. Are you going to tell Morghan?'

Clarice took longer to answer. 'Maybe?'

'I think you should,' Clover said, throwing sand on the fire to extinguish it. 'It's too much to keep from her, don't you agree?'

Clarice levered herself to her feet, feeling stiff and sore, as though she'd run a marathon, not just gone for a walk in the Otherworld and met her dead mother.

MORGHAN WAS IN HER OFFICE AT HAWTHORN HOUSE, AND Clarice paused in front of the door, trying to gather her wits about her when the door opened.

'Hello Clarice,' Morghan said. 'Are you all right?'

Clarice blinked, then frowned. 'Why do you ask?'

'Your energy feels like it's been through a blender,' Morghan replied.

Clarice's frown turned to a look of consternation. 'Through a blender?'

'Indeed.' Morghan smiled. 'Do you want to come in? I was just doing some planning.'

With a silent nod, Clarice followed Morghan into the room. It had been Selena's room once; Clarice remembered it from her childhood. Selena had had a table cluttered with her altar bits and pieces, and cushions on the floor for travelling. It had been a fantastic place for a child to nose about – when she'd been let in, of course.

Morghan kept it much more minimally. It was mostly a work office. Clarice took a breath and let herself look at the triptych of paintings at the end of the room, above the narrow table Morghan used as her personal altar.

The trio of encaustic paintings were Grainne's artwork. Clarice stared at them, seeing them properly for the first time in ages. There was the forest. And Wolf. She closed her eyes.

'You're not really all right, are you?' Morghan said softly. 'Tell me what has happened.'

'Mum,' Clarice said, and sniffed back the tears. She hated crying. Hardly ever did it. Refused to.

'Grainne?' Morghan stilled, turned and leant against her desk, looking at Clarice carefully. Clarice's energy was chaotic, as though she'd just been through something emotional.

'What about her?' Morghan asked. Then, forming the words carefully: 'Have you seen her?'

Clarice turned to look at her. 'How did you know?'

'Just a guess,' Morghan said. 'Just a guess.'

Clarice nodded, took a shuddering breath. 'There's a lot going on,' she said, echoing the words she'd said to Clover.

'There is,' Morghan agreed.

'There's...' Clarice lifted her hands, spread them apart, then let them drop. 'Everything.'

'Yes.'

'Clover and I – Clover asked me to help her.' Clarice closed her eyes. Squeezed them tight. 'I probably shouldn't be here. I probably shouldn't tell you. You've enough to think about.' She tightened her hands into fists and dug the short nails into the flesh of her palms.

'Morghan,' she said. 'It was like she was still alive.'

Clarice's face crumpled and she wrapped her arms around herself, swaying slightly.

Morghan put down the papers she'd been holding and went to her stepdaughter, put her arms around her and held her.

Clarice clung to her, breath coming in sobs.

'I'm sorry,' she said, between hitches. 'It was just a shock, that's all, seeing her. Such a shock.'

'It's all right,' Morghan said, and held Clarice's weight as she leant against her. 'These things are shocking.'

'I'm snotting all over your clothes,' Clarice said after a minute. 'God, I'm sorry.'

Morghan smiled. 'It's been a long time since you've done that. It still washes out, I'm sure.'

Clarice straightened, wiped the tears from her eyes. Morghan looked at her then reached over to her desk and plucked up a tissue, passed it to her.

'Thanks,' Clarice said. 'Wow, I'm such a mess.'

Morghan drew her over to the chairs in the room, sat her down in one and took the other for herself.

'Tell me,' she said. 'If you can. If you want to.'

Clarice sniffed. 'Krista wants to have a baby,' she said.

'Oh.' That hadn't been what Morghan was expecting to hear.

There was a lot going on, then. More than she'd known.

'She went over to Blackthorn House to ask Ambrose if he'd...you know...father it for us.' Clarice closed her eyes. 'Krista wants the child to be part of each of us, related to me as well as her, I mean.'

Morghan smiled. 'Does she? And what did Ambrose say?'

'I don't know.' Clarice shook her head, then mopped at her eyes with the tissue again. 'I haven't seen her yet.'

'You've said that Krista wants to have a baby, but you must want it too, if it's reached the stage of asking Ambrose such a question?'

Clarice gave a watery laugh. 'Goddess help me, but I do. Or I want to see Krista with a child in her arms.' She rubbed at her eyes. 'Can you imagine me bringing up a child?'

Morghan considered the question. 'I can, actually. I think you'd make a fine mother.'

'That's what Krista says.'

'You don't agree?'

'The concept of me as a mother terrifies me,' Clarice said. 'But...'

'But?'

'At the same time, I think I could do it. I think I could fall in love with a child.' She breathed deeply and looked at Morghan. 'You managed it – you were a mother to me.'

'I managed it?' Morghan was amused by the phrasing.

But Clarice just laughed. 'Come on, admit it, you and I, we don't come across as the most maternal of women.'

'Perhaps not, but parenthood is about love and responsibility. You've always known about love.'

'And I've learnt a lot about responsibility, the last year.'

'You have,' Morghan said. 'I'm very proud of you.'

Clarice gave a sly smile. 'You'd be a grandmother. Grandma Morghan.'

'Hmm.' Morghan smiled in return. 'It has a certain ring to it, don't you think?'

'I think it sounds terrible!' Clarice laughed. 'Look at me,' she said. 'Tears to laughter all in three minutes flat.'

'I wish your mother were here to see it,' Morghan said gently.

Clarice sobered immediately. 'I saw her, plain as day in my travelling.' She blew out a breath and shifted in the chair, shook her head. 'Clover enlisted my help in shepherding the gathered lost in the tunnels.' She glanced at Morghan to be sure she was understood.

Morghan nodded.

'Well, that was well and good, until we had to figure out what to do with them, and then how.'

'What did you decide?' Morghan wanted to hear about Grainne but suppressed her impatience.

'That they needed to be taken by boat to the Summer Lands. So, we went to the river to look for a boat.' Clarice's brow creased. 'Did you know that there's a lot less traffic on the river than there used to be? It was weird. No one swimming, no boats. That's not right – it shouldn't be that way.'

'Things have changed in the Otherworld as well as here,' Morghan said.

'And more numbers of gathering dead than ever,' Clarice said. 'I mean, I know there have always been some, but now they're practically clogging the tunnels.' She glanced at Morghan. 'When we were looking for a boat, two figures came towards us.'

Clarice closed her eyes. 'One was Clover's mum.' She opened her eyes and looked at Morghan. 'The other was Grainne. She called us her daughters of destiny.'

Morghan sat silent, absorbing this. She knew, of course, that Grainne lived on. Everyone did, one way or the other. The soul was, as far as she knew, immortal. Or near enough to. She didn't know everything about it.

But she knew that Grainne could still appear as herself. She closed her eyes and let the knowledge sink in that she had.

A touch on her hand. 'Are you all right?'

Morghan opened her eyes and nodded. Managed a smile. 'It must have been something, to see her like that.' She curled her fingers around Clarice's.

'It was. It was a shock, though.' Clarice looked at the

painting that took up the whole wall. Her mother's work, when she'd been alive.

'I couldn't take it, actually. Clover had to bring me back.' Clarice shook her head. 'It was just such a shock, that's all.'

She shifted in her chair again, looked back at Morghan. 'I mean, she's come to me in dreams, and that time in the cave. But this was different. So, I don't know, so matter of fact.'

'Did she say why she and Clover's mother had come?'

Clarice nodded. 'To help take the dead to the Summer Lands.'

Morghan nodded, and they sat together, hands linked, for a few minutes, listening to the quiet, giving themselves time to explore the reaches of love they still felt for Grainne in their hearts.

'I wish I had seen her,' Morghan said at last. 'My eyes would like to have sight of her again.'

'She looked just the same,' Clarice said. 'I thought I was forgetting what she looked like, that the image of her was fading, but no.' She shook her head. 'I realised when I saw her that I hadn't forgotten anything.'

Clarice moved, pushed her hair back from her face. 'I'd better go home,' she said. 'Krista will be back by now, I'm sure.' She checked her watch. 'Definitely I'd better get back. I have to open Haven soon.'

They stood and hugged, holding each other for a moment.

'Thank you for telling me,' Morghan said, then smiled. 'Both pieces of news.'

Clarice nodded. 'Of course,' she said, and pressed a hand to her own cheek. 'I love you, Morghan,' she said.

Morghan placed her palm over Clarice's and leant in, whispered a kiss on Clarice's forehead, then stood back and smiled. 'I love you too.'

When Clarice was gone, Morghan stood in the middle of her office for a long minute, then walked down to gaze at the painting Grainne had done for her.

There were the woods of Wilde Grove. There was the Wildwood. And Wolf. Morghan's fingers hovered an inch above the painted figure of Wolf, then dropped to her side to touch the head of the kin himself.

She looked for Hawk in the picture, found him on his branch. Looked for herself, and there she was.

The only person not there was Grainne.

Morghan closed her eyes. Listened to her slow, deep breathing, to the beating of her living heart.

'Oh Grainne,' she said out loud. 'I miss your presence beside me.'

25

'ROWAN?' GINGER PUSHED OPEN THE DOOR, SMILING DOWN AT Robbie. He'd been a little angel for her, no trouble at all. He'd even talked a bit – more than she'd ever heard him do before.

'Robbie!' Rowan reached out her arms for him, face lighting up with relief. 'Oh I missed you, darling.'

Ginger lifted him up onto the bed and the little lad snuggled into his mother's arms.

'Was he a good boy for you?' Rowan asked Ginger, then planted a kiss on Robbie's head. 'Were you a good boy for Ginger?'

Robbie nodded.

Ginger nodded as well. 'Good as gold,' she said. 'We had a nice evening together, didn't we, Robbie?'

Robbie sat up on the bed. 'Ginger got a dog,' he said, eyes shining. 'Dog's name is...' He frowned and turned to Ginger.

'Biscuit,' Ginger said with a grin.

Robbie nodded. 'Biscuit.' He leant closer to Rowan. 'He yellow colour,' he said. 'Are you better, Mummy?'

Rowan squeezed Robbie in a hug until he squirmed and then planted another kiss on his tousled head. 'I am,' she said. 'The doctor says I can go home.'

Robbie pulled away and looked at her, eyes suddenly dark. He shook his head.

'Don't wanna go home.' He looked Ginger. 'Want stay with Biscuit and Ginger.'

Ginger laughed. 'Glad I'm included in that sentence, buddy.' She reached out and swiped a hand over his head. 'You're coming home with me. You and Mummy both are going to stay with Biscuit and me. We've already organised it.'

Rowan sucked in a gulp of air. 'Are you sure, Ginger? I mean, really sure?'

'Really sure,' Ginger said. 'Now, let's get you dressed, shall we? I brought some clothes for you from what we got out of the house.' She set the bag on the end of the bed and lifted Robbie down. 'Hop down for a minute, buddy boy, while we get your mummy ready to rock and roll.'

'Wock and woll!' Robbie said, grinning.

'You betcha socks, wock and woll,' Ginger said, and she helped Rowan off the bed.

Robbie was pulling up his trouser legs to examine his socks.

'Did he have bad dreams?' Rowan asked in a whisper. 'Last night? He always has bad dreams.'

'Not a single one,' Ginger replied. 'Not a peep out of him all night, actually. When I checked on him, he was sound asleep and Bikkie was tucked in next to him snoring like a mad thing.'

Rowan closed her eyes in relief, and to keep the sudden tear from falling. She sniffed, took the clothing from Ginger and tried to smile.

'I can't thank you enough for this,' she said. 'I don't know what we'd be doing if it wasn't for you.'

'You don't need to know,' Ginger said. 'Because it's not how things worked out.'

Rowan nodded, swiped at cheeks that were wet despite her best efforts, and leant against the bed to draw her knickers and leggings on. Ginger passed her a pinafore dress and cardigan.

'There,' Rowan said when she was dressed and slipping her feet into her shoes. 'All upright and human again.'

'And it looks good on you,' Ginger said, laughing and picking up the bag. 'You've been discharged?'

Rowan nodded and took Robbie by the hand. He beamed up at her, and she gazed down at him, bemused by his good mood. Usually he was such a quiet, unsmiling little guy.

Her heart cracked a little more under the weight of guilt. She'd thought there might, in the deepest parts of her mind, be something wrong with Robbie. Something that she probably ought to take him back to a doctor about.

But she should have known. Should have been able to see it, figure it out. It wasn't anything wrong with Robbie. It was Paul and her that were broken, and Robbie was just trying to survive in the minefield that was their life together.

'I'm sorry, love,' she whispered. 'I'm so sorry.'

Robbie looked at her and smiled. 'I show you Biscuit,' he said. 'At Ginger's place.'

'Okay,' Rowan said.

Ginger looked back and grinned. 'I see a dog in your future,' she said. 'When you're set up in your own place.'

Ginger's words echoed around and around in Rowan's head on the drive from the hospital, perched awkwardly on the doughnut cushion she'd been given. She thought of the daydream that had been a constant through her life. The small dog in it.

The house that felt like the Well-Keeper's cottage in Wellsford.

'Are you okay?' Ginger asked, glancing across at Rowan, who seemed to have gotten only paler since leaving the hospital. 'The baby is still all right; you're not having pains again?'

Rowan shook her head and glanced in the back seat at Robbie. He was sitting head tilted in his car seat, gazing outside the window at the clouds.

'I haven't told him yet,' Rowan said.

Ginger nodded and mimed zipping her lips. 'Mum's the word.' But she glanced over at Rowan again. 'Are you okay, though?'

'Where are we going to live?' Rowan asked.

'You could probably get Paul to move out of the house.'

'It's just a rental,' Rowan said, leaning her head back against the headrest. 'So, I don't think that will happen.'

'Both your names are on the lease?'

Rowan shook her head. 'Just his,' she said.

'Ha.' Ginger narrowed her eyes but kept her sight on the

road and made no further comment. Little ears might be listening.

She turned down the next street. 'Look at that,' she said. 'The river's high – look at it. When was the last time you saw it like that?'

There was a little picnic area next to the river, and water sloshed about the legs of the picnic table.

'I've never seen it like that,' Rowan said. 'I hope it goes back down.'

'It'll have to stop raining first,' Ginger said grimly, and she got the car moving again, feeling a vague disquiet in her veins. It looked so wrong, she thought, with the water spread over the grass, lapping in the wind like it was a lake, not a river.

'There's probably something in the papers about it, or on the telly,' she said.

Rowan looked at her blankly.

'The river,' Ginger said. 'Overflowing its banks.'

'Oh, right.' Rowan tried to make herself focus, but the truth was, nothing felt quite real to her at the moment. She supposed that maybe such a violent and unexpected change in circumstances could do that to a person.

'Anyway,' Ginger said. 'You can stay at mine for as long as it takes to get you somewhere of your own. I've two bedrooms, so you'll have to share with Robbie, but that will be all right, won't it?'

Rowan nodded. 'Of course. And it's very generous of you. I don't know how to thank you enough.'

Ginger waved the comment away. 'I'm just glad I was coming along the road yesterday when I was. I don't even usually drive that way.' She glanced at Rowan. It was true, she didn't usually drive that way. It wasn't on the direct route to the shops from where she lived.

'The universe sometimes helps us out, doesn't it?' she said. 'It really does.'

'Does the universe even know we exist?' Rowan asked, resting her head on the heel of a hand. She felt very tired, and all of her ached as though she'd been hit by a car, not simply fallen down a step.

'Well,' Ginger said, pondering the question. 'If we believe it has a consciousness of some sort.'

'You're talking about God.'

'I don't go to church, I'm afraid,' and Ginger frowned, realising she didn't know if Rowan did, or anything much about her new charge at all.

Except that they needed help. She knew that, and really, she supposed, that was plenty to be getting on with.

'Nor do I,' Rowan said, and closed her eyes. 'That was why Paul and I were arguing. We'd just been to the Cornerstone Church for the first time and had pancakes afterwards with a couple from there.'

Ginger glanced at her. 'Pancakes don't sound too bad.' She needed to stop at the shop and grab another bottle of milk. Some other supplies. Perhaps she'd go when she'd gotten everyone settled.

'The pancakes were fine, but when the woman – I don't even remember her name, except that she looked very polished and put together – said that I'd have to take Robbie out of Ladybird Lane and put him in the daycare they ran at the church...' Rowan petered out.

'They wanted you to take Robbie out of Ladybird Lane?' Ginger was astonished. 'But he's so settled there.'

'He loves going there.' Rowan heaved herself gingerly more upright. 'I walked out, heaven help me, Ginger. I guess I...snapped, finally, or something. But I got up and walked out.'

Ginger turned into her driveway. It was just a parking space outside her house, but it did fine. She pulled on the break and looked at Rowan.

'Paul was livid,' Rowan said. 'And everything sort of went from there.'

'Good on you for walking out, that's what I say,' Ginger told her, turning the car off.

The engine ticked as it began cooling down. Rowan made no move to get out. She frowned down at the wedding ring on her finger instead. It was just a plain band. It had been her mother's. Paul hadn't bought her a new one, or even an engagement ring.

'It's just...' She faltered, then tried again. 'It's just that I'd been to Wilde Grove a few days before.'

'Wilde Grove?'

'I wanted to do their Stations of the Heart course.' Rowan closed her eyes. 'I ran out of there; too scared, I guess.' She shook her head. 'But to go from wanting that to Cornerstone – I just couldn't do it, Ginger. I couldn't.'

'They're pretty much polar opposites, for sure,' Ginger said, and she leant over and patted Rowan's hands. 'It's going to work out,' she said. 'I guarantee it. And for the best too.'

Rowan nodded, straightened, and found a watery smile for Robbie staring at them from the back seat.

'Come on then,' she said. 'Let's go see this Biscuit dog.'

Robbie's eyes lit up.

. . .

Winsome touched Erin on the arm. 'Remind me I want to call in on Rowan Sutherland before we leave.'

Frank, the orderly, overheard her. 'She's gone, she is. I took her down not past an hour ago.'

'Oh. You don't know where she was going, do you? Not back to her husband?'

Frank shook his head. 'Was a woman came to pick her up.' He lifted his hand to shoulder height. 'About yay high, quite round, black woman, she was. Had the little boy with her, skipping at her side.'

'I know who that is, I think,' Erin said and nodded at Winsome. 'That sounds like Ginger Lowry. She owns Ladybird Lane, where we did the garden blessing.'

'Of course,' Winsome said. 'It was Ginger who found Rowan when she was in trouble.'

'Not husband trouble, I hope,' Frank said, looking ready to go after the man.

'I can't say, I'm afraid,' Winsome told him. 'But thank you for letting us know she's okay.' She turned to Erin. 'Perhaps we will pop in on her at Ms Lowry's, then.'

Frank gave a mock salute and ambled off to his next job.

'That's really what we do?' Erin asked.

'What's really what we do?'

Erin frowned. 'Well, looking in on people, even though they haven't asked us to.'

'They don't have to invite us in, Erin,' Winsome said with a laugh. 'But yes, in essence, that's what we do, when it comes to chaplaincy.' She paused. 'And basic human caring, really. We check and recheck on those who might be vulnerable.'

Erin sighed. 'Which is just about everyone, these days.'

Winsome nodded and set off down the corridor, smoothing down the green stole. 'That's why community is so important. It's why we're doing the work we are with the Stations of the Heart.' She smiled slightly. 'The lighting of beacons. The keeping of the wells. All of it.'

'Are we doing it in time?' Erin asked.

Winsome lifted an eyebrow.

'My darling,' she said. 'What other time is there to be doing it?'

26

THE DAY WAS DARKENING, A FOG COMING IN FROM THE SEA, climbing the hills to wrap around the green land and hang from the branches of the dreaming trees.

Morghan stepped out of the warmth of the house and crossed the terrace. She stared out over the lawn for a minute, arms tightly crossed under her cloak, the hood pulled up over her head to keep her dry.

There was the well, she thought, that I fell down when I first came here. There is the path into the woods that Blythe took too late to escape the people pursuing her.

Morghan closed her eyes. It seemed to her as though all her history was there, bound up in the land surrounding her. She could barely recall her childhood years, her schooling. All that seemed another lifetime.

She smiled slightly. That was wrong, thinking it felt like another lifetime. Many of her lifetimes felt nearer than those early years did.

Particularly the lifetimes she'd spent with Grainne.

Morghan stepped off the paved terrace and took the path around the house to the summerhouse, the odd, fairy-tale-shaped house that once upon a time Grainne had used for her studio. Morghan didn't lift the latch, didn't go in. She'd given the building to Clarice, finally clearing out Grainne's things, giving away those she could bear to part with, keeping some she could not.

Still, she stood in front of the door, hearing in her mind the echoes of Grainne's voice. She leant her cheek against the cold wooden grain and closed her eyes.

That Clarice had seen Grainne in the tunnels of the Otherworld! How shocking that must have been, and how miraculous.

'Oh my heart,' Morghan whispered. 'Why did you have to go so soon?'

She thought about going into the tunnels herself, seeking Grainne.

But Grainne wouldn't be there. Even if Morghan paced the banks of the river that led eventually to the Sacred Isle of Apples, she likely would not come.

Would she?

Swallowing, Morghan straightened, turned around so that she leant against the door, feeling the room behind the door at her back, the way it used to be, the long table with Grainne's supplies on it, and Grainne herself, absorbed, her mind constantly moving, shifting like the tides.

Like the tides. Deep and unfathomable, like the ocean. Morghan breathed in, thinking she could taste the tang of salt from where she stood. It was make-believe, of course, but she didn't tell herself that.

Instead, she did something she had hardly let herself for

years now. She thought about that last trip out on the ocean that Grainne had made.

For Grainne had loved the ocean with a passion that had come from more than one lifetime spent upon it. Always it had called her to it periodically, making her leave them, Morghan and Clarice, to take to it as though a siren had called for her.

Morghan sank down onto her heels, rested her elbows on her knees, still leaning against the door, and put her head in her hands.

Had she known that trip would be her last? Is that why she'd had that faraway look in her eyes when she'd left? Morghan didn't know, and it didn't matter. She'd never come back, except fleetingly, in dreams and on breezes.

Without a sound, Morghan stood up, dropping her hands to her sides. She retraced her steps along the path, then crossed the lawn and headed into the woods.

She walked the familiar paths until they ran into the Wildwood, and the drizzling rain stopped. Still she walked, Wolf loping at her side in full view now. She paid him no mind, nor Hawk, who landed on a branch and looked at her from amber brown eyes.

She reached her clearing, the place in the Wildwood she thought of as hers, for so it had been since she was seventeen – so long ago now, and yet just a ripple in the river. She stopped, finally, and stood there on the ground that was soft with moss and leaf. The trees here were in their green finery, and sighed softly at her, spreading their garbed fingers above her.

'Amara?' Morghan stood and called for Grainne's kin, for she'd seen the great cat here before, hadn't she?

She looked toward the undergrowth, for the mountain lion to come padding out. She remembered when Grainne had first come to Wellsford, and they had walked together through the woods of Wilde Grove, and she'd felt Amara gambolling in the woods with them, bounding off to chase something, finally coming back to them.

'Amara?' she called again. 'Grainne?'

There was no answer. Had she expected one?

On impulse, Morghan turned and walked across the clearing, slipped between the trees, and made her way to the spot where there was a fence, and behind the fence, a house that had been blackened by fire.

Neither were there.

A movement behind her, and Morghan swung around.

'You won't find her,' Catrin said. 'She is not your business anymore.'

'She is always my business,' Morghan said. 'Our business. How can you say the opposite?'

Catrin sat down on a fallen log and shook her head. 'We played our part until it was done.'

Morghan looked down at her hands. She still wore the ring Grainne had given her.

'She has come back,' Morghan said, and lifted her chin to look at Catrin. 'Did you know that?'

'She has not come back for us,' Catrin said. 'For Clarice.'

'In the same way you are here for me?'

'Not quite, obviously, Morghan, since you and I are the same soul. Clarice and Grainne share a blood bond and one of love; they are not the same soul as we are.'

Morghan touched her fingertips to her forehead and

pressed them there. She knew what Catrin said was true. She had known it herself before even asking the question.

'I am not thinking straight,' she said. 'This news has... startled me.'

Catrin shifted on her log. 'Well,' she said. 'You'd best become used to it, and quickly.'

Morghan stared at her.

'We have more important things to concern ourselves with.'

'More important things?' Morghan was incredulous. 'This, from you who meddled and manipulated across centuries so that we would not lose her?'

Catrin stood up, smoothed down her clothes, and gave Morghan a sly look. 'Ah,' she said. 'And we did not lose her, did we? As for being manipulative, was not she, also, when it came to it? She wanted us to return to our soul family's council, and she got her wish.' Catrin pursed her lips. 'I got down on my knees before them, because of her, and asked them for their forgiveness.'

She, Catrin, who had made it her habit to bend her knee to no one.

Morghan was silent. Catrin's mention of the council reminded her of the Queen Bessanae's words, but she didn't want to be distracted by that. Not just yet.

She hadn't finished feeling sorry for herself, for the great loss she had suffered.

Her mouth quirked at the thought. She pressed her hand to her heart. Gave in.

She had not lost Grainne. They would be reunited.

'The Fae mentioned a council,' she said.

Catrin nodded.

'But that is not the same one as you refer to, is it?'

'Of course not,' Catrin replied. 'We keep our own councils, and the faerie keep theirs.'

'I want to visit the council the Queen spoke of,' Morghan decided.

'If they wanted our visit, they would have sent for us,' Catrin said, and sat back down, planted the tip of her sheathed sword in the soil.

Tipping her head to the side, Morghan looked at Catrin. 'Why are you here?' she asked suddenly. 'And why do you say *our* and *us*?

Catrin drew a spiral in the dirt. 'You have been meaning to come looking for me.' She glanced up at Morghan. 'I have saved you the trouble.'

Morghan folded her arms. 'I have?'

Catrin laughed. 'Why you set yourself against me, I don't understand.'

'Your underhandedness, perhaps?'

Catrin straightened. 'You forget several things, Morghan Wilde, Lady of the Forest.'

Morghan was silent.

'You forget that it was I who trained you.'

'Selena trained me.'

'Selena schooled you. I trained you – I led you about, made you remember everything you'd learnt over our lifetimes.' She raised her eyebrows. 'Which brings me to the second of the things you have forgotten, my Lady Morghan. That they were *our* lifetimes. Yours and mine. We are the same soul.'

'But we are not the same person.'

'That is quibbling. Do you not feel the parts of you that are mine?'

'Yes, and I have done my best to banish them.'

Catrin stood again, hooking her sword back upon her belt. She gazed steadily upon Morghan.

'I made a promise to the council – our council – that when our task with Broca – Grainne – was complete, I would take a step back, because there was a larger plan for you that I was not to interfere with.'

Morghan listened, felt a deep echo inside her that told her of the truth of Catrin's words.

'What was the plan?' she asked, her voice low.

'They did not tell me,' Catrin said. 'Only got my oath upon the matter.' She looked about her for a moment, then shrugged lightly. 'Obviously however, we know now that I needed to step aside so that Ravenna might come forward, and all that business might play out.' Catrin waved a hand in the air, as though the business in question had been inconsequential.

'But now you're back,' Morghan said, feeling the certainty of it even as she spoke the words.

And hadn't Catrin been at one side of her, and Ravenna the other, in her vision?

Catrin was right. She had been meaning to seek her out, exactly because of that vision.

'Why though?' Morghan asked, and her voice was suddenly low, as though the question and its answer would finally, irrevocably, change everything.

Catrin shifted on her feet as though impatient. She was impatient.

'Because there will be a war,' she said. 'And if there is

one of us who knows about fighting for our lives, our gods, our magic, and the very fabric of which the worlds are made, it is I.'

Morghan stilled, felt the woods around her, the living, breathing, singing trees, the air against her cheeks, felt the touch of Wolf at her side, the keen sight that was Hawk's from her perch in the tree nearby, the watchful gaze of Snake from the undergrowth.

She felt the Wildwood deepen into the paths of the Otherworld. She felt the warp and weave of the web.

She felt it all, then drew herself back together.

'A war?' she asked.

Catrin gazed steadily at her. 'What do you think it is that you have been seeing, my Lady Morghan? That darkness that stains the world in your visions? That spreading darkness that devours all it touches?'

27

Erin lowered her phone and looked at Winsome.

'Well?'

'We can go around there.'

'Both of them have said so?'

Erin nodded. 'Ginger's going to text me her address.'

Her phone vibrated and she glanced at the screen. 'That's it now.'

Winsome nodded, smiled. 'How fortunate for us that you still had her contact number from organising the blessing.' She touched Erin's arm. 'God is on our side.'

'God?' Erin asked uncertainly.

Winsome laughed. She'd come so far, she thought, in accepting the way Ceridwen had insinuated herself into her life. She with her cauldron of gifts. 'Indeed,' she said. 'Several of them, apparently.'

There was a noise behind them in the corridor, the sound of a throat clearing, and Winsome looked around, saw who was there, and immediately put her guard up.

She felt it, her guard going up, and she knew that it wasn't just a figure of speech, but instead it was the way Morghan had taught her, a contraction of her energy, her colours – aura – and around herself, Winsome wrapped a protective barrier.

Erin's heart sank. The Reverend Christie – wow but he must be tickled, she thought, to have Christ's name in his own.

But she expected that Jesus would have carried a lot more compassion in his heart than this man did.

She felt the immediate contraction of Winsome's energy and battened down her own hatches too. This man would siphon you off and spit you out, if he could.

'What did I just hear you say, Miss Clark?' he said, boring his gaze into Winsome's. 'How dare you undermine the divinity of the Christ.' He shook his head. 'I will be having yet another word with the Dean about you.'

'Another?' Winsome asked, and she shook her head. 'You forget, Christie, that I am not here as a priest of the Anglican diocese.'

His eyes drifted down her to look with contempt at the stole she wore with its entwined Celtic design and flame, which was probably the pagan symbol of one of those gods the woman had so brazenly spoken of. Then his gaze crossed to Erin his brows beetled even lower over his eyes.

Erin made herself stand tall in the face of his scowl.

'May we help you, Reverend Christie?' Erin asked, keeping her voice pleasant.

'There is only one God,' he said, swinging back to Winsome.

'That depends entirely on which religion you follow,' Erin said, unable to help herself.

'There is only one God in the true religion.' Christie answered Erin but continued to glare at Winsome. She was, he considered, the exact reason why women should not have been given any offices in the church. They changed their minds as often as their pretty frilly knickers.

But the Church was overrun with them now, and what was happening? There were empty pews in every diocese. He could barely tolerate it.

'If there is nothing we can help you with, Reverend Christie, then I'm afraid we must be on our way,' Winsome said, turning and walking away, welcoming the chance to get out from under that disapproving gaze.

'I've got a bad feeling about him,' Erin said, when they were safely out of earshot and leaving the building.

'What?' Winsome shook her head. 'He's just an old misogynist. I'm surprised he's allowed out in public, let alone around the wounded and dying.' She sighed.

But Erin was frowning. 'I don't know,' she said. 'He's been against us ever since we started working at the hospital.' She frowned, quieted, and tried to trace the source of the sudden uneasiness she felt.

'Are you all right?' Winsome had gotten her car keys out but now she stood still and looked at Erin. They were standing in the middle of the car park.

Erin blinked slowly, casting around for what was making her feel so oddly. She could feel the thread of it somewhere but couldn't quite grasp it.

Finally, she stopped trying and shook her head. 'I almost had it,' she said.

'Had what?' Winsome looked intently at her.

'Like, I don't know, I got a shiver or something, tried to follow the thread to where it came from.'

'A shiver?'

'A premonition, perhaps.' Erin dropped her head and frowned. 'A foreboding.' She laughed suddenly. 'I sound really freaky. I'm sorry.'

She took a deep breath and shook the last of the sensation off, coming back to the fact that they were standing in the car park.

'Oh no,' she said. 'Let's go, Winsome. Someone's got their phone out. I think they're taking pictures.' Erin looked around for Winsome's car, saw it, and made for it, forcing down the desire to cover her face.

But the young man holding up his phone intercepted her on the way there.

'You're Erin Faith, right?' he said. 'I saw you on the telly.'

Erin stopped her headlong escape and nodded. 'I am.'

The guy put his phone down suddenly and Erin realised, startled, that he was about to burst into tears.

'Hey,' she said. 'Are you all right?'

He shook his head. 'My girlfriend's in there,' he said, gesturing towards the hospital. 'She's real sick.'

His face took on a hopeful cast and Erin's heart sank.

'Can you fix her? You know, make her better? The doctors say she's not gonna make it this time – she's been sick since she was a kid.' He paused for a hitching breath. 'It's her heart, right?'

He noticed Winsome for the first time. 'What kind of God lets people die like this? Doesn't he care?' His gaze swung back to Erin. 'You can fix her, right? I saw what you did in Trafalgar Square. It was a miracle. You can do miracles; you can help her.'

Erin wanted to look at Winsome, to beg silently for her help, so that they could make their excuses and get in the car. But she didn't. Instead, she looked at the young man. He looked like he was in his late teens.

'What's your name?' she asked him, letting her spirit relax and touch his, feeling the pain and confusion.

'What?' he asked and was silent a moment. 'Nate,' he said at last. 'I'm Nate.'

'Hello Nate,' Erin said, and she reached out and took his hand, the one that didn't have the phone in it. 'I'm Erin, and I will be happy to talk to your girlfriend, but I can't fix her, I'm afraid. Bodies are complicated and fragile, and things go wrong with them.' She breathed out, closed her eyes for a moment, and imagined her heart open wide, letting Nate's pain touch her, transmuting it into love.

'But she's gonna die,' Nate said, in a whisper now.

'Maybe,' Erin answered.

'But I love her. What am I gonna do without her?'

'You'll miss her and be glad you got to love her,' Erin said.

Nate nodded, a tiny movement, then more certainly. 'Yeah,' he said. 'Yeah, I'm real glad I got to love her, you know? She's amazing.'

'She is,' Erin said. 'I can feel your love for her.'

She could. She threaded it out of his pain and let it gleam, precious, strong.

Nate frowned. 'She's scared. I don't want her to be scared.'

'You can help her,' Erin said. 'You can tell her it's all going to be all right. That she will be just fine.'

'Even if she dies?' This was little more than a whisper.

'We never really die,' Erin said. 'Only our bodies do. We live on.'

'What happens to us?' Nate seemed mesmerised by their conversation. He slipped his phone into his pocket and reached for Erin's other hand. 'After we're dead?'

'We go on home,' Erin said.

Nate nodded. 'Will I see her again? You know, when it's my turn to go?'

'You might well,' Erin said. 'Love never dies either, you see.'

Another nod from Nate. 'Yeah,' he said and took a deep breath, blew it out. 'Thanks. I'm gonna go be with her now. Sit with her.'

'Good,' Erin said. 'I'm glad. It will help her not to be afraid.' She let go of his hands and he took another breath, nodded again, and set off at a jog for the hospital entrance.

Winsome looked at Erin. 'Goodness,' she said.

Erin straightened, took a deep breath of her own. 'I don't know what I just did,' she said.

'You just helped that young man enormously, is what you did,' Winsome told her.

Erin placed a hand on her forehead, stood there a minute, slightly dazed.

'Are you all right?' Winsome asked, reaching out a hand to Erin's elbow, in case she needed steadying.

Erin dropped her hand and looked at Winsome, focusing on her. She smiled.

'I feel amazing,' she said, then laughed. 'Slightly wobbly, but amazing.'

Winsome dug into her pocket and pulled out a small package of crackers and cheese. 'Here,' she said. 'Eat this.'

Erin took the package and laughed again. 'Wow,' she said. 'Where's the car? I think I'd like to sit down.'

Nodding, Winsome checked out the distance to the car, then noticed something else.

'Oh oh,' she said. 'I think someone just videoed you doing...what you did.'

Erin lifted her head automatically and saw Winsome was right. A woman with a kiddie in a pushchair was standing not too far away, phone in her hand, arm outstretched, obviously filming her.

'Let's go, shall we?' Erin said, sighing.

'THAT'LL BE ALL OVER SOCIAL MEDIA BY THE TIME WE'VE pulled out of the car park,' Winsome said, buckling up her seatbelt and getting the car going. 'It happens to you all the time now, doesn't it?'

'Yes,' Erin answered. 'All the time. Pretty much everywhere I go.'

'Well,' Winsome considered. 'At least she got something worth seeing.'

'Why?' Erin asked, glancing at Winsome as they pulled onto the road, then opening the package of crackers and cheese.

She was, she thought, going to have to start carrying snacks of her own with her, if she started doing things like that.

'There wouldn't have been anything to actually see, though, right?'

'That poor young man was very upset,' Winsome said. 'You took his hands, and a minute later, he was feeling better. So, it might not be as flashy as getting covered in ravens in Trafalgar Square, but I think it will look as though something was going on.'

She flicked a look at Erin. 'What did happen?' she asked carefully, than glanced at Cu stretched out on the back seat.

Erin shook her head and placed a square of cheese on one of the crackers. Then just held it.

'I don't know if I can put it into words,' she said. 'I sort of...let my spirit flow. I felt all this compassion for him and let my spirit sort of gather him up into it, I guess.'

'You opened your heart to him.'

Erin considered that. 'Yeah, I did. I actually felt it in my chest, this feeling of being wide open, and his energy was full of pain and anguish, but it was full of love too, and I sort of...found that, and kind of...made it shine.' She blew out a breath. 'There aren't the words to describe this sort of thing.'

'You strengthened his love,' Winsome said. 'You made him feel love over fear.' She glanced at Erin, her face shining with excitement. 'Love over fear. That's what we need, all of us, in a nutshell.'

Winsome tapped her fingers on the steering wheel. 'There's got to be a way to teach people to do this themselves.'

Erin nodded slowly, chewing the cracker and cheese. She swallowed.

'I agree,' she said. 'And it really is about the stations of the heart, isn't it?'

'What do you mean?'

Erin looked down at the last two crackers, not really seeing them as she thought about it.

'Well,' she said. 'The heart holds the key, I think. Open hearted, strong spine, isn't that what you said?'

Winsome cast about for the conversation Erin was referring to, couldn't find it. 'That sounds like something I might say.'

Erin was certain now. 'The only thing that can overcome our fear,' she said, feeling she was really onto something, 'is being open-hearted.' She glanced at Winsome. 'And I agree – there must be a way to teach people this. Not just in theory, either. But to actually do it.'

'Yes,' Winsome said. 'To do what you just did, for themselves, and for each other.'

Erin laughed a little. 'You know what? I actually feel hopeful. We could do this. People – they could really learn and do this.'

'Hope,' Winsome said, smiling. 'Now there's something to keep us going.'

28

Morghan looked steadily at Catrin.

'But that, the spreading darkness, that is already what I am pushing against.'

'By doing what?' Catrin was intractable.

'By fanning the light of as many beacons as possible,' Morghan replied.

Catrin nodded. 'That is true. And really, you are right. The only way to shed darkness is with the shining of lights.' She sighed.

Morghan heard the sigh. 'But?' she said. 'There's clearly a but coming.'

'I am concerned, that is all.'

'Concerned?' Morghan was baffled. 'You come here, ready to draw sword and battle lines, and now you're merely concerned?'

Catrin held a hand up and Morghan stilled her tongue and watched her instead.

'When it was my time,' Catrin said, hand going to grip

247

her sword, 'the enemy was easy to spot. It came marching in orderly lines, it fought us in ways with which we were unfamiliar, but at least we understood it.'

'That's because they were men,' Morghan said. 'Trained soldiers. Other human beings, the same as you.'

Catrin put her head on the side and looked at Morghan. 'I have never,' she said, 'understood your willingness to judge your own actions as they were through time.'

Morghan sighed, accepted the rebuke.

'If we are to work together, then you must accept me once more.' Catrin looked at her, implacable.

'Once more?'

A nod. 'As you did when you were young, when you first came here.' Catrin paused for emphasis. 'I walked with you then. You looked through my eyes and I through yours.'

Morghan schooled herself to answer calmly. 'And if this were to be done, what then? What is your plan?'

'To teach you the magic as it was once done.'

'And how was that?'

Catrin gestured about her. 'We drew down mists,' she said. 'We moved stone. We brought forth from ourselves the spark of flame.'

Morghan tucked her chin down and crossed her arms, considering this. She felt Catrin's eyes on her, watching her.

'These things were normal once?' she asked after a minute.

'They were, for some of us,' Catrin answered.

Morghan shook her head. 'It is the wrong course.'

'The wrong course?' Catrin repeated this, incredulous. 'Even though I can feel in you the desire to relearn these things?'

Morghan let herself smile briefly. 'It is true – I would like to know once again, how to work such things.'

'But?' Catrin asked. 'Now it is you saying but.'

'But if we were to walk out into the public and perform such things, we would only create fear.'

Catrin was silent, looking at her, digesting this.

'The world view is that different now,' Morghan said.

'Your Erin performed such a thing,' Catrin reminded her. 'Or almost such a thing.'

'Yes,' Morghan said. 'And it stirred people to talk and even action. But if we kept doing things that people did not understand, they would feel threatened rather than inspired.' She sighed. 'I feel it is a delicate line.'

'Bah!' Catrin said and snatched her sword from her belt and drove it into the ground in front of her. 'How may we remind people of the power they have, if we may not show them!'

'It is a long game we are playing,' Morghan said, arms still crossed. She glanced up to where Hawk sat unruffled in the branches of an ancient oak, smelt the sweetness of bark and soil, then looked back to Catrin.

'I would have you by my side nonetheless,' she said.

Catrin stared at her.

A smile lifted Morghan's lips. 'You were at my side in my vision. Ravenna to my left, you at my right.'

As if saying her name had conjured her, Ravenna stepped out of the air and materialised in front of them. She gazed at the two of them with dark eyes, her hand holding not a sword as Catrin did, but a long staff, shells and feathers tied on leather thongs around it so that the breeze ruffled and rattled it.

Morghan closed her eyes at the sound. She thought of bones rattling, the resurrection of her many lives, and then the sound was just that of the constant tide that ebbs and flows against the shore, and she opened her eyes again.

'We are here, then,' she said.

Ravenna bowed slightly, and a moment later, Catrin did the same.

Morghan looked at them both, spoke to them.

'You strengthen me with your presence at my side,' she said. 'What we have worked for will come to pass, or I too shall die trying.'

For a moment, no one spoke, and Morghan's words hung in the air until she wished she could take them back, for they gained weight, the feeling of prophecy.

It was Ravenna who finally broke the silence. She looked to Morghan.

'You are expected,' she said.

Morghan looked at her. 'By whom?'

'The Queen's Council.'

GINGER OPENED THE DOOR, HUSTLED WINSOME AND ERIN IN, then looked hastily up and down the road before closing the door in relief.

'I think he's gone,' she said, and she sagged back against the door.

Perhaps, she thought, poor Rowan and Robbie ought to have gone to the refuge, because it was clear as day they couldn't stay with her now.

'What's the matter?' Erin asked. 'What's happened?'

Winsome followed the sound of sobbing into the small

sitting room, where Rowan was clutching Robbie to her on the sofa.

'Rowan,' she said.

Ginger followed her into the room. 'He's gone,' she said. 'You're all right, now. He got in his car and left.'

Rowan lifted a pale face and looked at Ginger, then Winsome. 'He came around. Paul. Banging on the door, screaming.' Tears stung at her lids. 'He wouldn't go away.'

'Not until I said I was calling the police,' Ginger said. 'How did he find out she was here?'

'Through the hospital, probably. He is her husband, after all,' Winsome said sadly. 'Next of kin and all that.'

'They still shouldn't have told him,' Erin said. 'It must have been a mix-up.'

Winsome sat down next to Rowan, smiled at Robbie. 'And what about you, sweetheart?' she said. 'Are you all right?'

Robbie stared at her with round eyes.

'Here, let me take him so you can put yourself to rights,'' Ginger said, stretching her arms out, even though she was shaken, her knees still feeling weak from the fright of Paul Sutherland bashing and kicking at her front door.

She'd thought for a moment that he was going to break the window to the sitting room and just come smashing in.

'He went around the side of the house,' she said, trying to keep her voice even as she hugged Robbie's small warm body. 'Stared in here where Rowan was. I thought he was going to crash through the window.' She smiled down at Robbie. 'But we're all right, aren't we?'

Rowan wiped her eyes on her sleeves, then looked at

Winsome. 'He was so mad,' she said. 'He kept screaming for me to come out.'

'Did you call the police?' Erin asked. She could feel the energy in the house, disturbed, jittery, and of course, she thought. How could it not be?

Tears streamed down Rowan's face again, and she reached for Winsome's hand, clung to it. 'I can't stay here,' she said. 'It's not safe.' She glanced up at Ginger. 'You've been so kind to us,' she said. 'And now look what's happened. I'm so sorry.'

Ginger just shook her head, bouncing Robbie up and down slightly, more to soothe herself than him. She was shaken, she'd admit it.

'I don't have anywhere to go, though,' Rowan said, and her chest hitched.

'There's still the refuge,' Ginger said, because it was true, Rowan and Robbie couldn't stay with her anymore. Not now that Paul knew where they were.

He'd backed off when he'd seen her through the window on the phone calling the police. But he would return, she was sure of it. When she was out, perhaps, her car gone from the driveway, just Rowan and Robbie in the house, or perhaps later that night, when they were all asleep.

She wished her dog was bigger. Biscuit, just a little yellow chihuahua, had barked at Paul, a high-pitched panicky barking that had been almost a scream. He was in the bedroom now, she'd had to shut him in there so he could stay out of harm's way.

'That's right,' Winsome said softly, stroking Rowan's

hand. 'We can give the refuge a call, and Erin and I can take you there.'

Rowan shook her head. 'I don't want to go to the refuge. I don't want to stay in Banwell. I won't feel safe, even there.'

'You'll be safe,' Winsome said, her voice low, soothing. 'They make sure of it – that's what they do.'

Rowan was silent, then lifted her arms to get Robbie back. Robbie wrapped himself around her like a small monkey. She felt his warm breath on her neck and let herself calm down a little.

'I've had enough,' she said after they were all quiet for a minute. 'I have. I've had enough of this.' She looked around at the three women, then settled on Winsome. 'Is there somewhere in Wellsford we could stay?' She drew breath, amazed at her temerity. 'He wouldn't look for us there.'

'Nowhere will be safer than the refuge,' Winsome said.

But Rowan was thinking about the Well-Keeper's cottage, and she looked over at Erin.

'Do you remember what you said to me when we met for the first time?'

Erin shook her head.

'I asked you who the well-keeper was,' Rowan explained. 'And you said I was, if I was coming in.' She closed her eyes. 'That's what I want,' she said. 'I want to become a Well-Keeper.' She looked at Winsome.

'I want to do the Stations of the Heart. I don't want to run away from it again.' She straightened a little, wincing on the cushion that shielded her tailbone. 'I've wasted too much time on Paul as it is. I want to get back to living. Properly.'

Winsome and Erin looked at each other.

'Is there somewhere she could stay, in Wellsford?' Ginger asked.

'We don't have a refuge there,' Erin said.

'I don't want to go to a refuge. I want to rent a house. For me and Robbie and the baby.'

Robbie looked up at Rowan. She gave him a watery smile and patted his back. 'I'm going to have a baby, Robbie. A little sister for you. We're going to be a lovely little family.'

She didn't know if he understood what she was saying, but there was plenty of time for that. For explaining it to him.

'I don't have any money, yet,' she said. 'But I'll sort that out, I promise.'

'I don't know that there are any houses to let in Wellsford,' Erin said, sifting through her knowledge of the village.

'Yes there is,' Winsome said. 'There's at least one.'

She looked at Erin. Then back at Rowan.

'I'll take it,' Rowan said. 'Please?'

'Are you sure you won't go to the refuge?'

'I don't want to,' Rowan said. 'I need something more than that. I need what you have, what Wilde Grove has.' She paused, and a voice at the back of her mind screeched at her. What the hell was she doing?

'I need it, that's all,' she said.

'We can't protect you like they can at the refuge,' Winsome said, but she was thinking about it. About the one house she knew for sure was still empty in Wellsford.

'I'll take out a restraining order on him,' Rowan said. Her tears were dry on her cheeks now. 'I'll have to deal with him one way or another anyway, whatever I do.'

'Yes, but he needs some cooling off time,' Winsome said. But still, she was thinking.

'He wouldn't know she was in Wellsford,' Erin said. 'He'd think she was at the refuge, if she wasn't here.'

'That's probably true,' Winsome agreed and looked back at Rowan. 'Would you mind if Erin and I had a private word, to see if this is something we can or should do?'

Rowan looked at her, shook her head.

'Good. Thank you.'

Winsome got up, raised an eyebrow at Ginger. 'We'll make some tea, perhaps, while we're discussing things, if you'll point me to the kitchen?'

Ginger nodded wordlessly and pointed in the direction of the kitchen at the back of the house.

'Thank you.' Winsome walked back that way without checking that Erin would follow.

Erin was right behind her.

'I'm confused,' Erin said as soon as they were in private. 'What house are you thinking about – and is this a good idea?'

Winsome looked around the kitchen, picked up the electric kettle and filled it at the tap. 'I think when someone is asking to learn what we have to teach them – that exact thing that we were just talking about in the car park of the hospital – I think we have the responsibility to do so.'

Erin flushed. 'I understand that,' she said. 'But physically, wouldn't she and her little boy be safer at the refuge?'

'Safer in body, perhaps,' Winsome replied, unerringly finding the teabags and cups. She glanced at Erin. 'But safer in spirit?' She raised her eyebrows. 'Why don't you check in with yourself?'

'Check in with myself?'

Winsome nodded. Touched her heart. 'Check in with yourself.' She paused, leant against the kitchen bench. 'I've seen Morghan doing it more and more often recently. She'll pause and sort of...'

'Turn inward for confirmation,' Erin finished. The kettle came to a boil, and she plucked it up. 'Yeah, I've seen it too. And Selena, she did the same thing.'

'There you go, then. Obviously, you'll be able to get the same results as they do.'

'Obviously?'

Winsome shrugged and grinned at Erin. 'With some practice, perhaps, but now seems a good time to begin that.'

'You do it too, then,' Erin said. 'We both walk the same path, more or less. You should be able to do it too.' She replaced the kettle. 'Whatever it is.'

'It's using the heart as your compass,' Winsome said promptly. 'To always take you down the path of spirit to your true north.'

Erin grinned. 'You're just as woo as Morghan,' she said. 'In your own way.'

'She rubs off,' Winsome agreed. 'But to live a deep life – I've never wanted anything else.'

That made Erin pause, and she looked at Winsome, nodded, closing her eyes to search for the guidance in the deep flow of her spirit.

'Nor have I,' she said quietly.

29

'MORGHAN,' AMBROSE SAID AND HELD THE DOOR OPEN. 'COME in out of the rain for the gods' sakes.'

Morghan nodded her thanks and stepped inside the warmth of the house. The afternoon had grown late and dim while she'd been gone, but Ambrose's house was warm, and Morghan shook off her cloak and let herself in to his study. There was a chair by the fire she was particularly looking forward to.

'Kurt and I are just having coffee,' Ambrose said. 'Would you like something?'

Morghan sat down with a sigh, smiled across at Kurt, then leant back and looked at Ambrose.

'A cup of tea would be welcome,' she said.

He looked at her with his senses wide. 'And some biscuits on the saucer,' he said.

'Thank you,' Morghan told him. 'That would be lovely.'

He nodded, eyed her for a moment longer, then left for

the kitchen. It wouldn't take but a minute to make a pot of tea.

'You look exhausted,' Kurt said.

Morghan stretched a hand toward the fire and nodded. The warmth curled around her, wrapping and drying her. It made her sleepy, and she sat up.

'I have had a particularly busy day,' Morghan said. 'How are you settling in?'

Kurt nodded. 'It is satisfying,' he said. 'To be working this way, making house calls, going to the people I serve.' He sipped at his coffee, and nodded again. 'Yes. There is no better way to know how to help those you wish to heal, than to see them inside their own lives.'

'I agree absolutely,' Morghan said. 'I'm very glad the routines are suiting you.'

'They are.' Kurt smiled, his face lighting up. 'Some though – I think they are getting me to come see them not because they are unwell, but so that they can ply me with cake and tea.'

'Everyone will be very interested in meeting you,' Morghan laughed, and turned when Ambrose came in, putting down the tray of tea things on the small table by her chair.

'Some of them are very interested,' he said, and grinned at Kurt. 'I found him at the vicarage today, and he was most anxious to get away.'

'Ah,' Kurt said. 'Veronica was a little more forward in her interest than I had counted upon.'

'She'll calm down, I should say,' Morghan told him. 'She has already done so, believe it or not, since she first came here.'

'She is Erin's mother?'

'She is. Veronica and her husband adopted Erin when she was born. Erin's birth mother grew up here in Wellsford.' Morghan looked hopefully at the tea, then poured some into her cup anyway, taking a biscuit from the plate. They were some of Simon's Afghans, ones Clover had given him the recipe for. They had turned out to be quite the hit in Wellsford.

'Just what I needed,' Morghan said, sitting back and feeling herself relax, warm up.

'Where have you been?' Ambrose asked, taking his own chair and frowning at her.

'To a council meeting,' Morghan said, looking at him and smiling.

'A council meeting?' Ambrose was momentarily confused, then his expression cleared. 'Ah,' he said.

'Yes,' Morghan agreed. 'It was extraordinary. You're going to need your notebook.'

'A council meeting?' Kurt asked. 'I do not understand.'

Morghan turned her smile to him. 'A council meeting in the Otherworld,' she said. 'Like nothing I've been to before.'

Kurt's eyes widened and he shook his head. 'Do you wish me to leave while you discuss this?'

Morghan gave his question the consideration Kurt deserved, then shook her head. 'I don't think that's necessary, do you, Ambrose?'

'Not at all,' Ambrose answered, coming back with notebook and pen. 'I would value Kurt's insight.'

'Thank you, both of you,' Kurt said.

'Where's Winsome?' Morghan asked. She hadn't been

into any other room, but she could feel that Blackthorn House was empty of Winsome's presence.

'She and Erin are busy still,' Ambrose said. 'With someone they helped at the hospital.' He pondered the situation for a moment. 'A pregnant woman and her little boy, who are coming to live in Wellsford, in Mariah's house, apparently.'

Morghan raised an eyebrow.

'Julia has given the go-ahead, of course. I believe the woman is getting away from an abusive husband.' Ambrose turned to Kurt. 'You'll be meeting her, I would think. Winsome will want you to check in on her.'

'If she is pregnant, and has been in the hospital, I will be desiring to, it is certain,' Kurt replied.

'Morghan?' Ambrose looked at her. 'Are you all right?'

Morghan nodded her head slowly. She had her eyes closed. 'I just have the oddest feeling, Ambrose,' she said. 'Something about this woman. She's moving into Mariah's house, you say?'

'That's what Winsome told me when I spoke to her on the phone,' Ambrose said. 'What are you feeling?'

'The cat among the pigeons,' Morghan said.

'What?' Ambrose frowned. 'This woman?'

But Morghan shook her head. 'No. She should be here. I feel strongly that she should be here.'

Her eyes were still closed, and Morghan was listening to the sensations within her, trying her best to interpret them. Selena had told her that it was possible that she would begin to feel her connection this way.

The connection with her own intuition and perhaps even her spirit kin. In her body. It was extraordinary.

'But?' Kurt asked. He was looking at Morghan with interest. Almost, he thought, he could feel her energy swirling around her in powerful gusts.

'But it will set off a chain of events,' Morghan said. 'Is that right?' She nodded. 'That's correct.'

'What sort of chain of events?'

Morghan felt light-headed. 'I have no more information than that,' she said and opened her eyes. 'What a day.'

Ambrose nodded. What a day it had been, for sure.

He drew himself back to the reason Morghan had come over. 'The council,' he said. 'Tell me about it.'

'Well,' Morghan said, straightening and going for the tea again. 'If we ever suspected that the Lady of the Ways worked with others, then we were right.'

'Did we suspect that?' Ambrose asked.

Kurt held up a hand. 'If I may interject,' he said. 'Who is this Lady of the Ways of whom you speak?'

'She is the Patroness of this house,' Morghan answered, then elaborated at Kurt's confused look.

'Long ago, when Wilde Grove was the Forest House, the priestesses followed the ways of the Deer Mother. Perhaps – probably – others, but the Mother is the one I am familiar with.'

'The Deer Mother?'

'Yes,' Morghan said. 'I call her Elen of the Ways now, although truthfully, she has never given me her name, but the Deer Mother is who she is, or was. Elen is a form and name she seems comfortable with, and indeed, in these times, it is a goddess of ways and paths that we need.' Morghan smiled at the memory that came up. 'I have run as a deer twice in this lifetime now.'

Ambrose scowled. 'The second time being this fool testing the Fae did to you.'

Morghan just shrugged and sipped her tea.

'Fine,' Ambrose said, letting that go, again. 'Tell me about the council.' He paused. 'It seems odd, does it not, that it is just mentioned for the first time the other day, and now you have been there.'

It was Kurt who answered. 'But that is what it is like,' he said. 'One word said with meaning, and the path opens in that direction.' He looked at Morghan. 'Would you not say so?'

'I would indeed,' Morghan said. She nodded. 'Let me think a moment, where to begin the story.' She looked at Ambrose.

'Have you seen Clarice today?'

Ambrose was perplexed at the change in subject. 'No,' he said, then flushed. 'I only saw Krista.'

'Yes,' Morghan said, and couldn't help her smile. 'That is also a conversation I will enjoy having, but I think we must stay on track for a minute.'

Ambrose nodded, glanced at Kurt who grinned widely at him.

Morghan finished her biscuit and took a sip of tea. She would leave out, for now, the part of the story to do with Grainne. That, she would address with Ambrose the next day. He needed to know it.

'I was wandering the Wildwood,' Morghan said. 'Speaking with Catrin, when Ravenna showed up.' She smiled at Kurt. 'These are two aspects of my own self. Past lives, if you will. One, Catrin, an iron-age priestess and

Ravenna, the second Lady of the Forest House, that is now Wilde Grove.'

Kurt's eyes widened.

Morghan nodded and turned back to continue her tale. She would tell Ambrose of Catrin's talk of war another time too. Right now, she was growing weary, and that story could wait.

'Ravenna told me that the council was waiting for me. When I asked which council she was referring to, she told me it was the Goddess's.'

Ambrose was stunned. 'The Goddess's?'

'Indeed,' Morghan agreed. 'I'm sure my face looked just the same as yours does right now.' She poured a second cup of tea and settled back into the chair. She was quite warm now, by the fire.

'Naturally, I made my way there with all haste.'

'Where is it?' Ambrose asked, opening his notebook. 'Where do they hold this council?'

'Somewhere in the labyrinth of tunnels in the Underworld.'

Kurt caught the name she'd used. 'The Underworld?' he asked.

'That's right,' Ambrose said. 'Not the Upper Realms?'

'No,' Morghan said. 'I'm aware that the soul family council is accessed through the Upper Realms, but this, this was in the tunnels.'

'Fascinating,' Ambrose said.

'Near the chamber where Alastrina and Elen took me when they drugged me.'

Kurt's eyes were like saucers. 'Drugged you?'

'That is exactly what they did. They made me drink of a

brew of some sort, so that I would have a travelling within a travelling.'

Kurt shook his head and leant back in his own chair. 'I do not know what I have been doing with my life,' he said. 'To have missed all this.' He gestured with a hand. 'To live among those who speak this way as a matter of course. I wish the whole world knew about this connection that is possible. I wish many conversations around the coffee cup to be like this.'

Morghan smiled at him. 'You'll find your wish come true here, then,' she said.

'And everywhere, if we ever achieve our aim,' Ambrose added.

That earned him a sympathetic look from Morghan. 'We will achieve our aim,' she said. 'As it turns out, there are a great many working towards it, and we are only one part of the effort.'

Ambrose nodded. 'The council.'

30

'HERE?' MORGHAN ASKED, BUT RAVENNA JUST LOOKED AT HER and pushed the door open.

'Go in,' she said. 'They are expecting you.'

Suddenly apprehensive, Morghan nodded, took a breath, and stepped into the room. The door closed behind her.

The chamber was oval-shaped, the same shape as the large table that stood within it, the walls smooth and high. Morghan gazed around at the people seated at the table, then sank into a deep bow.

She recognised no one. Elen was not there.

When she rose, the silence broke, and it was as though she were also absent, for no one greeted her, or paid her any attention; instead, they gathered themselves up and murmuring to each other, left the room, some filing past her to the main door, others going through a door in the far end.

Morghan watched them, not understanding at all what

was going on. There must, she thought, be twenty or so people. None looked human.

Finally, there were just four left at the table, two women who clearly were Fae, and a wizard who reminded Morghan strongly of Clover's stories of her wizards. Was he perhaps one of them?

Then there was the final person, who resembled Dwarf more than man, and was clearly in charge of the proceedings.

'Morghan of the Grove,' he said. 'We thank you for coming.'

'You are welcome,' Morghan said, bowing her head. 'I am curious as to what this place is?'

Her question was ignored. Instead, another asked in its place.

'You are satisfied with the work you are doing?' The Dwarf looked directly at her, and although, Morghan thought, he might have been smaller in stature than a man, she wasn't sure she'd ever met anyone with a greater radiance of authority about them. 'Its new direction?'

Nonplussed, Morghan ran his question through her mind, looking around at the other people in the room. There was a woman sitting beside the Dwarf, but she said nothing, only returned Morghan's gaze.

'I am,' Morghan said at last. 'But if there is anything you would rather I be doing, then I would like to hear it.'

The Dwarf pursed his lips. 'You signed a contract,' he said.

'Many years ago,' Morghan said, surprised at the mention of it. For it was true. Elen had led her, one travelling, to a small room, and bid her sign her name in a book, so that she might, Elen said, be supported for the work she would do.

It had been an office, Morghan had thought at the time. An accounting office. She had protested that she would do her healing work without compensation, but that had not been accepted, and in the end, she had written her name into the book.

'I feel myself well supported and compensated for the work I do,' Morghan replied, mystified.

Why this talk of contracts?

The Dwarf nodded. 'That is well, then. It shall remain in force.' He turned to the man standing behind him, who passed him something.

The Dwarf set it on the table and slid it across to Morghan.

It was a small wooden chest, and Morghan looked at it in surprise. 'This is for me?'

'If you will accept it.'

Morghan paused, frowning at the phrase that had been used. 'Must I accept it before I know what it contains?' she asked.

It was with some relief that she heard the answer come back in the negative. She drew the chest toward her, lifted the latch, and opened the box.

Inside, fit snugly and lying on its side, was a golden egg.

'What does this mean?' she asked, looking at the gleaming egg.

There was no answer, and Morghan laughed softly before bowing her head. 'My gratitude for the offer of this gift,' she said. Then, lips twitching. 'Am I then, to be your goose that lays golden eggs?'

The egg in the box was about the length and breadth of her hand. Bigger than a goose egg, but still. As in dreams, communication with those in the Otherworld ran on symbolism and wordplay.

But apparently her question was beneath notice, because the council members still assembled stirred, and it was obvious that she was dismissed.

Morghan closed the lid of the box, picked it up, bowed, and made her way to the door.

It wasn't until she was on the other side of it that she realised that by taking it with her, she'd accepted the gift from the Council without even knowing what it meant and certainly not what it was for.

Or what strings came attached to it.

'AND THAT'S ALL?' AMBROSE ASKED.

'That's all?' Morghan laughed. 'They gave me a golden egg!'

'The egg holds weight as a symbol of the pause before creation,' Kurt said. He had leant forward in his seat to listen to Morghan's tale, fascinated. He had thought, when applying for the job as doctor in this little village in England of all places, that he would enjoy a place that wanted him to do his work in the midst of community, but there was, it turned out, even more to appreciate about the conditions in Wellsford.

Morghan nodded. 'In my world, it also symbolises the soul and is probably the most personally important symbol I work with.' She touched the crystal egg she wore around her neck. 'It's been relevant to me in many ways over the years.'

'What do you think it means that these people gave you a golden egg?' Kurt asked.

Morghan looked down at her right hand. It too was golden, to her vision. A golden hand and now a golden egg. The egg in a chest, like treasure.

'I think it means there is no more important work we can do, than to awaken people to the fact that they have souls.' Morghan considered her words, then nodded.

'I also think,' she said, 'that it is expected that this work will show dividends.'

Kurt mulled upon these words. He glanced at Ambrose, who nodded, encouraging him to speak his thoughts.

'People do not know this?' he asked, then shook his head. 'You need not answer this, for I know this myself. Individually, perhaps, many still do. But as culture and society – maybe it is forgotten.'

Morghan nodded. 'I envision a world that is ensouled again. One in which the numinous is as real as the clothes we wear and the chairs we sit in. One in which wisdom comes from the heart and soul.'

'That's what we're trying to do, I think,' Ambrose said. 'With our Stations of the Heart books – to give people a blueprint for how to regain this state.'

Kurt nodded. 'What about for those people who do not like to read?' he asked. 'Learning from books does not suit everyone.'

'We have the website so far,' Ambrose said. 'An online presence.' Thanks to Krista. He flushed at the thought of her, of what she had asked him.

Kurt nodded, looked at Morghan. 'And you have been on

the television.' He straightened. 'That is good. The interviews were good. I watched them.'

'I hate doing them,' Morghan confessed. 'There is something about television that feels like it trivialises things.'

But Kurt was already shaking his head. 'No,' he said. 'This is the way to reach people. Through the videos, Erin, for example, going viral. That has made change, that one thing.'

'Yes,' Morghan agreed. 'It has brought us to the attention of so many.'

There was a quiver in her awareness, a rising up of sensation through her body and she stilled, listening to it.

'What is it?' Ambrose asked.

Morghan shook her head. 'That feeling again. That something is going to happen. That...' She shook her head.

'I don't know.'

'I can't believe it,' Rowan said.

She turned slowly around the sitting room, shaking her head. 'I didn't expect all this.'

Julia's brow wrinkled. 'I can have the furniture removed, I guess, if you don't want it.'

'Oh no, please don't,' Rowan said. 'I didn't mean for you to do that.' She patted Robbie's head as he stood beside her, one arm hooked around her leg. 'And we don't actually have anything. Nothing, practically, except the clothes we're standing up in.'

She turned her suddenly worried gaze to Winsome. 'I don't have any money yet, either.'

Julia cleared her throat. 'You can start paying rent when you've sorted that.'

'And I'll sign you up for the grocery subscription and take care of that, so you'll be able to eat for the first couple of weeks while you're figuring everything out. Plus, Julia has already stocked the fridge for you.'

Rowan stared at them, then burst into sudden tears. 'You're all so kind,' she said. 'Why are you all being so kind? You don't know Robbie and me at all.'

'Yes we do,' Winsome said. 'You're the living expression of beautiful souls, as are we all.'

'And you're in need,' Erin said. 'We're in a position to help. So we are.'

'But this,' Rowan said, shaking her head. 'This is more than I could ever have hoped for. A whole house?'

'For however long you need,' Winsome said, and she looked at Julia.

'Yes,' Julia said. 'That's right.' In truth, she thought, it would be a relief to have something to do with the place. Empty, Mariah's house sat on the street and haunted her every time she walked or drove past. There, she always thought, there were the windows that looked into rooms murky with sadness and fear and anger. There was the garage where petrol had been siphoned into milk bottles.

Julia blinked away the rest of the thought. Soon, she hoped, she'd be able to walk by and see the house where a little boy played, where a young woman rebuilt a life into something nourishing. Julia thought of her plants, her small but thriving business, and felt the relief that flooded through her every time she reminded herself that this was where she belonged now.

She could even cope with the spirit cat that would be waiting at home for her.

With that, she passed Rowan the set of house keys and nodded. 'Let me know if there's anything you need – or tell Winsome, and she'll pass it on.' Julia frowned, glancing at Winsome. 'Wen does the lawns, but he can keep on with the job, I think.'

Winsome nodded. 'That would be wonderful.' She glanced out the window at the grey clouds that clung to the spire of Bridget's Sanctuary across the road. 'Not that the lawns are in any state for mowing right now.'

'Can we do anything else for you tonight, Rowan?' Erin said. 'Do you need anything else?'

Rowan shook her head. 'No, we've everything and more we could need. Don't we Robbie?'

'Would you like me to stay with you a while?' Winsome asked.

But Rowan shook her head. 'I've kept you long enough,' she said. 'I think I'd just like to put our things away, and then have a rest. I'm very tired, and I think Robbie is too.'

'You've had quite the day,' Winsome said. 'I'll pop around tomorrow, then, and see how you're getting on.'

In five minutes, Rowan closed the front door to her new home and turned to look wide-eyed at Robbie.

'All right, love?' she asked. 'What do you think about our new house?'

Robbie looked around, clearly overwhelmed.

Rowan nodded, took a wavering breath, and smiled. 'I know,' she said. 'I feel the same. Let's get something from the fridge and have an early tea, shall we?' She glanced at the television in the corner. It wasn't large, but the remote, at least, would be all hers. 'Then we can snuggle up on the couch and watch something on the telly for a while.'

Winsome had not been kidding when she'd said that the fridge had been stocked, and Rowan almost started crying again when she opened the door to it and the freezer.

'Oh, Robbie,' she said. 'There's enough here for a feast!'

She made them eggs and bacon on toast, with ice cream for afters. They ate at the dining table, then snuggled down in a nest of blankets on the couch to see what was on the telly suitable for Robbie to watch.

Robbie though, was asleep inside five minutes, and Rowan turned the television off, and lay back, Robbie safely in the crook of her arm. She looked around the room, listened to the rain on the roof as the sun went down, and the crackling of the fire that had been lit for her before she'd even stepped foot in the house.

She and Robbie were warm, she thought. And safe. Paul would have no idea where she was. She wouldn't have to worry about him.

And tomorrow, or the next day, if she was feeling better, she and Robbie would walk down to the Well-Keeper's Cottage and do exactly what Winsome had suggested.

They'd give an offering of thanks at the sacred spring.

Who knew, Rowan thought drowsily as she went off to sleep on the couch. Perhaps she could be a Well-Keeper.

Perhaps she could at that.

31

PAUL SLAMMED THE DOOR TO THE HOUSE AND TURNED around and kicked it for good measure.

Why was she gone? Why had Rowan gone and left? He hadn't done anything wrong – she was the one who had behaved badly. What had she been thinking, getting up and walking out on their lunch?

She'd made a fool of him. Right there in front of people he'd wanted to impress. She'd walked out, leaving him sitting like a lame duck, his fork halfway to his mouth, syrup dripping from it.

And she'd thought she'd been justified!

'Fuck!'

Paul stomped into the living room and turned the TV on. There wasn't anything he wanted to watch, but he'd been about to go over the fact that she, Rowan, his wife, had called the police on him.

Well, truthfully, it hadn't been Rowan who'd done that. It was that big interfering cow Ginger, who'd done that, who'd been stood there right behind the police with a smug look on her face when he'd had to open the door before they'd beaten it down.

And how had Ginger come to be in on it anyway? Paul threw himself down on the couch and stared up at the ceiling through narrowed eyes. They'd planned it, hadn't they?

He nodded, not hearing the television blaring the theme song to his favourite Ancient Aliens show.

That's what had happened, he thought. Ginger had put Rowan up to it. They'd planned it between them.

It had to have happened that way. Rowan would never have left him, otherwise. Never.

It was Ginger, with her vegetable garden blessings and Wilde Grove voodoo. That's who was behind this.

He squinted at the hairline crack in the ceiling paint. Then he sat up, slowly, carefully, as though it would dislodge his next thought if he made a sudden move.

Wilde Grove. Them. If Ginger was behind Rowan's sudden leaving, then it was those Wilde Grove women who were right behind her.

A smile spread slowly across his face. He knew where she was, then. Not at Ginger's anymore. Ginger had been more than pleased to tell him that – after she'd threatened to call the police for the second time that day, of course.

No, she'd told him Rowan was no longer with her.

So, someone else must have taken her and the kid. Some other interfering bitch.

He nodded. Made sense. Made complete sense. She was up in Wellsford.

Somewhere, in the recesses of his mind, didn't that ring

a bell? He concentrated, hand absently seeking the remote to turn the volume of the telly down.

Another nod. Yeah, that's right. Rowan had been spouting off something about Wilde Grove. Hadn't she? Going to something they were putting on, some women's group.

Paul closed his eyes, scanned through his memory, came right up with what he was looking for. Yeah. She'd said, in that stupid timid voice of hers – how had he ever thought she was something special, something big and bright? – she'd said she wanted to go to something there, and he'd told her no, of course not, that they were a bunch of lesbians there, didn't she know?

A jangling tune cut his train of thoughts short.

His phone was in his pocket. He dug for it, looked at the number, didn't recognise it.

He'd already left about fifty messages on Rowan's phone.

'Yeah?' he answered.

'Paul?'

'Yeah, who's this?'

The voice on the other end of the line answered him.

'It's Malcolm, Paul. We had lunch after services on Sunday?'

For a moment, Paul didn't know what services the guy was talking about, then realisation came flooding in and he stood up, ran a hand through his hair to tidy it.

'Right, of course, yes, sorry. How are you?'

'I'm good,' Malcolm said. 'You sound a bit on edge though.'

'Ah, no,' Paul said. 'I'm good too.'

'Right. Well, I thought I'd be brotherly and let you know

that our men's study group is getting together at my place tonight, and we'd love it if you came along.'

'Study group?'

'Bible study,' Malcolm elaborated. 'And we sit around having a bit of fellowship, it's true. No man is an island, Paul, as I'm sure you can appreciate.'

Paul swallowed. 'Ah, yeah, of course. I'd love to come. Cheers for the invitation.' He held up his wrist as if to check the time. 'When should I come?'

'Starting at 7, Paul. I'll text you the address. See you then and there.'

'Righto. Is there anything I need to bring?' Paul looked around the room, pounced on the remote and turned the television off, thankful, by God, that he'd turned the volume down earlier.

'Nothing but the Good Book and your own self,' Malcolm said cheerily.

It took a moment for Paul to figure out which book was the Good Book and when he went to reply, he realised that Malcolm had already disconnected.

Paul stood in the middle of the room and smiled. Yeah, he might have hung up without saying goodbye, but hadn't he called in the first place?

By God, Paul thought. Rowan hadn't ruined everything. This was what he needed. A bit of brotherly support. A bit of fellowship. He'd been to these study groups years ago, before Rowan, and he knew they were good. Made him feel good.

He might even tell them about Rowan being coerced into joining Wilde Grove. He nodded to himself.

Yeah. He could tell them that. They'd be outraged for him.

And rightly so. It was an outrage. A travesty. Those folk – that woman, whatever her name was, - he'd seen her on the telly, spouting all her do-good love and light shit. Saying how it was time to draw together in communities, how it was time to remember who we really were.

Well, that's exactly what he'd do. Except his community would be the righteous one.

Paul smiled, sank back onto the couch and turned the television back on. There was time to watch the rest of Ancient Aliens before getting something to eat and having a shower. He lifted an arm and sniffed his pit. Definitely needed a shower.

Getting angry in the name of the Lord was a sweaty business.

But he'd see it right. Him and the new friends he'd make later, at the study group. They'd be behind him one hundred percent.

They'd help him get his wife and kid back home where they belonged. Out of the clutches of that lesbian bitch.

He fixed his gaze on the TV screen. Would he want Rowan back?

Maybe it should be Robbie that he should be outraged about?

His son. His heir.

Paul nodded. That sounded good.

But Rowan was pregnant, wasn't she? That was his kid too. He wrinkled his nose.

Maybe, he thought, she didn't tell him about that. Maybe he didn't know about the baby yet.

That made sense. It should be Robbie he had concerns for. His son he needed home. Yeah.

Rowan would be tainted goods anyway. He wouldn't want her after she'd gone and done that to him.

What man would?

Paul imagined Rowan entwined naked like a snake around another woman's body. The image made his mouth dry, and he tried to push it away.

Robbie, he thought. He needed his son back. That was the line to take.

But the picture of Rowan with someone else, the woman from the telly, snagged on something inside his head, wouldn't quite go away.

His breath quickened. Perhaps he should go have that shower now, he thought.

That was a good idea.

'Paul, glad you could make it!'

Malcolm came up to him, arm outstretched, and gave his hand a vigorous shake, then led him through the large and well-appointed house.

'You've got a nice place,' Paul said, aware that he was gazing around a bit star-struck, but it was a nice place. Real nice.

'Thanks Paul,' Malcolm said. 'Jemima did all the decorating. I just bring home the bacon.'

'Must be a lot of pigs in your line of work,' Paul said.

Malcolm looked at him funny for a moment and Paul wished he'd kept his mouth shut. Only, he couldn't remember the last time he'd been in such a nice house.

Detached place, and all. There was probably a swimming pool or something similarly fancy outside. A pergola or something. Outdoor kitchen, all that.

Malcolm laughed. 'Oh,' he said. 'I get it. Yeah, plenty of bacon for the takin' where I work. What do you do?'

Paul decided he didn't need to laugh at Malcolm's joke, that it was time to start telling his story.

'I'm between jobs at the moment,' he said. 'Been real hard to find a new one. This economy, you know?'

Malcolm nodded as if he did know. 'I'm sorry to hear that, my friend,' he said. Then clapped Paul on the back. 'Come and meet the guys.'

Paul nodded and followed him to a living room that was probably twice the size of his own. He shook hands with the ten or eleven men ranged around the seating. The all told him they were pleased to meet him again. He nodded along, said the same.

And he was, pleased to meet them. When he sat down, he was feeling a bit more optimistic.

They opened with prayer, Malcolm doing the out-loud bit, bidding the Lord to look down upon his servants and find them worthy.

Paul nodded along, trying to catch hold of the feeling that he'd used to have before he'd quit going to church and went after Rowan instead. He was sure the feeling was still inside him somewhere. He just had to dig it out and dust it off.

He went through almost the entire evening before he got the opportunity to say anything about Rowan, about what had happened. But finally, Malcolm asked if anyone was in need of particular prayer.

Paul nodded, moved slightly to the edge of his seat and Malcolm gave him a sympathetic smile.

'Tell us,' he said. 'We are your brothers here.'

Paul nodded again, cleared his throat, and kept his gaze on his hands.

'You probably met Rowan, my wife, at church last Sunday,' he said.

There were nods all around, an expectant silence.

'Well.' Paul fiddled with his wedding band. It was supposed to look like platinum, but it was only silver with a diamond chip in it.

'It's all right, Paul,' Terry, one of the younger guys said, his Adam's apple bouncing up and down. 'You can trust us to have your back.'

'I've got a son,' Paul said, looking around the circle and seeing the sympathetic faces. 'Robbie. That's his name, see?'

'Has something happened, Paul?' Malcolm asked, his voice calm and warm.

Paul nodded. 'She's up at Wilde Grove,' he said, the words blurting from his mouth. 'She's taken Robbie, my own son, and taken him to those people. Those women.'

There was silence, and Paul straightened slightly. There, he thought. There was the reaction he was hoping for.

'She's left you for the blasphemy that is Wilde Grove?' Malcolm asked.

Paul nodded, looked miserably down at his hands again. 'They're why I brought us to church on Sunday,' he said. 'Because she'd been talking about them, those people, and how she wanted to do their course, or some nonsense.' He lifted his head and gazed around the circle, his expression wounded.

'I knew that was wrong, that she would be taking us down the wrong path if I let her do that, and so...' His voice petered out.

'And so, you came along to Cornerstone,' Malcolm said, nodding. 'A wise move indeed, and one we are very glad you made.' He looked around the room. 'Aren't we all?'

There was a chorus of yesses, with a few amens thrown in, and Paul dredged up a smile, wiped the stray tear from his cheek.

'I can't thank you enough,' he said. 'Your support makes it an easier burden to bear. You can't believe how my heart aches for my son in particular, how much I wish I could have him back at home with me where he belongs.' He cleared his throat, rubbed it in. 'He's only...' For a moment, Paul was blank about Robbie's age. 'Ah, only two. Two years old.'

'Have you tried getting the police involved, Paul?'

It was the young guy again. Paul didn't remember his name.

He gave him a bitter look. 'The police!' Paul shook his head, heaved a sigh. 'They're no use – they're the ones who let her pack Robbie up in the first place!'

'What's this?' One of the older men this time. Paul groped for his name. Roger, that had been it. Firm hand-shake, warm, dry hand, not posh, a lorry driver. 'The police, you say, they let her go to Wilde Grove?'

Paul was affronted at the very memory of it. He nodded. 'They kept me in the sitting room while she packed her things. They delivered her right into their hands!'

'The woman who runs the place? Morghan Wilde?'

Paul shook his head. 'No,' he admitted. 'Although she

was behind it, for certain. It was one of the group who took her away.' He wrinkled his nose and spat the name out. 'Ginger. She runs Ladybird Lane.'

He was met with blank looks.

'The daycare centre where Robbie goes, or where he used to go. I bet it's where Rowan was recruited.'

Now he got nodding heads.

'Recruited, and then enabled by the very police force supposed to protect us,' Roger said, and leant back in his own chair, looking up at the ceiling, as though inspiration would be found there. Or God. 'This is grave,' he said, and looked over at Malcolm. 'Pastor Stoat needs to know about this.'

Paul perked up. 'Pastor Stoat?' he asked. 'Who is Pastor Stoat?'

Malcolm nodded, his face relaxing into an almost beatific smile. 'Of course,' he said. 'And the Pastor would have been with us himself tonight, if he'd been more rested.'

He turned to Paul. 'John Stoat,' he announced. 'Has come all the way from America especially to deal with the scourge that is Wilde Grove. To nip it in the bud before it can spread any more than it already has.'

A satisfied smile. 'And I think Pastor Stoat will be very interested to hear your story.

'Very interested indeed.'

32

IT WAS DARK, WET, AND CHILLY BY THE TIME WINSOME WAS ready to head through the woods to Blackthorn House.

If only, she thought, that there was a way to drive to the house on a night like this.

'Are you sure you want to go venturing out there?' Veronica asked from her perch at the kitchen table where she was enjoying a cuppa while leafing through a magazine. She eyed Winsome. 'It's nasty out. You'll trip and break your neck.'

'I've got a light,' Winsome said, and if she didn't want so much to see Ambrose, she'd be more than happy to stay put.

'Well then, on your head be it,' Veronica said. 'Do you have your phone?'

Winsome patted her pocket.

'Good. Tell your boyfriend to put a driveway in.'

'That would mean cutting down trees.'

Veronica rolled her eyes. 'Heaven forbid we do any of

284

that.' She sighed. 'Well then, go and have fun, we both know he's worth the broken neck.'

'Veronica!' Winsome gave her an exasperated look.

'Speaking of dishy men,' Veronica said. 'I had a home visit from the new doctor.'

Winsome's brow furrowed. 'You're not well?'

With a smug smile, Veronica touched her throat. 'Dreadful sore throat,' she rasped, then smiled more widely. 'Don't worry,' she said. 'I paid for the appointment, and happily. He was worth every penny, with those tall scrumptiously good looks of his.'

'You're not sick?' Winsome looked at her uncertainly.

'I'm feeling much better for sitting and having coffee with a handsome doctor,' Veronica said.

'But he's what, not even forty yet!'

'Thirty-eight on the 6th of August. A Leo, which makes sense of the beard, I suppose.'

'It does?'

'I've never much liked a beard on a man, but I have to admit, Kurt Lundquist wears it well.' Veronica sighed happily. 'A big strong Viking of a man.'

'You're not...' Winsome couldn't quite think of the words needed for the situation. 'Making passes at him?'

Veronica laughed. 'A little flirting never does any harm, but no, Winsome. I'm not making passes at our lovely new doctor. I'm not even going to flirt with him anymore – that was just a bit hard to avoid. I just wanted to meet him properly. He'll make some woman very happy though, that I can tell you for free.'

She waved Winsome off. 'Go on, go and make yourself very happy; you deserve it.' She gave Winsome one last, critical look. 'Although you look a bit done in. Be careful on that walk, okay?'

WINSOME HAD BARELY MADE IT INTO THE WOODS BEHIND Bridget's Sanctuary when she saw a light coming towards her.

'Hello?' she called.

'Winsome.' It was Ambrose's voice.

'What are you doing out?' Winsome said, looking up at him with a wide smile.

'I came to walk you back,' Ambrose said.

'But I hadn't even said I was on my way.'

He looked at her in the torchlight, the dark, dripping woods around them, and drew her into his arms, kissed her hello.

'I felt you,' he said, releasing her after a moment.

'You felt me?'

'Yes. I just had the idea that if I left and walked down here, I'd be in time to meet you.'

'And you were.' Winsome was impressed.

'And I was, and I'm very glad of it.'

Winsome found his hand, held it, and turned for the path again. 'You're on the Winsome Wavelength.'

Ambrose laughed. 'I guess I am.' He gave her hand a squeeze and then sobered. 'Winsome, Krista came to see me today.'

'Krista?' Winsome ducked her head to avoid the knobbly fingers of a branch. 'How is she? We've been doing so well with the Stations of the Heart group; Krista is such a natural teacher. I love her to bits.'

Ambrose cleared his throat. 'Well, she, er, had something she wanted to ask me.'

The path widened, and Winsome slipped herself under Ambrose's arm, feeling his warmth and watching their torchlights bobbing along together, small twin beacons in the dark.

'What was it?' she asked. 'You sound as though it were very serious.'

'It was,' Ambrose said. 'It is, I mean.'

Winsome looked up at him, and saw he meant it. She stopped walking and shook her head.

'What is it? You can tell me.'

Ambrose took a breath. 'Krista and Clarice have decided they wish to have a child.'

Winsome's eyes widened. Whatever she'd been expecting, it hadn't been that.

'Krista hasn't mentioned anything,' she said.

Ambrose rubbed at his face. 'Well, I suppose it's a bit delicate, since they obviously need, ah, outside help.'

Winsome stared at him, confused for a moment before understanding dawned. 'Oh my goodness,' she said.

'Yes,' he answered.

Winsome swallowed. 'They want you? To, erm...'

'Yes.'

'Gosh.'

'Indeed.'

The wind gathered up its breath and blew a shower of raindrops at them.

'Let's get to the house,' Ambrose said. 'It's cold out here.'

Winsome nodded automatically and turned her feet to the path again.

'What did you say?' she asked. 'Did you say yes?'

'I haven't given any answer yet,' Ambrose said. 'I wanted to talk to you about it first.'

Winsome nodded, staring at the ground, barely seeing it.

'Right,' she said. 'Thank you. I appreciate that.' She shook her head. 'Wow. This has really come out of left field. Krista has never mentioned it at all.'

She frowned. Was that right? She had the vague memory of Krista talking about babies, or children, but she hadn't paid it any mind.

It had never registered with her that Krista might be thinking of her own maternal wants.

'I haven't been paying attention,' she said now, frowning into the darkness.

'What do you mean?' Ambrose asked.

'Well. I've been working right alongside Krista, and yet I had no idea this was coming. I feel like I should have paid more attention.'

Ambrose shook his head, steered them onto the path that led to Blackthorn House. 'She said she needed to speak to me, before she could make too much of it to you.' He cleared his throat again. 'You can see why.'

Winsome nodded. 'Because I would have asked, you know, who or how...'

'Yes.'

'And they want you.'

'They do.'

'Because you're related to Clarice,' Winsome said. 'You're her uncle.'

'And Krista wants the baby to be a blood relation to Clarice, yes.'

Winsome nodded again, was glad to see the lights of the house appear in the distance. The sun had set now, she wanted to warm herself in front of the fire.

And she wanted a cup of sweetened tea. She felt a bit like she'd had a shock.

They walked the rest of the way in silence.

Ambrose opened the front door, ushered Winsome in, took her coat from her and hung it up.

'Cup of tea?' he asked.

Winsome nodded. 'Thank you. That would be welcome.' She followed him down to the kitchen and warmed herself in front of the fire while he moved about the room, making tea.

He was dishy, she thought, using Veronica's word. She was lucky to have him in her life.

'Ambrose,' she said.

He turned to her, a look of inquiry on his face.

'I love you,' she said.

He put down the cups he was holding and came over to her, touched her cheek, pushed back a strand of hair.

'Winsome,' he said. 'I've loved you from the moment I saw you.' He tipped his head on the side. 'Possibly even before that, who knows?'

She reached up and pressed his hand to her cheek, leant into it, looked into his green eyes.

'Do we want children?' she asked.

Those green eyes widened.

'I've startled you,' Winsome said, letting his hand fall away.

'Yes,' Ambrose said simply. 'I hadn't thought of that.'

'You haven't?' Winsome gave a shaky laugh and slid away to sit at the table. The kettle boiled.

'You have?' Ambrose asked, going to pour the water into the teapot.

'No,' Winsome admitted. 'Not until right now.'

'Because Krista wants to get pregnant, have a child...'

'Your child,' Winsome said.

'Clarice's child,' Ambrose corrected.

Winsome thought about it for a moment, nodded, smiled. 'Yes,' she said. 'It would be Clarice's child, wouldn't it. But biologically yours.'

'I would be the baby's great uncle in practice,' Ambrose said.

'You've been thinking about this,' Winsome told him.

Ambrose brought the tea things to the table and sat down opposite her. 'It's been difficult to think of anything else,' he said.

'I can imagine,' Winsome answered. 'I feel like it's blown everything else from my mind.'

'Are you angry?'

Winsome looked at him, astonished. 'No,' she said. 'Not at all. Just...shocked, I suppose, but only because it had never entered my mind that this could happen.'

Ambrose nodded. 'I feel similarly.'

'What are you going to tell her?' Winsome asked.

'Nothing, until you and I have discussed it, and come up with an answer we're both comfortable with.'

His reply made Winsome reach across the table to him. She touched his hand, saw the ink stains on his fingers and smiled.

'You are so dear to me,' she said. 'My heart is full of you.'

She curled her fingers around his.

'If we want children,' she said. 'We'd have to decide soon.' She shook her head. 'I'm not getting any younger.'

Ambrose tried to imagine what it might be like to have a child running around Blackthorn House.

'Do we have the space and time for a child?' he asked.

'I think they're the sort of thing one makes the time and space for.'

'We've both taken on a lot of extra work recently,' Ambrose said, watching Winsome's face carefully.

'Are you saying no?'

He shook his head. 'I'm saying only that we've both taken on a lot of work recently. With the Stations of the Heart.'

Winsome nodded. 'It's true. That's our baby, currently. You writing the books, me teaching the courses.'

'Our own baby – that's not something we need to decide upon tonight, is it?'

The question broke the tension inside Winsome and she laughed in relief. 'No,' she said. 'Absolutely not.' Smiling, she poured tea for them both.

'But I expect Krista will need an answer sooner than later,' she said. 'It would be cruel to keep her waiting.'

Ambrose nodded but said nothing.

Winsome looked at him as she spooned sugar into her cup. 'What is your inclination?' she asked. Then added something. 'Not taking me into account.'

'That is not possible,' Ambrose said. 'It isn't possible for me not to consider you – us.'

His reply made Winsome feel soft and warm inside.

'There really is an us, isn't there?' she said.

'There really is.' Ambrose lifted his teacup and held it up. 'Here's to us, you and I, who walk together our path through this life.'

Winsome smiled, clinked her teacup against his in a toast. 'To us,' she said. 'Let our destinies be entwined.'

'So be it,' Ambrose said, letting the words float and settle upon them, weaving them into the fabric of the world, and he sipped his tea to seal the deal.

Winsome did the same, then raised her eyebrows. 'I think you should say yes.'

Ambrose looked at her. 'You're sure?'

'I think so.'

'Why?'

'You don't agree?' Winsome looked at him.

Ambrose shook his head. 'I'm not saying that, necessarily; I just want to know your line of thinking.'

'Well,' Winsome said. 'In that case – I think it would be a lovely thing to do for two people we care deeply about. I think Krista's desire, and Clarice's too, since she must have agreed to it also – their desire to have a child that belongs in this way to both of them, since it's possible for them to, - I understand it and think it's marvellous. I'd do it no differently if I were either of them.' She paused, thought a moment more.

'And if, for instance, we were to choose not to have our own family, for whatever reason, it would be lovely to have a baby around that is part of our extended family. We'd sort of be grandparents.' She wrinkled her nose. 'Only better.'

'Better?'

Winsome pondered it, lit up. 'Do you think there's a possibility the child could inherit your green eyes?'

33

Erin blinked gummy eyes open and grimaced.

'Burdock! Get your face outta mine,' she said, freeing an arm from the blankets so that she could push him away.

He licked her face. She curled her arm around his neck.

'You silly old horse,' she whispered. 'How long have you been waiting for me to wake up?'

Burdock whined a little. He'd been up for hours.

Erin searched for Stephan's warm body with her other arm, found only cold sheets.

'Where's Stephan?' she asked.

Burdock stood up, knocked his butt against the wall, decided he was going to get wedged into the small room if he wasn't careful, and so leapt up onto the bed instead.

'Oof! Mind your clodhoppers, you clodhopper!'

Burdock jumped off the bed on the other side and made it to the door, where he reversed and stuck his head back in the room.

'Woof,' he said. Get up get up!

'Okay,' Erin grumbled. 'I hear ya.'

She scrubbed at the drying lick on her cheek and shoved back the blankets, reached for her dressing gown, pulled it on, and thick socks too. Winter was apparently not done with Wellsford yet, even though Imbolc had been and gone and Ostara, the spring equinox, was right around the corner.

Burdock bounded down the stairs, and Erin would have sworn only three of his giant feet actually landed on them.

'Oh wow,' she said, following him. 'What's that amazing smell?'

Stephan turned at the sound of her voice and grinned. 'You finally noticed my new aftershave, then.'

She came up to him and slid an arm around his slim waste, kissed him on his cheek. 'You shave?'

Stephan rubbed at the stubble on his chin and wrinkled his nose. 'All right,' he said. 'You win. The delicious smell is your breakfast.'

Erin sighed happily. 'What on earth did I do to deserve you?'

Stephan pretended to consider the answer. 'Well,' he said. 'You gave me a home and a dog, I guess.'

'Woof!' Burdock said. He knew the word dog. It was one on the list of his favourites. The rest included walk, picnic, and his best above all others – biscuits.

But he'd already had those that morning.

Erin laughed and made to spin away. 'That's it?' she asked. 'That's all?'

Stephan caught her up and hugged her to himself. 'No,' he said. 'Not quite all.' He kissed her, then kissed her again, more slowly. 'There's quite a lot more to it, in fact.'

Erin felt the strong push of his energy and hers rose to meet it, twining together, until they were both breathless.

'May we never forget how to do this,' Erin whispered, putting her hands on Stephan's shoulders to steady herself.

He muttered something in her hair, held the tension of their energy for a moment, then let it break over them like a waterfall.

After a minute to recover, Stephan shook his head. 'We are never going to forget how to do that,' he said, and blew out a breath, then found Erin's lips again for another kiss. 'Good morning, fair Lady.'

Erin extricated herself from his arms and wobbled away on jelly legs to the table where she sat in relief.

'Good morning,' she said, smiling at him from the safety of her chair. Then, 'so, what is that yummy smell?'

'Breakfast rolls, with rosemary, marjoram, and lavender baked in.' Stephan peered at the cooker, then pulled the tray from it. 'And as usual, you have impeccable timing.'

'And you've been up since midnight making them,' Erin said. 'What's up?'

Stephan set the tray down to cool and turned to make coffee. 'I got up at 4, and nothing's the matter,' he said.

'Then why did you get up at 4?' Erin asked. 'Usually, Burdock has to trample all over you to get you up in the morning.'

Burdock, hearing his name, got up and moved to lean against Erin, lifting his head at the yeasty herby smell from the kitchen. It smelt good, but it was missing the meaty yums.

'I forgot to turn my phone off,' Stephan said, and spooned out the coffee.

'So? It's not like you have a 4am alarm.'

'Nope,' Stephan said, bringing over two cups, setting them on the table and ruffling Burdock's ears. 'But I'll tell you what I do have.'

Erin gazed at him. 'Okay then, tell me.'

'I have a Google alert set for new videos of you.'

Erin was confused. 'What?'

Stephan went back for the coffee things, then slid two rolls onto a plate and nabbed the butter. He slid onto a chair at the table and shrugged.

'People are always taking videos of you now,' he said. 'You know that, right?'

Erin groaned. 'Oh, I know that, all right. Every time I go anywhere outside of Wellsford, someone always pulls their phone out in case I do something astonishing.' She paused. 'Which of course, I never do.'

'Except you did yesterday,' Stephan said.

Erin stilled, stared at him, then her eyes widened as she remembered. 'No, I'd forgotten. This was outside the hospital, right?'

Stephan nodded, tore open a roll, buttered it, and put it on a plate in front of Erin.

'Wow.' Erin shook her head. 'It wouldn't have looked like anything on the video, though, right?'

Stephan laughed. 'You wish,' he said and buttered his own bun. 'Nope, it looked like something, that's for sure. The guy you were talking to?'

'Yeah, he was really upset and mad,' Erin remembered. 'His girlfriend has cancer, or something, been sick for a long time.'

'You can see he's really upset,' Stephan said, then took a

bite of the roll, chewed thoughtfully and nodded. Just the right amount of lavender. You had to be careful with that stuff.

'I felt so bad for him,' Erin said, tearing a piece of her own roll off, and leaving it on her plate to pour the coffee into their cups. 'He was hurting.' She passed Stephan the cup. 'Is this why you've been up since the unfathomable hour of four in the morning?'

'Eh, yes and no,' Stephan said. 'The phone woke me up with its stupid noise, and then when I saw what it was, I watched it, which was a bad idea because then I was awake.'

'So you decided to get up and do some baking?'

Stephan shrugged. 'Baking is relaxing.'

'You're very strange and marvellous, you know that, right?'

Stephan laughed. 'There's nothing quite as magical in my bread rolls as there is in whatever you did for that guy at the hospital yesterday.'

Erin nodded, frowned, the laughter gone. 'What did it look like on the video?' she asked. She could, of course, just look for herself, but she'd discovered a severe aversion to watching the videos of herself that popped up all the time now.

It creeped her out a bit, made her feel nervous of who was watching. She didn't want to feel that way, so she didn't watch the videos.

'I don't know what you said to the guy,' Stephan said. 'But whatever it was, it transformed him.'

Erin nodded slowly. 'It was a little weird, actually. It wasn't so much that I said anything to him – in fact, I can't remember what I said to him.'

'You were doing something else. It looks like you were doing something else.'

Erin closed her eyes, grimacing. 'I'm sorry,' she said, and looked at Stephan. 'I feel like I am making everything more complicated.'

But Stephan laughed. 'Don't you dare apologise. Everything was already complicated. You're just being a Beacon of the Grove.'

Erin looked dubiously at him. Then had a thought. 'Can I see if I can do it again?'

'Do what? What do you mean?'

'I want to try it on you,' Erin said. 'What I did with the guy at the hospital. I want to see if it was just some one-off fluke, or if I can do it again.'

'Sure,' Stephan said without hesitation. 'But what was it that you did?'

'Well, it's not going to be the same with you, because you're not hurting,' Erin said, thinking it swiftly through. 'But I want to try anyway.' She looked hopefully across the table at Stephan. 'All I did, was I opened up my heart to him.'

'Opened your heart?'

Erin nodded. 'Yeah, but in this really big, accepting way. I felt his pain, I mean, really accepted it, let my spirit flow all around it in like, this cloud of compassion and acceptance.'

Stephan leant back and considered her words. 'Where did you learn to do that?'

'I didn't,' Erin said. 'Or not like that.' She picked up her piece of roll and held it. 'Following Winsome about has been a wonder.' She bit into the warm roll, chewed, swallowed. 'Gosh that's good,' she said. 'Wow. Delicious.' She smiled at Stephan. 'I think I ought to marry the guy who made those.'

She looked at Burdock, still sitting beside her. 'What do you think about that?'

Burdock thought whatever she was talking about was an excellent idea. She smelt of love and bread rolls and everything good and warm.

'I absolutely think you should do that,' Stephan said, grinning.

They looked at each other across the table for a minute, smiling, reaching for each other's hands before returning to their coffee.

'I didn't know what to expect,' Erin said. 'When Morghan told me that she wanted me to work with Winsome. I couldn't understand why.'

'I remember,' Stephan said, and didn't mention how much energy Erin had put into wondering why, and what good it would do.

Erin laughed. 'I bet you do,' she said. 'I whined about it, didn't I?'

'Maybe a little.' Stephan picked up his coffee cup and grinned into it.

'But Morghan was right, as usual. I've learnt so much from trailing around behind Winsome. About how to listen to people, how to be with them.' She paused, thinking. 'I mean, about how to truly hold space for them.' She shook her head. 'I'm not perfect, or even great at it yet. I make mistakes, but I'm getting there, I think.'

'If this video is anything to go by,' Stephan agreed. 'Then you're definitely getting there.'

Erin stood up. 'Let me try it on you,' she said.

Stephan put down his cup and stood too, rolling his shoulders, loosening up as he came around to Erin's side of the table to stand smiling at her.

She shook her head. 'No,' she said. 'You have to hold that in check. This is not another sexy session.'

That made Stephan laugh. 'Okay,' he said. 'Not easy, but okay.'

She poked him in the chest. 'I mean it, Stephan Reed.'

He held up his hands. 'I'm not doing anything.'

'Good.' Erin nodded, growing serious. 'Let me hold your hands.'

Stephan gave them to her. 'Do you want me to think about anything in particular?'

Erin shook her head. 'No, I don't think so. I just want to see if I can do it, and if you can feel anything change.'

'Gotcha.'

Burdock watched them with interest, his head cocked to one side. Perhaps, he thought, they'd go outside for a bit after this. It wasn't raining, although he could still smell water in the sky, so it would be again before too long.

'Are you ready?' Stephan asked.

Erin nodded, couldn't decide whether to keep her eyes open and look at Stephan, or close them.

She decided to keep them open. At least for the first try. Took a few deep, calming breaths.

'It's like the same opening up that you do when you flex the spirit and step to the side,' she said, still breathing deeply, calmly, letting herself relax on each exhale, letting herself open up, open her heart wide to Stephan on each exhale. She imagined energy beaming out from her heart, felt the sensation of it, of being open wide, of being filled with love.

She could feel him. Could feel the swirl of his feelings, his being, his love and all the rest of him. She didn't question any of it, just accepted it all, and wrapped herself around him.

'It's...' She hesitated, trying to find the words for what she was doing. 'It's being so vulnerable,' she said, and then frowned slightly. Because that wasn't right, was it?

She hadn't felt vulnerable there in the car park with the young guy whose girlfriend was dying.

It had been her heart, she remembered now. The girl's heart was weak; it wasn't cancer.

She straightened, kept her heart open, but strengthened her spine, felt it at the back of her, strong and straight. Unafraid.

'It's just like Winsome said,' Erin told Stephan. 'An open heart and a strong spine.'

She breathed slowly. 'Everything that you are,' she said. 'I accept it. All the wounds and doubts and fears you carry, I accept them. All the things you don't know, I accept them. All the things that made you who you are, I accept them.'

She felt them all, made space in her heart for them. Wrapped them in love. Radical, unquestioning acceptance.

Erin brought Stephan's hands to her lips and kissed the knuckles. Then, on another exhale, she relaxed, brought herself back to her normal state, and stepped into the circle of Stephan's arms.

'You were hurt in places once,' she said in a whisper, and looked up at his face to find tears on his cheeks.

'We all have been,' Stephan said.

Erin reached up and touched her fingertips to the wetness on his cheeks, then dampened her own cheeks with his tears.

'Younger Stephans,' Erin said. 'Who were once scared, afraid, and feeling alone.'

Stephan nodded. 'They're part of who I am,' he said.

'They're not that way anymore,' Erin said. 'I could feel the memories of it, not the...' She didn't know how to finish the sentence.

Stephan caught up her hand and kissed it. 'Teresa helped me,' he said. 'She helped those parts of me to let go of the fear they'd felt. She found them and loved them, accepted them – just like you were doing.'

'Teresa?' Erin smiled and rested her head on Stephan's shoulder. Her grandmother.

She felt Stephan's nod. 'Her only regret was that she couldn't do that for her own daughter.'

Becca. Erin thought of Becca, her mother. Of finding her and bringing her back to wholeness.

'She's all right now,' she said. 'Becca.'

Stephan wrapped his arms around Erin, and they stood like that for a minute, feeling the world flex and shimmer around them, feeling the breadth and depth of their own hearts, and all that each of them was inside, singing.

'We're all going to be all right.'

34

ROWAN ANSWERED THE DOOR, AND WINSOME SMILED AT HER. 'I've brought Veronica along for a minute,' she said. 'She runs the charity shop, among other things.'

Veronica, standing just behind Winsome gave a little wave.

'Good morning,' Rowan said, then hurriedly backed up, holding the door open. 'Please come in.'

'How was your first night?' Winsome asked and took off her coat. 'It's so nice and toasty in here.'

Rowan flushed. 'There was wood stacked by the fireplace, so I kept it going – it's been so cold and damp lately.' Her face crumpled. 'I shouldn't have, I know I shouldn't have, I'm sorry. I should have asked.'

'Of course you should have kept the fire going,' Veronica said. 'The wood was there to be used.'

Rowan's cheeks reddened further. 'Of course, you're right. Sorry.'

Winsome looked at her for a moment, then glanced away and smiled at Robbie playing on the couch with his barnyard. 'Hello Robbie. Did you sleep well in your new room?'

The little furrow between Rowan's brows finally smoothed. 'He did,' she said. 'Although actually we fell asleep on the couch last night, so when I woke up, I just tucked the both of us into the bed in the big room.' She swallowed, tried to remind herself that this was her place.

She could light the fire, and she could have Robbie sleep in her bed if she wanted.

'I've just put the kettle on, if you'd like a cup of tea or coffee?'

'That would be lovely,' Winsome said, throwing a warning glance at Veronica. They'd just come from the vicarage and breakfast, but another cup of tea wouldn't kill them.

It was more important to set Rowan at ease right now, to accept her hospitality.

Besides, the young woman looked as nervous and skittish as a kitten. Fussing about the kitchen would give her something to do.

'Veronica's come to drop you off a welcome pack, and I'm here just to see you're settling in,' Winsome said, helping herself to a seat at the dining table.

'A welcome pack?' Rowan asked.

'That's right,' Veronica said. 'There are quite a few things going on in Wellsford, so Winsome and I have put together all the information you'll need about them, so you and your little lad won't be at sea.'

She laid the folder on the table and patted Winsome on

the shoulder. 'I have to go,' she said. 'I'm meeting Erin to talk about this handfasting of hers.'

Rowan came around the corner with the teapot she'd found in the cupboard, and the loose tea blend that was in a beautiful ceramic jar on the counter.

'A handfasting?' she asked. 'What's that?' She hurried to explain herself, tripping over her words. 'I'm sorry. You weren't talking to me. I've met Erin though; she's been very kind.' She set the teapot down. 'Everyone's been very kind.'

'Erin's my daughter,' Veronica said proudly. 'And she's getting married.'

The thought of it made Veronica laugh. 'It's not what I had envisioned for her.' She shook her head. 'But then, living in a vicarage in a tiny village isn't what I had envisioned for myself either.'

Rowan looked at Veronica but didn't say anything. She wanted to know more, but didn't know what to ask, or how to ask it.

'Stephan couldn't be lovelier,' Winsome said, and turned to Rowan. 'You'll probably meet him at some stage. He made the tea in your pot.'

Rowan blinked. 'He made that? How do you know...'

'I can smell it, and it's delicious,' Winsome said.

'It is,' Veronica said. 'But I really must be going.' She looked kindly at Rowan. 'Perhaps we'll see each other later. I run the charity shop; you've got a pamphlet about it in your folder there. We've lots of children's things.'

Rowan nodded and tried to smile as Veronica let herself out.

'What's wrong?' Winsome asked, when the door had closed behind Veronica.

Rowan shook her head. 'I have hardly any money,' she said, and she looked over at Robbie, who was sitting on the couch looking at her. She gave him a watery smile. 'We, well, it was Ginger, really; she grabbed some of Robbie's things, but there wasn't time to get his toys and so on.'

Winsome patted the table in front of an empty chair. 'Sit down,' she said. 'Let me fetch the cups, and we'll work out what needs doing, and how we're going to do it.'

Rowan frowned and looked down at her hands knotted in front of her. If only she could relax, she thought. Last night, she'd been so happy to be where she was, to have this amazing house.

But today – today she remembered the reality of her situation. No money, none of her things except what she stood in, really. All her clothes bar a few bits and pieces, were still at the house she and Paul had rented.

'Sit,' Winsome said, watching the emotion flood Rowan's expression. She got up and scooted into the kitchen, grabbed two mugs, and came back.

Rowan was seated, listing slightly to the side without her doughnut cushion, but not nearly as uncomfortable as she had been. Fortunately, her tailbone had only been bruised, not fractured.

'Okay,' Winsome said, sitting back down and digging in her pocket for a pen. 'We've got some paper in here.' She opened the folder and found the notepad she'd slipped in, thinking it might be useful.

'You pour the tea; it's probably ready by now. And we'll make a list.'

'A list?' Rowan picked up the teapot and filled the mugs.

Robbie came over and she set him on her lap. He was hugging his barnyard, and she hugged him.

'I'm very fond of lists,' Winsome said. 'Now, first things first, I would say. Clothes, money, Robbie.'

Robbie looked at Winsome and she smiled at him. 'That's right, I said your name, didn't I?'

Robbie nodded. Put his toy on the table for Winsome to see. 'I got barnyard,' he said.

'So you do, and it's a beautiful one. Does it have animals in it?'

Robbie gave a solemn nod and undid the zip.

'Lots of animals,' Winsome said when he held it open for her to look. She glanced up at Rowan. 'What a lovely toy, and it's obviously a favourite.'

'I made it,' Rowan said. 'He takes it just about everywhere.'

'You made it?' There had to be eight or nine different animals inside. 'I'm very impressed,' Winsome said, leaning back in her chair and putting her pen down. 'What a wonderful thing to be able to do.'

'I like sewing,' Rowan said.

Winsome looked at her, eyes lit. 'Well, there we go then, I've just had an excellent idea.'

Rowan didn't know whether to shrink back, or sit forward.

But Winsome was nodding to herself. 'Yes. It could work out.'

'What?' Rowan squeaked as Robbie lined up his animals along the table.

'There's a couple who lives here in the village,' Winsome said, regaining her pen and tapping it on the paper. 'Marshall and Lynsey. They make clothing, both of them. Marshall knits the most fabulous garments, you wouldn't believe it. What that man can't make with wool and a pair of needles isn't worth making.' She looked at Rowan. 'But it's Lynsey I'm thinking of. She weaves and sews and embroiders clothing. Ritual wear, mostly.'

Rowan frowned. 'What is ritual wear?' One of the horses took a tumble from the table and she caught it, put it back into the ranks of Robbie's animals.

'Hmm.' Winsome thought for a moment. 'Do you remember the stole I was wearing at the hospital? It has embroidery on it.'

Rowan was blank. 'I don't remember much about that day,' she said. 'I'm sorry, it's just a blur to me.'

'Of course it is,' Winsome said. 'I should be the one apologising.' She smiled at Rowan. 'Anyway, let's just say that Lynsey makes the clothes that Erin wears – that you saw her and the others wearing on the Trafalgar Square video.'

Understanding lit up Rowan's face, and she felt a quiver of excitement. 'I know what you mean! And does she have a shop? I saw one the day I came to Wellsford.' Rowan's smile faded as she remembered.

'She does,' Winsome said, and leant forward to pat Rowan on the arm. 'Now, what I'm wondering is this: Lynsey is looking for a sewist to help her. Since that video blew up the internet, she can't make clothes quickly enough, and of course, all the embroidery is done by hand.'

'She doesn't use a machine for that?'

Winsome shook her head. 'She might down the road, but not at the moment.' Winsome considered it, shook her head again. 'Her whole thing, and Marshall's too, for that matter, is to make things slowly, with intention. She weaves in prayers and blessings as she sews.'

'Oh.'

Winsome smiled. 'But never mind that, she's looking for someone, I know she is. Perhaps you'd like to meet her later?'

Rowan nodded. A job, she thought. She might end up with a job.

'The prayers, though,' she said hesitantly. 'I don't know any.'

'That's how Lynsey does it. She and you would find out how you can do it, what would be comfortable for you.'

'They're not...' Rowan took a breath, remembering Cornerstone. 'They're not Christian, are they?'

Winsome laughed.

'Not that I have anything against Christians, on the whole,' Rowan hurried on to say. 'But I thought it might be, well, Wilde Grove stuff.'

'It's definitely Wilde Grove stuff.' Winsome pursed her lips. 'Which reminds me, perhaps you'd like to go down to the Sacred Well later?'

Rowan nodded, swallowed. 'I think I'd like that very much.' She paused. 'I wish I hadn't run out on the class the other week,' she said, dropping her head over her cup. 'I'm so sorry for doing that.'

But Winsome shook her head. 'Oh no,' she said. 'Things can take some time, and you had an awful lot going on.'

'Yes,' Rowan agreed on a sigh, then hope sparked within her. 'I'd like to learn more about the Stations of the Heart.

There were some handouts for the class that I didn't have. Could I have some of those?'

'Absolutely,' Winsome said, beaming now. 'We'll pick up the book from the Well-Keeper's Cottage. In fact, that's a marvellous idea, because the First Station is all about finding a space of belonging.'

'That's right,' Rowan said. 'I read that somewhere.'

Winsome nodded. 'We all need to feel a sense of belonging and identity in the world, and that there is meaning to our being here.' She lifted her hands. 'That there is meaning to everything, really, so I've made this the First Station.'

'You made it?' Rowan was surprised, even though, a second later, she knew she oughtn't be. Winsome had been teaching the course, hadn't she?

'Well, not just me. Ambrose and Morghan, too.'

Rowan blinked. Ambrose and Morghan. She knew the names from all the coverage on the television, and in the magazine articles that had been written about them. They'd had a lot of publicity over the last few months, since the Trafalgar Square video.

Rowan had followed it all with an intensity she hadn't understood. But something about it spoke to her, touched her, well, her heart.

She looked around the room. Shook her head.

Winsome, watching her with a little smile, felt the energy in the room shift with Rowan's thoughts.

'I can't believe I'm here,' Rowan said with a small, self-conscious laugh. 'It can't be true. Here in Wellsford. Staying here.'

'Living here for as long as you need,' Winsome said.

Rowan nodded. 'Living here.' She took a big breath, hugged Robbie tight. 'You have no idea how much I wanted to come here, to learn more about it all.'

'And now, here you are,' Winsome said.

'Will I...do you think...' Rowan trailed off, embarrassed.

'Will you what?' Winsome asked. 'There are no silly questions, Rowan. Not when you're just learning your way around.'

That made Rowan nod and try again. 'Will I get to meet them, do you think – Morghan and Ambrose? Is there a chance I might meet them?'

Winsome reminded herself not to laugh at the awe in Rowan's voice. To her of course, Morghan and Ambrose were dearly loved friends. But to others now, they were, she suspected, near mythical personalities seen from a distance in the media.

'There's a good chance,' Winsome said. 'For starters, Ambrose is my partner, and Morghan my dearest friend.'

Rowan's eyes went saucer-round. 'Ambrose is your partner?'

'Yes.'

'Gosh,' Rowan said softly. 'This is all real, isn't it? I'm really here?'

'It's all real, I assure you.' Winsome drew the pen and paper towards her again. 'Now,' she said. 'We'll pop along and see Lynsey soon, on our way to the Well, perhaps. And I'll give Henry a call, and we can go into Banwell to see whoever he recommends.'

'Henry?' Rowan asked, and she shivered at the thought of Banwell. She didn't know if she was ready to go there. 'What about daycare?' she asked, remembering Ladybird

Lane, suddenly. 'It's nice for Robbie to have other children to play with.'

'There's a playgroup here you'll be able to take him along to, and there's the bus to Banwell, of course.'

Rowan nodded and sank back in her seat. Robbie, his animals safely back in the barn, slid off her lap.

'Okay. I don't think I'm ready to go to Banwell,' she said. 'I don't want to run into Paul. He'll be looking for us at Ladybird Lane.'

'I understand,' Winsome said. 'And that's where Henry Block comes in. Henry's the Grove's solicitor. He'll be able to put us onto a good Family Court person.'

'Family Court?'

Winsome nodded and touched Rowan's hand. 'I think it would be wise to get custody of Robbie sorted out sooner rather than later, don't you?'

35

—————

John Stoat smoothed down his hair, then surveyed his reflection in the large round mirror of his host's bathroom.

'My Father was generous indeed,' he said, pitching his voice low in case someone was passing outside the door. But his smile was wide. 'The face of an angel. That was what my mother always said.' He mimicked his mother's voice with satisfaction. 'God has laid his hand on you, Jonny.'

He straightened his jacket, patted an imaginary piece of lint off his lapel, then washed his hands for a good twenty seconds, until the water was running almost scalding. Then he dried them, fussing the towel about the heavy gold rings he wore, and settled the cloth back on the rail, making sure it was folded just so.

'God does not love slovenly housekeepers,' he murmured, and pushed the door open, his mouth arranging itself in the smile of fellowship, ready to join the family for the gift of their meal.

The Masons had three daughters, each one scrubbed

clean, fresh faces wide-eyed as they waited for him to take his seat at the table. He'd been given the seat at the head of the table, he saw, and was glad that he didn't have to make another scene so soon in the scheme of things.

He sat, reached out his hands to either side. The eldest daughter placed her hand in his with an almost unseemly haste that made his lips twitch in a suppressed smile. Perhaps, he thought, his stay with the Masons would be gratifying in more than one way.

'Dearest Father and Angels of Light,' he said, bending his head in prayer. 'My gratitude knows no bounds for the fact that you have seen fit to set me here with this fine family. That they will be steadfastly behind me as we begin this holy war brings me the deepest pleasure.'

He risked squeezing the daughter's hand.

'May your divine countenance look ever approvingly upon us who do your work here on earth. May your love sustain us through this bounty of food prepared for us by these upright women of your flock here today.'

He paused, considered whether to squeeze the girl's hand again, then decided its growing dampness in his was not something to continue, and finished the Grace.

'Amen.'

There was a flurry of Amens around the table, and John Stoat nodded, satisfied, then picked up the bowl of mashed potatoes.

Pastor Eric Mason cleared his throat and John frowned over at him. When he'd first arrived in this place, a meal at this table had been a chattering bore, chaos that he couldn't abide. Soon, though, he'd schooled the four women to hold their tongues and keep their gazes on their plates, which was, as far as he was concerned, the only place they belonged.

But Pastor Eric. Jonny smiled inwardly. He thought he made the good pastor nervous.

'What is it, Eric?' he asked now, after a moment had passed in which the man had not spoken up.

'I was ah, wondering how you might want to start things off?'

Jonny lifted his brow in a delicate look of inquiry. 'Start things off?'

'Yes. Your ah, purpose for coming here.'

'Do you whiffle waffle like this in the pulpit, Eric?' Johnny asked.

Eric's eyes grew round. 'Whiffle waffle?'

'Yes. Vacillate, waver.' A pause, nicely placed. 'Flounder.'

'I'm perfectly at home in the pulpit,' Eric said, his indignation rising.

'I shall like to see that, come Sunday,' Johnny said, unperturbed and stabbing at a piece of something on the plate that he hoped very much was a piece of cauliflower. 'When you introduce me to your flock.'

Eric stared at him, then gave a curt nod and flicked a glance at Patty, his wife. She ignored him, except to tuck her head down lower and continue slicing her meat into ever smaller pieces.

John Stoat, Eric thought, had been in their house and their lives for less than a week and that had been too long already.

With a start, Eric realised he couldn't stand the smug, prissy bugger. And the way he was flirting with Emily - that had Eric's blood boiling.

Still. The man was here, he reminded himself, to do God's purpose. To tackle Wilde Grove and their already-growing network of Beacons.

Beacons, thought Eric. The trouble with that, was it was catchy. Who wouldn't want to be a beacon of light in this dark world?

'You had something else to say, perhaps, Pastor Eric?'

Eric gave a start, straightened. 'Yes,' he said, careful this time not to appear to waver, vacillate, or heaven forbid, flounder. 'One of our newest members is having some, ah, domestic problems.'

John Stoat rolled his eyes. 'That sounds rather tedious,' he said. 'Still, you must do your duty as broody hen as well and coddle them all.'

Eric put his knife and fork down. Yes. He was absolutely decided.

He despised John Stoat. There wasn't an ounce of the man he'd met so far that he didn't despise.

And what was crazy about that, was that he thought John Stoat knew this, and liked it.

'This man,' he said, trying to clear his mind of all but the matter at hand – although perhaps Emily would be best sent to stay with her Aunt Jane for a number of weeks. While the good Pastor John was with them.

'Has a wife and child who have been taken in by Wilde Grove,' Eric finally finished.

John Stoat put down his knife and fork. Something had been said at last that was worth hearing.

Jonny pushed away his plate. These heavy lunches were not to his taste. He'd have to speak to Patricia about it, get her to make him something he liked better.

'Now you've said something interesting,' he said, looking down the table at Eric. He tapped his long fingers on the table. 'Can you elaborate, please? Have you met this man?'

Eric shook his head. 'He came to service for the first time last Sunday. I haven't met him personally yet.'

John Stoat nodded along.

Eric continued. 'Malcolm – you've met him, one of our finest deacons.' Eric nodded at the thought of Malcolm. He was a good, upright man, and an excellent deacon. Funny, he thought, there was another reason for using the word Beacon. The fact that it rhymed with deacon, and therefore would automatically seem more legitimate. He wondered if there mightn't be a way to claim the word off Wilde Grove and for themselves?

'Malcolm, yes. I remember the man.' Jonny waited for Eric to continue, reminding himself that patience was supposed to be a virtue.

Eric nodded. 'Malcolm takes a men's study group on Tuesday nights. Invited this new man along. Paul, that's his name. And Paul tells him the most extraordinary story.'

'Extraordinary?' Jonny Stoat looked dubious. He felt dubious. But still, he was willing to be surprised.

'His wife got upset at the suggestion that their little boy, aged two or three, would be better off coming to our daycare here at the church, rather than continue at Ladybird Lane, where recently the Wilde Grove priestesses had blessed the new vegetable garden.'

Stoat regarded him with narrowing eyes. 'Blessed the new vegetable garden?'

Why on God's green earth would a vegetable garden need blessing?

Eric nodded. 'They've been doing a lot of things like that, as you probably know.' He paused. 'Not that we care, necessarily, about a little daycare centre, but the land healing ceremonies and blessings they've been doing alongside the council, that's what grates my nerves.'

'Grates your nerves?'

'Yes,' Eric said, making his voice firm. 'They're always in the newspapers, on YouTube, on the television. You can't get away from them anymore.' He paused, made himself meet John Stoat's eyes, which seemed as beady, he thought, as the animal in the man's name.

'That's why you were invited here, to give us some guidance in how to deal with these people.'

'I was invited here?' Jonny threw back his head and laughed. 'Begged, more like it. Begged to come across the ocean and show you how to deal with the scourge against Christ that are these Wilde Grove people.'

A hand crept onto Eric's leg and gave him a squeeze. Eric looked gratefully at his wife, but she didn't return the glance, just added a pat to the squeeze, then her hand vanished, reappeared on top of the table.

Eric couldn't help it, and he cleared his throat. 'Well, it seems to me that these people aiding and abetting a wife to separate from her husband, to keep their child from him, that seems to me a good opportunity for us to not only support the man, but to make a good case against them.'

'I agree,' Stoat said. 'Absolutely, one hundred percent.' He picked up his fork again, and thought he'd give the food another go. He always thought better on a full stomach. 'When can I meet this fellow?'

. . .

Rowan smiled up at the sky. 'I feel like the sun has come out just for me,' she said. 'To say it's glad for me being here.' She tucked her chin back down. 'I know it's a silly thought.'

'I understand the sentiment completely,' Winsome told her. 'You're glad, and the world seems glad right along with you.'

Rowan nodded and they turned up the driveway to the Well-Keeper's Cottage. 'You're being very kind to me, bringing me here, showing me around. Don't you have to work?'

'Erin and I are only part-time at the hospital. The rest of the time Erin works at the care home and with Morghan, and I roam about the village really, helping where I can.'

'I can't believe I might have a job already.' Rowan glanced down at Robbie, who sat forward in his pushchair, a new – new to him, at least – bulldozer clutched tight in his hand, from the charity shop. 'Lynsey was so nice, and the clothes she makes are beautiful.' Rowan's eyes rounded at the thought of them. 'That I might help make things like that, to have even a part in it.' She shook her head. 'I'm sounding silly, now.'

'You're appreciating what ought to be appreciated. Joy, delight, and thankfulness are things we should let ourselves experience fully when they come our way.'

'My mood is all over the place,' Rowan confessed.

Winsome smiled. 'It will settle in time. Everything is very new, yet.'

Rowan nodded, and when they got to the door of the tiny cottage, she parked the pushchair and unbuckled

Robbie. 'It's very small in there,' she said. 'And the sun is out, so I can leave this here.'

She didn't think anyone would pinch it. Not from there.

'Good idea,' Winsome said.

Rowan nodded and when Winsome held open the door to the cottage, she took a breath and stepped inside, Robbie holding her hand.

It was just as it had been the day they'd last been there, except it wasn't Erin who rose from the small table in the corner and came to greet them, but a petite young woman with curly fair hair and the bluest eyes Rowan had ever seen.

'Rowan,' Winsome said. 'I'd like you and Robbie to meet Clover Wilde.'

'Hello,' Clover said, smiling.

Rowan managed to find her voice. 'I saw you, at Ladybird Lane last week.' She blinked. 'That's where Robbie goes, you see.' She glanced at Winsome, frowned. 'Or where he went, at least.'

'Rowan and Robbie are renting Mariah's old house now,' Winsome said.

'Ah.' Clover knew the story of what had happened to Mariah. She glanced at Winsome. 'You cleared the place first, I take it.'

'Thoroughly,' Winsome answered, and frowned at the memory of Mariah. Someday, she thought, they'd find the woman's bones under a tree somewhere. Perhaps.

Rowan was confused. 'The place is wonderfully clean,' she said. 'I've not found a speck of dust anywhere. Everything's lovely.'

Clover nodded. 'Are you here to visit the well?' she

asked, then gestured at the books lining every wall. 'All these are available to purchase, but we've copies to borrow, if you'd prefer.'

Rowan glanced at Winsome and felt suddenly shy. 'I'd like to see the well, if that's okay,' she said.

'More than okay,' Winsome said. 'Why don't you go with Clover, and she'll show you it.'

Rowan and Robbie stepped out into the back garden with Clover.

'We're lucky the rain has stopped,' Clover said. 'Although it's set to drizzle again come this evening.'

Rowan nodded, feeling the pale sun on her cheeks and breathing in the scent of damp grass and soil. She laughed, nervous.

'Everything seems a little unreal,' she said.

Clover looked curiously at her, and let her senses flare wider for a moment, then clamped down on them fast. Rowan was a mess of chaotic energy.

One thing seeped through however, and Clover frowned a moment over the vision of a woman spinning around and around in the sunshine, a small white dog at her heels.

'It does?' she asked.

Rowan nodded. 'Just a couple days ago I was lying in a hospital bed.' She put a hand on her belly. It was getting rounder now. 'I thought I was going to lose the baby I'm carrying.'

Clover nodded. 'But she's all right.' The child's energy was strong within her mother's.

Rowan looked at her in surprise. 'How did you know it's a girl?'

'Oh, I didn't really,' Clover said and gave an awkward

shrug. 'I just don't like calling babies 'it', do you?'

'No,' Rowan answered. 'Not really, I suppose.'

'The well is in the orchard, just down this little pathway,' Clover said, and herded the two in front of her. 'Unlatch the gate, and we'll see her.'

'Her?' Rowan asked again, and discovered she was smiling as she lifted the gate.

Clover laughed. 'Apparently it's not just babies I don't like to be called it.'

'Oh,' Rowan said, seeing what she supposed must be the well. 'It's a spring.'

'Yes,' Clover said.

'Water,' Robbie said.

'Yes,' Clover said. 'Water.'

The little boy turned his face towards her and smiled, and Clover saw him there in the weak sunlight, glowing with the radiance of the young, his aura a small swirl of yellow and orange around him.

'You like it?' she asked.

He nodded, and turned back to the spring, dropped onto his knees in front of it and looked at the wide basin of water.

'It's lovely,' Rowan breathed. 'It's so peaceful here.'

'We keep it that way as much as we can,' Clover agreed, and she watched Rowan's aura smooth out, regain some of its lustre. It had dark pieces in it still, however, like debris picked up along the way.

She'd benefit from a healing ceremony. Perhaps, Clover thought, she should suggest it to Winsome, who had obviously taken Rowan under her wing. A good thing. The woman needed protection.

Rowan turned a puzzled gaze on her. 'You keep it like that? What do you mean? How can you keep a place peaceful?'

'It's a sacred space,' Clover answered, making herself attend to the conversation. 'So, we approach it as such and tend it as such.'

'A sacred space,' Rowan echoed and looked around, nodding. 'Yes, I can see that.'

Ancient rocks were placed around behind and in front of the spring, so that water collected in a natural bowl in the earth, in the bottom of which someone had placed a fitted dish tiled in a swirling pattern of blue and green glaze.

'Who she?' Robbie asked, pointing to the statue beside the well.

'That's our Lady Coventina,' Clover said. 'The Goddess of the Sacred Waters.'

Rowan stared at the statue, the Goddess's kind face, and fell in love with the place. The gently sloping meadow, the lichen-covered trees – apple, she thought, and the ancient spring. Something inside her opened up to it all, and she felt as if she'd drunk of the water.

And it was sweet on her tongue.

36

CLARICE SLIPPED INTO THE WELL-KEEPER'S COTTAGE, THAT had once been called Apple Tree Cottage, and found it empty. She went out the back door into the garden and discovered Clover wandering the garden.

'Hi,' she said. 'Are you almost ready?'

Clover startled at the sound of the voice, shaded her eyes, then smiled. 'Yeah,' she said. 'Sorry, I was miles away.'

'Anywhere interesting?' Clarice made for the gate into the orchard field. She wanted to contemplate the well first, before doing anything.

Clover's expression was ambiguous, and Clarice narrowed her eyes. 'Come on,' she said. 'Spit it out. Rue isn't here to interrogate you, so the duty falls upon my shoulders.'

Clover burst out laughing. 'I was not expecting you to say that,' she said.

Clarice walked the few steps to the well, dug into the

small bag at her waist, and drew out a tiny herb bundle. Crouching in front of the wellspring, she lit it and blew out the flame a moment later, watching the smoke curl up into the sky. Air, fire, water, and herself, heavy as the earth, made of flesh.

'Everything in one,' she murmured. 'One with everything.'

Clover stood behind her, waiting for her to finish, and Clarice felt her there, and the cottage behind that, and then the trees spreading out over the hills, the lane winding down past Ash Cottage, the paths through the forest criss-crossing.

There was Blackthorn House, she thought, feeling its presence in the woods. There was Hawthorn House, the well in its lawn.

She felt the land all around her, large and solid and lovely, and she herself, one tiny part of it all, small and significant. Then she felt the worlds layered upon this one. Filled with spirit and energy.

'May I be worthy of the depths you offer me,' she said at last, bowing her head to the statue. She touched her fingers to the water, lifting them damp with the fresh spring water to her forehead in a blessing.

'Okay,' she said to Clover when she was done. 'I'm serious. I can feel something going on in that head of yours. Cough it up.'

They went inside, met Stephan there, come to take over the keeping of the well from Clover.

It was a new thing, the keeping of the well like this, but even though it meant staying over for the night at the cottage, everyone had taken to it more than they'd expected to. There was a sense of gravity about the business. And an opportunity to be alone to contemplate that gravity.

'Hi Stephan,' Clarice said. 'Thanks for coming an hour early.'

'No problem,' Stephan said and grinned. 'I'm always glad to come here – gives me a chance to sit down and study.' He raised his eyebrows at the pair. 'Which reminds me, Erin and I are going to have a knees-up at The Green Man sometime soon.'

'To celebrate the big news,' Clarice said.

'Yep, to do just that,' Stephan smiled.

Clover stood on tip toes and kissed Stephan on the cheek. 'Well, I think it's wonderful. Have you set a date, yet?'

Stephan shook his head. 'Nope. Only had the idea a few days ago.'

Clarice grinned at him. 'Which of you proposed?'

'One or the other of us,' Stephan said airily, matching Clarice's grin. 'It wasn't planned, or anything.'

'You're teasing him,' Clover said. 'Don't tease him.'

'Stephan and I have known each other practically our whole lives,' Clarice said, laughing. 'He can take it, I hope, since he's the closest thing I have to a brother.'

Stephan nodded. 'And that brings us around to the next question.'

'What's that?' Clover asked. She could feel the exhilaration and joy that thrummed through Stephan, wave after wave of it. And underneath the wave, there was something else. Solid ground, she thought. The foundation of his excitement – he and Erin, Finn and Macha, all the others they'd been – it gave them a solid footing.

Stephan smiled at her, then turned to Clarice, his handsome face suddenly serious. 'Will you be my best man?' he asked. 'Well, best woman, I guess I should say.' He paused, then the grin appeared again. 'Ring bearer. Will you be my ring bearer?'

'Me?' Clarice's eyes widened. 'What the heck? I didn't expect that.'

'We're going to have a hand fasting, but there will still be rings involved,' Stephan said. 'Come on, what do you say?'

'Yeah,' Clarice said, dazed. 'Yes, I mean. Sure. Of course I will.'

Stephan snatched her into an embrace, twirled her around then let her go. 'Thanks, Clarice. Thanks so much.'

She laughed, swatted him away, then turned to Clover.

'Hey,' she said. 'Clover?' She straightened, glanced at Stephan, who sobered immediately.

Clover was having one of her episodes.

Or so it seemed.

She was stiff and straight where she stood, lips slightly parted, but her eyes – they were, Stephan and Clarice saw, gazing at nothing in the small, warm room.

Clover was in the white mist.

It wafted around her in an unseen breeze. She stood there in it, still, waiting. Waiting for something.

It seemed an age that she waited, watching the white mist swirl and eddy, and then she sensed something behind it, and reached for it, and the picture burst into her, made her gasp.

'Five by five the thunderclaps boom,' she said. 'The seas heave and run ashore, and safe from all, the Golden Children are born. In a rabbit hole they lie, in a nest on high. The trees themselves sing their lullaby.'

Clover blinked, and the mist cleared so that she stood once more in the small library at the Well-Keeper's Cottage. She looked at Stephan and Clarice.

'What?' she said.

They stared at her. Finally, Stephan spoke.

'What was that?' he asked.

'What was what?' Clover replied.

'You don't know what you just said?' Clarice shook her head.

'I said something?' Clover sucked in a breath, let it back out, slowly. 'I saw something, I don't know what, though.' She frowned, trying to catch the vision again, but it had slipped away like an unremembered dream. 'Did I say what it was?'

'I don't know what you said,' Clarice told her. She looked at Stephan. 'What about you? Did you understand any of it?'

'What was it?' Clover's curls shook as she looked from one to the other of them. 'Why can't I remember what I said?'

'Five by five the thunderclaps boom,' Stephan said. 'The seas run onto the land...'

'Heave and run ashore,' Clarice corrected him. 'And safe from all, the golden children are born.' Clarice swallowed. 'Oh shit.'

'What?' Stephan looked at her in alarm. 'Are you okay?'

'I gotta sit down,' Clarice said, and promptly did that.

'The golden children are born?' Clover looked at them. 'I said that? What does it mean?'

And why couldn't she remember what she'd seen?

There had been the white mists, and then they'd cleared a little...and then nothing.

'We haven't told you yet, the rest of the news,' Clarice said. 'Because we've only just found out for sure.'

'Told us what?' Stephan asked.

Clover put her hand over her mouth. 'Oh my goddess,' she said.

Clarice nodded, looked at Stephan. 'Krista and I are going to have a baby.'

Stephan's eyes widened. 'The golden children,' he said. 'Already?' he asked. 'When's it due?'

'No, Krista's not pregnant yet,' Clarice said. Clarice drew breath, looked around the room, glad no one had seen fit to visit just then. 'Ambrose has only just told us, you see, that he'll, like, donate the sperm. So that the kid can be related to me. That's what Krista wants.'

Clarice shook her head, still unable to quite believe that she'd ended up there.

'Ambrose?' Stephan tipped his head back to the ceiling and thought about it. Krista hadn't breathed a word of this part of the plan. 'Wow.' He looked back at Clarice. 'I mean, this is fantastic. Wow. I can't believe it! There's going to be a baby in Wilde Grove!' He laughed. 'I'm getting handfasted, and you're having a baby.'

He pulled Clarice off the chair and into another hug, spread out an arm, and tugged Clover into it as well, so that they stood there, the three of them, letting the joy of the moment sink in under their skins.

'I can't believe it,' Stephan said happily, when they finally stood back.

But Clarice was looking at Clover. 'What was the rest?' she asked Stephan. 'The rest of Clover's...prophecy?'

'Prophecy?' Clover shivered, although it was warm in the room. 'I don't know that I like the sound of that.'

'An oracle. That's what you said the fairy Queen called you.' Clarice nodded. 'And believe me, that's exactly how you just acted. Like an Oracle.'

'I don't know anything about oracles,' Clover said, and this time it was she who sat down, her legs giving out from under her. 'What are they even for? Why would something like that even be needed? It makes no sense in this world.'

'That's exactly why it's needed, maybe,' Stephan said, thinking about it. 'Because of this world, which, let's face it, barely believes in the soul, let alone a universe in which a person might have visions and glimpses of the meaningful future.'

But Clover was still shaking her head. 'No. Listen, it doesn't work. We're all walking along our soul's path, right? We have our relationships with our kin, and we're guided through our lives. What use do we have for an oracle, when we already know what we're doing?'

She dropped her head into her hands. 'I don't know, guys. I guess I'd better read up on what the heck an oracle does or has done in the past when there were some.'

Clarice nodded. 'Seems a good place to start.' She looked at Stephan. 'We should write down what Clover said, though. Before we forget it.'

Stephan's eyes widened, and he went over to the table where the guest's book was, and the prayer cards. He picked up one of those and the pen.

'We can write it on the back of this,' he said. 'What was the line after the golden child being born?'

Clarice thought about it for a moment, then recited it with a dry mouth.

'Golden children,' she corrected. 'Not just child, thank goodness, which lets me off the hook, right?' She looked around at the other two, but they just shook their heads. Clarice sighed. 'I don't know either. But this was what you said, Clover: Five by five the thunderclaps boom, the seas heave and run ashore, and safe from all, the Golden Children are born. In a rabbit hole they lie, in a nest on high. The trees themselves sing their lullaby.'

'My god, you have a good memory,' Stephan said, scrawling down the verse. 'There.' He held out the card to Clarice. 'You should probably take this,' he said. 'Since it seems most relevant to you.'

'It could be about anyone,' Clarice said. She took it and made to pass it to Clover. 'You should take it. You said it.'

'I don't remember saying it!' Clover shook her head and regarded the card like it was on fire. 'No. You keep it.'

'We should give it to Morghan,' Stephan said. 'Or Ambrose.'

'Good idea,' Clarice said, and poked it into Clover's hands. 'You're at Hawthorn House, so you'll likely see Morghan before we do. I guess it's yours to take.'

'You don't want it?' Clover said, reluctantly letting Clarice pass it to her. 'You're having the baby, after all.'

Clarice snorted. 'Believe me, I don't need the card to remember what you said.'

She patted Stephan on the arm. 'Okay, Bear Fella, we're going to get on with things. See you later, all right?'

Stephan nodded. Looked at Clover. 'Let us know what Morghan says about that, won't you?' He gestured at the card she held.

'It'll be the full moon shortly,' Clarice said. 'We'll all be getting together then. Perhaps we can talk it over as a group.'

Clover's mouth turned down. She fumbled the card into a pocket and sighed.

37

MAXEN WAS IN THE CAVE WHEN CLARICE AND CLOVER reached it. He bowed to them in greeting, and they returned the gesture.

'What are you doing here?' Clover said, then she blushed.

'How is your young man?' Maxen asked, a smile playing about his lips.

Clarice had the lamp lit and settled herself in front of the fire to light it. Outside, the afternoon had turned grey and soon the air would be wet with drizzling rain. They'd want the fire, a beacon to set them on their way – and to return to.

She laughed up at Clover, who still stood awkwardly on the cave floor. 'Good question. I've been meaning to ask how you're both getting along.'

Clover lowered herself to the mat in front of the fire and Maxen followed suit, lithe despite his great age.

'We're fine,' Clover said. 'It's good.'

Maxen replied with one raised eyebrow.

'Okay,' Clover said and shook her head. 'Alex is pretty fantastic, actually. He is surprisingly open-minded.'

'You should invite him along to Stephan and Erin's shindig whenever they have it,' Clarice said, setting flame to the dry kindling.

Clover nodded. 'I will. I'll do that.'

'Have you danced with him yet?' Maxen asked.

His question got a frown from Clover, and a coughing splutter from Clarice.

'Maxen,' she said. 'Good grief.'

'Danced?' Clover looked from one to the other. 'I don't get it. Why would you ask if we'd danced?'

'He's asking if you've had sex yet,' Clarice said, shaking her head. She looked at Maxen. 'The Fae consider love-making both a sacred dance and a fun pastime. Don't you?'

Maxen bowed his head in acknowledgment. 'It is true. We are not shy about celebrating the great gift of life in this way.'

Clover nodded, feeling her cheeks flaming. 'Well, we haven't, no,' she said, then bit her lip. 'I've never slept with anyone.'

Maxen nodded wisely. 'Then you have many pleasures to look forward to.'

Clarice rolled her eyes. 'Ignore him.'

'What I say is true,' Maxen said with a grin. 'Is it not, Clarice?'

'It's true, but that doesn't mean Clover wants to talk to us about her sex life.'

Maxen grinned, his white teeth gleaming in the low light.

'It's...difficult,' Clover said, with her head tucked down, frowning. 'I'm getting better at not seeing everything all the time, but I'm...worried what it would be like if I...'

'Let go in the way that would mean the most enjoyment from the act.' Maxen nodded. 'I can see why you would hesitate.'

'I really like Alex,' Clover said, sighing now. 'And he's being so sweet and understanding.'

'As he should be,' Clarice said. 'I don't know why we have to praise people for behaviour they should show as a matter of course.'

'He is showing it as a matter of course,' Clover said. 'I didn't say he wasn't.'

Clarice nodded. 'Sorry,' she said. 'Of course he is.' She paused, then decided it was time to change the subject. 'You should ask Maxen about the oracle business.'

They'd talked of nothing else on the walk to the cave.

'What is this?' Maxen asked. 'Oracle business?' He looked inquiringly at Clover.

'You were there when Queen Bessanae said the things she did about me,' Clover said. 'When she called me an oracle, and spoke of some plan to do with it.' Clover drew breath. 'Well,' she said. 'I want to know what it means.'

'Because you certainly said something today in the manner of an oracle,' Clarice said.

Maxen was interested. 'And what was this which you said?'

But Clover shook her head. 'No,' she said. 'We can talk about it later. Right now, we need to go and do our chosen job.' She was jittery and needed normality for a moment. To go into the Otherworld and help shepherd the spirits there. A task, simple and heart-led. That was what she needed.

'As you wish it,' Maxen said. But he found himself vastly interested. The machinations of everyone were weaving their own colours into the web of the worlds, and he was fascinated by it all.

'I shall sing you there and back with my flute,' he said.

'Thank you, Maxen,' Clover said, relief flowing through her voice. She'd ask him afterwards, she thought. Because there was a good chance he would know and would tell her when not everyone else could be counted on to do so. But she and Maxen were close, she thought. They were friends.

'I'm nervous,' Clarice admitted finally. They were in the tunnels, making their way to the river, to ensure there was a boat.

'Nervous?'

Clarice nodded. 'To see Grainne again. My mother.' She pressed a hand to her heart. 'It's...difficult to think of working alongside her.'

Clover understood. 'It was a shock,' she said. 'Seeing them here last time. Even for me, and I've never really known my mother in this lifetime except in spirit.'

'It was just so unexpected.' The light that Clarice had conjured to guide them bobbed up and down. 'Nothing is ever straightforward, is it? The more we do, the more questions come up, the more of a puzzle it becomes.'

Clover stopped walking and waited until Clarice faced her.

'It's true,' she said. 'All those things are true. We've not chosen the easiest path, you or I.'

'But?' Clarice smiled.

'But there's you and I, and all the rest of us, all in it together. Beacons on a dark night. Well-Keepers in a shallow world.' Clover sighed. 'Is there any other way we'd rather it?'

Clarice looked at her for a long moment, then shook her head and turned to keep walking. 'Come on, let's get on with the job at hand, then.'

Grinning, Clover hurried after her. They were almost at the river.

It was deep and wide and unfathomable in the dim light of the cave. Clover could smell the mineral tang of it.

'How strong is the current, do you think?' she asked Clarice in a whisper.

Clarice shook her head. 'Strong enough,' she said. 'But I don't think you and I can row them to the Summerlands anyway.' She swallowed. 'That's why they've come.'

She didn't need to point out who she referred to. Clover could see them very well, twin heads in a boat, gliding smoothly down the river.

'Wow,' she breathed. 'They look like goddesses.'

There were tears on Clarice's cheeks, but she made no move to wipe them away. Let her mother see them there.

The boat came close, and she realised it was no longer Grainne within the craft. She glanced at Clover. Nor was it Beatrix, Clover's mother.

And yet, there was the same feeling of connection, she realised, as the boat glided up to the edge of the river where they stood upon a small jetty.

The two women stepped from the boat and bowed a greeting at Clarice and Clover.

'We are well met this day,' Broca said, her eyes upon Clarice.

Clarice returned the bow. 'I was expecting Grainne,' she said.

'And Beatrix,' Clover whispered. 'But I recognise you.' She spoke to the other woman, whom she'd known once, millennia ago, when she'd been Rhian. She shook her head.

She didn't think she'd ever get used to the way the worlds were so intricately woven.

'Ula,' she said. 'You are Ula.'

'Yes,' Ula said, and bestowed a radiant smile upon them. 'We thought we would come in these aspects.'

Broca reached for Clarice's hands. 'Do you know who I am?' she asked.

'You're Grainne,' Clarice said.

'An aspect of the same soul, yes. A past life, as you would say.'

Her touch was cool on Clarice's.

'I am Broca, and I am glad to meet a daughter of mine.'

'Broca.' Clarice said the name and shook her head. 'You are Catrin's...' She didn't know how to phrase the rest.

'Catrin's heart, yes,' Broca said. 'As she is mine.'

'I'm not sure this is any better,' Clarice stuttered, throwing a wild glance at Clover.

Broca threw back her head and laughed, the light from Clarice's floating orb catching the wildfire of her hair.

'Come,' she said when her laughter had died down. 'We have a job to do, is that not so?'

Clarice glanced again at Clover, who stared still at Ula.

'Clover?' she asked.

But Clover shook her head. 'One thing first,' she said. 'A question.' She pressed a hand to her heart. 'Since one of my elder priestesses is with us.'

Clarice looked at Broca – Broca! – then examined the other woman. Ula, Clover had called her.

'You may ask,' Ula said to Clover. 'But I may not know the answer.'

'You were one of the mother priestesses,' Clover said, and smiled at the soul who later, had come back to the world to be her own mother.

Ula acknowledged the statement with a nod.

'And must have been in Ravenna's confidence.'

'My bond was more tightly with Mother Wendyl,' Ula said. 'But once Ravenna came, we all worked together, it is true.'

'What does me being the Oracle mean?'

Ula shook her head. 'I cannot attest to the years you spent before joining us at the Forest House.'

Clover considered this. 'You mean the years I spent with the Fae.' She remembered the fairy woman in the recent delegation who had seemed so familiar. There was another to question if it were at all possible.

'Yes.'

'What did they do to me?' Clover asked. 'During that time?'

'I cannot say,' Ula said, sympathy in her eyes.

'Cannot or will not?' Clarice asked.

Ula shifted her gaze to Clarice. 'Cannot,' she repeated. 'None of us knew the true extent of those years.' She paused. 'Except Ravenna, perhaps.'

Clarice looked immediately to Broca. 'Ravenna,' she said. 'Also known as Catrin.'

There was a pause.

'Yes,' Broca agreed finally, with a smile playing about her lips. 'And Morghan.'

'Whoa,' Clarice said, stunned by the implications to what Broca had just said.

She shook her head. 'This makes me feel dizzy. Everything just goes around in circles.'

'The Wheel turns,' Ula said. 'And we turn with it. The endless spiralling of the worlds.'

The four stood in silence for a minute, while beside them the great river flowed on, smooth on the surface with barely a ripple to disturb its skin, but underneath, the current surged deep and strong.

Clarice shook herself out of her daze and touched Clover on the arm. 'We should do what we came here for,' she said.

Blinking, Clover grounded herself where she was and stood straighter. 'Yes,' she said. 'Let us be shepherds for the spirits who huddle in these passages.'

She looked at the two dead women. 'What are your tasks?' she asked.

'We will take them across the river, across the sea, to the Summerlands,' Broca said.

'It's going to take more than one day to take them all,' Clover warned.

It was Ula who answered. 'I cannot think of a better use for my time,' she said.

. . .

'HOW DO WE GO ABOUT THIS?' CLARICE ASKED ONCE THEY were in the tunnels, the river at their backs.

Clover was still distracted. 'Can you believe this?'

Clarice glanced behind them, but the two women were no longer in sight. 'Wait until I tell Morghan,' she said. 'I thought it was complicated enough when it was just my mother Grainne involved.'

Clover looked at her curiously. 'I don't understand,' she said. 'Why would it be more complicated now?' She hesitated. 'Do you think Morghan knows what the oracle business means?'

Clarice shook her head. 'You'll have to ask her,' she said. 'But do you know who Catrin is?' Clarice asked.

Clover frowned. 'I might have heard the name, but no, I don't think so.' She reached for the knowledge with her spirit, but all she got was an impression of an intricate and complicated weaving.

Clarice flapped a hand. 'I'll have to tell you some other time, what I know of it, anyway. It's a pretty twisted story.'

'Twisted?'

'Catrin walked with Morghan for years. She schemed and schemed for a certain outcome.'

'Did she get it?'

'Oh yes, in the end, and thanks finally to Morghan.' Clarice paused. 'It began with Broca and Catrin and ended with Grainne and Morghan. But I'll tell you the rest some other time, because we're there.'

They were there. As they'd been talking, they'd arrived at the first group of lost spirits.

Clarice eyed them, asked Clover from the corner of her mouth. 'Any idea what we do now?'

Clover nodded. 'The same as always, Clarice,' she said. 'We follow our open hearts.'

343

Back in the waking world, Clarice slipped out of the warm air of the cave and into a mizzling rain. 'I'll come with you,' she said, wrapping her cloak more warmly around her. 'I need to break the news to Morghan about Broca.'

'Broca?' Maxen asked.

Clarice looked at him. 'Don't tell me you knew Broca as well.'

But Maxen shook his head. 'I cannot tell you that, because for once, I do not know of whom you speak.'

'And it's way too complicated to tell you,' Clarice said. She rubbed at her neck and stretched, yawned. 'That was tiring.'

Clover nodded. The spirits of the dead had taken rather more persuasion than she'd anticipated. They felt safe in the tunnels. It had taken a lot of effort to gain their trust.

And there were so many of them. Clover thought she might regret taking on the task except the relief and satisfaction of seeing them in the boats to be taken across the river filled every part of her with a deep and quiet joy.

Maxen was smiling at her. 'The job of shepherd is a difficult one,' he said. 'But worthwhile.'

Clover nodded. 'It is. I don't think I'll rest well until we've helped all of them we can.' She paused. 'Can you walk with us a moment?'

Maxen bowed slightly. 'It would be my pleasure.'

The fell into line along the path towards Hawthorn House.

'Maxen,' Clover said. 'You know the history of your people, don't you?'

'Clover,' he said and sighed. 'I cannot answer the question you have for me.'

She turned large blue eyes on him, and he regretted that he was unable to give her what she wished for.

'I do not know the answer,' he said. 'Believe it or not, it was before my time.'

Clover stared at him. 'You weren't around then?'

Maxen smiled at her. 'It was a long time ago.'

'Oh.' Clover's heart fell. Then lifted. 'But you could ask the Queen?'

Maxen frowned at the idea. 'I do not know if that would be possible,' he said. 'I am not one of the Queen's close counsel. I am not in her confidence.'

'Well, who can I ask?' Clover all but wailed. 'This is me they were talking about, the two Queens. And today... today...' She stood on the path in the rain, not noticing it wetting her hair, her hands clenched into fists.

'What happened today?' Maxen asked her, his voice gentle.

Clarice nodded. 'Tell him,' she said, then lifted the hood of Clover's cloak over her head and took her hand, led her under the shelter of the trees. The rain was cold.

'The mist,' Clover said, collecting herself. 'I was standing back in the mist, just white all around.' She lifted her shoulders in a shrug. 'Then, I woke up.'

'That wasn't all you did,' Clarice said.

'I said something,' Clover said. 'But I don't remember it. All I remember was getting a glimpse of something.' She sought out Maxen's gaze. 'Like I'd touched the web and seen a pattern.'

Maxen nodded. 'Perhaps you did,' he said.

'But I've never done that before,' Clover protested. 'Not like that. I've seen it - I can picture see it. But I've not touched it, and, and, downloaded it, or whatever.'

'Well, you did this time,' Clover said. 'Come on, let's get on to the house. It's getting dark and cold.'

But Clover was still looking at Maxen. 'But why?'

Maxen smiled at her. 'I do not know,' he said. 'Perhaps to see the path of the spirit more clearly?' He waved a hand in the air. 'To be, a, what do you call it? A signpost along the way.'

Clover looked at him, lips flattening into a line. She shook her head and sighed. 'I don't know,' she said. 'I don't know what to think. But thank you for accompanying us today, Maxen.'

Bowing, Maxen smiled at her, then stepped back into the folds between the worlds.

. . .

MORGHAN AND ERIN WERE IN MORGHAN'S OFFICE, GOING over the new slew of requests for interviews, from bloggers, streamers, podcasters, morning chat shows, and everyone besides. They'd sorted those into piles of possibles and never-evers and were now onto requests for blessings and healing ceremonies.

There was a lot more paperwork to Wilde Grove that there had used to be.

The latest video of Erin outside the hospital had done exactly as Winsome had predicted and gone viral. She and Morghan had already spent over an hour thinking of ways to cope with that and turn it to their advantage, if that was possible.

Morghan lifted her head at the tap at the door and smiled.

Burdock rose in anticipation.

'Clover,' Morghan said, then saw Clarice behind her. 'And Clarice too.' She smiled even as she digested the state of their energy. A little less settled than usual.

Burdock made a bee line for Clover and pressed himself against her.

'What has happened?' Morghan said to them.

'Can we go in the drawing room?' Clarice asked. 'We need some tea and toast or something.'

Erin stood up, glad for a different task. 'I'll go make some.' She gave Burdock a pat on the way past. The dog had adored Clover from the first time they'd met each other.

Clover spied something on Morghan's altar and her eyes widened. 'May I look at that?' she asked.

Morghan glanced at the small wooden chest and nodded.

'Why is this such a powerful thing?' Clover asked, going to stand over the wooden chest, which was open to display a golden egg.

Clarice looked too. 'Is this out of a fairy tale or something?' She looked at Morghan and grinned. 'Did you steal Jack and the Beanstalk's golden goose?'

Morghan couldn't help her returning smile. After all, she'd had much the same thought. But she shook her head. 'I don't know what it is,' she said. 'Or what it means. It was given to me in the Otherworld, and then Erin and Krista were kind enough to make me a facsimile of it.'

'A golden egg in a treasure chest,' Clover whispered, then looked over at Morghan. 'Why is everything from the Otherworld and those in it shrouded in such confusion?'

'Confusion?'

'Well.' Clover tried again. 'No one ever says straight out this or that, do they? It's always a bit cryptic.'

'That's because it never is just this or that,' Morghan said, and she ushered everyone and the dog toward the drawing room. 'That's why symbolism is used. There are always layers of meaning. Various tasks, differing outcomes.'

Clover went straight to the fireplace and warmed herself. What she really wanted to do, she discovered, was to go upstairs to her room and throw herself on her bed. She was exhausted.

She also wanted to hear Rue's voice. Even though Rue would flip out if she knew about what had happened today. The oracle thing.

Clover frowned. Was she making pronouncements upon the future? To what purpose? She couldn't see a purpose for it.

'We went into the tunnels again today,' Clarice said to Morghan when Erin came in with the tea tray.

Erin put down the tea things and straightened, feeling a change in the atmosphere of the room. She took a slow, deep breath and opened her heart to the people in the room and was overwhelmed with love for them. She took a cup of tea to Clover and gave it to her with a smile.

'You saw your mother?' Morghan said and she also took deliberate breaths, anchoring herself where she stood so that she would not be rocked by the conversation.

Clarice flicked a glance at Clover. 'Sort of,' she said.

Morghan looked questioningly at her.

'They didn't come in their previous aspects,' Clarice said. 'Not as Beatrix and Grainne.'

Morghan decided to sit down. She took another breath, keeping herself composed, and listened for a moment to the rain outside. It was coming down harder, a storm rolling in, perhaps.

The fire shifted in the grate.

'Who did they come as?' There was a stirring inside her, and Morghan felt Catrin with her.

'Ula, from the Forest House.' Clarice looked at the sofa, thought about sitting down, then decided her legs might be too feeble to carry her over to it. She could see, in her memory, as clear as day, Grainne sitting in her usual perch on the arm of Morghan's chair, tugging playfully at the escaping strands of Morghan's hair, a smear of paint on her cheek and smiling her wide smile at Clarice.

Clarice looked down at the cup in her hand.

'Ula, and instead of Mum, Broca.' Clarice swallowed.

'They said perhaps it would be easier for us, if they came in these aspects.'

Morghan turned her head and gazed at the fire. She felt Catrin's presence.

'Broca?' she asked.

'Yes,' Clarice said.

'It is not easier,' Morghan said after a minute. She closed her eyes, trying to think this new development through. It was difficult, over Catrin's sudden, silent howling inside her.

She took a breath, felt a hand upon her shoulder and looked up to see Erin's face, gentle and full of love looking upon hers. She nodded silently and accepted the flow of strength and warmth from Erin, until she had to smile.

'That is new,' she said, and covered Erin's hand with her own. 'A new skill and one I thank you for.'

Clover and Clarice exchanged a confused look.

But Morghan shook her head, and Erin removed her hand, went and sat down.

'What else has happened?' Morghan asked, directing her gaze at Clarice, then Clover. 'Something else has happened for Grainne and Beatrix to appear as Ula and Broca.' She managed to keep her voice steady.

'Why?' Clarice asked. 'What do you mean?'

'But something else did happen,' Clover said to Clarice, her hand on Burdock's warm neck.

'Yeah, it did,' Clarice agreed, but she was still looking at Morghan. 'How do you know that, though?'

Morghan shook her head. 'Here's something we forget all too easily in our modern lives - we live in a world full of meaning.'

Erin frowned and turned the phrase over in her mind. A

world full of meaning. 'But isn't that, I don't know, sort of superstitious to think that way?'

Morghan smiled. Her heart had stopped its great thumping in her chest, and Catrin had quietened, become attentive. Somewhere behind them both too, she could feel Ravenna's presence, or memory.

'That the knowledge of meaning in our world has been reduced to superstition is a tragedy,' she said. 'We don't take it seriously because it has become nonsense – don't walk under a ladder, a black cat crossing the road in front of you is bad luck.' She paused, looked at her hands on the arms of the chair, the unfamiliar age spots on the left, the golden gleam of the other, then continued.

'But the silliness hides a greater truth. Our world is full of meaning. Things are intrinsically meaningful, and the world is also always in conversation with us. Only its language is one we are too lazy to learn, the language of symbol and omen.'

'So Ula and Broca didn't come for the reason they said – to make it easier, so that we wouldn't feel our loss so badly?' Clarice asked.

'Undoubtedly they did,' Morghan said, and she leant forward. 'Did it work?'

Clarice was startled. 'Ah, yeah, it did.' She looked at Clover, who nodded as well. 'It was much easier, not to look over and see my dead mother, even though intellectually, I knew it was still her.'

'Good,' Morghan said. 'I'm glad.'

'But?' Clarice asked, sure she was hearing a but there.

'But it raises more questions, which is why I need you to tell me what else has happened.'

'What questions?' Erin asked. She was fascinated, and marvelled once again, for the hundredth time perhaps, over the way Morghan's mind worked. The way she was trying to train her own mind to think.

'Why, of all the soul aspects there are to choose from,' Morghan said. 'Did they choose Ula and Broca?'

'Because we'd recognise them?' Clover asked. She was now feeling wide awake, despite the heat of the fire at her side.

Morghan nodded. 'Perhaps that was part of it,' she said, and she looked at Clover, saw the tiredness in her energy, and the great strength of sight at the centre of it. The way her energy was connected almost directly to the web.

'You spoke as an oracle, didn't you?' she asked.

'What the hell?' Clarice exploded as Clover paled. 'How on the Goddess's green earth did you know that?'

Morghan spoke to Clover. 'Your connection is stronger,' she said and nodded thoughtfully. 'Not just stronger but woven into the strands of the web in a way I didn't see before today.'

Clover remembered to breathe, sucked in a lungful of air. She nodded. 'It happened today,' she said, almost whispering. 'I was surrounded by the mist. I thought I was having another of my episodes, you know?' She shook her head. 'But it was different. I don't know what happened. There was just the mist, and then there was the web, and I put my hands on it, and when I opened my eyes, Clarice told me I'd said something.'

She put down her cup and saucer with unsteady hands. 'I don't remember saying anything.'

Clarice broke in. 'And before we tell you what she said,

before I forget, Broca and Ula said you are the only one who knows what went on with Rhian before the Fae handed her over to Brynn.'

Morghan's brow rose. 'A puzzle within a puzzle,' she said. 'I wish Ambrose were here.'

'You don't seem very shocked,' Clarice said.

But Morghan leant back in her chair and closed her eyes. She and Catrin turned to look for Ravenna. They felt her presence, but it was far away.

She opened her eyes. Looked at Clover. 'What did you say?' she asked.

39

ROWAN SHIFTED SLIGHTLY ON THE DOUGHNUT CUSHION AND wrinkled her nose. Her tailbone wasn't painful so much now as it just ached. She could sit without the cushion, but having it helped.

She sighed and got up, loaded another piece of wood onto the fire, and went to check on Robbie. He was in her bed again, but that was okay, and Rowan leant against the door frame watching him sleep. His barnyard was on the pillow, but tucked in his arms was an old teddy they'd gotten from the charity shop. It already looked like it had been well-loved, but Robbie had taken a shine to it, and Rowan hadn't had the heart to get him to pick something else.

'I love you,' she whispered and blew him a kiss before turning and wandering through the house. She could hear the rain at the windows but elsewhere it was muffled. The house was good, solid. And hers.

'My house,' she whispered, going back to the living

room and looking around. 'My sanctuary where I can stay as long as I need to.' She cleared her throat.

It wasn't her house, in the sense that she owned it, but maybe that was okay. She and Paul hadn't owned the place they'd lived in either. She'd never owned a house. When her parents had died, there'd been no inheritance, because they hadn't owned anything past a few sticks of furniture and knick-knacks.

It was hard to trust that she'd ever really have a place where she could stay as long as she needed.

The thought made her frown, go back to the table where she'd been reading the book Winsome had dropped off to her. She sat down again, squirming on the cushion, trying to ease the ache, and turned again to the beginning.

Stations of the Heart: Belonging.

Belonging. Rowan rolled the word around in her mouth for a moment. It felt good. It sounded good. She tipped her head back and tried to imagine it as a reality. Belonging. Did anyone anymore really feel like they belonged somewhere?

Perhaps if you were religious, you did, she thought. Then remembered Cornerstone Church and shivered. They taught belonging, but at the expense of others. Rowan didn't want to live in a way that said she could belong but not them, not that other person over there.

She wanted a world where everyone belonged.

'The very first part of our journey back to belonging,' she read, 'involves the willingness to enter a great maze.'

We've wandered far from our natural centre, from that place where we plant our seed and see ourselves clearly, reflected in the sacred water of life. And so, we must enter the maze that will lead us back there, to that centre, and then we must refashion our life into one of belonging and wholeness.

Why a maze? Because it's not possible to walk blindly through a maze and get anywhere. We must think about where we are going, engage all our senses, look for clues, actively find our way.

So come then, let us enter this maze. It is a sunken one, because we are entering the realm of our soul, leaving our daytime self behind us for a while, and finding our way through to the discovery of our true nature.

The way into the maze is down wide stone steps, then, wide so that anyone might see and descend them. This is not a hidden process, only for a select few.

The journey back to our whole selves, to our hearts, is for all of us.

There was a link then, a website address to download a guided meditation to lead her into and through the maze. Rowan frowned down at the website address. She'd never done anything like that before. Should she do this one, now?

She thought of the sacred spring in the orchard field then touched a hand to her heart. Just thinking about it made her feel good. Why was that?

Getting up, she decided to check on Robbie again, but he was fast asleep, the teddy clutched to his chest still. She smiled at him from the doorway and looked around at the dimly lit bedroom. It was old fashioned, with wallpaper in a tiny floral pattern, and otherwise simply a bed, drawers, wardrobe. She'd nothing with which to personalise it – yet.

In the bathroom, she used the toilet, washed her hands. Finally, she returned to the living room and the tablet

Winsome had lent her. The internet had been reconnected to the house that morning. Rowan pressed her hands to her hips and took a breath.

She would do it, she decided. Wasn't this why she'd pushed to come to Wellsford? So she could learn some of the Wilde Grove ways? Well, she'd been all around the village, signed up for the grocery subscription, looked around the community garden, been to the charity shop – whose proceeds went right back into the village, - and everywhere else besides. Haven for Books, where Robbie had been fascinated by the silver talismans dangling from the ceiling.

And Bridget's Sanctuary, which was the old church, and now still a place of peace and prayer and it seemed, plenty else besides.

But this, she thought. This was the heart of the community. This idea of belonging. The First Station of the Heart.

Rowan turned the tablet on and brought up the browser, typing in the address in the book. It brought up the Stations of the Heart website and there was the recording of the guided meditation.

She'd need earphones for this, she realised, but Winsome had seen to that as well, and given her a pair. Rowan picked them up and took everything over to the couch, looked at it a moment, then lay down, shifting about until she was comfortable and there was no pressure on her tailbone.

The rain, hard against the window, muffled to nothing when she put the headphones on, and she promptly took them off again and sat up.

What if Robbie cried out and she didn't hear him? He

had cried out every night at home, waking screaming from a bad dream.

She couldn't do it, she thought. There was no way she could relax enough. Not worrying about Robbie calling out.

Finally, on a sigh, Rowan picked up the tablet and head-phones and went into the bedroom. She changed into her nightclothes, put the tablet and headphones on the bedside table, then straightened and looked around again.

Why was she so jumpy? Everything was okay.

Actually, she thought. Everything was terrific. She had a new home, a safe place just for her and Robbie and the baby when it came. She had a new community, and she was sure she'd be able to make friends.

She even had a new job.

Everything was set. She couldn't have planned it better.

She checked the time on the tablet, then walked back out to the living room and the table there where she'd left her phone. Picking it up, she looked at it for a moment, trying to ignore the 24 new text messages from Paul.

That was what was making her nervous, she thought. All those messages coming in. Even though she had the phone set to silent, it still vibrated when they came through, and she thought she could feel that vibration, even while she was in a different room.

She sat down on the doughnut and looked at the number. The amount went up suddenly, and the phone vibrated in her hand, startling her, and making her throw it down on the floor as though it was a poisonous snake.

She was not going to look at those messages, Rowan decided. She was going to follow Winsome's advice and not read them. Keep them, in case they were useful later on, in the family court maybe. But she wasn't going to read them.

Rowan glanced at the windows and nodded at the closed curtains. Paul didn't know where she was. He couldn't come barging in, no matter what.

There was an old landline phone in an old-fashioned nook in the wall, and she stepped gingerly over her mobile on the floor, even as it vibrated again, and picked the receiver up and held it to her ear. There was a ring tone, and she listened to its buzzing drone for a moment, then gently set the receiver back down.

She didn't need her mobile. There was still a phone in the house. The house was tucked up tight, and no one in their right minds would be lurking outside on such a wet and miserable night.

And Paul didn't know where she was.

'Please,' she whispered to the house. 'Keep us safe.'

A log shifted in the fireplace, making the flames hiss, and Rowan let out a shaky laugh. She'd take that as a yes, she decided, and looked at her cheap little phone lying on the floor.

Then, in a swift movement, she snatched it up and held it dangled between two fingers as though it were indeed something poisonous, and she let herself out the front door, careful not to lock herself out. A flash of lightning brightened the night for a fleeting second.

Rowan stood on the top step for a moment, peering into the darkness. Then, on a deep breath as though she were about to go underwater, she dashed down the steps through the rain, running for the door to the garage.

She pushed it open, scrabbled around for a light switch

as thunder rumbled somewhere overhead. She found the switch and the garage flooded with very welcome light.

There was no car in the garage and Rowan stood with the door pulled loosely to behind her, gazing around. She saw the lawnmower, various buckets and the usual detritus that ends up in old garages. There was a shelf on the back wall, and Rowan made for it and put the phone down on top of an old rag there.

She stood back, nodded. Now she wouldn't hear it buzz, and she wouldn't feel its vibration, and she wouldn't even have to think of it, because it was out here where no harm would come to it, but where she wouldn't have to deal with it.

She wouldn't even have to think of it, unless she needed to. She'd take it to the lawyer's office when it was time for her appointment, but until then, it could stay here and go flat.

Rowan nodded again with satisfaction and turned around to hurry back to the house. She opened the garage door, wrestled with it for a moment as the wind tried to bluster it closed, and got it open in time to see the world light up in a blinding white flash.

Something moved in the brightness, in the back yard, and Rowan shrank back against the door, the rain pelting into her. She blinked as the sky turned dark again, trying to make out what it was she'd seen.

Or thought she'd seen. Thunder rolled across the sky, so close that Rowan flinched back against the door behind her.

'Robbie,' she said, and wanted to run inside to him.

But lightning flashed again, and there it was, in the back yard. Rowan's mouth fell open, Robbie forgotten about for a moment, Paul too, everything that had been on her mind forgotten.

The night went dark again, and Rowan cringed as the thunder crashed and boomed.

But there was still something there, in the back garden, where she could see it. Just. Like an after image, she thought, and blinked again.

The lightning, she decided, unaware she was even thinking. The lightning had done it, had burnt the image into her retinas, or something.

She pushed away from the garage and stepped down the path toward the back garden. Rain smashed down onto her, but she was barely aware of it, just lifted a hand and pushed her hair back from her eyes.

Yes, she thought. It was still there. Moving across the tiny patch of lawn. Something.

Graceful. Something graceful.

'Dancing,' Rowan croaked, unaware she was speaking out loud. But she nodded and stood at the corner of the house, the rain pouring down upon her, and she watched the figure move around and around the lawn.

Dancing.

There were no features to make out. Just the vaguest idea of a figure. Dancing.

Lightning zigzagged across the sky again, and Rowan's back garden was lit brilliant white and she gasped, eyes rounding, and her hand flew to cover her mouth.

A woman. She saw a woman in the brief second of dazzling light. Slim and beautiful, hair long and dark, and she'd been...

Dancing.

The thunder struck with a crashing, discordant boom-ing, and Rowan flinched, staring at the spot where she'd seen the figure.

It was gone now, though, and as much as she blinked the rain out of her eyes, she couldn't see even a hint of it.

When the lightning came again, the garden was empty, and Rowan, realising finally that she was standing outside in the rain in a thunderstorm, turned and scurried back to the house, let herself in, then stood dripping water onto the carpet.

What had she seen?

It hadn't been real.

It wasn't a real person. She shook her head, sending water spraying, her wet hair slapping against her cheeks. Rowan looked down at herself. She was soaked, she realised. And cold.

Rowan kicked her shoes off and padded through to the bathroom, stopping for a moment to look in on Robbie.

He was sound asleep.

The shower filled the room with steam, but Rowan didn't care. She stripped off and stood under the hot flow of water, warming up again, her mind still filled with the dazzle of lightning.

Still seeing the woman dancing.

40

Winsome slipped her phone back into her pocket and stared at Ambrose.

'Is she all right?' Ambrose asked.

Winsome nodded.

'I only heard your side of the conversation,' Ambrose told her. 'But, Mariah?'

Winsome swallowed finally. Nodded. 'Sounds like it, yes. Don't you think so?'

'Dancing?'

Winsome nodded again. 'Dancing in the back garden.'

'In physical form?'

Winsome shook her head. 'Like seeing a ghost.'

Ambrose's gaze turned even more thoughtful. 'Is Rowan all right?' he asked. 'It must have been a shock.' He picked up his plate to begin clearing the breakfast things away.

'She seems more excited than anything else.' Winsome gave a helpless shrug. 'I guess there's been so much on the news and things about Wellsford and Wilde Grove, that people expect odd things to happen here?' She looked over at the corner where Cù was lying, head on his paws, looking at her. 'And let's face it. Odd things do happen here.'

'They do?' Ambrose paused, holding plates in both hands.

'You don't think so?' Winsome laughed. 'You've been here a long time, my love. It all looks very normal to you, I'm sure.'

Ambrose smiled and took the breakfast things through to the sink. 'What are your plans for the day? Can you make it here this afternoon for the planning session for the next Station?'

Winsome pushed her chair back and beamed at him. 'Can you believe we're onto the next Station of the Heart already? You've done such a wonderful job writing them.'

Ambrose came back to look at her. 'Do you really think so?' He frowned. 'I've sent everything through to Molly and she thinks I'm doing really well but I wish she was able to come to Wellsford to work on it with me.'

But Winsome was shaking her head. 'You don't need anyone to write this with you, Ambrose. You're doing an excellent job.' She got up and moved over to him, threading her arms around his waist and leaning into his warmth. 'I knew there was a writer inside you, and sure enough, I was right. The material is excellent.' She sighed happily. 'Everything is going rather swimmingly at the moment. Even Veronica is happy as a clam, although she won't tell you so.'

Ambrose kissed Winsome's forehead, then searched out her lips and kissed those as well. 'You're still happy with our...decision?'

'About the baby?' Winsome looked up at him and

smiled widely. 'I am,' she said. 'In fact, it gets more exciting each time I think about it. A baby in Wilde Grove.' She shook her head in wonder, curls bouncing. 'That's a thing to celebrate.' Her brows rose. 'When are you needed to play your part.'

Ambrose's cheeks coloured. 'I, ah, next week,' he said. 'She said she'll be ovulating next week.'

Winsome squeezed her arms tighter around him then let go, smiling. 'Yes,' she said. 'It is exciting. I think it's wonderful. Make sure you donate each day that she'll be at her most fertile.'

Ambrose nodded, cleared his throat. Cast around inside his head for another topic of conversation, fell upon it gratefully. 'So, will you be able to come over this afternoon? Around 4? Morghan will be here, and we need to make sure I've not missed anything out for the second and third Stations.'

Winsome glanced at Cù, gave him a wink and almost wiggled in excitement. She looked back at Ambrose. 'This is an amazing project, don't you think?'

'It was an excellent idea,' Ambrose agreed. 'You had an excellent idea.'

Winsome grinned but she shook her head, enjoying the conversation, the cosy domesticity of the kitchen when outside the wind was still rushing double time around the house, throwing splats of rain at the window.

'We came up with it together, you, me, and Morghan,' she said, then paused, frowned. 'I haven't had a good catch up with Morghan for days. I should do that.'

'You'll see her this afternoon,' Ambrose reminded her.

But Winsome was already picking up the rest of the

breakfast things to wash. 'I think I'll head over to Hawthorn House anyway,' she said. 'I worry about her sometimes.'

'Morghan?' Ambrose asked, then nodded. 'I do too. These trips to see the Fae Queens. They're dangerous with their idiotic tests.'

'No,' Winsome said, squeezing past him carrying the teapot and mugs. 'That's not what I mean.' But she put the tea things down and frowned at him. 'They're not really dangerous, are they? These trips to the Fae lands, and the testing? Morghan acts as though they're not a big deal.'

'Morghan acts as though nothing is a big deal.' Ambrose frowned at Winsome. 'If you didn't mean that, then what were you referring to?'

'Morghan is lonely. I worry about that for her.'

'Oh.' The answer stopped Ambrose short. 'Lonely?'

'Yes,' Winsome said. 'All of us around her have paired off. But she is resolutely on her own.'

'She misses Grainne,' Ambrose said, his voice low. 'I miss her too.'

Winsome entered the circle of his arms again. 'What was your sister like?'

'She carried such burdens when she first came here, Winsome,' Ambrose said. 'She shifted here, there, and everywhere so fast and so often, I could barely keep up with who I was talking to.'

Winsome straightened. 'Who you were talking to?'

'Mmm.' Ambrose breathed a deep sigh. 'She'd been diagnosed with dissociative identity disorder.'

'Isn't that something like multiple personality?'

'The same thing, really.' Ambrose moved into the kitchen, ran water into the sink, added detergent. 'I'd been begging her to come and stay with me. It was a relief when she finally did, her and Clarice.'

'Clarice was just a baby?'

'A little girl. Three or so, I think.' Ambrose dipped the plates into the soapy water, scrubbed at them.

A gust of wind rattled at the window.

'And Morghan met Grainne, and they fell in love?'

Ambrose smiled. 'They did.' He laughed a little. 'Being near them was...it was like when you and I met, and the atmosphere around us was charged, filled with strong energy.' He put the plates in the dish drainer.

Winsome picked them up, dried them, put them on the shelves. Her lips twitched in a smile. 'I remember,' she said.

He glanced at her and felt the whisper touch of her energy. 'Yes,' he said. 'Like that.' Ambrose forced himself to look back at the dishes in the sink. 'Only ten times stronger. They'd known each other so often.'

Winsome cleared her throat. 'In past lives, you mean?'

Ambrose nodded. 'Yes. They had a lot to work out with that also, but first there was, well, the state Grainne was in when she arrived.' He straightened, his hands covered with bubbles in the soapy water.

'I remember, not long after she got here, she looked at me and said *I'm not broken*.'

Winsome stared at him, eyes filling with sudden tears.

Ambrose looked down at the water, shook his head. 'She wasn't broken, either, but she was in pieces. She was fighting so hard to find wholeness.'

'What happened?' Winsome whispered.

Ambrose glanced at her, gave her a smile. 'She and Morghan, that's what happened. Morghan went and retrieved all the children, and that took enough pressure from Grainne that she could recover.'

'Retrieved the children?'

'The childhood trauma,' Ambrose said. 'It had fractured her, which is what it does, of course.'

Winsome nodded.

'Those children were stuck there, back there where they'd been hurt. Grainne had gathered some of them up herself. She was nothing if not strong, resourceful, but there were still some.'

'And Morghan fetched them, didn't she? She did the same thing she did for Wayne.' Winsome covered her eyes. Shook her head.

Ambrose huffed out a breath. 'How did we get onto talking about this?'

'I asked, I think,' Winsome said. 'I'm sorry.'

'Don't be sorry,' Ambrose said, turning to her. 'Grainne was wonderful, and she found her way back to strength. I miss her too. I wish you and she had been able to meet. She would have loved you.'

Winsome nodded, wiped the tears from her cheeks. Gave a tremulous smile. 'I think I'll pop over to Hawthorn House, if that's all right. Before the day gets hectic.'

Ambrose nodded, leant over to kiss her, his breath warm on her skin. 'Have a good day, all right? I'll see you this afternoon.'

'Elise,' Winsome said, popping her head into the kitchen and breathing in the heavenly scent of baking bread. 'Do you know where Morghan is?'

Elise looked up from her baking and smiled. 'Hello Winsome. Rotten day again, isn't it?'

'It is, yes,' Winsome said, and frowned at the window. 'I hope it stops, this incessant rain.'

'Wettest March in memory so far,' Elise said, then sighed, sliced a knife through a block of butter. 'Morghan's gone to the cave, I'm afraid.'

'Oh.' Winsome's heart sank. 'I was hoping to catch her.'

'She only left ten minutes ago.'

Time enough perhaps, to catch her before she went somewhere Winsome couldn't follow her.

'Thanks, Elise,' Winsome said, and withdrew, picked her coat back up and let herself out again.

The cave was empty. Winsome looked at the fireplace and knew it hadn't been used recently. She ducked back out into the wind and looked around.

Morghan could be anywhere. Winsome hadn't passed her on any of the paths below the cave, however. She hadn't been at the stone circle, where Winsome knew she liked to go to dance.

The path continued past the cave to Winsome's left, and she looked at it, at the way it wound up into the hills. Morghan was like a mountain goat, she thought, climbing these ways and paths each day.

For a moment, Winsome fought the impulse to go after her. It was a bit of a climb, and she had other things she needed to do that morning.

But she wanted to see Morghan, and Cù, standing a few steps up the path told her Morghan had climbed the hill.

'Okay,' Winsome muttered to him. 'But if you're wrong, I'll be plenty mad about it.'

The wind pushed and shoved at her, picked up the tail ends of her coat and flapped them like flags. She ripped them from its grasp and hugged them to herself more tightly.

When she reached the top of the way, she was breathless, the muscles in her thighs aching. She'd gotten a lot fitter since she'd come to Wellsford, but she was no mountain goat.

Cù was sitting in the sloping meadow, tongue lolling, and Winsome gave him a glare as she passed. He thumped his tail soundlessly.

'Winsome,' Morghan said. 'This is a surprise.'

'Cù led me here when I was looking for you.' Winsome bent over to catch her breath.

Morghan looked for the spirit dog, found him, and gave a nod before turning back to Winsome. 'Are you all right?'

Winsome flapped a hand at her. 'Fine,' she wheezed. 'That's just some climb, is all, and I've been spending a lot of time sitting down at people's bedsides lately.' She sucked in a great gulp of wind and straightened.

'Erin has told me how valuable she's been finding the chaplaincy work,' Morghan said, and she bared her teeth in a grin. 'I knew it was the right thing to do, to have her learn from you.'

'She's a pleasure to work with,' Winsome said. She gazed out over the view, at the sea far away beneath them. 'Did she tell you what she did the other day?'

Morghan shook her head. 'Yes. Someone caught it on video. There's been a great deal happening in all directions.'

Winsome glanced at her. 'Is that why we're standing here being battered about by the wind?'

'It is,' Morghan said, and lifted her face to its gusting blows. She closed her eyes. 'Selena can read the secrets and stories that the wind carries.'

Winsome raised her eyebrows.

'But I can't,' Morghan admitted.

'So, what are we doing, then?'

'Thinking.'

'Couldn't you think in front of a nice warm fire?' Winsome stuck her hands in the warmth of her coat pockets.

Morghan laughed, then elaborated. 'In my visions, I stand upon a tor, which this place reminds me of.'

Winsome looked at her but said nothing. Waited for her to continue.

'I stand here watching the lights of the world go out,' Morghan said.

Winsome's eyes widened.

'Then into the darkness shine the lights of the beacons,' Morghan said. 'And I stand here and watch, Catrin to one side of me, Ravenna to the other.'

Winsome looked around. 'Where I'm standing now?' she asked, then more nervously, 'Are they here now? Do I need to move?'

Morghan smiled kindly at her. 'They are not,' she said. 'You do not.'

Winsome nodded, relieved. Then she chewed on the inside of her lip a moment. 'That's what you're thinking about here then, today?'

'Yes,' Morghan said. 'The puzzle of it all.' She closed her eyes against the wind again. 'The gift of a golden egg, the proclamation of an oracle telling of the birth of golden children.'

Winsome frowned. 'Golden eggs and children? What does that mean?'

Morghan opened her eyes, watched Hawk fly wings spread, riding the air currents.

'We've walked this world for generation after generation,' she said, musing upon it. 'And will do so until the golden children are born.'

She tipped her head back, spread her arms wide and conjured the image of the golden egg in her mind.

'And then, Winsome,' she said. 'Perhaps we will walk all the worlds once more.'

41

ROWAN LEAPT UP AT THE TAPPING UPON HER DOOR AND LET
Winsome in.

'Thank you for coming over,' she said, backing up so Winsome and Erin could enter.

'Winsome told me what you saw,' Erin said, and glanced at Winsome. They'd not had any time to say anything else to each other yet.

Robbie looked over at Robbie playing on the living room rug, his toys organised in a circle around him. He looked at the visitors then went back to his game.

'What was it?' Rowan asked, then shook herself to let some of the tension out. 'I hardly slept last night. I just kept replaying it over and over in my mind.' She looked about the room, rather wildly, then took a breath and smiled at her guests. 'Please, sit down. I'm sorry; I should let you sit down before I start raving like a lunatic.'

Erin laughed as she took a seat at what was once Mariah's table. 'You sound like me when I first came to Wellsford,' she said. 'Everything I was seeing and needing to do meant I had to think in an entirely different way or go crazy.'

Rowan looked at her hopefully. 'I'm not crazy?' She sank down at the table and looked from Erin to Winsome. 'Tell me I'm not crazy.'

'Absolutely, you're not.' Winsome exchanged a look with Erin, then turned back to Rowan. 'This is Wellsford, I'm afraid, and it's easier to see things here.'

'Things like ghosts?' Rowan asked, then looked over at Robbie and lowered her voice. 'That's what I saw last night, isn't it? A ghost? This house is haunted, isn't it?'

But Erin shook her head. 'Not as far as we know.'

Rowan leant forward. 'But I saw a ghost last night - dancing outside. Every time the lightning flashed, there she was.' Rowan sat back up and shivered, hugging herself. She shook her head. 'I knew this place was different,' she said. 'Magical even, but this is well beyond my expectations.' She drew in a deep breath and blew it out between her lips. 'Do you know who she was? The ghost? She was young, so she can't be the woman whose house this was. Julia said her aunt was an old woman when she passed.'

Passed being the right word, Erin thought. Passed into a different world.

But how were they supposed to answer Rowan's question? It was a bit early to go telling her that well, yes, it likely was Mariah, who instead of being allowed to set fire to Hawthorn House, was taken by the Fae to dance eternally in their world.

How would that go down? Even Erin thought it was crazy.

But Mariah's body never had been found. As far as Erin knew, the missing persons investigation was still an open case. Gathering dust perhaps, but still open.

And Mariah apparently was still dancing.

'She was young?' Erin asked. 'The spirit you saw?'

Rowan nodded. 'Teenager young, I think. Maybe eighteen, or early twenties, I suppose. But young.' She looked from Erin to Winsome. 'Do you know who she is? What do we do about her? Shouldn't we do something about her?' Rowan looked down at the embroidered tablecloth on the table. She'd found it folded neatly in one of the drawers and thought it was too pretty to be hidden away.

'Do we do something about ghosts – spirits – here?' she asked. 'Or do we just let them wander about?'

A voice inside her piped up to marvel that she was having this conversation.

Life had changed in several significant ways. That was for sure. That she was even considering the reality of ghosts!

Erin and Winsome looked at each other, neither knowing what to say.

It was Winsome who turned to Rowan and spoke first.

'No,' she said on a sigh. 'We don't generally just let them wander about. Not unless that's really what they want to do.'

Rowan sat back in her chair and shook her head slowly from side to side. 'Oh my goodness,' she said then leant forward again. 'This is really real, isn't it? Do you know who the ghost is?'

'We've got an idea, yes,' Winsome said.

'Who?' Rowan's voice was a high-pitched squeak again, and she looked over at Robbie. He was lying on his tummy though, having a serious conversation with his barnyard donkey. Rowan's lips quirked in a sudden smile. Robbie was always having trouble with those donkeys.

She looked back at Winsome. Modulated her voice to a normal, low, speaking tone, and asked again. 'Who?' she said.

'Probably Mariah,' Erin said reluctantly.

'But Mariah was old,' Rowan said, gaze wide. 'Julia said so.'

'Indeed, yes.' Winsome attempted a smile. 'She was in her eighties. But spirits don't have to keep their aspect as it was when they...passed.'

'They can look younger,' Rowan said, and nodded. 'Why was she outside, do you think? Wouldn't it have been more usual to see her inside?' Rowan shivered a little at the thought and looked around the room. She wouldn't like to see a ghost inside, but...

But on the other hand, she could almost feel the world she thought she'd known splitting wide open and becoming so much more.

She'd wanted that. Hadn't she? She'd felt so stuck before, in a situation she'd felt she hadn't really even chosen.

But even so, she just hadn't expected this would be the way getting unstuck would happen.

She looked shyly at Erin, remembering suddenly who was sitting at her table: a priestess of the Grove, the one, in fact, who had conjured the ravens in Trafalgar Square. The one who, it was said, would one day be head of the Grove.

'I don't think you'll see her inside the house,' Erin said, and she looked at Winsome. 'Do you agree?'

'Absolutely,' Winsome said. 'And we cleansed and

blessed this house quite thoroughly when it became offi-cially Julia's.' She paused for a moment, thoughtful, then turned to Rowan.

'There's little separation of the worlds in Wellsford – barely any veil between them.' She paused, decided the best way forward was to be perfectly frank. 'I expect we should have told you this, in no uncertain terms, but well, we're all getting used to things and there's been a lot to deal with.' She looked at Erin for support and Erin nodded.

'Wellsford is different,' Erin said. 'Some people fit right in, and they may or may not see...unusual things. Would you prefer to go back to Banwell? It isn't too late to go to the refuge there.'

Rowan was horrified. She shook her head. 'Absolutely I want to stay. Seeing...what I did – it makes me feel like I can touch the magic too, like you do.' Rowan was feeling quite giddy all of a sudden. Perhaps it was just hormones, or the fact that the last week had been such a wild, up and down ride, but she found that her emotions were veering all over the place. One minute she was feeling crushed under the weight of everything, the next she was near ecstatic over the fact that she was living in Wellsford, which was something she knew plenty of people wouldn't mind doing, and would do, if there were houses available.

But she let herself grin anyway, fiercely glad suddenly that she'd seen that gossamer figure outside in the lightning flashes. Already she wanted to know everything there was to know about Mariah.

Perhaps, she thought, she'd pay a call to Julia Thorpe later. Mariah's niece.

Erin reached out across the table and touched Rowan

on the arm. 'I wonder,' she said, 'if we could ask you not to take this sighting to Julia.'

Winsome looked at Erin with raised brows.

'How on earth did you know I was thinking about going to see Julia Thorpe?' Rowan asked, astounded.

But Erin just shook her head. 'I didn't,' she said. 'Not really, anyway. I just caught the impression of it, I think.'

'You can read minds?'

Now both women were looking at her in consternation.

Erin laughed and held her hands up. 'No,' she said.

'But you just did,' Rowan told her. 'I had just thought about going to see Julia to ask her what her aunt was like.'

Erin shook her head. 'I just caught the...colour of your thought,' Erin asked carefully. 'Of what you were thinking.' She wished she'd just denied it all together. It would have been a reasonable thing to say, logically, to ask her not to go to Julia.

But she hadn't done that.

'The colour of them?' Rowan frowned at her.

'Like, there was a shift in your energy,' Erin said, trying desperately to explain now. The trouble was, she didn't know how it had really happened. 'And I caught that shift and something in me, within a split second, equated it with Julia.' She shook her head. 'I'm sorry,' she said. 'I didn't mean to be intrusive.'

Erin sat back a little in her chair and thought then of Clover. All she'd done was catch a sudden change in colour or timbre of Rowan's thoughts. What must it be like to be Clover, then, and see much more than that about a person?

The question she was asking herself made Erin think of

something else. Rowan was pregnant. It wasn't just Krista and Clarice who were going to have a baby. Rowan was too.

And probably, of course, a million other women Erin didn't know.

Would these be the golden children?

She still didn't understand well what Clover's...declaration meant. Except maybe, that there was hope after all, for a shift back to the life of the spirit.

'Okay,' Winsome said. She turned to Rowan. 'Julia has complicated feelings about her aunt. And she's a very private person. I don't think she'd feel comfortable answering a lot of questions about Mariah.'

Rowan nodded. 'I understand,' she said. 'That's fair enough, too. I think it would be quite a shock if someone came to me saying out of the blue that they'd seen the ghost of my mother or someone.' She placed her hands on the table and tried to smile, took a breath. 'What were you going to tell me about the first Station? I'm not far through, I'm afraid. I was going to do the guided meditation, the one about going through the maze, but then I decided to take my mobile out to the garage, and I saw Mariah.'

'You decided to take your phone out to the garage?' Erin asked, trying to make sense of that.

Rowan's face darkened. 'Paul,' she said shortly, with another glance at Robbie to make sure he wasn't listening. 'He won't stop calling and texting.'

'He's harassing you?'

Rowan shrugged. 'I guess so. He's trying to find out where I am.' She swallowed. 'So, having my phone around was making me tense, which was why I decided to put it outside in the garage.'

Winsome nodded. 'I understand,' she said. 'I think I would have done the same thing if I were in your position.' She paused. 'He doesn't know where you are?'

Rowan shook her head. 'I'm pretty sure he doesn't.' She remembered him beating on Ginger's door and closed her eyes. She should call Ginger, let her know she was all right, make sure Paul wasn't bothering her.

'I don't want him to know, either. He was in such a rage the other day.' Her voice dropped to a whisper. 'I think he'll try to take Robbie from me just to hurt me, when we go to court. And that would be the worst thing that could happen. He's never even played with Robbie, let alone done anything else for him.' Rowan looked down at the table, feeling the familiar shame sweep up through her body in a hot flush. That she could have stayed with Paul so long.

That she could be in this position now.

She felt a hand upon her shoulder and looked up to see Winsome standing now, smiling at her.

'You're going to be fine, Rowan,' she said. 'Everything's going to work out.' She squeezed Rowan's shoulder. 'I'll pick you up later like we arranged, and we'll go into Banwell to meet with the Family Court lawyer, to draft up your custody agreement.' She nodded at the sudden alarm on Rowan's face. 'We'll tell her about the harassment, too.'

'I'm scared of running into Paul,' Rowan confessed, all the buoyant feelings deflating.

'We will all be with you,' Winsome promised. 'And he won't know about your appointment.'

. . .

'Well,' Erin said when they were out on the footpath. 'What do you think we should do?'

They were across the road and walking up to the vicarage door before Winsome answered. She paused on the path and looked towards the old church. The Sanctuary as it was now.

'Let's go in there for a moment,' she said. 'May we do that?'

Erin looked at the church in surprise, then nodded. 'Of course,' she said.

Winsome smiled at her. 'Old habits,' she said. 'Always, when in doubt, or when the way is not clear, then I just want to kneel in prayer for a minute.'

Erin nodded again, and this time she smiled. 'I know what you mean,' she said. 'If I'm feeling wound up, or unsure, or whatever, I just want to go into the garden and centre myself.'

She followed Winsome across the lawn between the old gravestones, and into the cool dimness of Bridget's Sanctuary.

The lovely old church wrapped its atmosphere of the sacred around them and Erin smiled. You can take the church out of the building, but you couldn't take the sacred away.

She let Winsome walk away up the nave to find a quiet spot for prayer and turned to the sacred well that had once been the baptismal font, and contemplated the water.

There was light shining through the stained-glass window and falling on the water in a shower of red and blue. Erin stared at it, fancied she could see the blessing that Winsome had spread over the water, and closed her eyes.

'Blessed Goddess,' she murmured. 'Travel with me the ways and paths it is my task to walk. Leave me not alone, but let me be always in your presence, and that of my kin. Let me be strong and brave and capable. Let my thinking be clear, my heart open and full of love, world to world to world.'

She breathed slowly out and opened her eyes, dipped a finger into the water and touched her forehead with it.

'From sky to root, through all worlds.' Erin sighed, smiled.

'My life dedicated, my service freely given.'

42

Paul hesitated at the front door and wondered about the rent payments. Rowan ought to be paying them, of course, but knowing her now, she'd probably stopped them going through.

He bounced the car keys in his hand and turned away from the issue. He'd deal with it later.

Right now, he had a different task.

Should he take his car? She'd recognise it, wouldn't she? Rowan.

The ungrateful bitch who had stolen his son away from him.

Paul tightened his fist around the keys so that they bit into his skin. Yeah, he thought. He'd take the car, and if she saw him, then well and good. It would give her a scare, and he liked the idea of that.

Maybe, if he saw them, he could even snatch Robbie from her.

He turned and glanced behind him, up the stairs that

led to the bedroom. The house was quiet without Robbie, who had always been underfoot with his damned toys, but Robbie was his son, and he ought to be home where he belonged.

Rowan ought to be too, for all that. She was his wife, after all.

Yeah. He decided. He'd take the car. He could go along to Malcolm's and ask to take his car instead - the guy had a pretty nice ride to go with his nice house – but he thought that Malcolm wouldn't be so keen on that idea. He might even want to play tag and come along, and when Paul thought about it, he knew this was something he wanted to do himself.

Paul parked the car outside the village, under some trees. When he looked back at it from under the hood of his raincoat, he nodded in satisfaction. It was barely recognisable as his car. He smiled; he'd even had the foresight to smear the numberplate with mud, so that it wasn't easy to make out.

There were maps of Wellsford now – you could find them all around Banwell. Paul had picked his up from the tourist office (ha! He'd thought – that was a joke – who would want to come to Banwell?) and had spent the whole of the previous evening going back and forth from it, studying it until he'd memorised every detail.

Not that there were many details. Wellsford was only a village and not a big one. There was a small school for the youngsters, the thought of which made Paul twist his mouth in a grimace. He didn't want his boy going there.

He didn't want his boy anywhere near Wellsford.

The map was in his pocket now, but he didn't put his

hand to it, draw it out. Instead, he patted his other pocket, nodding in satisfaction when he felt the brand-new smart phone there. He'd signed up to a data plan, so he could go on the internet if he wanted to.

But it was mostly the camera he was interested in right now. He'd had to spend quite a bit to get one with a decent camera. He'd wanted an iPhone since they were supposed to have the best cameras, but he'd balked at the price.

Still, he was happy with what he'd gotten. It was fancier than anything Rowan had let him have before.

His shoes squelched on the wet lane and Paul cursed the rain that had come in after lunch, then remembered that it was a good thing. Rowan was less likely to be out and about, if it was raining.

A gust of wind smacked him in the face, and he shouted at it, then looked around, hoping that no one had heard him.

There was no one around. Just the bloody trees, which, according to the map, surrounded the village on practically every side.

Haunted place to live, if you asked him.

The trouble was, he thought as he kicked a stone off the road, that no one was asking him. Everyone was doing what they liked to him, with never a by your leave.

Well, he'd decided that morning over a bowl of cold, stale cereal, he'd change that.

He'd not only get his wife and kid back, but he'd bring down the whole Wilde Grove thing. He'd expose them for what they were – a bunch of lesbians and witches.

Sniffing, Paul bent his head against the wind and

consulted the map imprinted in his mind. The Well-Keeper's Cottage should be right up ahead.

He stopped and tipped his head to the sign.

Stations of the Heart, it said. The Sacred Well.

Paul lifted his lips in a snarl. What were the stations of the heart? What sort of namby pamby business was it?

And a well? Who cared?

It was a bunch of pagan blasphemy. Hadn't all witches been burnt at the stake? Why were they suddenly out in the open now?

With his wife tangled up with them.

Paul grunted and turned up the driveway towards the tiny cottage he could see at the end of it, a swirl of smoke rising into the greyness from the chimney. He walked past the three cars parked in the gravel drive and up to the front door, which had a welcome mat in front of it. He stomped his feet on the words.

He was going to visit all the places marked on the Wellsford map. There was this one, the so-called sacred well, then there was the old church. Bridget's Sanctuary as they called it now.

Paul rolled his eyes.

John Stoat, the American guy, had had quite a bit to say about that one.

Which was part of the reason why Paul was here today. He patted his pocket for his phone again before pushing the door open. He was going to get photographs of the whole place for Stoat.

What the pastor was going to do with them, Paul wasn't entirely sure, but he'd be able to use them to expose the place in some way.

Paul felt a frisson of excitement as he stepped into the cottage. Stoat would do something about an outfit who would steal a wife and son from their loving home.

He was grinning when he entered the softly lit room and stood there to take it in.

There was a fire in the grate. Nice touch. He'd seen photos of the place, of course. He'd done his research. Read everything he could find online about Wilde Grove and Wellsford – and there was plenty, that was for sure.

But still, he pulled out his phone, opened the camera app, and clicked a picture. Stoat had mentioned wanting their own evidence. He clicked another one of the books. The place was full of bloody books. He looked around, eyes narrowed, ignoring the two others hovering around the shelves, grabbing this book and that book from them.

Nothing much interesting here, Paul thought. He sidled over to a table and squinted down at the printed material on it. Snapped another picture. Picked up one of the cards and grimaced.

Some sort of prayer card, by the looks. Stoat would want to see that. Paul tucked it into his inner pocket. He pocketed the flyer for their study course as well.

Then looked around. The other two people were studiously ignoring him and Paul nodded to himself. Good, he thought, glad he was making them uncomfortable.

This place was nothing but a trickster's nest. A, what do you call it? Den of inequity. Paul nodded, pleased with himself. That was exactly it.

There was something on the floor, under one of the chairs at the back of the room, and Paul sidled up to it, then bent and snatched it up. It was one of the prayer cards –

someone had dropped it, obviously. He grunted in disappointment, stuck it in his pocket with the other one. Took another photo, then poked his head in the other room - that was boring. Just a bunch of tables and chairs, a coffee machine and a basket of muffins.

Maybe he wouldn't mind nipping in and grabbing one of those muffins. He took a photo and did so. Sniffed it. Banana choc chip, he reckoned.

Would eating something made by a witch turn him into a frog or something?

Laughing at his own joke, Paul took one and let himself out into the back garden, where a sign pointed down a path to the famous well.

Another photo. He finished the muffin in four huge bites and watched the people in the field behind the house, nodding to himself.

Stoat would want to see this, for certain, he thought, and snapped another picture of the small knot of three people bending over something. The well, he supposed.

From the pictures of it online, it was only a puddle of a thing. He couldn't see the appeal, himself. There was nothing sacred about a ditch.

But still, he'd promised himself he would go around the whole place. Try to figure out why Rowan wanted it. And take photos for Stoat, of course.

And if he happened on the place where Rowan and Robbie were staying, then that would be well and dandy also.

The guy and girl came back from the field, and he nodded to them, hands in his pockets. Then sauntered down the garden path himself, through the gate into the field and stopped in front of the well.

It wasn't the well that he was looking at, though. He tried to sneer at the woman standing by some statue of another bloody woman, but it faltered on his lips, and he settled for a glare instead.

Then remembered that he was supposed to be incognito.

'Can I take a photo?' he asked the woman. The queen bitch herself, nonetheless. The big lesbo leader of them all.

Resentment curdled in his stomach, making him regret the muffin.

'No,' Morghan replied. 'Of the well, certainly. But not of me.'

Paul sniffed, lifted his phone camera, pointed it at the puddle of water that was supposed to be the sacred well, then turned it swiftly and took a shot of her.

He shrugged. 'Sorry,' he said, one side of his mouth jerking upwards in a lopsided grin. 'Slipped.'

She didn't say anything, just stood there looking at him.

Paul wanted to laugh, to sneer at her, or even better, to ask her where his wife was. But instead, he found himself shifting from foot to foot, unsettled by the look she was giving him.

'What?' he said at last. 'What are you looking at?'

Morghan shook her head. She could feel the twisting and turning of his energy, could see it, murky and unsettled. Here, she thought, was a man carrying many unhealed wounds around with him.

'Are you all right?' she asked, ignoring his question.

Paul stared at her. 'What?'

'Are you all right?' Morghan repeated.

Paul spluttered. 'No,' he said finally. 'No, I'm bloody not all right. I came here to see what this bollocks is all about.' He turned his head and kicked out a foot at the puddle of water. 'It's nothing, is it? Just some dirty old spring someone stuck some tiles under and a pile of rocks behind.' He spied the statue. 'And who's that, then? You're worshipping the devil, that's what you're doing.'

'The devil's a woman?' Morghan asked.

'Ha!' Paul shook his head. 'If you're not with me, you're against me. That's what Jesus says, in the bible. But you wouldn't know that, would you? You haven't read the Holy Book, have you?'

Morghan sighed inwardly. She had read the book in question, actually, but didn't see any point in saying so to this man who was wearing his anger like armour.

She gestured to the wellspring and dug back into her memory of all the studying she'd once done on the subject of wells.

'The well is a symbol for the life of the spirit that dwells in us all and does not distinguish between us from our religion.' Morghan paused then spoke again. 'Whoever believes in me, as Scripture has said,' she recited, 'rivers of living water will flow from within them.'

Paul stared at her in shock. 'What's that from?' he asked.

'The gospel of John, I believe,' Morghan said.

43

ROWAN LET OUT A SHAKY BREATH AS THEY CAME OUT OF THE solicitor's office. Winsome smiled at her.

'That's good,' she said. 'You could even give yourself a little shake like a dog does. They do it to shake off tension, and I find it works for people too.'

Erin eyeballed her. 'It does?'

Winsome laughed. 'Try it some time. Yes, it can work.'

Rowan shimmied her shoulders, then squared them. 'That's that done, then,' she said, and tickled Robbie under the chin before looking at the others. 'Now, just to get my things.' She grimaced. 'I'm not looking forward to this part.'

Erin shook her head. 'I'm sure you're not.'

'I can't take Robbie there, not even under these circumstances.' She closed her eyes briefly and tried to breathe out the tension. 'Thank goodness for Ginger.'

As if conjured by her words, Ginger's car pulled up to the kerb, and Ginger got out, grinning.

'You're doing it!' she crowed as she enveloped both Rowan and Robbie in a hug, then lifted Robbie from his mum.

'I am, but I'm nervous,' Rowan said.

Ginger shook her head. 'It'll be okay,' she said. 'I went past the house on the way here and the car isn't in the driveway.' She gave Robbie a good squeeze. 'And this little fella will be just fine with me.'

'Where are you going to take him?' Winsome asked.

'Not back to Ladybird Lane, because I don't want any bother with the other kids and teachers if Paul turns up.' Ginger smiled at Robbie. 'I think we'll go for a drive, yeah? See what we can find to do while Mummy's busy?'

Robbie nodded.

Rowan blew out another breath. 'I'm ready,' she said. 'I think.' Then double checked. 'The police will be with us?'

'Bryce and Andrew are on their way already,' Erin answered. She'd gotten to know the two officers over the last few months, and liked both of them, even if there was never anything they could do about the protesters who seemed to follow the priestesses wherever they went. She glanced about for people looking at her, but there were none.

'Okay, then,' Rowan said. 'Let's go get my things from the house, and hopefully Paul won't get back while we're there.'

PAUL GOT BACK TO A SILENT HOUSE, UNLOCKING THE FRONT door and pushing it open. His jaw ached and he knew he'd been clenching it all the way back from Wellsford.

He went into the kitchen to put the kettle on and

stopped dead in the centre of the room. Something was different about the place. He frowned, then spun on his heel and made for the stairs.

'Bitch!'

He stormed into Robbie's room and shook his head, unable to believe what he saw.

'You bloody cow!'

He stood with his hands fisted on his hips. All Robbie's things – not the furniture but everything else – had been stripped from the place.

Rowan. She'd been in there and taken everything while he was out. Damn her to hell and back!

Paul went back into the bedroom he'd shared with Rowan and stared at the empty wardrobe. His jaw ached abominably.

His eyes were stinging. There was a hitch in his breathing and Paul tried desperately to hang onto his anger, blinking rapidly so that the tears wouldn't fall.

It was all that woman's fault. He squeezed his eyes shut and saw her face again behind them. The grey eyes that seemed to laugh at him. Her voice, pretending to be calm and reasonable, when really, she'd been goading him, he knew.

Paul groaned and left the room to go downstairs, where he sat on the couch and reached automatically for the TV remote. Then clicked the mute button and put his head in his hands.

In a minute, he thought, he'd call Malcolm, tell him the latest. Tell him about his run-in with the Wilde woman. The so-called high priestess, or whatever she was.

Tell him to pass it onto Stoat that she'd tried preaching the Bible at him.

He shook his head, remembered suddenly the card he'd stowed in his pocket and reached to pull it out.

Yeah. It was some sort of prayer card. That Stoat guy ought to see this too, he thought, reading it. It was blasphemy, pure and simple.

May the spirit of water flow
Clean and bright through us.
May the sacred flow of spirit
Be pure from world to world to world.
Let us not forget who we are,
That we are not alone,
But eternal as the spring,
The clear and joyous bursting
Of sacred life from sanctified ground.

Paul's lips twisted as he read, and he turned the card over in disgust. On the other side was just a printed symbol, meant to be a well or something, he supposed, but someone had written something.

Another verse or prayer, he guessed, and turned the card slightly so he could read that one too.

'Five by five the thunderclaps boom, the seas heave and run ashore, and safe from them the Golden Children are born. In a rabbit hole they lie, in a nest on high. The trees themselves sing their lullaby.'

He stared at the card. What on God's green earth did that one mean? It wasn't a prayer.

Paul stared at the piece of writing, a deep frown beetling his brows. Just what in the hell was it talking about?

Thunderclaps? Seas heaving?

It was weird. It was written weirdly. Almost like a...

Paul strained for the description, what it reminded him of.

He stood up slowly, gaze still fixed on the handwritten message.

That's what it was, he thought, nodding now. A message. A what do you call it?

A prophecy.

Sudden excitement flooded through him, and he shook his head, paced the room, holding the card out in front of him while he thought furiously.

He went into the kitchen. Back into the living room. Stopped and stared blankly out the window. Thinking. Furiously.

Yeah. He nodded. That's what it was. Someone in Wilde Bloody Grove fancied themselves a – he couldn't remember the word for it. His only experience of prophecies was from the Bible, and from the telly, from Game of Thrones.

Paul paced some more, tapping the card against the palm of his hand, his mind grinding, spinning.

He had to do something with this. He nodded, stopping to stare out the window at the street. The glass was wet. It was raining again. The town would bloody flood if it continued.

Paul looked down at the card. *Seas heave and come ashore.*

Wasn't that kind of like flooding?

Paul was in two minds about climate change, but this, it meant flooding and that sort of thing, right? Maybe.

Paul had another thought. Stoat would want it. The card, this prophecy. He'd want it. Paul shivered at his memory of meeting the man. Stoat was a slimy bastard, a mean son of a bitch under his smug, poncy attitude. Paul wouldn't have admitted it to anyone, barely even voiced it to himself, but the American preacher scared him.

But still. Stoat had been intrigued to hear Paul's story. Had given him the whole of his attention, even said some real flattering things. Paul had found himself preening under the attention, even while his skin crawled. It had been a meeting both uncomfortable and exciting.

Stoat, Paul thought, would definitely want to see this card.

But was there something else he could do with it first? Paul resumed his pacing, nodding to himself.

Five by five the thunderclaps boom. He nodded his head five times. Then five more.

The seas heave and run ashore.

Now he stopped moving again. Stood staring into space. He should share this with his buddies online. The guys in his favourite forum would have a field day with it.

His mouth curved in a smile at the thought of the discussions they'd have. Everyone would clamour after him for more information.

That would be great, he thought. He'd do that. He'd give the prophecy to Stoat for sure, but he'd share it on the forum too.

He got moving again, into the living room, pacing the length of it, turning, a glance out the window, then out into the narrow passageway and through into the kitchen, where Rowan had left him the kettle and toaster, but taken the tablecloth and bits and pieces of her gran's old dinner set.

Which was okay, because they'd been prissy girly things and just for display.

Back into the passageway, not glancing upstairs where the real evidence of Rowan's betrayal was.

On into the living room again. The telly was playing silently, something about the shitty weather. He ignored it, straining his mind to think. Think think think.

And wasn't there something else he could do with the prophecy? Something that when he hit upon it, made such exquisite sense that Paul stopped his pacing to stand grinning.

Yeah, he thought. 'Yeah,' he said out loud. 'That's it.'

A gust of wind rattled the window with rain and Paul stared for a minute at the smeared glass, then turned and left the room, ran up the stairs and threw open the door to his office.

Sure, he'd give the card to Malcolm to give to Stoat.

Actually, scratch that, he'd insist on giving it straight to the man himself. Along with all the photographs.

Paul nodded, booted up his computer.

He'd share it to the forum too. That was for certain. He'd do that after seeing Stoat, when he was back home, when he could spend a few hours at the screen.

Paul grinned again. Yeah. He'd get a bottle of brandy to celebrate. Order a curry. Make a real celebration of it. Chat to the other guys in the forum right through the night.

Wait till they got a load of the prophecy. They'd go nuts.

He navigated to his browser, typed in the address he wanted, waited for the page to load.

If he was lucky, he thought, maybe he'd be able to buy a new computer. Something fast. Get two screens, perhaps.

Something he could game on as well.

The page loaded. The big heading stared out at him. Paul curled his lip.

Welcome to the Wildewood.

Sure dude, whatever you say. Paul shook his head, clicked on the small 'contact me' link at the bottom of the page. Tapped his fingers on the desk while he waited for that page to load.

How was he going to do this? He had to do it right. Properly. Get the guy's interest.

Bait the hook, so to speak.

The website was run by a fella whose thing for the last five months was a running commentary on Wilde Grove and Wellsford. Paul had read it through only the night before. He'd known about it before that, of course – some of his own fame on the forums came from living in Banwell, just down the road from Wellsford, so he knew about the Wildewood site.

He stared at the contact page, eyes narrowed. How to get the guy begging for the card and its prophecy? That was the trick.

Finally, Paul put his fingers to the keyboard and typed. He put his phone number at the bottom and ended the message PHONE ME.

Satisfied, he moved his mouse, proved he was human, hit submit, then leant back in his chair, hands behind his head, a wide smile on his face.

All this was going to work out, he thought. Sure, he might have lost Rowan, but there were other women, if he wanted one. Plenty of them at Cornerstone. He'd be famous too, so he could have his pick.

Paul's phone warbled and he snapped forward, picked it up, hit answer.

'Yeah,' he said, then listened, nodded his head. 'Sure, you can have it.'

He leant back again, grinned at the ceiling.

'For a price.'

Krista slid her phone slowly back into her pocket.

'What?' Minnie asked, coming out from behind the table where she'd been arranging the Station of the Heart books. 'What is it? You look like you've seen a ghost or something.' Her eyes widened. 'Did you hear about this new woman in town seeing Mariah?'

'Mariah?' Krista was confused.

But Minnie nodded sagely. 'She's the one who Winsome's moved into Mariah's old place – well, she saw the old bat...' Minnie scrunched up her face and tried again. 'I mean, she saw Mariah outside, as a ghost, like. She was dancing.'

'Dancing?'

'Uh huh. Guess she's still with the Fae, right? Apparently neither Winsome nor Erin think there's anything to be done about it, but I reckon we're all going to start seeing her dancing about the place.' Minnie gave an elaborate shrug. 'You know, as the energy here gets stronger.'

Krista closed her eyes. Mariah sighted? Dancing? She guessed it was possible. Anything had become possible, it seemed. And what could be done about it? About Mariah? Nothing, most likely. The Fae, as Clarice had said, would keep her, or send her back.

Krista shook her head, steadied herself. 'Have you seen Clarice?'

Minnie wrinkled her nose at the change of conversation. 'Yeah, but that was half an hour ago, something like that. She was off to Hawthorn House.'

That made Krista draw in a breath. Of course. She remembered Clarice's plans now.

'Can you hold down things here for a couple hours?'

'No problem,' Minnie answered. 'But is something wrong? Has something bad happened?' She looked consideringly at Krista for a moment. 'You're a bit pasty.' Her eyes widened. 'You're not...you're not pregnant already, are you? You haven't just been given the news?'

Krista's face relaxed into her usual humour for a moment, and she shook her head. 'No,' she said. 'We won't know about that for a few weeks yet.'

'Oh, okay.' Minnie nodded and moved around behind the counter. She touched light fingers to the cash register, the stack of Haven bookmarks with Erin's artwork on them. But she was still looking at Krista. 'So?'

'I need to go,' Krista said, and raked her fingers over her head. 'Yeah. I'll be at Hawthorn House. Call if you need me, all right?'

'Okay,' Minnie said, trying not to be disappointed that Krista wasn't telling her what was going on, what the phone call was about, who had been on the other end. She stepped ruthlessly on the growing need to know. 'Everything will be fine here. I'll take care of the shop.'

The bell over the door tinkled and Minnie looked to see who was coming in. She hoped it would be the seekers who flooded Wellsford every weekend now – heck, who wandered about the village practically every day, weekend or not.

But it was just old Humphrey Barton, who'd be looking for his next science fiction adventure. She reached beneath the counter for book six in the current series he was reading and waved it at him, grinning. It looked like an absolute corker of a read. When she glanced back to Krista, she'd already moved, was heading upstairs to the flat above.

KRISTA LOOKED AROUND THE ROOM. 'DID YOU KNOW THAT THE woman Winsome's helped to move into Mariah's old house happened to see Mariah last night, dancing in the storm? She thought she was seeing a ghost.'

'What?' Clarice stared at her, surprised. 'She's back? Maxen said she was happy to stay with them. Did you know about this, Morghan?'

Krista interrupted. 'I heard it from Minnie, so the details might not be strictly true.'

'Winsome called me,' Morghan said. 'We decided that nothing needed to be done about it.'

'What could you do, anyway?' Clarice asked. 'Things bleed through here. If this woman's going to stay in Wellsford, she'll have to get used to it.' She shrugged. 'It's not like we can go get Mariah back. It isn't up to us.'

'The woman's name is Rowan,' Morghan said. 'And she seems to not be too perturbed by it all.'

Krista shook her head, sighed. 'Anyway, that's not why I'm here,' she said. 'Jack Newton has Clover's prophecy, which is exactly what he's calling it, and he's publishing it. Some guy found it at the Well-Keeper's cottage apparently and gave it to him.' She felt the shock wave from the announcement. 'He asked me if I had any comment.' Krista looked from Morghan to Clarice and back again. 'Do I?' she said. 'Do we have any comment to make on this?'

'What's going on?' Clover asked, coming in and seeing everyone standing in a knot in the drawing room. She narrowed her eyes, reading the perturbation in the atmosphere. 'What's happened?'

Morghan turned to look at her, gestured for her to come in. 'Krista's had a phone call from Jack Newton.'

Clover scrunched her brows together trying to remember who Jack Newton was. Finally, her eyes widened and the hand holding her offering bag dropped to her side.

'Right,' she said, and coloured slightly. 'Alex knows him, says he's a good guy. What did he want?' she asked, now with a growing sense of consternation blossoming inside her as she took the psychic temperature of the room. 'It was something bad, wasn't it?'

Clarice answered. 'Someone found the card with your... oracular pronouncement on it. Long story short, they gave it to Jack, and he's printing it on his blog, wanted to know what we thought of it.'

Clover was frozen. 'But I put the card in my pocket, didn't I?'

Clarice shrugged. 'Must have fallen out.'

'But...' Clover looked helplessly at Morghan. 'But it was just, like, a verse or a poem or something. Why does he think it means something?'

'Because it reads as though it means something,' Krista said, gentling her voice in the face of Clover's obvious shock. 'He has already written the blog post about it, was just calling to see if I wanted to add anything.'

Krista fielded all Jack Newton's calls, got along well with him. He was fascinated with what he called the Wilde Grove phenomenon, but this time she'd not had a clue what to say to him. Not one single idea.

She'd said she would give him a call back, although now, thinking about it, she realised she probably shouldn't have done that, because he'd know exactly what she was doing – going and checking with Morghan.

And that would mean that he had something big in his net.

She huffed out a breath. She should have just said that the card was meaningless, that she didn't even know who wrote it.

Except that would have been a lie and a fabrication, and for all she knew, this public exposure of it was needed, intended, part of the weaving.

'So,' she said now, turning to Morghan. 'What do you think I should tell him? I'm supposed to be calling him back in twenty minutes.'

Morghan tucked her chin down, thinking.

'We can't tell him anything,' Clarice said. 'Tell him it means nothing.'

'But it does mean something,' Krista insisted.

'But we don't know what that something is,' Clover said,

shifting on her feet, uncomfortable. 'I don't know what it means.' She looked at Morghan. 'Do you?'

Morghan felt the weight of all three gazes upon her and lifted her head. 'If I do,' she said, perfectly aware that Clover was asking about the whole oracle business rather than just her utterance while in trance. 'Then it is a memory buried within a different lifetime.'

'Ravenna's,' Clarice said flatly.

Morghan inclined her head. She turned to Krista. 'There is no way he will wait on this?'

'No.' Krista was certain of her answer. 'He said he was giving me an hour, then he'd hit publish.' She pursed her lips. 'It's too juicy, he said.'

'But whatever he says about it will be just speculation,' Clover cried. 'He doesn't know what it is.'

'Does that matter?' Clarice asked. 'It sounds like something. Reads like something, I suppose I should say. It's got that...weight to it.'

'Because it is something,' Morghan said.

'We don't know what, though.' Clover shook her head, blonde curls shivering. She was upset.

Morghan looked at Krista. 'Tell him he will have to go ahead without a comment from us at this stage.'

'He'll say that, though. That we refused to comment upon it.' Krista pulled her phone out of her pocket.

'Just tell him that at this stage we do not have any comment to make on the matter,' Morghan insisted. 'Which is the truth, because we do not have enough wisdom on the subject to be able to say anything definitive.'

Krista gazed at the phone in her hand then nodded. 'All right,' she said. 'I'll tell him that.' She paused a moment, then continued. 'But he has a lot of readers, and I've a feeling this might blow up into something big.' She looked over at Clover, an apology on her face. 'I'm sorry,' she said. 'It just reads like it's something. Like what it is, really, an oracular pronouncement. There's no way around it; that's just what it sounds like.' But she shook her head and left the room, already pushing the buttons to call Jack back.

'We will deal with whatever unfolds,' Morghan said. 'As do we always.' She glanced at her watch, calculating the tasks for the day, their possible rearrangement. Then looked at Clarice and Clover. 'You were going back into the tunnels to shepherd more spirits?'

Clover nodded, then glanced at Clarice. 'I don't know if I can now,' she said. 'I feel a bit off-balance.'

'We should do it another day, then,' Clarice said immediately. It was hard enough to travel between the worlds, let alone deal with frightened dead people when you were feeling off-kilter. She looked at Morghan, pale brows arched. 'What are your plans?'

Morghan tapped her fingers against her thigh, feeling a tightness inside herself that she knew would serve no good purpose.

'I will go for a walk,' she said after a beat. 'I need to seek some clarity.'

Clarice nodded. 'Company, or not?' she asked.

Morghan gave the question the consideration it asked for, then shook her head. 'Perhaps not, this time.'

'I want to see the Queen,' Clover said, interrupting things. 'I do,' she said, when Morghan looked at her. 'She has the answers and I need them.' Clover clenched her hands. 'She did it, whatever it was. To Rhian. I need to know.'

'She's not going to tell you,' Clarice said, not unkindly. 'That's not what it's like. She won't give you any straight answers.'

Clover looked at Morghan. 'You then,' she said. 'Ula said you would know. Rhian never had any memory of what happened to her before she joined the Forest House.'

'Yes, perhaps Ravenna would know,' Morghan conceded. She nodded and offered Clover a smile. 'I will endeavour to find out; will you give me the space to do that?'

Abashed by Morghan's gentle tone, Clover nodded. 'Of course,' she said. 'I'm just antsy, feeling like there's a puzzle and for once, I don't know the missing piece.' She paused. 'I am the missing piece.'

Clarice stepped in, touched Clover on the shoulder. 'All right, then,' she said. 'Missing Link here and I will find something grounding to do.' She nodded at Morghan.

Krista came back in, her mobile pressed to her chest.

'Well?' Clover asked. 'What did he say?'

'His post is going live as we speak,' Krista said. 'Two of them, actually.'

'Two of what?' Morghan asked.

'Two posts,' Krista explained. 'The second one is more of his usual thing. This one featuring a video of Erin outside the hospital. She's comforting some guy, apparently.'

'Ah.' Morghan nodded. Erin had told her what had happened, what she'd done.

And that someone had had their phone out, recording it. Which pretty much made it inevitable that it would end up on Jack Newton's website. The title of which – Welcome to the Wildewood – said it all, really.

'I will leave my phone at home, then,' she said on a sigh. That she would come back to a full voicemail box, she had no doubt.

'We should get a publicist,' Krista said.

'A what?' Clarice stared at her.

'A publicist.' Krista turned to Morghan. 'You need a proper assistant, and we could do with a publicist to help us navigate all this, so that we're properly promoting all we're doing.' She lifted her shoulders in a graceful shrug. 'We have to make the most of it, after all. That Trafalgar Square business opened up the world to us. We can't squander the opportunity.'

'We're not,' Clarice said. 'We're doing stuff all over.'

'But it's still piecemeal,' Krista insisted. 'We can do more, and better, and control the narrative better.'

'Control the narrative?' Clover frowned. 'What does that mean?'

'Just be more organised,' Krista said, sighing now. 'Be on top of it all. I feel like we're spread out all over the place and we could do with someone sort of coordinating it all.' She shook her head. 'I'm going to give it some thought.'

Morghan smiled at her, even though just the idea of an assistant made her nervous. 'You've been doing very well so far,' she said.

'Well maybe.' Krista grimaced. 'I think hearing from Jack just threw me. I thought we'd be able to keep the oracle business between us until we knew more.'

'I thought I'd put the card in my pocket,' Clover said.

'I know,' Krista said.

"The Wheel turns,' Morghan said finally. 'Things fall into their place. Remember, my dear ones. We are not alone here. This is not just our task.' She thought of Elen and Alastrina's council. 'We're just one part of it, and we'll play that part as it falls to us.' She drew herself up. 'I will go seek what may be found, and we all need to remember to stay upright and centred.' She smiled at Clover, reached out to put a hand on her shoulder. 'Perhaps it might be nice to call home, talk to Rue and Selena for a while.'

Clover nodded, although she didn't think she'd do that. Or not straight away. First, she'd do some grounding exercises. Shake off the stress she could feel nipping at her.

'Wanna go dance, Clarice?' she asked.

A slow grin crept over Clarice's face. 'I thought you'd never ask.'

MORGHAN WENT INTO HER OFFICE. SHE HAD THE SENSATION of events tumbling, things moving into place, into arrangements wrought by others, not herself.

She hoped those others were their allies.

Grainne's painting was in front of her. Morghan reached out and let her fingers hover above its surface.

'I wish you were here, darling,' she said. 'I could do with one of your pep talks.'

She smiled sadly. Grainne had always been ready with encouragement when Morghan had needed it. Going without her as a sounding board and as someone – probably the only person – willing to give Morghan a good push when needed, was a lack Morghan still sometimes felt keenly.

She pressed fingers to her heart, then her lips, sent her love to Grainne. Then sighed and looked down at the golden egg in its wooden box.

'The goose who lays the golden egg?' she murmured,

then snorted a laugh. What did it matter if she was said goose? The golden eggs were the prize, were what mattered.

The return of the soul-led life.

'We are making a difference,' Morghan said, still out loud, to herself, perhaps, or to her kin.

But there were other hands stirring the cauldron besides hers. Was this oracular business part of that?

Another sigh, then Morghan turned to her altar, anointed herself with a dabbing of scented oil, and whispered the words that ruled her life.

'From each birth to each death, my life dedicated, my service offered.'

She closed her eyes. *Help me follow the path you have set for me.*

In the woods, Catrin appeared at Morghan's side. Morghan looked at her over her shoulder.

'You should be spending your time with Broca,' she said. 'Not with me.'

Catrin glanced at her. 'Love has its time,' she said. 'As does duty.'

Morghan looked at the path ahead, aware that she was crossing from the trails of Wilde Grove to those of the Wildwood. She caught a flash of white, knew the Stag was there in the shadows.

'Love drives everything,' Morghan said.

Another glance from Catrin. Morghan felt her attention focus on her face, then flick away.

'There are many flavours of love, and the bonds you talk of, those between Broca and myself, you and Grainne, they do not break once tied, but instead make room for us to do the things that are necessary.'

Morghan drew breath, let it out. The air had warmed once they'd stepped into the Wildwood, fragrant and soft against her skin.

Catrin looked at her again. 'In ordinary circumstances,' she said. 'I would tell you to take a lover, let yourself find joy in another's arms a while.'

Morghan stared at her, wordless.

But Catrin shook her head. 'These times, however, won't allow that sort of distraction, I think.' She put her hand on the hilt of her sword. 'But you are distracted anyway.'

'A lover?' Morghan echoed.

'You're shocked.' Catrin laughed. 'Why are you shocked?'

Morghan shook her head. Such things as lovers had never crossed her mind. 'I am bound to Grainne,' she said.

'Love overflows,' Catrin responded. 'It does not break bonds.'

'Nonetheless,' Morghan said, and stopped walking, pausing in hope of regaining her equilibrium.

'Did you take lovers?' she asked Catrin. 'After you and Broca were parted?'

Catrin gazed away between the trees. 'On occasion,' she said, then straightened. 'But that is by the by. It is now that we must consider, and I do not think this is a good time for the distraction.'

Morghan shook her head. Looked at the soft mulch of the ground on which she stood. 'I miss her,' she said, voice low, and the trees sighed in unison in the background.

'You are with her,' Catrin said, but she didn't speak sharply. 'In spirit, in other lifetimes.'

Morghan gave a sad smile. 'You didn't let that stop you, when you missed Broca.'

'It was not that I missed Broca, but that I wronged her. I risked everything between us.' Catrin stared at Morghan. 'You and Grainne could not be what you are together, if I had not righted my error.'

Morghan blew out a breath, nodded. 'Come,' she said. 'Let's do what we came here for.'

Catrin walked after her. 'What would that be, then? Where are we going?'

Morghan didn't answer but posed another question instead. 'Grainne told me once that when it looked like she might not survive her life long enough to do her task, and her kin came to fetch her bright spirit, they called it the Golden Child.'

Catrin, listening, did not say anything.

Morghan turned her head toward her. 'The Golden Child,' she repeated. 'Clover's declaration said that golden children would be born.'

'Every child is a golden child,' Catrin said.

But Morghan shook her head. Not because she didn't agree. She did, in fact. 'I think this means something different,' she said. 'More...nuanced.'

They came to a cliff's edge and stopped to cast their gaze over the far view.

'That city there,' Catrin said, speaking of the far-off vision of a city of buildings, low-slung, small-windowed, made from the orange soil that surrounded them. 'It reminds me of the life we spent with Broca when she was part of the cat women's cult.' Her lips twitched in a smile. 'She never lost that aspect of herself, I think.'

'Perhaps it is where Amara came from,' Morghan said, referring to the mountain lion that was Grainne's kin. She glanced at Catrin. 'You spend your time with me and miss her too,' she said, and this time it was not a question, but a plain statement of fact.

'I do,' Catrin said, and started for the steps down the cliff face. 'So let us achieve our purpose here, that we might be all the closer to returning to her side.'

Morghan watched for a moment, then started after Catrin. 'I told you she has appeared to Clarice, to help with the task of shepherding the lost spirits to the Summer Isles.'

Catrin nodded, her feet crunching on the dry dirt as she followed little more than a rabbit track across the cliff face.

'That is not our concern,' she said.

'You do not wish to go and look for her?'

Catrin turned and looked at Morghan. 'Why?'

'She is so close.'

'No.'

Morghan swallowed. 'Why not?'

'To what purpose?' Catrin asked, turning back to continued walking. 'She comes to aid Clarice. She does not come for us.'

Catrin reached the tunnel opening, stepped into it onto firm ground, then waited for Morghan to join her.

'What is it?' Morghan asked, blinking in the sudden dimness.

Catrin shook her head slightly. 'You wish to feel her with you again.'

Morghan looked down at the dirt at her feet. 'My memories of her fade,' she said. 'I do not see her face as clearly.'

'That,' Catrin said, 'can be a boon.' But she moved suddenly and pressed a hand to Morghan's chest.

Morghan's eyes widened as Catrin's energy flowed into her, and with it, her visions, memories.

Visions of lifetimes spent with Grainne.

Lying inside a nest of grasses, the sun hot on their backs. Grainne the shape-shifting cat woman, Morghan as she was then, running her fingers over the scars on Grainne's neck, put there as part of her initiation.

Broca, stroking her face, her wild green eyes gazing into Catrin's, laughing.

Then Grainne was a man, looking over his shoulder at her, that same smile, that same look in his eyes.

Life after life, together, snapshots of them together, the memory of laughter, tears, touches.

Many Morghan recognised, many she had only the vaguest idea of. Herself a farming man, in love with Grainne who was slight, fair-haired, mother to a brood of their children.

Ravenna, the swirls serious upon her cheeks, with Grainne, black-haired this time, eyes dark, deep pools, the resemblance to Rhian unmistakable.

Morghan tore Catrin's hand from her chest.

'Stop,' she said. She squeezed her eyes shut. 'Ravenna?'

'What are you asking?'

'Ravenna,' Morghan repeated. 'All those lifetimes – you and Broca, Grainne and I. And Ravenna, with a dark-eyed Grainne. I swear it was her.'

'Of course,' Catrin said.

Morghan straightened. 'You knew that Ravenna had known our Grainne?'

Catrin considered this. 'We have known her over and over. There are many lifetimes I have not needed to pay particular attention to. Where I was content simply to be with her.'

'Ravenna lived earlier than you,' Morghan said, and went to lean against the tunnel wall.

'The flow of time only matters when we are flesh.'

But Morghan shook her head.

'Why is this important?' Catrin asked, impatient. 'You wanted to see her face again; I showed you how often we have seen her, how dear she is to us, how close, even when the memory seems to fade.'

'Do you have Ravenna's memories?' Morghan demanded.

'Ravenna keeps them herself,' Catrin said. 'I can touch them, as you can, but I do not carry them.'

Morghan closed her eyes. She didn't have time to worry about the intricacies of how soul aspects worked.

'I need to find Ravenna,' she said instead, then looked around at where she was. Why had she come to this place?

To see the Queen, to question her about Rhian. About what had been done to the child in the time the Fae had her.

But now, she thought, shaking her head, putting her hands to her temples as if to hold everything inside when it seemed it would spill over out of her. But now, it seemed that she had stumbled upon one piece of the puzzle – whose child Rhian had been.

Morghan straightened. There was no reason not to continue with her planned visit to the Fair Lands.

'Where are we going?' Catrin asked, striding after her.

'To see the Queen,' Morghan said.

'MORGHAN,' QUEEN ALASTRINA SAID, AND TURNED TO WALK to her favourite seat under the perpetually flowering bower. 'I was not expecting you.'

Morghan lowered her head. Catrin had declined to enter the Fair Lands, so she was alone.

'My visit is impromptu, for which I apologise,' she said.

'It is important, then,' the Queen said, a smile playing around her lips, her tone faintly mocking.

Morghan decided to get straight to the point. She cleared her throat.

'Will you explain the matter of Clover being called an Oracle?' she asked. Then added, 'please.'

Alastrina gazed up at her. 'Sit,' she said. 'You make me crane my neck.'

The Queen's skirts took up the length of the bench, so Morghan nodded, sat down upon the grass. Then turned her expectant gaze back upon the Fae Queen she had known for most of her life.

'You wait for me to answer,' Alastrina said.

'I do,' Morghan replied.

The Queen gazed out over the green fields. 'There is a shadow over your town and village,' she said. 'My people, those whose business it is to walk the edges of the worlds, they have seen this.'

Morghan looked at her. 'A shadow?'

'Darkness gathers,' Alastrina said. 'It will come to a head shortly.'

There was a buzzing inside Morghan, an instant discomfort. 'I don't know what you're talking about,' she said.

'Darkness gathers, the edifice cracks, tumbles.' She paused, changed subject. 'The Oracle's purpose is to bring hope. Her message is one of hope.'

'The Golden Children?'

Alastrina inclined her head. 'If you are quick enough.'

'Quick enough with what?' Morghan tamped down her impatience. They were lucky, she knew, that they understood each other even imperfectly, coming together as they did as two different races with two different histories, and two completely different experiences of the flow of time.

'The Great Returning.' Alastrina turned her gaze to Morghan's face. 'You have everything you need. You know what it is we want. You must become it. In the midst of the great disruptions coming, there must be a soul-change.'

Morghan thought of the council that had met deep within the caves. Of the golden egg in its treasure chest.

'The Great Returning,' she said, half to herself.

'Yes,' Alastrina said.

'It will take centuries,' Morghan said. 'As it did to turn in the first place.'

'Perhaps,' Alastrina said, and she turned her head away. 'Perhaps not.' She looked back at Morghan, and Morghan had the fleeting thought that she wasn't being told the whole story.

'And what matters time when the soul is involved?' the Queen asked. 'It is only important that we each perform our tasks, that the beacons are lit, that the light shines out the way through the darkness.' She paused. 'That is the urgent task, thanks to the carelessness with which your people have treated our home.'

'I could do more?' Morghan asked.

Alastrina's eyes were blue as the sky overhead. 'There is always more that could be done.'

Morghan accepted this, nodded. 'The Oracle,' she said, making a return to the subject. 'Rhian's mother.'

'Do you need the details?'

Morghan considered this. 'I don't know,' she said after a moment. 'Perhaps it would help.' She nodded. 'Help Clover, for certain, to know her...history.'

'It is there if you wish it,' Alastrina said.

'But you do not think it important?'

'She has spoken?'

'Who?' Morghan asked, momentarily confused.

Alastrina was impatient. 'The Oracle?'

'Clover?' Morghan took a breath. 'Yes.'

Alastrina paused, gazed out over her summer-filled garden. She nodded, a smile on her lips. 'I had faith,' she said.

Morghan waited.

'It is good,' Alastrina said. 'We took her and broke her open, and from her pours forth the greatest thing: hope.'

But Alastrina's voice was gruff when she turned back to Morghan. 'You must leave this and tend to the darkness that gathers in your own back yard.'

Morghan's eyes widened. 'Over Wellsford and Banwell?'

Hadn't she felt this too, the insistence on being poised on the brink of something? When had she felt this intimation? She could not remember. Something had brought it on, however. Something particular.

Alastrina stood, a sign that the interview was over. Her face was stern. 'Have I not said so? Go and look for it, and ready yourself.'

Her gaze lit on Morghan and softened slightly. 'Mind your way, Morghan of the Grove. We have known each other long and well. I would not care to lose you.' She paused, reached out to touch Morghan's golden hand.

'It is time to burn brightly, but not to the point of perishing in your own fire.'

She smiled briefly, then turned and stepped away, her skirts rustling like the breeze in the trees.

Morghan stared after her, but unseeing. Behind her eyes, she beheld her vision once more.

Upon the tor, Catrin to one side, Ravenna to the other.

And herself in the centre, burning bright with the light of her soul.

Burning white and hot and brighter than ever before.

46

STOAT TOOK THE CARD FROM PAUL'S HAND AS THOUGH IT would burn him. His lip curled in distaste as he read the prayer printed upon it.

'The other side,' Paul said. 'It's on the other side.' He was wishing, just a little, that he hadn't handed the card over. It felt as though things had just passed for good out of his own hands.

But he had sold the story to the blogging guy first, hadn't he? A tiny bit of pleasure ticked at his insides. And he'd told the others on the forums to watch out for the post when it came out, which it probably had by now.

He had to admit, it had been a stroke of brilliance to sell the thing to Jack Newton. The blog post the guy had written would also be a stroke of brilliance.

Sure, Jack Newton was a little more pro-Wilde Grove than Paul liked, but at least he'd get the news out there that they were now dabbling in prophesying. Which had to be dangerous ground, whichever way you looked at it.

But still, right up until now, Paul had had the actual card, the real thing, in his keeping. He thought now, with dismay, that it wasn't likely to come back into his direct possession.

'I found it at the Well-Keeper's Cottage,' he said, and glanced at Malcolm, and at Eric Mason, the pastor of Cornerstone, who was looking a bit gaunt and green around the gills.

'And did you take the photographs of the well-keeper's cottage and other places as I asked?' Stoat quizzed, finally turning the card over.

'Yeah, I did,' Paul said, and held out the photographs he'd had printed out at his own expense.

But Stoat didn't so much as glance at them, and after a moment, Paul dropped his arm back to his side.

John Stoat turned his back on the men gathered in Eric Mason's study and read for the second time the item on the reverse side of the card.

'It's something, isn't it?' Paul asked. 'I mean, it's really something.'

'Hush,' Stoat said, and hunched deeper over the hand-written lines.

It was something, he thought. It was indeed something.

Eric cleared his throat, wishing he could go back out of the room and get in the car to go to his wife, rest his head against her soft breasts again for comfort, away from this horror that was John Stoat. The man had been with them two weeks now, and Eric felt as though his life had imploded.

It had been a wisdom to send their oldest daughter out of the house and away from the wandering hands of John

Stoat, but it hurt Eric's heart, even as he understood and agreed, that Patty had decided she and the other girls needed to accompany her.

'What does it say?' he asked now.

Stoat flapped a hand at him.

'It talks about golden children being born,' Paul said.

Stoat rounded on him, long narrow face flushed with sudden anger. 'I said hush your stupid mouth,' he hissed.

Paul took a stumbling step backwards, eyes widening. 'These are the people who have my wife and boy, remember,' he said, then wished he hadn't spoken, because his voice was thin, like that of a mewling child.

Stoat straightened. He hooked a finger in his collar, resetting it on his clavicle.

'Of course,' he soothed. Paul Sutherland was a fool and an imbecile, but his situation provided a golden opportunity. A smile stretched across John Stoat's mouth. Golden children, golden opportunity.

He drew in a nice, deep breath, and nodded. Spread out his arms in an expansive gesture, as though he were on the pulpit.

'My friends,' he said. 'We must make our move against this abomination to God and the sanctity of the family.' He held up the card, waved it back and forth. 'Now, not only do they hide a wife from her God-fearing husband and a son from his loving daddy, but they claim to see that which only God and his prophets may know!'

'What's that?' Malcolm demanded. He glanced at Eric, but Eric only looked at him blankly, so he turned his attention back to Stoat.

But John Stoat was calculating the next move, tapping

the card against his fingers, eyes narrowed as he considered. Finally, he realised everyone was staring at him, and he smiled at them.

'We will take this into the public arena,' he said. 'We will hold a public service, in which we will expound upon the evils that confront us.' He turned his blazing gaze to Paul. 'We will demand your child is returned to his father. We will expose them for what they are – the diabolical plan of the devil himself to pervert the course of the world along his lines.'

Stoat lowered his arms. He would save his energy. But still, he wanted for a moment to dance and caper about the room.

He contented himself with nodding instead. 'We will enjoin every congregation across the country – no, the world – to come out and stand up against this hideous threat that is Wilde Grove.' His grin widened and there was a damp spot of spittle on his chin. 'It will be glorious. The real soldiers of Christ coming once more to the rescue of the world.'

Malcolm glanced at Eric, but the pastor had his head down gazing at the floor, the skin on his cheeks slack, defeated.

Then he looked at the man, Paul, who was grinning also, all but pumping his fist at Stoat's words.

'We'd need a permit to meet in public,' Malcolm said, hoping to inject a modicum of sense to the proceedings.

Stoat turned to him. 'No permit will be necessary. We meet with the approval of Jesus himself.'

'I'm not sure the town council recognises that.'

'Then they must begin!' Stoat roared and he spread his

arms apart, wide. 'We will be the martyrs, if necessary, but we will blaze with the fire of righteousness, of that everyone will be certain.'

Malcolm looked at Eric again. Hadn't Eric told him that Stoat was a crazy man?

Perhaps he'd been right.

'The rain...' he said, helplessly.

'The rain?' Stoat screeched at him, and now he did a small shuffle of the feet. He grinned at Malcolm. 'The rain is God's tears that we have strayed so far. Don't you understand that?'

Malcolm blinked at him.

'The rivers rise,' Stoat cried. 'The rivers rise, the storms come, God cries, weeps tears of agony and fury!' Stoat calmed, smiled beatifically. 'But we will triumph. Armies of angels will come pluck us from the waters, take us to higher ground where we will continue to preach God's will.'

Malcolm stared at him, then looked at Eric, touched the pastor's elbow. 'Can we have a word for a minute, Eric,' he said.

Stoat raised an eyebrow. 'Erica is behind me one thousand percent, aren't you, Erica?'

The way he pronounced Eric, emphasising the last sound, made it seem to Malcolm as though he was calling Mason Erica. Malcolm was humiliated for him.

But Eric had lifted his head, at least, although he wasn't looking at Malcolm. He was nodding, though.

'We'll do whatever Stoat deems necessary,' he said, his voice dull. And then he shook off Malcolm's hand and turned on his heel, leaving the room.

'Well, how's that, then?' Stoat said, that horrible grin

back on his face. 'Whatever I say? You're my people now. My church.'

'We are God's church,' Malcolm said.

But it was as though Stoat hadn't heard him. He had already turned to Paul.

'I need your help, I think,' Stoat said. 'We need video equipment, and that's just for starters.'

Paul glowed with pride. Just wait, he thought, until this all goes public. Then it would be him on the telly and in the papers, and wouldn't that be something? The guys on the forums would be bright green with envy.

'Whatever you need,' Paul said.

Stoat nodded and tucked the card delicately away in his jacket pocket.

ROWAN STOOD IN THE MIDDLE OF ROBBIE'S NEW BEDROOM, holding him in her arms. He had his sweet little head on her shoulder, and she could hear him snoring softly in that snuffly little way she loved so much.

She squeezed her eyes together, took a deep steadying breath and whispered in her sleeping son's ear.

'I've never been so happy, Robbie, since the day I first held you.'

He stirred, rubbed an eye with a small fist still pudgy and baby-round, then settled again. Rowan smiled, gazed around the room. She had spent the last hour, with Robbie's help, putting all his things away and making the bed with the sheets and quilts she'd made while she was pregnant.

She had her own bed in the next room freshly made too,

with another patchwork quilt she'd done. Paul had grumbled when it was finished and on their bed; he'd said it was like sleeping in a salad. Rowan shook her head and banished Paul from it. No more thoughts of him, he no longer signified.

She tucked Robbie into his bed for his afternoon nap and kissed his warm little cheek. 'You'll see,' she whispered. 'Everything's going to be so much better now.'

Straightening, Rowan left the room and went back to the dining table where the Stations of the Heart book was.

There is a village in the Otherworld, close by an ancient forest where lost souls seek shelter. The village has many houses, enough for us all, and a church, in the bell tower of which hangs a glowing egg, its light shining out as a beacon to all with eyes and the desire to see it.

In the village square, there is a once-magnificent fountain. Now however, it is clogged with leaves, and the water does not flow, just as the houses stand mostly empty.

You can see however, that we have begun the job of clearing and cleaning the fountain. One day, the water will flow bright and clear once more.

The village is one of shadows, except for the glowing light of the egg in the bell tower and a warmly lit window here and there, where someone such as yourself, determined to live an ensouled life of connection and joy, is making their home.

It is here, in this lost and found village, that you must come and make your home. Walk down the cobblestone lanes and choose yourself a house, for it is time we returned to this place, made ourselves at home once more in the village of life and refuge.

A bird cries out from the woods, and it is a lonely sound

within the quiet of the village. It takes courage to come back to this lost place and determine to make your home in it.

It takes courage and heart – but we have that, don't we? We are souls as bright as the shining egg that I have put in that tower.

Come, my dear one, you who wishes to return to the true life of the embodied soul, walk these lanes, choose yourself a house, push open the door, and move in.

Clear a corner of your new home, sweep it and polish it, set a candle there, an offering of gratitude, a reflection of light that says, here I am, where I belong.

Rowan stood up, realised that even though she was no good at visualising things, since she only sort of felt them instead, that it seemed strangely that she was in the village she'd just read about, and it was in her.

There were candles in one of the kitchen drawers, and an old candlestick – where had she seen that? She found it, stood in the living room looking around, seeking a good spot.

The windowsill, she thought. There was only a hedge beyond the window, but Rowan nodded. The hedge, she told herself, imagining it, was the forest, and she wiped down the sill, set the candlestick there on one of her gran's pretty doilies.

Yes, that was right. Rowan smiled. Just right. She'd light the candle, and the light would shine in the window to show she'd moved in, that she was claiming her place in the village.

The match rasped and lit, and she touched it to the candle wick. The flame caught, bobbed in an unseen breeze, then steadied, brightened.

Rowan imagined the bell tower, felt the radiance of the egg's glow. The egg for the soul. It felt right – all that potential, all that life. Touching her palm to her chest, she felt for the beat of her heart, eyes closing.

Here she was, she thought, and inside her mind she was spinning in the golden light.

Here she was, claiming her belonging, on the path of her spirit.

47

Erin parked the Mini outside the vicarage and got out, frowning.

'Is it just me,' she asked Winsome, 'or are there more people than usual?'

Veronica came out of the front door in time to hear the question. 'It's not you,' she said. 'They've been gathering since that man's blog went live.'

Winsome looked at her. 'What man's blog?'

Veronica gazed over the milling, buzzing group of people clustered around Bridget's Sanctuary, and sniffed. 'You might want to go inside, Erin,' she said. 'Before they see you.'

But it was too late. A woman pointed, gave a shout, and the small crowd moved towards them in a wave.

'Was it you?' someone shouted, while heads all around him bobbed.

'What does it mean?' another asked.

'Tell us what it means!'

Winsome glanced at Erin. 'What what means?'

Veronica scowled. 'Where have you been all day?'

'In Banwell, at the solicitors with Rowan, then we had to go back there to the hospital after we dropped her at Mariah's.' Erin shook her head. 'I mean, at...'

'We know what you mean,' Veronica said.

'Well?' called another from the crowd, a woman with a small child in her arms. She held the baby up. 'Is he one of the Golden Children?'

Winsome stepped forward, held up her hands, and the crowd hushed.

'I'm sorry,' she said. 'Erin and I have been busy all day. We don't know what you've heard.'

'Read,' Veronica said.

'Or read,' Winsome echoed.

The woman with the baby tucked him back against her chest. She was looking at Erin, confusion on her face. 'You didn't say it then?'

'Say what?' Erin asked, and then understanding dawned, and she covered her mouth with a hand, eyes widening.

'The prophecy,' someone else in the crowd said. 'The Wilde Grove Prophecy.'

'Yeah. If you didn't say it, then who did?'

The Wilde Grove Prophecy. Her head suddenly buzzing, Erin looked at her mother. 'How did it get out?'

'Someone found the card Stephan had written it on. Gave it to Jack Newton.'

Erin glanced at Winsome, who stood there, mouth a

perfect O of surprise. 'I'm sorry,' she said. 'Hold the fort, okay?'

Winsome nodded wordlessly, while the crowd of fifteen or twenty people rippled with excitement.

'Tell us what it means,' an older man called out. 'What does it mean?'

The woman beside him nodded and recited it, her voice high and clear. The others in the crowd moved out into a loose semi-circle to listen, nodding along, faces bright with excitement.

Five by five the thunderclaps boom,
The seas heave and run ashore,
And safe from all, the Golden Children are born.
In a rabbit hole they lie,
In a nest on high.
The trees themselves sing their lullaby.

THE WORDS ECHOED IN ERIN'S EARS AS SHE PICKED UP HER skirts and got back into the Mini. She'd thought, in the daze of her mind that she ought to walk – she was so used to walking everywhere – but the car would be quicker.

She backed the Mini out of the driveway and pointed it towards Hawthorn House.

'Please be there,' she said.

There were other cars on the driveway. Erin got out and glanced at them. It was almost a replay, she thought, of the aftermath of the Trafalgar Square incident. Would this sort of thing keep happening, she wondered?

The front door opened, and Burdock bounded out to

greet her. Erin took a moment to give him a good rub then looked up at Stephan in the doorway.

'You heard, then,' he said.

She nodded. 'There's a small crowd at Bridget's Sanctuary. They told Winsome and me.' She winced slightly. 'I left Winsome and Mum to deal with them. That probably wasn't kind.' Erin thought of the woman who had held up her baby. 'What does it mean?' she asked. 'The prophecy? I know everyone's been trying to figure it out. Does Morghan know?'

Stephan flattened himself in the doorway and gestured for Erin to come in. She paused, rested her hand against his chest for a moment in connection, and Stephan covered it with his. She gazed up at him, let their energies twine together for a minute, then she smiled, and he followed her into the drawing room.

Morghan looked up at Erin's entrance. 'Ah,' she said. 'You've heard, then.'

'I saw,' Erin said. 'Crowds. How do they turn up so suddenly?' She shook her head. 'What happened? Mum said that someone passed the prophecy on to Jack Newton?'

'He wrote a big article about it,' Krista said.

'It's not a prophecy,' Clover said miserably.

Erin looked at her, went over and hugged her. 'It's okay,' she said. 'It's going to be okay.' She turned to Morghan. 'Isn't it? What are we going to do?'

Ambrose cleared his throat. 'Is Winsome all right?' he asked.

Erin winced, then nodded. 'I kind of abandoned her, but between her and Mum, they'll deal with it.'

Ambrose frowned then also looked to Morghan. 'Still,' he said. 'We need to decide how to handle this, and quickly.'

'They want to know who said it,' Erin said, and gave Clover's shoulders a squeeze when Clover let out a groan.

Ambrose moved closer to Morghan. 'We're going to have to say something about this. Make some sort of public statement.'

Krista nodded. 'I've already had the TV stations calling. The Breakfast Show wants you back on.'

Morghan closed her eyes, took a breath. Things happened so swiftly, she thought. Then another thought tumbled over that one.

Not quickly, she realised. This had not come to pass quickly at all. It had been planned. Millennia ago, when the woman she knew as Grainne gave birth to a child and gave the girl to the Fae, to Alastrina.

Catrin was at her shoulder then, and another presence stepped to her other side. Ravenna.

You knew, didn't you, Morghan whispered in her mind.

Ravenna tipped her head. After the fact.

For this also? Morghan asked. Not just the ability to hold back the veil, but for this prophecy?

For it was, no matter Clover's protestations, a prophecy.

For this, Ravenna confirmed. They broke the child open so that she could not help but see.

Morghan, eyes still closed, nodded. She had suspected as much. She remembered Clover's other vision, the one of the possible future, poverty, starvation, suicide. It had already begun.

We are the living beacons, Morghan said to Catrin and

Ravenna. 'Not just Clover but all of us. We are the bell tower with the egg shining its soul light to the world.'

Ambrose caught Morghan's low murmur and glanced at Clover. 'That's a lot to ask of us,' he said, pitching his voice equally low.

'The soul chooses its purpose,' Morghan said, opening her eyes. She reached for Ambrose's hand and beckoned the others in the room to draw together. Krista, Clarice, Clover, Erin, and Stephan. She looked them over, her heart warmed at the sight of their glowing faces.

'We are the Grove,' she said. 'The living breath of the spirit's path in this world. We have chosen this path, and we must not turn back now.'

Clover swallowed over the lump in her throat. She did want to turn back, she thought suddenly. She wanted to go and hide, go back to Rue, duck her head down and pretend she had no role to play.

Morghan smiled at her. 'We must not turn back now. Remember, when things are difficult, when our task tests us, that this is just a blink in the flow of our soul's span.' She breathed slowly, deeply, quoted a line from a poem she remembered suddenly that Grainne had written under the wax of one of her artworks.

'Why are you afraid?' she said. 'Press your hand to your chest.

'- Even broken, a heart goes on beating.

'Every tear can be mended, and death is only something from which wild-eyed daisies grow.'

Clarice lifted her head. 'Mum wrote that,' she said. 'It was in one of her paintings.'

Morghan nodded. 'She did. She was a very smart

woman, and we're going to take her poem to heart, and we will not be afraid.'

Erin gave a nervous laugh. 'You sound as though we're going to battle or something.'

Clover frowned and let herself look properly at Morghan. Widening her senses, she saw the ghostly figures of two women with Morghan, one on either side. Ravenna. She recognised her and swallowed. Ravenna held her staff, from which swung shells and feathers. In her mind, Clover could hear their rattle, like small bones.

She didn't recognise the other woman, who stood so calmly beside Morghan, even while she held a sword in her hands, the point resting on the floor.

'We are going to battle, aren't we?' Clover said. 'In a manner of speaking.' She cleared her throat. 'Against the order of things as they stand now, against the darkness.'

Morghan smiled at her. 'A battle?' She shook her head, despite Catrin's presence beside her, she with her great sword with which she had once fought, blade in her hands, magic upon her lips. 'Let us call it a great unveiling instead.'

The Great Returning.

She looked at Ambrose with love, at each of their number, her heart full. These women and men, she thought, were light bearers. Way showers. Well-Keepers in a shallow world, a world that had forgotten for the most part its true depths.

These women and men and those outside who were gathering together under the calling of a prophecy, coming together to give birth to a better world even amidst the turmoil that would come with the change.

She knew the odds were stacked against them. That any

and all change would likely be slow in coming, happen in fits and starts, but, Morghan knew, they weren't the only ones involved in this work.

There were bright lights shining all over the world, people doing the work, living by their hearts, building community, staying steadfast.

'And we will stay steadfast,' she said. 'Even into death.'

STOAT TURNED ON ERIC AND MALCOLM WITH NARROWED eyes. 'How did Mr Newton get hold of it?' he asked, making an effort to keep his voice calm but unable to help the little sneer.

He always thought he sounded more dangerous when calm than he did shouting. The sign of a true leader was keeping a clear head when events were spiralling.

In reality, of course, his blood was boiling. 'It was that fool, wasn't it?' He shook his head. 'I wonder how many pieces of silver this Judas was paid?'

Eric was glad Malcolm was with him. Stoat's face had turned an alarming shade of scarlet, and he was rather afraid that if Malcolm hadn't been present during the telling of the bad news, then Stoat might have slapped him backhand across the cheek again. He pressed his hand there as though the deed had been done.

'I can't see what difference it makes,' Malcolm said, blissfully unaware that John Stoat's temper was rising like mercury in a heatwave.

'Of course it makes a difference,' Stoat spat at him. 'How can we control the narrative when someone else has beaten us to the punch?' Spittle flew from his lips, and he turned away. 'I wish to be left alone,' he said, his back to Eric and Malcolm. 'I need some time to ascertain the Lord's plan.'

Eric made immediately for his study door, relief making his limbs feel almost boneless. In the hallway of his home, he kept going, putting a shaking hand to the front door, opening it and stepping outside.

'Where are you going?' Malcolm asked on his heels.

Eric shook his head, patted his pockets. His wallet and car keys were in there, and he wondered why. Was it God's work? He thought it might be.

'Can't stay here,' he said. 'Going to go join Patty, I think.'

Malcolm frowned, turned and closed the front door, then stared at Eric in disbelief. 'What?'

Eric shook his head. 'He's crazy.' The words were hissed, under his breath so that Stoat wouldn't hear.

'Crazy?' Malcolm looked at him in disbelief. 'He's American,' he said at last. 'They do things differently, that's all.'

But Eric was shaking his head. 'No, that's not all. It's just Stoat. He's...weird and crazy. He talks to himself when he thinks no one's around.' Eric swallowed, thought longingly of Patty and the girls. 'And he's abusive. Verbally. Physically.'

Malcolm was taken aback. 'Physically? He hit you? Is that what you're saying?' Malcolm shook his head. 'No, I can't believe that. Stoat's a bit eccentric, I give you that.'

'He thinks he's the second coming,' Eric said flatly, and he got his car keys from his pocket.

'You've misunderstood him, obviously.'

Eric looked at Malcolm and laughed. It was high-pitched, slightly hysterical, nothing like the calm, joyful man he'd used to be.

'I haven't misunderstood a thing,' he said, and turned to

walk to his car. He opened the driver's door, paused a moment before climbing in. 'Whatever scheme he comes up with, Malcolm, do yourself a favour and don't go along with it.'

Malcolm shook his head. 'But what about the church? You can't just leave.'

But the pastor of Cornerstone Church didn't hear him. He was already reversing out of the driveway.

48

'Mummy,' Robbie said, from his perch standing on the couch. 'I hear people.'

Rowan glanced at him and nodded. 'So do I,' she said, and went to the front door, opened it, and stepped out upon the stoop. A gust of wind caught at her and whipped her skirt about her legs, then took off down the street. Rowan didn't notice.

She was looking across the street at the church and vicarage. Bridget's Sanctuary, she corrected.

Winsome was there, and a crowd of twenty or so people clustered around her.

Robbie pointed at her. 'Winsome,' he said.

Rowan nodded, then looked down at Robbie in surprise. 'Yes,' she said. 'You're right. That's Winsome. Well done learning her name!'

Robbie beamed up at her, and she scooped him up into her arms. Really, he had become like a different child the last couple of days. Happier. Chatty, even.

'Let's go see what is going on,' Rowan said on impulse, and moved off the stoop and across the road before she could change her mind. She joined the cluster of people around Winsome.

'What's happening?' she asked.

The woman next to her, holding a baby whose sweet face poked out of a swaddle of blankets, looked at her. 'You haven't heard?'

Rowan shook her head. 'Heard what?'

'About the prophecy,' the woman said. 'About the Golden Children.'

Rowan looked automatically at Robbie in her arms and thought about the child, the little girl, growing inside her. 'What are the Golden Children?' she asked.

The woman shrugged. 'We're trying to find out. The fella on his blog who writes about Wilde Grove, he reckons the Golden Children are the next generation, the ones who will save the world.'

'Save the world?' Rowan was bewildered, and wished she could catch Winsome's eye, but Winsome had her head bent in conversation with Veronica, who had a phone pressed against her ear.

'Yeah,' the woman with the baby agreed. 'That's my kid, and yours too, right? We bring them up differently and that's what they'll do.' She pressed a kiss to her baby's plump cheek. 'The Golden Children will save the world.' She nodded and looked earnestly at Rowan. 'You agree?'

Rowan hugged Robbie closer. 'Bring them up differently?'

The question earned a beatific smile. 'To be Beacons, you see?'

And suddenly, Rowan did see.

'You get it,' the woman beside her said, looking at her and nodding her head. 'I'm Carly, by the way.'

'Yeah,' Rowan said. 'Hi, I'm Rowan. This is Robbie.'

Another nod, and the woman thrust a small piece of card at Rowan. 'Here, Rowan, I printed out a bunch. You can have one.'

Rowan took it and looked down at it.

'It's the prophecy,' Carly said.

'Who...' Rowan didn't know how to ask. Did someone just say a prophecy, or announce it, or proclaim it, or what?

'Who said it?' Carly shook her head. 'We don't know, yet.' She nudged an elbow into Rowan then. 'Wait up,' she said. 'Winsome's gonna speak.'

'You know Winsome?' Rowan asked, looking up.

'Everyone knows her,' Carly said. 'We know everyone in the Grove, right?'

Rowan nodded. She guessed Carly was right. It was hard not to know the Grove now. She looked at Winsome, who had her hands up, gesturing for quiet.

'Thank you, everyone,' Winsome said when the small crowd hushed. 'As you can probably tell, this latest event has taken us a bit by surprise.'

'You knew though, right?' one of the men in the group asked. 'About the prophecy? Someone must have said it, I mean, and written it down?'

Winsome nodded. 'Morghan and others have known about it, but it was only...' Winsome floundered for a moment. How did one describe how a prophecy was delivered? 'Well, it was only pronounced a few days ago.'

'So, who said it?' It was Carly who asked this, rocking

her small child in her arms. She glanced at Rowan, who found herself nodding and looking at Winsome in hope of an answer.

'I'm afraid I can't tell you that, yet,' Winsome said. 'As I said, this event has overtaken us somewhat.'

'You mean you weren't going to tell us?' The older woman who asked this shook her head, frowning, and a low murmur rippled through the people gathered outside the vicarage.

'Oh,' Winsome said. 'Of course it was going to become public – it's important for us all. It just didn't come out in the way the Grove had planned.'

This got some nodding heads in the crowd, and another ripple of comment, this time in agreement.

'So, when do we find out who said it and what it means?' Carly asked. 'Although it's pretty obvious what it means, isn't it?' She hugged her baby with a sudden, tender smile on her face.

'Well,' Winsome said, looking around at the people gathered there and seeing Rowan, Robbie on her hip. She smiled at them and Robbie promptly waved at her. Her smile widened, and she nodded at the crowd. 'I expect there will be an announcement about it on the Wilde Grove Website before the day is out.'

This sent a rather disappointed grumble through the men and women assembled.

'We want Morghan to talk to us about it,' Carly said. 'And the priestess who said it. We want to see them.' She looked inquiringly about herself and was met with nods all around.

Even Rowan found herself nodding. She hugged Robbie

closer and looked down at the printed card Carly had given her.

And safe from all, the Golden Children are born.

Her heart lifted at the line. Golden Children. Surely Carly was right, and that meant Robbie, and Carly's baby, and the one even now growing inside Rowan's womb.

Winsome hid her sigh. She'd rather anticipated this would be the case and was sure Morghan and Ambrose had had the same thought already. She lifted her hands for quiet again.

'I was talking to Morghan on the phone just a minute ago,' she said. 'She wants me to ask you all to please check the website to keep up to date with things, and that there will be some sort of event or discussion around the prophecy at the Ostara festivities next week.' Winsome paused, brow creasing thoughtfully.

'I believe something special has happened,' she said, pressing her hand to her chest. 'I personally believe that. I think we are being given hope in a world that needs hope, and a blueprint for the future that will serve us well.' She smiled. 'And now, I'm afraid I need to attend to some things. As always, Bridget's Sanctuary is open to all. Light a candle, say a prayer, support each other.'

WINSOME STEPPED AWAY AND INSIDE THE VICARAGE WHERE Veronica met her, brows raised.

'What is it?' Winsome asked.

'Someone just called for you – on the landline.'

'A parishioner?' Winsome asked. That was still how she thought of the people she ministered to in Wellsford. As parishioners, and why not? Bridget's Sanctuary still sat within a community. A parish of the heart.

Examining the contents of Ceridwen's cauldron had meant a lot of looking at things from a different perspective.

But Veronica was shaking her head and cleared her throat. 'Afraid not. It was a woman named Bethany, who said she was the secretary for Dean Morton.'

Winsome stopped on her trek down the hallway to the kitchen and turned to gape at Veronica. In the doorway to her study, Cù stood, tongue lolling.

'Dean Morton?'

Veronica nodded. Ignored the odd way Winsome was looking into the room she used as a study. Winsome was always peering about as though she could see things no one else could. Which of course, she could, although Veronica was resolute in her own determination not to go down the same road. Witnessing it second hand was plenty close enough.

'He wants to see you.'

'When?'

'Now,' Veronica said with a grimace. 'You don't have to, though, do you? He's not your boss or whatever now.'

Winsome swallowed down the sudden lump in her throat. 'Did Bethany say what he wanted?'

'Just the pleasure of your company,' Veronica told her. 'Do you want me to come with you?' She flattened her lips; she hadn't yet forgiven the man for wanting to bundle Winsome off to a convent, there to be wrapped in moth balls to gather dust. 'I can see already you're going to go.'

Cù walked down the hallway, straight through the

unsuspecting Veronica's legs to the front door where he turned to wait.

Winsome watched him silently for a moment, then sighed. 'You're right,' she said. 'I am going.'

'I'm coming,' Veronica said decisively. 'Don't argue. I'll drive.'

'Okay,' Winsome said, knowing that any arguing with Veronica was an exercise in futility. 'All right. I guess we'll just go now, then.'

'I'll grab my handbag,' Veronica said.

ROWAN WALKED BACK ACROSS THE ROAD, ONE HAND CUPPED around Robbie's ears. The wind was getting up again and she was sure it was going to rain. Again. She could hear the trees all around, their branches swooshing as the wind swept them this way, then that.

'Let's hope there's not going to be another thunderstorm,' she said to Robbie as she let them into the house, stepping over the threshold with a thrill of delight that this was her place. Hers and Robbie's, and...

Grace. Hadn't she decided at the hospital to name her Grace?

Robbie slipped from her arms and ran to the circle of his toys on the rug in front of the sofa. Rowan watched him, a great bubble of love rising inside her and bursting, making her cry out to him.

'I love you, Robbie,' she said, and he looked up at her and smiled, his orange hair tousled, his sweet face glowing.

A cup of tea, that was what she needed, Rowan decided, and moved into the kitchen, glancing out the window that looked out onto the road. Raindrops were turning the tarmac dark in great splotches, and in the churchyard, there still milled a group of people, Carly and her baby among them, coming together in clusters to speak, then spreading out again, then coming back together, as though they were part of something larger than themselves, something that lived and breathed.

Rowan shook her head and put the kettle on to boil. The rain fell harder, and the group across the road finally dispersed, chased away by the weather. Rowan made tea, glanced over at Robbie's sweet head bent over his toys, and then she wondered idly if she would see Mariah dancing on the lawn again later, at night, glowing gently in the rain as she pirouetted.

'Thank you,' she whispered. 'For letting me have your house.' In her mind, Mariah danced again, young and beautiful, thick dark hair in a waterfall down her back. Rowan poured a cup of tea and took it over to the table, then went to stand in front of the candles she'd set up on the windowsill.

The afternoon was growing dark from the rain and on impulse, Rowan picked up the battery-powered candles she'd gone and bought from Haven and switched them on. They were safer to use during the day while Robbie was about.

Robbie lifted his head, watched the two candles glow, yellow light radiating, then smiled to himself and went back to his playing.

Rowan looked at the lights in satisfaction, then remembered something, and went into her bedroom to fetch it. She found what she was looking for among the things she'd retrieved from the house she and Paul had shared, and she took it back to her little windowsill altar.

It was a jewellery box, given to her when she was small by her gran. Rowan wound up the key at the back then set it on the sill and opened the lid. A small ballerina twirled to the music.

Robbie came over and climbed on a chair to look, then did a wiggling dance to the music. Rowan laughed and copied him.

'We love to dance, don't we?' she asked.

He nodded and smiled widely at her. Rowan hugged him to her side. 'The lady who used to live here – she loved to dance too.'

Robbie pointed at the slowly spinning ballerina. 'Like her.'

'Yes,' Rowan said. 'Just like her. I'm playing this now to say thank you to her for letting us live here.'

Robbie looked up at her, a slight frown wrinkling his forehead. 'Fank you?'

Rowan gave him a squeeze. 'That's right. We've got a lot to be thankful for, that's what I think.'

'That's what I fink,' Robbie echoed, and Rowan laughed and popped him back on the floor where he could go back to his toys.

She looked at her little windowsill setup, and drew the card out of her pocket, the one that Carly had given her. Carly had done a nice job of printing it out, Rowan thought. There was the verse – the prophecy – and she'd put flowers and trees around it to decorate it. Rowan leant it against one of the candlesticks as the music wound down and the ballerina came to a graceful stop, one leg still lifted, foot pointed.

'Golden children,' Rowan murmured, and she put her hands against her gently swelling belly. She didn't know what it meant, but something about it gave her hope. For the future, hers and her children's. For the future of everyone, perhaps.

Rowan nodded. Hope. That's what the prophecy sounded like. Even in the midst of upheaval, there was going to be hope.

You just had to keep sight of what was precious.

49

Cù waltzed into Dean David Morton's office like he owned it. Winsome frowned at the spirit dog, grimaced at Bethany as the woman waved her straight in, and glanced back at Veronica who had threatened a scene if she wasn't allowed to accompany Winsome into the meeting.

Winsome wasn't sure what good it would do to have Veronica's company, but she had to admit that she appreciated the fierce loyalty of it.

She had, however, elicited Veronica's solemn promise that she wouldn't say a word when they were in there.

Cù parked himself beside Morton's desk and narrowed his doggy eyes. Winsome followed his gaze and came up short.

'Reverend Christie,' she said, and looked at him in confusion. 'What are you doing here?'

The resolutely erect figure of the reverent sniffed and looked at her with disdain.

'Keeping my promise,' he said in answer. 'To disclose your appalling actions.'

Winsome turned to look at the Dean. 'Why am I here?' she asked.

David Morton sighed, picked up a sheaf of papers from his desk and shuffled them, returned them to the same spot on his desk, then sighed again.

'Please,' he said finally, 'sit down, ladies.'

Winsome glanced at Veronica, turned back to the Dean. 'This is Veronica Faith,' she said. 'A friend.'

David nodded. Gestured at the chairs. 'Please sit.'

Winsome and Veronica sat. Christie stayed standing, back to the wall of the office.

'How can we help you, David?' Winsome asked.

Christie gave a little growl in the back of his throat. Winsome ignored him, kept her gaze on the Dean behind his great desk.

David Morton cleared his throat. 'Wilde Grove,' he said as preamble. Then he cleared his throat again. 'This prophecy business.'

Another snarl of contempt from Christie. Both Winsome and David ignored him. Veronica treated him to a look of pure disdain.

Winsome took an unobtrusive breath. 'What about it?' she asked.

'What's it about?' David wanted to know. 'Everyone is talking about it.' He shifted uncomfortably in his chair. 'The Archbishop wants to know what it's about.'

Winsome's eyebrows all but disappeared into her hair-line. 'The Archbishop?'

'Of Canterbury, yes,' David said.

'Of Canterbury?' Winsome echoed, and beside her, Veronica frowned. The Archbishop, she knew, was top dog in the church.

David swallowed, sighed. 'In fact, he wants to talk to you.'

'To me?' Winsome's voice came out as a squeak.

'Probably it would be better to talk to Morghan Wilde herself,' David said, running distracted fingers through his hair and leaving it in disarray. 'But the Archbishop isn't quite prepared for that yet. You're the next best thing.'

Now Christie launched himself forward. 'I object,' he said. 'Most strenuously.'

David looked wearily at the man. 'This isn't a law court,' he said.

'Nonetheless, the Archbishop talking to this woman is absurd. Out of the question.'

'Why?' Veronica asked. This pompous man was not endearing himself to her. Not one little bit.

'Because she's a scourge upon the church!' Christie roared. 'Because she's taken the teachings of the church and spat all over them!' Spittle flew from his mouth.

'Christie,' David intervened. 'Perhaps you'll leave me to it now. I've noted your concerns, but I'm afraid the Archbishop has told me his desire.'

The Reverend Christie worked his mouth around more and greater retorts, but no sound came out, fortunately. A moment later, he stormed towards the door.

'Who on earth was he?' Veronica asked, completely forgetting her promise to hold her tongue.

'He's the Anglican Chaplain at the hospital,' Winsome

said, and she looked at David. 'And totally unsuited to offering solace to those ill and dying.'

David leant back in his chair and looked at the ceiling. Another sigh welled up inside him. He snapped back upright. 'Will you see the Archbishop?' he asked.

Winsome considered him. 'When?' she asked, feeling pale at the suggestion and doing her best to hide it.

'He's expecting you in his office tomorrow morning at 8a.m.'

Winsome nodded, looked at Cù, who sat grinning at her. 'All right,' she said.

One did not say no to an audience with the Archbishop. And she was after all, still technically a clergywoman.

'All right,' David echoed, then cleared his throat. 'And if you could er, ask your friends about this so-called prophecy, that might be a good idea.'

Winsome nodded again, gave a slight smile. 'I can do that.' She stood up. 'You're looking well, otherwise, David,' she said. 'I'm glad to see it.'

'Long may it last,' David said sourly and stood to end the interview.

Veronica let them into the vicarage, shaking her head. 'Good grief,' she said. 'When is this rain going to end?'

At least it had chased away the crowds.

She glanced back at Winsome, took in the preoccupied expression and decided then and there. 'Right,' she said, briskly now. 'Something to eat, a cup of tea, and you can tell me why everyone is going bonkers over this so-called prophecy.' She shook her head. 'After all, I've met Clover and she's lovely, but no one can tell me she's not a bit odd.'

Veronica stalked through to the kitchen, put the takeaway curry on the table and got plates down. 'We should get Erin here to explain it to us,' she said, dipping into the cutlery drawer. 'Although I expect you'll be off to Ambrose's soon, and you can get your answers from him.' She pursed her lips, set two places at the table and glanced out at the rain. It was coming down in heavy silver sheets. She'd never known a spring like it. Was this global warming, she wondered?

The seas heave and come ashore.

Veronica shivered. She was not a fan of the prophecy. She never could have babies, and the two she'd adopted were grown now.

Winsome sat down at the table in front of one of the settings and watched wordlessly as Veronica filled a plate for her.

'I'm going with you tomorrow too,' Veronica said, her tone making it clear she would brook no argument on the matter.

Winsome nodded, mustered up a smile. 'Thank you,' she said, then finally blew out a breath. 'Is this real?' she asked.

'Which part?' Veronica asked, mouth turning down.

Winsome spread her hands. 'Any of it. All of it.' She picked up a fork, held it. 'The Archbishop.'

'The big cheese himself,' Veronica agreed, picking up her own fork and tucking in. Truthfully, she felt rather invigorated by it all. She wasn't interested in the prophecy, didn't even believe in prophecies, but the rest of it? Going to

Lambeth Palace to visit the Archbishop of Canterbury? That she could appreciate.

'It's all real,' she assured Winsome. 'Weird, of course, as everything Wilde Grove is, but real.' She ate a mouthful, swallowed, and smiled at Winsome. 'We're really getting up tomorrow morning at the crack of dawn to go down to London to see the Archbishop of Canterbury.' Veronica's eyes widened and she put down her fork. It clattered against the plate.

'What?' Winsome asked.

'Great balls of fire,' Veronica said. 'What on earth are we going to wear?'

AMBROSE MET HER UNDER THE SHELTER OF THE TREES.

'I don't know how you keep doing this,' Winsome said.

'Doing what?' Ambrose asked, frowning.

Winsome smiled up at him in the dimness. 'Meeting me. Knowing when I'm on my way.'

Frown disappearing, Ambrose grinned at her. 'I'm on the Winsome Wavelength, remember?'

She tucked her arm through his and laughed. 'You really are, aren't you?' Her laughter died and she watched Cù's ghostly form leading the way along the wooded path.

'What is it?' Ambrose asked. 'What's happened?'

Winsome shook her head. 'Oh, Ambrose,' she said. 'Where is this all leading?'

'Where is all what leading?'

She shook her head again, curls bouncing. 'This prophecy business. I'm not sure that I like it.'

'Why's that?' Ambrose asked.

Winsome didn't answer his question, but asked one of her own instead. 'What do you think of it, truly?' A small pause and she spoke again before he could muster an answer. 'I can't help feeling that prophecies and so on are so...superstitious. Like something we did well to leave behind.'

'Leave behind?'

A loose shrug, then Winsome burrowed closer to Ambrose. The evening was cool from the incessant rain.

'I'm not expressing myself very well, am I?' Winsome sighed. 'It's just, I don't know. Prophecies? They seem so Dark Ages.'

Now it was Ambrose's turn to laugh. 'Oh, Winsome,' he said. 'I'm sorry. I shouldn't be laughing.'

She poked him in the side, a smile wide on her face. 'Then stop.'

He did. 'There have always been prophecies,' he said. 'About twenty seven percent of the Christian Bible is prophetic in nature.'

Winsome's shoulders slumped. 'I know,' she said. 'Perhaps I'm just not used to them happening so close to home, and outside of fantasy novels.'

Astonished, Ambrose looked at her. 'Are you calling your bible a fantasy novel?'

'Oh goodness,' Winsome shook her head. 'No, of course not. That didn't come out right, did it?'

Ambrose laughed again. 'Not quite,' he said, and took her hand as the path widened onto the lawn of Blackthorn House.

They dashed across to the front door and tumbled inside damp and glad for the fire in the grate.

'I'll put the kettle on,' Ambrose said. 'And you can tell me what happened today.'

Winsome followed him to the kitchen. 'It's not so much what happened today,' she said, 'as what's going to happen tomorrow.'

She slumped into a chair. 'Ambrose, the Archbishop of Canterbury has asked me to present myself to his office tomorrow morning at 8a.m. because he wants to talk to me about this bothersome prophecy.'

Ambrose put down the tin of tealeaves and turned slowly to Winsome. 'The Archbishop?'

'Uh huh.'

'Of Canterbury?'

'Yup.'

'Thats...' Ambrose searched for the word. 'Extraordinary,' he said. 'Absolutely extraordinary.'

'It's terrifying, you mean,' Winsome said, and grimaced at him.

Ambrose came and sat down opposite her and reached for her hands. 'But Winsome,' he said. 'It's marvellous.'

She looked at him as though he'd grown a second head. 'What do you mean it's marvellous?'

Ambrose was nodding. 'I said you'd be the bridge, didn't I?' He smiled at her. 'A prophecy of my own come true.'

Winsome frowned at him. 'You really think this is marvellous?' she said after a good minute.

He nodded.

'But what am I going to tell him about it? I don't know what it means.'

Ambrose squeezed her hands and straightened. 'Yes,

you do, darling. It means hope.' He stood up, kissed her on the forehead and went back to finish making the tea.

He brought the pot to the table, set a cup and saucer in front of her. 'Winsome, the Archbishop wants the same thing as we do.'

'He does?'

Ambrose nodded. 'He wants people taking care of themselves and each other, minding their spiritual life, being the beautiful, blossoming souls that we are meant to be.'

That was what they were supposed to be, Winsome thought. People living in the grace of God. She thought of Ceridwen and her cauldron. People living deep and inspired lives.

'Will you come with me?' Winsome asked. 'If you come, you'll be able to tell him these things much more eloquently that me.' Winsome sighed. 'I'm going to trip over my tongue and make a fool of myself.' She nodded. 'Besides, you know Wilde Grove much better than I.'

But Ambrose was already shaking his head. 'The Archbishop hasn't reached out to Morghan or I, Winsome. He's reaching out to you.'

'But I'm terrified!'

Ambrose smiled gently and poured the tea. 'He's just a man like any other, Winsome.'

'No, he's not,' Winsome countered. 'That would be like saying Morghan is just a woman like any other.'

'Isn't she?'

Winsome frowned, her mouth turning down. 'She'd say so,' she admitted. 'She'd just say her path is the path that anyone can follow and has just led her more deeply into the Wildwood.'

Ambrose's smile widened. 'You know her well,' he said. 'I think that's exactly what she'd say.'

Winsome wrinkled her nose. 'Your point?'

'The Archbishop is just a man like any other,' Ambrose said.

He smiled. 'Whose path has led him further into the Wildwood.'

50

______

VERONICA PULLED INTO THE DRIVEWAY OF HAWTHORN HOUSE and looked at Erin as she hopped out of the car.

'Good thing I called Erin last night, isn't it?' Veronica said to Winsome who was fidgeting in the seat next to her. 'And such a lucky coincidence they needed to go to London as well.'

Winsome blew out a breath. 'I don't think I can do this.'

'That's the fifth time you've said that this morning.'

Winsome deflated. 'That's because I don't think I can do this.'

Erin came back to the car, Morghan beside her. Winsome got out. 'Here,' she said to Morghan. 'You can take the front seat.'

But Morghan shook her head. 'I'd rather the back,' she said, then reached out and touched her hand to Winsome's arm. 'Are you very nervous?' she asked.

Winsome groaned. 'I don't think I've been this nervous since I was fifteen years old and waiting for Alan

460

Reynolds to kiss me behind the science block at high school.'

Morghan tipped her head back and laughed. 'Sit in the back with me,' she said. 'We can talk about what you're going to say to the Archbishop.'

'Oh thank Jesus,' Winsome said, and scrambled into the back seat of Veronica's car.

'It was one of our priestesses, yes,' Morghan said.

The Breakfast Show host switched his attention to Erin. 'You?' he asked.

'No,' Erin said with a smile. 'Not me, not this time.'

'Well, we all want to know who, then,' Anthony asked, and he raised his eyebrows at Jillian, his co-host. 'Don't we?'

Jillian nodded. 'We do, but maybe even more than that, we want to know what it means. Let's go over it, if that's all right by you, line by line.'

Erin swallowed, not noticeably, she hoped and wanted badly to look at Morghan sitting next to her. She was finding it difficult to keep her energy calm, and exhaled slowly, letting herself feel Morghan's presence beside her, the steadfastness of it.

There, she thought, while trying simultaneously to listen to what the woman, Jillian was saying. There was that word again. Steadfast.

That was what Morghan had said to them all the afternoon before.

Steadfast, even into death.

Erin couldn't help her shiver. Even while she knew she'd lived and died over and over, there was still a small piece of her that was frightened by the thought of dying. She knew it was silly, knew even in her heart that death was only a transformation, as natural and necessary as breathing. But still.

Steadfast. She closed her eyes for a moment, let Morghan's presence wash over her, felt for Macha and found her, not at her shoulder as she did when Macha wished to guide her, but inside herself, Macha's strength within her own.

Erin tuned back in to the host's talk.

'Why does it have to be so cryptic?' Jillian asked. She laughed and turned to Anthony. 'I've always had this problem with Nostradamus's prophecies as well, and who was the other?'

'Mother Shipton,' Anthony said promptly. They'd done their homework, of course, scripted out the bones of their interview. He smiled at Morghan. 'You're aware of Mother Shipton's pronouncements?'

'I am, yes,' Morghan said. 'There have always been soothsayers, throughout history.'

Jillian nodded emphatically. 'So, you're not denying that this is a prophecy, then?'

Erin looked at Morghan, held her breath.

But Morghan did not let her calm demeanour change. Instead, she smiled and let the course of history change. Was this enough to change the course of history, she wondered? Not on its own, perhaps, but it was a signpost to a different place, a better outcome.

'No,' she said. 'I am not denying it.'

Erin watched the expressions of the two hosts. It was obvious that they didn't know what to think of the matter, and Erin was with them on that one. She wasn't sure she knew what to think of it either. She wished suddenly for Stephan. It now really felt as though they were on the brink of a shift. Perhaps, she thought, they were finally moving from what she knew many had been calling Tower Time, into...into whatever it was that came next.

There was a sensation within her then, as though she had been dipped in something warm and comforting. It spread like warm milk through her and the thought came within the wash of it: the time of the Star. That's what came next, she thought. After the Tower, then the Star. The shining of them all, the spread of beacons through the land, guided by the North Star, nourishing both the earth and all on it.

The star would shine upon them as they picked through the rubble, as they gathered themselves to build a new world.

She swayed slightly where she sat and felt Morghan's attention shift suddenly to her. Erin licked her lips, steadied herself, and tried to look as though nothing had happened.

Morghan though, had felt the subtle change in Erin's consciousness, and Erin's correction of it, and it was an effort to make herself turn her attention back to their hosts.

'So, the first line,' Jillian was saying. 'We're going to go through this line by line, and you can tell us all what it means.'

Anthony nodded. 'We know Jack Newton has already speculated on the meaning behind it – in fact, everyone is abuzz doing the same.' He turned to the screen on the wall between them, where social media comments from the various platforms were now scrolling slowly by, each of them propounding different meanings.

'As you can see,' Anthony continued. 'There's a lot of speculation, so we're hoping you can put that speculation to rest for us.'

Morghan inclined her head, still aware that Erin wasn't quite all with her. 'I can do my best,' she said.

'You don't know for certain?' Jillian said, pouncing on her.

'Symbols are like onions,' Morghan said with a smile. 'There's always another layer to them.'

'Tell us what the first two lines refer to, then,' Jillian said. 'It sounds like they're talking about weather – climate change, perhaps. Would you say that's a fair assessment?'

Morghan glanced briefly at Erin, then turned and took a breath. 'That would be my immediate understanding of it,' she said. 'But it also works on another level, as most symbolism does, which is why so many prophecies through the centuries are uttered in this way, as it takes only a few words to draw a large and nuanced picture in which the meaning can be divined.' She paused. 'Rather like the way our dreams speak to us.'

'Our dreams?' Anthony asked. 'You mean the dreams we have at night, asleep.'

'Yes,' Morghan answered.

Anthony laughed. 'I always put those down to having too much pepperoni pizza.' He laughed again, and Jillian joined in.

Morghan smiled slightly and waited, scoping out how Erin was faring.

Erin was dazed, but lucid. She looked at Morghan and nodded slightly at her inquiring look.

'All right,' Anthony said, making himself continue. He didn't believe in prophecies, or Wilde Grove, for that matter. They were a bunch of kooks, for the most part, he thought, but he had to admit, that the two women sitting opposite him and Jillian, well, they did kind of have an atmosphere about them. He didn't know what he meant by that, exactly. It was as if they were wearing perfume that wafted about and made everything seem a bit different.

A bit special?

He sniffed. 'So, if it's not just talking about climate change, what is it talking about?'

Erin felt Morghan's pause to let her answer, and she found her voice. 'It's not only the climate that's been changing,' she said. 'But us, over centuries. We've become disconnected, from each other, from our own essential natures.' She glanced at Morghan, continued. 'From our souls, the magic that is within us, that we can do. These lines tell us that the turmoil in this world is also within us.' She closed her mouth and resisted the urge to nod emphatically.

'You've been preaching against materialism for some time now,' Anthony said, trying and failing to tamp down his irritation. 'But I like my car and my house, and all the stuff I have. It makes me feel good, having all that.' He shifted slightly, felt Jillian's disquiet. Yeah, he was going off script. 'I don't know whether I'd bother swapping that for the ability to be a lamp post for a bunch of ravens.'

Erin found herself laughing and smothered it quickly. 'Ravens are the least of it,' she said. 'What we're really suggesting here, is that we find our value as humans in something deeper, older, and more meaningful than how much we own.'

But Anthony was shaking his head, not knowing why really that he felt so suddenly argumentative. It wasn't how this was all supposed to go. 'Are you calling me shallow?' he asked. 'Because I like having a fancy car?'

'You can like having a fancy car as much as you want to,' Erin said, frowning a little. 'You can like all sorts of things. We're simply advocating for something deeper to measure our intrinsic worth against.'

Jillian interrupted, throwing Anthony a furious look that made him snap his mouth shut and shift uncomfortably on his buttocks.

'What about the Golden Children, then,' Jillian said. 'What can you tell us about them? Who are they?'

'Yeah,' Anthony said. 'Peel a few onion layers back on that one for us.' There was a warning mutter from his earpiece.

Morghan stepped in to field the question, with a gentle smile. 'We are the Golden Children,' she said. 'Each and every one of us who develops a deeper connection with our own hearts and souls.'

Jillian raised her finely plucked eyebrows. 'It's that easy?' She checked the sheaf of paper in her lap. 'Why will we be in rabbit holes and bird nests, then? That sounds a bit obscure to me.'

'It means that everyone with such a connection will be also connected to the earth, in a symbiotic relationship that ultimately is nourishing for both.'

A blank look from Jillian. 'Nourishing for both what?'

'Ourselves and everything on the planet, including the planet itself,' Morghan said.

'DID THAT GO WELL?' ERIN ASKED OUTSIDE THE STUDIO. 'I don't feel like that went especially well.'

Morghan shook her head. 'It could have gone better.'

'That's what I think,' Erin agreed. 'It could have gone better. Ugh. That long drive for nothing much. I hope Mum and Winsome are getting on better.' She shook her head. 'What was wrong with Anthony Chisholm, then?'

'We challenged his view of himself,' Morghan said. She stretched slightly and sighed. 'I'm afraid his response will be echoed up and down the country.' She glanced through the doors to the street and her mouth turned down. 'There are people out there,' she said.

'In the rain?' Erin asked. 'I wish the weather would be helpful for once and put everyone off.' She risked a peek. 'Protesters,' she said, heart falling.

Morghan pulled out her phone, checked her messages. Nothing from Winsome. 'We'll go and wait in the cafeteria, I think.'

They slipped through the building, knowing the way from previous visits to the television studio.

The woman who served them their coffees gazed at them wide-eyed, but didn't say anything but the amount they needed to pay. Erin was relieved.

'I didn't enjoy that interview,' Erin said as they chose a table in the mostly empty cafeteria and sat down on the hard plastic chairs.

'What happened?' Morghan asked. 'I felt something change in your energy.'

Erin nodded. Picked up a spoon absently and scooped some of the froth from her cappuccino.

'I was thinking about the prophecy and Tower Time, and how what Clover said maybe marks the change that is coming, from the time of the Tower to that of the Star.' Erin gazed over the table at Morghan. 'And when I had that thought, it was like it washed through me – a sort of confirmation, I guess.'

'Washed through you?'

Erin nodded. 'Yeah. Like I was suddenly dipped in something warm. It was a bit weird, now that I think about it.'

But Morghan was smiling broadly. 'Not weird at all,' she said. She picked up her cup and looked delightedly over the rim at Erin. 'One of the things I think happens when you follow the path in the way that you have been learning to, is that you become in yourself, something of a divining rod.'

'A divining rod?'

'Yes, receiving confirmation, or otherwise, in your body.'

'Huh.' Erin thought about this. 'Has this happened to you?'

Morghan nodded. 'When I seek confirmation on something, I feel it like something pressing against my face.' She took a sip of the coffee. It was strong and hot. She smiled. 'And when I get a negative answer, I feel a sinking in the pit of my stomach.'

'Who needs pendulums, then,' Erin said, bemused.

'Pendulums are a great tool,' Morghan said. 'But sometimes you don't end up needing them.' She paused, thought about what else Erin had said. 'The Star,' she said.

Erin nodded. 'I think that's right too. Isn't it? Follow the North Star, shine like a beacon.'

'Yes,' Morghan said. 'I believe you're correct.'

'Sort of like the dawning of the Age of Aquarius,' Erin said with a laugh, thinking of the song her jet-setting grandmother had once told her she hated more than any other. 'Except it's the Dawning of the Age of the Star, because let's face it, the Age of Aquarius was a bit of a washout.'

She sobered then, thinking of the interview they'd just done, and the protesters outside the building. 'But Morghan,' she said. 'How can I feel that we'll be moving onto the next stage of things, when I'm really not sure we're getting the message through?' She paused. 'Or at least we didn't this morning.'

But Morghan was shaking her head. 'We are,' she said. 'But so far only to those receptive to it.' She glanced at the cafeteria windows, but they opened up onto an interior courtyard so she couldn't see the street, thankfully. 'Things are crumbling – the tower, as you say, is falling. We will soon be wandering about in the mess from it and gearing up, I hope, to enter the rebuilding phase. That could take a long time.'

Erin thought of the protesters that seemed to follow them everywhere they went. 'But there are so many who are against us – no, not even that. They hate us.' She frowned at Morghan. 'Are we just making things worse? We're creating this huge divide, and we're doing it by promoting unity and community.' She shook her head. 'I'm just not sure I understand how things are going to work out. What are we doing?'

'We're following the pincushion,' Morghan said. 'Following the path of spirit.'

'You know,' Erin said, leaning back and looking at Morghan. 'I was doing some reading recently, and the spirit paths were what they called the path everyone walked from church to cemetery. That doesn't make it sound good, you know.'

Morghan tipped back her head and laughed. 'From church to cemetery,' she said. 'But that is it, you know, and I think it's marvellous.'

Erin stared at her, frowning. 'How can you laugh? How is it marvellous?'

'From life to death, Erin,' Morghan said. 'That's the journey we all take, and it is what we come here to experience, in a way we just can't anywhere else.'

Winsome stuck out her hand. 'Look,' she hissed. 'I'm shaking.'

Veronica took the hand in her own and gave it a good squeeze. 'He's just a man, Winsome. Once upon a time some tired and rather marvellous woman changed his nappies and rocked him through the night, just as happened to us all. You're going to be fine.'

Winsome nodded, gave herself a shake and looked around for Cù. She'd hoped he would have the good sense to stay at home, but when Veronica had parked the car and they'd gotten out, she'd seen him standing on the steps, tongue lolling, grinning at her like it was all a grand joke.

Now, the spirit dog was nowhere to be seen. Winsome smoothed down her skirt, a sober charcoal wool, with matching jacket. It was her smartest outfit, no matter that Veronica's mouth had turned down at the sight of it. She tucked her finger in the high collar then stuck her hands resolutely in her lap. She'd worn the blouse with the high collar deliberately, as a sort of reminder – to whom, she wasn't quite sure – that once she'd worn the collar of a clergy person.

'I want to go home,' she said.

'What?'

Winsome stood up. She couldn't stand it anymore. They'd been sitting in the finely panelled waiting room for twenty minutes and she didn't think she could do it a minute longer.

'I need to get out of here.' She stuck her finger in her collar again, wishing to all heck and back that she'd chosen something else to wear. 'I think I'm having a hot flush,' she said.

Veronica looked at her critically, shook her head. 'Anxiety attack, more likely. Sit back down and take a few deep breaths.'

'No.' Winsome shook her head. 'I have to go. Where's the way out?' She looked around in a growing panic.

'Miss Clark?'

A young man in clerical garb stood in the doorway. 'The Archbishop will see you now, if you'd like to follow me?'

Winsome's eyes widened, and she looked frantically at Veronica, who stood up and smoothed her own skirt.

'I'm afraid you'll need to wait here,' the young man said to Veronica, who blinked at him, not understanding.

'I'm here to support Winsome,' Veronica said.

'She'll be fine,' he replied. 'I promise.'

Winsome found her voice. 'It's okay, Veronica,' she said, and gave a sudden, resolute nod. 'I'll be all right.'

Veronica looked at her through narrowed eyes, then

sighed and sat back down. One didn't, she supposed, argue with the Archbishop of Canterbury. 'I'll wait for you here.'

Winsome gave her a smile that was more grimace, then allowed herself to be ushered out of the room and into another.

A man came toward her, hand outstretched. 'Reverend Clark? I'm pleased to meet you.' He took Winsome's hand, shook it gently, and smiled at her deer in the headlights look. 'I need to thank you for coming at such short notice.'

Winsome nodded, then felt like her head was bobbing foolishly on a rubber neck and made herself stop. 'I'm glad to be of any assistance possible, Your Excellency.'

The Archbishop nodded and gestured for Winsome to take one of two chairs placed conversationally together, a small table between them.

Winsome sat, tucking her knees together and risking a glance at the other men in the room. There were only two, one of whom was obviously ready to take notes. Winsome gripped her hands in her lap, hoping no one would see their shaking.

'I'm glad you said that, Reverend Clark,' the Archbishop said. 'It will be helpful, I think, to get your perspective on recent events. You are in the position of having a unique insight, I think.'

'You are kind to call me Reverend, Excellency,' Winsome said. 'But you must also know that I've been removed from holding a position in the Church.'

His Excellency nodded, then leant forward a little in his chair. 'But you are still a member of the Church, are you not? You do still call yourself a Christian?'

Winsome took a breath. Here was the question she'd

been expecting, and right up front, too. Well, she couldn't blame the man for asking. She tried not to look at Cù, who had planted himself right at the Archbishop's side.

'Living in Wellsford has been an education,' Winsome said, trying to make a beginning in answering what was by no matter a straightforward enquiry.

The man not taking notes at the side of the room cleared his throat. 'You were removed from your position for joining in the Wilde Grove's rituals, I believe.'

Winsome looked at him, saw the censorship in his expression. 'You know that I was,' she said, her nerves suddenly calming. She loosened the knot her fingers were in and looked back to the Archbishop.

'You know that I was,' she repeated. 'And also that I have come to know Morghan Wilde very well.'

'And Ambrose McKeon, so we hear.' The same man to the side again.

'Yes, and Ambrose McKeon,' Winsome said. She drew breath and focused on the lively, intelligent face of the Archbishop. 'Wellsford has been a unique opportunity to discover the world in a way I had always yearned to, but not known how.'

The priest opened his mouth to retort but the Archbishop waved a hand to quiet him, looking intently at Winsome instead.

'In what way have you discovered the world?' he asked.

'I have learnt of its great depths, Excellency,' Winsome said, and she allowed herself a smile. 'I have learnt what it looks like when people live lives of soul-led purpose and understanding.' She shook her head slightly. 'When I lived in the contemplative community, I thought I had come close to living a life filled with God's Holy Spirit, but now that I have spent a year in Wellsford, I realise that I had only touched the surface of it.'

His Excellency nodded thoughtfully. 'What are they trying to achieve?' he asked. 'Morghan Wilde. What is she trying to achieve?'

'The same thing the Church wants, Excellency,' Winsome said. 'For people to live deep, meaningful lives that are expressions of connection, community, and love.'

'She believes in reincarnation,' the Archbishop said.

'Yes.'

'Do you now share this belief, among others of hers that the Church does not accept as true?'

'Does it matter?' Winsome asked, brows raised. 'I will soon be leaving the Church.'

'Hmm.' His Excellency leant back, contemplating the woman in front of him. 'Perhaps it does,' he said.

Winsome couldn't see how, but she decided to answer anyway. 'I have seen how living with what Morghan and others would call the knowledge of their continued and repeated lives colours their experiences and choices in this lifetime,' she said. 'I appreciate the value and purpose they find in that.'

The Archbishop's lips twitched. 'A very diplomatic answer, Reverend Clark,' he said. 'But not quite the answer I was looking for.'

Winsome smiled back at him. There were still nervous flutterings in her stomach, but she felt remarkably calm now that she was in the room talking to the man.

Like Ambrose had told her, the Archbishop was just a man. Just a man who had dedicated his life to going down the path of the spirit.

'The direct answer, since that's what you wish, is that it makes no difference whether I might have lived a hundred lives, or if this is my one precious time here on earth.' Winsome nodded gently. 'I am called to live well and deeply, to be of service in every way that I may, to hold and console, to preach peace and healing, to follow the stations of my heart and to love from the very depths of it.'

His Excellency leant back in his chair and contemplated the woman in front of him. She'd calmed down since they'd begun talking to each other properly, and he could feel the depth and breadth of her convictions. She was not doing what she was for politics or applause, but for the love of God.

'The Apostle's Creed?' he asked.

Winsome smiled. 'I believe in God, the Father almighty, creator of heaven and earth. I believe in Jesus Christ, his only Son, our Lord.'

She smiled again. 'Amen,' she said.

'Amen,' His Excellency echoed. 'All right, then. Winsome – may I call you Winsome?'

'Please,' Winsome said.

He nodded. 'The Wilde Grove prophecy,' he said. 'What can you tell me about that? Do you know who said it?'

'Yes,' Winsome said. 'I know who said it.'

'It was not Morghan Wilde, or – what is the name of her one-day successor?'

Winsome was sure he knew Erin's name, but she responded anyway. 'Erin Faith,' she said.

'Ah, yes. The one who commands ravens.' He leant forward. 'I've watched all the videos, many times. How did she do that?'

'Unintentionally,' Winsome said with a wry twist of the lips.

'Seriously, though.'

'I'm sure you've also watched the interviews on television in which Erin herself answers that question.'

The Archbishop sighed. 'I have. So, the prophecy, then.' He blinked. 'Should we call it a prophecy?'

'I think so, yes,' Winsome said. 'That is what Morghan is calling it.'

'And Ms Wilde explains it how?'

'I believe she is on The Breakfast Show right now doing just that,' Winsome said.

The Archbishop's eyebrows rose toward his thinning hairline. 'Indeed?'

'Yes.'

'I shall watch that with interest. But in the meantime, indulge me, please. Who are the Golden Children?'

Winsome thought of her conversation with Ambrose the night before, with Morghan in the car that morning. 'The prophecy is simple,' she said. 'We are the Golden Children, all of us.'

'In what way in particular?'

'You and I would say we are the children of God, and thus are precious souls each of us.'

His Excellency considered this. 'And the rest of it is about the climate?'

Winsome inclined her head. 'Yes, but with the implication that if we realise and live soul-led lives, that we will enter into a new relationship with the world.'

The black-clad priest against the wall spoke up again. 'One in which, presumably, the trees sing to us.'

Winsome smiled. 'Yes,' she said. 'One which is reciprocal, rather than one in which we are placed in dominion over everything.

52

ROWAN PUSHED OPEN THE DOOR TO THE MEDICAL PRACTICE and ushered Robbie in. They'd walked, not even taking the pushchair because everything in Wellsford was right around the corner.

'Hello,' she said to the receptionist. 'I have an appointment?'

Mrs Bagshaw nodded. 'Rowan Sutherland? You're right on time.'

Rowan nodded, but suddenly she was wondering if she had to spend the rest of her life being Mrs Sutherland. Perhaps she could change back to her maiden name? Or wasn't it important? She found it hard to tell.

'Take a seat in the waiting room, please. Doctor Lindquist will be with you shortly.'

Rowan sidled into the waiting room, Robbie hanging shyly onto her leg. 'Oh,' she said, when she saw who else was in there.

Julia put down her gardening magazine and smiled awkwardly. She didn't remember the young woman's name.

'Hello,' Rowan said. 'It's Julia, isn't it? Mrs Thorpe?'

'It's Miss, but Julia will be fine,' Julia said on a sigh. 'I'm afraid I don't remember your name.'

'Rowan.' Rowan nodded, smiled, and stroked Robbie's head. 'This is Robbie. I can't thank you enough for letting us rent your house.'

'My aunt's house,' Julia said.

'That's right. Your aunt's house. I'm so grateful. Robbie loves it too.'

Julia smoothed the magazine in her lap and shook her head. 'It's better if it's not just sitting empty.'

Rowan nodded. 'Your aunt,' she said tentatively.

Erin and Winsome had warned her away from talking to Julia about Mariah, but wasn't this too good an opportunity to miss? She swallowed and dove on in.

'How did she die, if you don't mind me asking?'

Julia's hands clenched on her magazine and she made herself smooth it out again. There was a lovely photograph of a rose on the front. One of the old-fashioned tea varieties she was so fond of. She looked at its soft salmon colour and felt better. A pre-1940 variety. She murmured the name to herself. 'Sparrieshoop.'

'I'm sorry?' Rowan said.

Julia straightened. 'My aunt went missing last year,' she said. She may as well tell the girl, who was bound to find out anyway. Anyone who lived in Wellsford could tell her. 'She's not been found and is only presumed dead.'

Rowan's eyes widened, and she shook her head, stunned. 'Missing?' she asked. 'But...'

She'd been about to say that she'd seen her. Rowan hauled Robbie onto her lap and shook her head.

Julia nodded. 'Winsome's told me you've seen her.'

'She did?' It came out as little more than a squeak.

Julia nodded. 'She said you saw her dancing. That she looked young again.'

'Oh, she was young,' Rowan told her. 'She was beautiful.'

Julia's mouth flattened and she looked away.

'Where...where did she go missing? Was it around here?' Rowan winced as she asked the questions, but she'd thought Mariah was dead. That made her pause. She expected Mariah must be dead, if she was seeing her ghost. 'Oh my goodness,' she said, pressing a hand to her mouth. 'I'm sorry. You must have hoped she was still alive.'

The nurse popped her head around the doorway and smiled at Julia, who stood up in relief and looked at Rowan.

'She is alive,' Julia said. 'For her sins.' She rolled up the magazine and followed the nurse out of the room.

Rowan was still sitting, baffled by the conversation, when a tall man filled the doorway.

'Mrs Sutherland?' he asked, brows raised.

Rowan blinked at him, then stood quickly, putting Robbie on her hip. 'Yes,' she said. 'That's me.'

'I am very glad to meet you,' Kurt said, and smiled at her. 'Will you come this way, please?'

'Jack Newton's written about you and Morghan on his blog,' Stephan said, sitting at the table in Ash Cottage and looking at Erin over the screen of her laptop.

'Of course he has,' Erin said. 'He reports everything we do.'

'Mostly fairly, to his credit,' Stephan said, and put out a hand to ruffle Burdock's ears. 'He wants to know what happened at the nine minute 21 second mark of your interview on The Breakfast Show.' Stephan smiled. 'I wouldn't mind knowing, either.'

Erin's eyes widened, and she came over to peer at the computer screen.

'He embedded the YouTube recording of it in his blog,' Stephan said. 'The better to dissect it.'

'I'll bet,' Erin said, then bent, dropped a kiss on Stephan's forehead before stalking back to the kitchen where she was trying, nonchalantly, to whip up a batch of cupcakes. It wasn't really going well, and she was starting to doubt the wisdom of testing her baking skills.

'You need to cream the butter and sugar some more,' Stephan said.

'I've about broken my arm doing it already,' Erin said, hands somehow sticky and gritty with the mixture.

'And then beat after each egg goes in.'

Erin groaned. 'Why doesn't this come naturally to me?'

Stephan laughed then looked back at the screen. 'Nine minutes and 21 seconds,' he reminded her.

Erin wrinkled her nose and picked up the mixing bowl again. 'Okay,' she said. 'I'll tell you that, if you tell me why this is so hard?'

'Because it's hard,' Stephan said, then grinned at the look she threw him. 'I mean it – your butter's too hard. It needs to soften to room temperature. Makes it much easier. You can't cream butter straight out of the fridge.'

Erin groaned again. 'How do you get to be an expert on cooking, baking, and gardening?'

'I'm naturally keen on cooking, Teresa taught me to garden, and Simon taught me to bake.' Stephan grinned. 'I bribed him with fresh fruit and veg until he agreed to teach me.'

Erin put down the bowl and narrowed her eyes at him. 'You what?'

Stephan gave a graceful shrug and Burdock shifted closer, under Stephan's arm. 'That's what I did.'

'You're a bit of a kitchen wizard, aren't you?' Erin said. She put the bowl down and washed her hands. She'd leave the butter to warm up now. Better than trying to beat it into submission.

She sat at the table. 'What does Newton say about it?'

Stephan didn't even have to look at the blog post. He'd read it twice already. Watched the video through the whole thirty minutes of the interview.

'Quite a bit about the prophecy, of course, and some speculation on who the Oracle is,' he said, straightening and rubbing Burdock's shoulder with one hand. 'But he's really interested in the fact that something obviously happened, that you went woo woo and that Morghan noticed it, even as the Breakfast pair obviously didn't.'

'No, they didn't.' Erin pushed back a strand of hair. 'Is that what Jack Newton called it? I went woo woo?'

Stephan smiled at her. 'Direct quote,' he said.

'Huh.' Erin paused, thought about it. 'Well, I had this thought, that was all, that the Tower – you know, the Tarot card, Tower Time, and all that?'

Stephan nodded.

'Well,' Erin said. 'I just had the thought that the tower is about to finish its fall and that we'll all soon be bumbling about all shell-shocked in the rubble.' She shivered at the thought of what possibly might be the thing that would bring the tower finally completely down.

Stephan thought about that, nodded again. 'Yeah,' he said. 'Could be.'

'And on the heels of that thought, I guess,' Erin said. 'Was that we would be getting onto the next card in the deck.'

'The Star.'

Erin shrugged. 'Yeah. And when I had that thought, this sort of great wave of confirmation washed through me. Like, I could feel the agreement. It was a physical response.' She got up and went back to her mixing bowl. She wanted to take the cupcakes with her for her early shift at the care home the next day.

'I think that's what Clover's prophecy is about too,' Erin said.

'How's that?'

'Well,' said Erin. 'Isn't it? Rebuilding the world? The Great Returning as Morghan and the Fae call it. Living differently. We've broken it, we will need to rebuild it.'

'Which won't be easy,' Stephan said, his tone one of warning. 'Others will fight against our vision of the future. There's plenty out there against it. And it's still crumbling about us all.'

'And there are plenty who will get caught in the middle of things too, through little fault of their own,' Erin said. She closed her eyes, then opened them and grinned at Stephan. 'But first,' she said. 'We have Ostara the day after tomorrow, then next week we get to celebrate our engagement with our friends.'

'I'm looking forward to that,' Stephan agreed.

'We've got to keep celebrating the wins, don't we?' Erin asked, coming over to bump her hip against Stephan's shoulder. He put his arm around her and hugged her to him.

'We absolutely do,' he said.

'And then we just keep on walking the Way, wherever it takes us,' Erin said, resting her head on his.

Steadfast even into death.

She closed her eyes.

'MORGHAN SAID…'

Veronica harrumphed. 'I know what Morghan said. I was there, remember. Driving us back from London.' She looked at Winsome, brows raised. 'I want to know what you think of it.' She touched a hand to her chest, above her heart. 'Here, what do you feel about it in your heart?'

Winsome stopped pacing and gazed at Veronica. It was funny, she thought, how good a friend Veronica had become. It hadn't been too long ago since she'd been consoling Veronica in the churchyard, and now here Veronica was, doing much the same for her.

'I don't know,' she said now.

'Then you'd best find out,' Veronica said. 'I'm going to go put my feet up for a while. That was an early start and an eventful day.' She looked pointedly at Winsome. 'You give it some good consideration,' she said. 'And make up your own mind. You don't have to do what Morghan tells you.'

'Morghan didn't tell me what to do,' Winsome said, while thinking that she wished that Morghan had done exactly that, in the car on the way back, when she'd repeated what the Archbishop had asked.

'I think I'll go over to the Sanctuary,' Winsome said.

It was cool and blustery outside and Winsome glanced up at the sky, a frown above her eyes. Surely, she thought, it wasn't going to rain some more? The ground was already drenched.

Bridget's Sanctuary was blessedly empty when she went in, and she stopped at the font, dipped her finger into the water of Bridget's sacred well, which was how she thought of it now, funny how fast that had happened, and blessed herself with it before moving up to the front of the small church where she lit one of the candles – Bridget's sacred flame – and got down on her knees.

The Archbishop's words swam round and round inside her head, little fishies darting around their fishbowl. Winsome closed her eyes, tried to breathe steadily, tried to pray.

Who to, though? She shook her head. Hadn't she sorted all this out over the last few months? Hadn't she come to terms with her strange dual life? Jesus on one hand, Ceridwen with her cauldron, Bridget with her bright flame on the other? They didn't have to cancel each other out.

Winsome snorted, startling herself, and she glanced quickly around the building. Still no one in it. That was good. Just five minutes to pray, that was all she asked.

About the Archbishop's request. Suggestion. Which had it been?

Winsome shook her head. She knew what Ambrose was going to say. He'd be gleeful. Tell her she was the bridge.

Maybe she was or maybe she wasn't. It seemed though, that she had to decide now. Officially.

'Lord of my heart and soul,' she whispered. 'Show me how to be of service to the world.'

The thought came straight on the heels of the short prayer. Hadn't He just potentially done so?

The interview with the Archbishop had gone on for quite a while. The man had had a lot of questions, most of which Winsome had been glad to answer. They'd been thoughtful, considered questions, despite the obvious animosity of the other priest in the room, who had never actually been introduced to her.

She frowned. Perhaps, when she had a minute, she'd see if she could spot him on the church website. He should be somewhere on it since obviously he had the ear of the Archbishop.

Whoever he was, he'd been against His Excellency's suggestion.

Request.

Whatever it had been.

'Stay a clergywoman in the Church, Winsome,' she whispered, repeating his words. 'Help us understand what is happening.' She heaved a sigh.

Well, she thought, still on her knees and gazing at the altar candle she'd lit. It was a ballsy move, keeping her in the Church fold so she could feed them information about what the Grove was doing, what their aims were.

'They're taking us seriously,' Morghan had said in the car when she'd heard the news.

'Extremely seriously,' Winsome had replied. 'I'm not sure though, whether as threat or ally.'

She'd asked the Archbishop that. Which they viewed the Grove and their spreading influence as. He'd taken his time answering that one, she'd give him that. He'd thought, or appeared to think about it, before giving his answer.

'I honestly don't know, Winsome,' he'd said. 'That's what we're hoping you can help us with.'

A gaggle of young men came in, then, and Winsome stood up, roused from her thoughts to watch them. They stopped in front of what had used to be the baptismal font and bowed their heads, pressing their hands against their chests, over their hearts. Astonishment bubbled up inside Winsome.

The men moved their hands outwards then, to hold them palm upward in front of themselves; then they relaxed and she saw them smile at each other.

'Hello,' she said, letting herself walk up to them, then. 'I'm sorry to bother you.'

They turned as she came down what had once been the centre aisle and smiled at her.

'You're Reverend Winsome,' one of them said. 'It's brilliant to meet you.'

The other four nodded their heads.

'Thank you,' Winsome said, biting her tongue on the impulse to tell them she was no longer a reverend.

Because she wasn't sure it was true anymore.

'We know you're not really part of the church anymore,' another of them said. 'But I don't know, it still kind of feels right to call you that.' He glanced at his companions. 'You don't mind, do you?'

His friend piped up. 'It's pretty cool, if you ask us, that you changed sides.'

'Changed sides?' Winsome asked, wanting to make sure she understood.

The guy shrugged. 'Left the Church for the Grove. That's what you did, right?'

'They kicked you out, that's what I heard.' The young men looked at each other and nodded.

'If that's the case,' Winsome asked, trying to pick her words carefully. 'Why do you still call me Reverend?'

'Dunno,' one of them answered. 'It still seems kinda right, I guess? They won't let you have the title, but we will, sort of thing.'

'You think it's an us against them sort of scenario?' The small hairs on the back of Winsome's neck were standing up.

More shrugging. 'Isn't it?'

Winsome shook her head. 'I hope not,' she said. 'I hope it doesn't have to be.'

They shifted on their feet in front of her, not knowing what to say.

Winsome spoke again, nodding towards the sacred well. 'Can you tell me what you were doing?' she asked. 'The gesture you made? What does it mean?' She mimicked it.

'Oh, that,' the first one said, relaxing into a grin. 'I mean, that's what we've seen Morghan Wilde do, right?'

'Do you know what it means?'

Emphatic nodding. 'Yeah, we do.' Suddenly they were all serious. 'It means sort of like, my heart is open to the world and its calling.'

Winsome's eyebrows rose. 'You're right,' she said, willing

to admit she was more than a little surprised. 'Do you feel a calling?'

More nodding. 'We all do,' one of them said. 'We want to be part of the Grove.' He looked at his mates, then back at Winsome. 'We are part of the Grove.' He reached to pull something out of the satchel slung over his shoulder and held it out to her. 'We're learning, right?'

Winsome looked at the book. At the embossed lettering on the cover. Stations of the Heart, it said.

'You helped write this,' he said to her. 'With Ambrose and Morghan.' He turned the book toward him and looked down at it.

'It's not an us or them thing,' Winsome said, feeling her heart sink even as the words came out of her mouth. 'I'm not being stripped of my position in the Church. I'm going to be finding a way to bridge the divide between Church and Grove.'

They looked at her in surprise. She nodded.

'Hey,' one of them said at last. 'That's cool, right? That's brilliant – working together. If it's possible.'

'Yes,' Winsome said.

It was brilliant.

If it were possible.

53

Rowan slid out from under the bedcovers and went to the window. The weather might still be cool and wet, she thought, but the sun was definitely rising earlier. She glanced back at Robbie still asleep, his little cheeks round and plump on the pillow. Rowan had discovered that she didn't care at all if he slept in the double bed with her. He'd grow out of it eventually, and right now it brought them both comfort.

She belted her dressing gown around her growing middle and thought of the doctor's appointment the day before. The baby's heartbeat had been good and strong, and the doctor had explained to Robbie all about it. Robbie had taken a real shine to the big Swedish doctor who wore an interesting pendant around his neck. Rowan reminded herself again to see if she could look up what it was.

Slipping her feet into her shoes, she eased the front door open, not wanting to wake up Robbie, then made sure she wasn't going to lock herself out, and walked around in the softness of the dawn to the back garden.

How had Mariah gone missing, she wondered? It seemed impossible that she wasn't dead. How could she have seen Mariah's spirit, if she was still alive? Rowan wished that she'd been able to ask Julia more questions.

Mariah had been so lovely, Rowan thought, remembering the dancing figure in the stuttering lightning. Graceful, long, young limbs, thick dark hair.

The grass was wet from rain and dew, but Rowan stepped off the path onto the lawn anyway. She felt vaguely silly, but didn't give up the sudden impulse that made her do it. Instead, she closed her eyes and remembered the dancing girl, and smiled, moved about on the lawn, danced.

She laughed, hummed the tune from her music box, and swept her arms about, stepped in time to the tune, and imagined she was dancing with Mariah.

Then she was the dancing spinning woman in her old, dearly loved imagining. She could feel the sun on her arms, the bright freedom of it, the music that spun through her mind and into her blood.

For a moment, Rowan thought she felt the sudden presence of others dancing with her. Tall, even more graceful than Mariah had been; she felt them come close, dance away again, and her steps slowed until she stood on the lawn, eyes closed, holding onto the sensation, her skin prickling.

Rowan blinked her eyes open, looked around where she was standing, in the middle of the small lawn. She shivered suddenly and rubbed her arms. That had been strange, she thought. For a minute there, she could have sworn others were dancing with her. On impulse, she danced another step and swept her arms down into a bow with a great flourish.

'Thank you,' she called, then giggled at herself, shaking her head as she went back inside.

'WHAT HAPPENED TO HER, DO YOU KNOW?' ROWAN ASKED. Robbie was safe for an hour with the other children at the little playgroup run by Bridget's Sanctuary. Now she was in the back room of Lynsey's shop, having a cup of tea before they went over her first day on the job.

'To Mariah?' Lynsey put her cup down and started hanging up her new stock of cloaks on a rack ready for the Ostara market. She shook her head. 'Winsome or Erin didn't tell you?'

'No, but I'd taken them by surprise saying I'd seen her ghost.'

Lynsey laughed. 'That would take anyone by surprise, I suppose.'

'And we were busy. There wasn't much time to discuss it, really.'

'Hmm.' Lynsey shook out the last cloak, bottle green wool embroidered with a great snake. 'It's a bit of a story,' she said. 'Are you sure you want to know? It might make you think differently about Mariah.'

'Differently about her? How?' Rowan asked, frowning.

'I kind of get the impression you like her.'

'I do,' Rowan said. 'And I'm so grateful to be living in her house.' She smiled. 'It has a really good feeling to it.'

'Well, that's thanks to Winsome, I can assure you. Not

Mariah.' Lynsey came back to her seat and picked up her cup, considered whether she ought to tell Rowan the story or not. Gossip was frowned upon in the Grove, but Rowan was living in Mariah's house. She'd seen her spirit dancing, for goodness sakes.

'Okay,' she said, deciding, then she sighed. 'Mariah wasn't well liked in the village,' she said, and watched with a pang of regret as Rowan's face fell. 'She had a few old cronies, and Julia was pretty much completely under her thumb, but she was a pretty horrible person.'

'Horrible?' Rowan asked. How could that be?

Lynsey shrugged. 'There's an old story that she was lovely when she was young, but her mother abused her or something, and it soured her like an unripe apple.'

'What?'

'I should probably start at the beginning,' Lynsey said with a glance through the doorway into the shop. Right now, there were no customers. 'Here in Wellsford, it's kind of a rite of passage to sneak up to the stone circle at solstice or Samhain to dance with the Fae, right?'

Rowan's eyes widened, and she felt goosebumps rise on her arms. 'Dance with the Fae?'

Lynsey nodded. 'Wilde Grove has this long alliance with the local Fae tribe, and some of them usually come and dance at the rituals.'

Rowan blinked. 'They come to the ritual?'

She thought of that morning, how for a moment she had been sure she wasn't alone on the lawn, spinning and dancing. There had been others with her; she'd felt them, felt their presence, how tall and somehow bright they'd been.

Had she danced with the Fae? Was that who they'd been? Her mouth went dry, and she gulped at her tea.

'Yeah, they come and dance,' Lynsey said. 'So, the story goes that when Mariah was young, she sneaked up there and danced with the Fae.' A smile lifted Lynsey's lips. 'And sometimes, with the Fae, a dance can mean a little more than that, if you catch my drift.'

Now Rowan's mouth dropped open. 'You mean, like…'

'A bit of a roll in the hay? Yeah. So anyway, when Mariah got home her mother went off her nutter, although by all accounts she was already well off her rocker, and she locked Mariah in her room for, I don't know, a month or two or three, something like that.'

Rowan was appalled. 'But that's terrible! Poor Mariah.'

'For sure. Mariah was never the same after that. And when Winsome moved here, Mariah took against her in a big way, and got her fired, basically.' Lynsey blew out a breath. 'Mariah was on her way to Hawthorn House to burn it down when she disappeared.'

'Hawthorn House?'

'Where Morghan lives, yes.'

'To burn it down?' Rowan hadn't thought the story could get much worse, but it just had.

'Uh huh. But the Fae stepped in and took her to dance with them for all eternity.'

'What?' Rowan was almost whispering now. 'What do you mean?'

'Exactly that. The Fae stopped Mariah and Julia, who was with her, and they took Mariah to their world.'

'Julia saw this?' Rowan felt as though her brain had just exploded. 'This isn't real, surely?'

'This is Wellsford,' Lynsey said with a smile. 'It's all real.' She stood up. 'Now, let's get things ready for tomorrow's market, shall we?' She shook her head. 'I am going to be so glad of the help, I can tell you.'

CLOVER KNOCKED QUIETLY ON THE DOOR TO MORGHAN'S office, then poked her head around the door that had been slightly ajar.

'Do you have a minute?' she asked.

Morghan, who had been standing facing Grainne's painting, her hands resting loosely on her staff, turned her head and smiled at Clover.

'I do,' she said. 'Come in.'

Clover took a breath and entered the room. She glanced at the great paintings of the Wildwood on the far wall and stopped in surprise. 'Is there something different about the painting?' she asked.

Morghan looked at it. 'You see it too?'

'I don't know.' She glanced at Morghan. 'Did you paint them in?'

'No.' Morghan looked at the oak tree in Grainne's painting. The one she'd always thought of as the Guardian Tree. 'I didn't paint them in.'

'But...' Clover shook her head. 'How, then?'

'Miracles and magic,' Morghan said. 'It strengthens.'

'It's getting stronger?'

'Yes,' Morghan said, and looked for a moment more at the tiny golden eggs hanging gleaming in the shadows of the forest from the Guardian's branches. She turned to

Clover and considered her. 'You want to go home,' she said at last.

Clover dragged her gaze from the artwork and made herself look back at Morghan without flinching. 'Yes,' she said.

Morghan nodded. 'Why?'

That was the question, Clover thought. The one she'd grappled with all night, tossing and turning beneath the covers.

'Because,' she said, then stopped and cleared her throat, began again. 'Because I think I've done what I was supposed to here.'

'The prophecy?' Morghan asked.

Clover nodded. 'Don't you think so?'

Morghan ignored the question, asked one of her own instead. 'You don't think you have more to say, in your capacity as Oracle?'

'I think I'm one and done, as Oracle, actually,' Clover said.

Morghan lifted her head and thought about this. 'You're basing this on what knowledge?' she asked after a long minute.

'On the basis of what else is there to say?' Clover answered. She wrapped her arms around her middle and hugged herself. 'Anything else would be just details.'

Morghan didn't say anything.

'And,' Clover went on when she realised Morghan wasn't going to comment. 'And well, when I turn to look into the mists, I can see the web, but there is no compulsion to put my hands on it, to read what is in its weaving.' She shrugged. 'A one prophecy wonder, that's me.' She took a breath. 'And I'm okay with that. I'm good with it. I'm glad.' She paused, choosing her words carefully, knowing how much Morghan and Selena cared about speaking intentionally. 'I wanted to run back to Rue, I admit that,' she said. 'It took me a little while to come to terms with this...' She waved an arm. 'Prophecy business. But I have. We've all got parts to play, I know that. Except, when I look for mine, I find that I've played it already.'

She groped around for more to say, for something that would convince Morghan to let her leave.

Of course, she knew she was free to leave and go back to New Zealand whenever she wanted. Morghan would never stop her.

'I want your blessing,' she said. 'I want you to tell me it's okay for me to go back home.' She swallowed. 'You're the Lady of the Grove. I need your wisdom.'

Morghan almost laughed, but she stopped herself and looked at Grainne's painting again instead. The golden eggs hanging from the tree. Grainne had not painted those there while she was alive. They had not been there, small dabs of gold under the wax, when Morghan had prayed in front of her altar the night before.

She looked at Clover, at the brightness of her aura, belying the slightness of her figure.

'What will you do back at home?' she asked, able to see that whatever else Clover might think had been played out, her psychic ability remained untouched.

Clover closed her eyes for a moment, relief washing through her so that her knees were suddenly weak with it. She was going to go home. Morghan was going to give her blessing. For a moment, Clover felt regret at having to leave

Alex, and she knew she'd have many more moments of regret and loss over him, but it was not enough to dissuade her.

She opened her eyes and looked at Morghan. 'I will continue what Clarice and I started here,' she said. 'Shepherding the lost souls. There are enough of them, unfortunately, to keep me busy the rest of my life.'

'Yes,' Morghan said. 'I rather think you're right.' She nodded, then tried one more time. 'You're sure?'

'Yes,' Clover said. 'I'm sure. I'll go after the Ostara celebrations tomorrow.'

Morghan smiled at her. 'Then you will take my heart and my blessing with you.'

54

PAUL HADN'T LOGGED OUT OF THE FORUMS UNTIL THREE IN the morning. It had been too intoxicating, having everyone defer to him as the one who had all the inside info, who had fed Jack Newton the lead about the prophecy. He'd posted all the photos he'd taken in Wellsford and was especially proud of the one he'd snapped of Morghan Wilde herself. Everyone had lapped it up when he'd told them she'd said he couldn't take her photo and he'd done it anyway.

That had made them laugh and cheer – well, post emojis that showed they were laughing and cheering.

He hadn't added the bit about her quoting the Bible at him. He'd looked it up, though, and she'd been right, it was there, about water. John chapter seven, verse whatever.

Still, she oughtn't have perverted it for her own uses. It wasn't right. That was the Holy Bible she was polluting with her filthy mind.

Paul stretched, yawned, and made himself coffee, sitting at the table to drink it, have a bowl of cereal, and scroll a bit on his phone. He navigated to the forums – this phone was worth every penny – and grinned as he read the comments that had come in while he'd been catching up on his kip.

Finally, though, he closed it all down and set the phone on the table. He'd slept in almost to lunch time and now he'd have to hustle a bit. Everything was set for the afternoon, but he had to get to the rental place and make sure the coaches were ready. Stoat had got them to hire three of them. Paul grinned. He'd scored the job of driving one of them.

A sweet deal indeed.

Wellsford and all its apostates would not know what had hit them.

Paul was still grinning when he grabbed his keys and wallet and headed out the door. Half an hour later, he was turning the big coach into the street and pulling to a stop on the road in front of Cornerstone. The two coaches behind him braked in a great wheezing huff. Paul slung himself out of his seat and out the door, revelling in the feeling of being in the midst of it all.

In the midst of all the righteous mayhem to come.

'All right, then?' he asked Malcolm, who was standing in front of the doors, looking at the three big buses. He looked around for the pastor. 'Where's Stoat?' he asked.

Malcolm jerked a thumb back at the building behind him. 'In there, getting ready,' he said. 'He's going to come out and give a speech before everyone boards the coaches.'

Paul nodded. Stoat had given him what-for, after discovering he'd sold the prophecy story to the blogger guy, but that hadn't lasted, not when the American had seen how that had just made the story all the more widely known, and everyone exponentially angrier. Paul put his hands on his hips and happily surveying the row of coaches that took up almost the whole road. Selling the story had been a great thing. Those bitches had even been on the telly again, yakking it up about the golden children.

Like it was actually meaningful. He rolled his eyes thinking about it. Nothing but a waste of airspace that was. Same with them, the uppity priestess bitches and their pathetic, fawning men. Paul blew out a breath between pursed lips. He had to keep it together.

Then, when destruction was raining down upon Wellsford, he had his own, quiet little mission.

'Where's Pastor Eric?' he asked now.

Malcolm shook his head. 'He was called away to his wife's side.'

'What?' Paul frowned. 'Sick, is she?'

Malcolm gave a jerking shake of his head. He thought he might have a slightly better understanding now of Eric decamping. John Stoat was a crazy bastard.

But he had decided that sometimes crazy bastards got done what needed to get done.

'I don't know the details,' he said, straightening. He was in charge of Cornerstone now, notwithstanding Stoat. He checked his watch. Time to get the show on the road.

'You're ready?' he asked Paul.

Paul nodded. 'Me and the others,' he said, referring to the fellas driving the other two coaches. 'Ready to lock and load whenever you are.' He looked about them. There were clusters of people milling all over the street. He'd be willing to bet the church was full too.

'Good turnout,' he said, baring his teeth in what he hoped was a wolfish grin.

Malcolm looked around. 'Yes,' he said. 'We'll fill all three of the coaches, I think.' Thanks to ringing around the other evangelical churches in Banwell and neighbouring towns, sending out the rallying cries. They would probably fill the coaches, and a bunch would follow in their own cars too. 'We'll drive the witches out of Wellsford,' he said and smiled, liking the way that sounded. Maybe he'd suggest that to the reporters that were bound to turn up, like flies to the dung heap.

Paul went back to the lead bus, his chest puffed out importantly. He swung into the driver's seat and honked the horn sharply, three times, to get everyone's attention as he watched Stoat, wearing a flash green suit, came out of the church, arms raised for attention.

It was almost time to roll.

ROWAN HELD ROBBIE SECURELY BY THE HAND. SHE DIDN'T want to lose him in the eddy of people who streamed up and down the main street of Wellsford. Lynsey grinned at her.

'I can't believe it's not raining,' Rowan said. 'It's like a miracle.'

'It really is,' Lynsey agreed and nodded her head at all the stalls set up along the street, including their own. 'The atmosphere is really festive.'

It sure was, and contagious, thought Rowan, as her own spirits were lifted and buoyed along with the happy faces all about her. 'I can't believe the turnout!'

There was a grand amount of people for sure. She could smell sausages and chips and suddenly her mouth watered. 'Can I go get us something to eat?' she asked. 'Those sausages smell amazing.'

Lynsey smiled at her even while she shook her head. She was vegetarian and looking forward to some of Simon's loaded veggie nachos in a little while. 'You go and have a bite and a wander about. Marshall and I are good here.'

Rowan gave her a grateful nod and led Robbie across to the sausage sizzle. Something to eat – they could sit in the green and listen to the band, then have a wander about, looking at all the stalls. Rowan didn't have much in the way of money to spare, but they could look, couldn't they?

She put Robbie on her hip and tucked the box with sausage and chips for each of them under her arm and wondered, not for the first time, how on earth she was going to manage when baby Grace was born. It was a happy thought, though, and she was grinning as they wove their way towards the green.

'You're looking happy,' Erin said, turning and spotting Rowan and Robbie. 'Is that your lunch?' she asked Robbie. 'It smells delicious!'

Robbie smiled shyly and nodded. Erin patted the table. 'Share with me, if you like,' she said.

Rowan sat down and got Robbie settled with his sausage. 'Thank you,' she said. 'It's so busy here!'

'I know; so many people have come to celebrate with us.' Erin tipped her face towards the sky. 'I think it helps that the sun has actually come out from behind the clouds for us.' She grinned at Rowan. 'How's your poor tailbone?'

Rowan shook her head. 'I hardly feel it now. It healed

quickly, thank goodness.' She looked toward where the band was playing. 'Gosh, they're great, aren't they?'

Erin nodded and looked at Stephan, who was singing up on the stage. She pressed her hands to her heart when she saw him looking back at her and relished his sudden smile. She went to reach for Burdock, then remembered he was spending the day out at Oak Tree Farm where things would be a little quieter.

'Erin?' Rowan said, leaning forward over the little table and speaking quietly so as not to get Robbie's attention, which was so far happily occupied with his sausage and chips. 'Can I ask you something?'

Erin turned to her. 'Of course.'

'It's about Mariah,' Rowan said, then wasn't sure how to go on from there.

'Hmm,' Erin said. 'I can imagine. What have you heard about her?'

Rowan's eyes widened with the thought of the things Lynsey had told her. She wasn't sure which one to begin with. 'She was going to burn Morghan Wilde's house down?'

Erin nodded. 'She was a very unhappy woman, whose thought processes had gotten corrupted.'

'But...burning the house down?' Rowan shook her head. 'Lynsey said the Fae took her.'

'To stop her, yes,' Erin said.

'But...I don't understand,' Rowan said. 'The Fae? Like... fairies?'

'Yes.' Erin smiled at her. 'But not the sweet little things with wings like we see in old picture books.' Her smile faded. 'The real ones are quite intimidating.'

'They're real?'

'Very much so,' Erin said.

'But...' Rowan shook her head. 'Will I ever see them?'

'Possibly,' Erin said. 'Probably.' She glanced up and saw Clover, Krista, and Clarice, gave them a wave. Watched them come over.

'Hi guys,' she said, then gestured at Rowan. 'I'd like you all to meet Rowan and Robbie. They've moved into Mariah's old house.' She looked at Rowan. 'This is Clarice, Krista, and Clover.'

'Ah,' Clarice said to Rowan before she could make a reply. 'I heard that you've seen Mariah. Is that right?' She pulled a chair closer and sat down.

In a moment, Rowan was surrounded by people she'd only seen on YouTube videos and the television. She hoped she didn't have tomato sauce on her chin like Robbie did. She wiped it away and tried to find her voice.

'Ah, yes,' she said, clearing her throat. 'During the thunderstorm we had recently. She was dancing. In the back garden.'

Clarice sat back and considered this, shook her head.

'She looked really good,' Rowan said hurriedly. 'Young.'

'That makes sense,' Clover said. 'Doesn't it?' She raised an eyebrow at Clarice. 'She won't be as she was, not after spending this long with the Fae.'

'That's fascinating,' Krista said, smiling at Robbie as he knelt on his chair gazing from one of them to the other, little mouth hanging open. He looked back at her and returned the smile.

'What's the mechanics of that, though?' Erin asked. 'I

mean...' She thought about it for a moment, shook her head. 'How?'

Rowan tried not to stare at everyone. When she went to contribute to the conversation, her voice was barely a squeak. 'Is she...I mean, is she still alive?'

'Almost certainly not,' Clarice said, and nudged Krista. 'Cute kid, huh?'

'Not alive?' Rowan said. 'You mean she's...?'

'Dead?' Clarice leant back in her chair, shading her face from the sun. It was good to feel the great burning orb's warmth, but the brightness was a pain, even with sunglasses on. 'I'm surprised we haven't stumbled across her remains, to tell the truth.'

Clover was considering this. 'I think you're right,' she said, then frowned, and squinted at Rowan. 'Do you think you'd mind if I tried something?' she asked.

Rowan was startled. 'What do you mean?'

'It won't hurt or anything, I practically promise it. I just want to hold your hand for a minute.'

'You think you can find her?' Erin asked. 'Mariah?'

Clover shrugged. 'Maybe.' She nodded reassuringly at Rowan. 'You've seen her, and you've been spending time in her house, so there's a connection there between you. Possibly.'

'You want to hold my hand?' Rowan asked, still gobsmacked.

Clover shrugged. 'Worth a go. It would do Julia good, probably, to have Mariah's body. Certainly would help the police if we could give them that, or maybe not, depending where it is.' She shrugged. 'I'm still curious, anyway.'

The band started playing a new song, and the group of

Morris dancers clapped their hands, lifted their sticks, stepped in time to the music.

Rowan looked at her hand, then stretched her arm across the table to Clover, her hand palm up.

Clover's fingers were warm and dry against Rowan's. She cupped Rowan's hand in her palm and covered it with her other hand. Rowan watched her close her eyes and let out a deep breath.

Rowan closed her own eyes. Her skin was prickling where Clover held it. She thought of Mariah, dancing while the storm raged around her, electricity lighting up the sky.

'That's good,' Clover murmured. 'Hold her in your mind. There is a connection, just like I hoped.'

Rowan tried not to think about that, or the mechanics of it. There'd be time for that later, at home, after this extraordinary day was done. She immersed herself instead in the memory of what she'd seen: Mariah, dancing in the silver rain.

She blinked her eyes opened when Clover let go of her hand. She looked at her palm for a moment, then rubbed it.

'Did you get a fix on her?' Krista asked. Rowan noticed that Robbie was in Krista's lap now, still delicately eating his chips, one by one, and leaning happily against his new friend.

It seemed surreal to Rowan suddenly. Sitting there in the sunshine, the smell of sausages in their air, a band playing, Morris dancers performing, everywhere chatter and laughter.

And there at her table she was talking with the famous priestesses of Wilde Grove about the whereabouts of a woman who had been taken by the fairies.

'Sure,' Clover said. 'You know that super old oak where the paths branch off, one to the stone circle, the other to Hawthorne House?'

Everyone except Rowan nodded.

Clover nodded. 'There's an old foxhole under it. The opening's long caved in, so there's nothing to see at all, but she's in there. If we dig between the tree's roots there, we'll find her.'

There was silence for a minute while everyone digested this.

'We should have asked you this sooner,' Krista said at last.

But Clover shook her head and nodded toward Rowan. 'I wouldn't have had that link to lead me until Rowan here.'

'What...' Rowan cleared her throat again. 'What will you find, if you, um, dig there?'

'Bones,' Clover said. 'That's all.'

'So, she really is dead?' Rowan asked.

Clover shook her head. 'Body, yeah. The rest of her is with the Fae.' Clover's face lightened. 'Except when she's dancing with you, that is.'

Rowan's mouth fell open.

She wanted to ask why Mariah was showing herself to her, but there was a sudden commotion in the street behind them and she turned to look.

55

John Stoat nodded to himself. Yes, Jonny, he thought. We're in our element now, aren't we? Born for this, we were.

He nodded again and let himself have a wide smile, even while he smoothed his hands down his suit. Unlike the others in front of him, he was not wielding a sign.

He needed his hands free.

The sun was out. That was a nice surprise. God himself was smiling upon them. He felt the crowd surge forward in front of him and heard the sudden, surprised shouts.

The band stopped playing, and Stoat smiled even more widely, lifting his eyebrows and bringing his hands up as though he were directing an orchestra.

Right on cue, his crowd began singing. Stoat did a little dancing step, throwing his arms into the air and letting exaltation sweep through him.

Onward Christian Soldiers, marching as to war,
With the cross of Jesus, going on before.

'Yes,' he said out loud, the singing drowning out his

voice. War. That's what it was. A holy war against sinners and all their filth.

They continued their surge up Wellsford's main street, Stoat leering at the people shrinking back against the shops, and he let himself dance another little jig and then laughed.

'That's right, people!' he called out. 'The jig is up!'

His singing army came to a stop and Stoat nodded his head in time with the stirring tune for another minute, before straightening, clearing his throat, and putting out his arms to also clear a path through his crowd, gratified beyond measure when they parted like butter for a knife, like the red sea, like a crowd ushering up their saviour.

He stepped out of the sea of righteous Christians, saw they were at the village green just as they'd planned. His lieutenants had enacted his instructions perfectly.

And the best thing of all – there were no police about to stop them from doing what needed to be done.

Whatever needed to be done.

Stoat looked up at the stage set up, at the namby pamby fella looking back at him with his curly girly hair and mouth hanging open. He laughed as his people's song ended.

Glory, laud, and honour, unto Christ the King,
This through countless ages, men and angels sing.

Stoat laughed, then swept into a great bow, knowing here was about to come the performance of his life. He laughed again, looking at all the silly, startled faces around him.

'Renounce!' he shouted. 'Renounce and repent the way of the Devil! For here is a prophecy of my own!'

His voice carried across the stunned masses admirably.

His mama had always told him he had a good voice, a voice meant to be heard.

And he was being heard.

'Your temples will burn, your goddesses will be ground to dust! Your wells will dry, your trees will be felled! There will be no golden children among those who follow the ways of the Serpent! You will not stand in any right-eousness! We will not let you!'

He leered at them. 'We will stand in your path and we will not let you pass!

'Your way is not the way of God but is instead an abom-ination!'

Stoat turned and grinned at his people and raised his hands to them.

'We are the way, the truth, the word!' he said, and swept up a cheer from them. 'No one may come to the Father except by me!'

Stoat turned again and flung his hands to the heavens. 'God said to suffer not the witches! To let the little children come only unto Him!'

He danced over to the nearest table and shoved it, sending cake and coffee and chips flying. He squealed in delight.

'We are the Way!' he screamed at them all. 'The Ancient and Holy Way of Jesus Christ in Heaven!' Stoat spun around and whipped his arms at his good and holy army. 'To war, my friends! To war with God and His Son at your side!'

THIS WAS WHAT PAUL HAD BEEN WAITING FOR.

He'd spotted Rowan, the absconder and traitor, straight

away. She was sitting at a table with a bunch of women. The same women who were always on the TV and internet now. He shook his head, eyes narrowed at her, ignoring Stoat's rallying cries, the crowd going crazy, all of it. He was like a sniper, he thought, eyes on the target.

And hadn't she been easy to find? Right there, out in the open, hanging out with the vipers. He'd been right all along, of course. There she was, sitting in the bosom of the Grove.

With Robbie.

Paul's lips flattened into a line. Look where his son was, sitting in the lap of the black lesbian bitch no less. Paul let himself growl in the depth of his throat, then sidled a few steps farther away from the crowd from his coaches.

He'd have to move quickly, keep his eyes sharp once the crowd moved, and they would in a moment, he could feel it, could feel it tense like it was an animal.

Tensing before the pounce.

And wouldn't that take these stupid Grove Do-Gooders by surprise? Paul grinned and moved away a little more, slipping into the shadows, not shifting his gaze an inch from Robbie.

The crowd heaved, screamed, and surged.

Paul broke free and ran, across the road from the green, watching as Rowan did exactly what he knew she'd do – scoop up Robbie and skedaddle from the scene.

He lost sight of her as the crowd filled the street and poured into the green. There was feedback from the band's amps on the stage, and some shouting. He didn't bother to listen, he was busy scooting. Along the edge of the street, searching, letting his gaze tick back and forth, back and forth.

And there she was, and Paul laughed at the look on her face.

This was nothing, he promised, as to how she'd feel later. Then she'd really regret her choices.

The crowd surged out from the green and down the street, overturning stalls, scattering people before it, rending and tearing and singing again. Singing *Onward Christian Soldiers*. Paul knew they'd be making for the church now, the building in which once, Stoat had told them in his speech before everyone had boarded the coaches, God had lived, but now The Almighty had been toppled in favour of a craven goddess, an abomination.

The sun went behind a cloud, but Paul didn't care, barely noticed. He was watching Rowan and nodding to himself as she scuttled up a driveway opposite the church and disappeared.

He followed, but slowly now, finding the shadows in which to hide himself, from which he could watch. The sun, as if on his side, had hidden its face behind the clouds once more.

Rowan was at the front door, throwing frantic glances over her shoulder, seeing nothing. Certainly not seeing him, Paul, crouching by the garage, watching around the corner as she got the key in the lock and the door open, all but falling into the house.

The door slammed shut and Paul straightened, pleasure washing through him. He stepped behind the garage, and leant against the brickwork, head tipped back, listening to the day, to the shouts and yells, the singing, the destruction.

·   ·   ·

'WHAT ON EARTH?' WINSOME LIFTED HER HEAD IN ALARM AND looked at Ambrose, Kurt, and Morghan. 'What's that noise?'

Morghan turned and looked through the trees in the direction of the noise. She shook her head even while understanding dawned.

'That's not the band,' Ambrose said, and he stepped instinctively nearer Winsome. They'd been able to hear the band, Stephan's singing, even from where they were in the small clearing behind Bridget's Sanctuary in which the summerhouse temple stood.

'It is absolutely not the band,' Kurt agreed.

The overflowing stream forgotten, Morghan shook her head. 'I should have known,' she said.

'Known what?' Winsome asked, not liking how her voice was suddenly shaking. She reached out to touch her fingers to Ambrose's sleeve.

'The Queen said I needed to look to my own backyard.' Morghan was already striding from the clearing, the water sucking at her boots. She made for the path that would come out at Bridget's Sanctuary.

If she was fast enough...

'Morghan,' Ambrose called. 'Wait!'

Winsome looked at him, eyes wide. 'The Sanctuary,' she said.

Kurt shook his head. 'Surely not. Who are they?'

But they could make out the singing now, and it certainly wasn't Stephan anymore. It was a crowd chanting a song.

Winsome closed her eyes for a moment, recognising the old hymn. Sudden hot tears soaked her eyelids, and she dragged in a breath, took off after Morghan, Ambrose and Kurt on her heels.

Paul saw Rowan's pale face at the window, and he smiled, eying Robbie on her hip. He drew in a breath. Rowan, he didn't care about, but he'd be damned if he was going to let her bring up his kid in Wilde Grove.

He shivered slightly with excitement, imagining the future that stretched out in front of him now – fame for going against Wilde Grove and winning, sympathy for all his son had gone through, and admiration for him, how brave he'd been, taking things into his own hands and getting his son out from the grasping hands of Satan's minions.

Paul smiled wider, imagining now how the women at Cornerstone would crowd around him, showering him with their soft willing glances, offers of help, all of them wanting him and Robbie.

He hadn't forgotten he had another child on the way. But that was all the better. He could fight for that one too, when it was born.

He'd be able to milk this for years.

Rowan disappeared from the window and Paul eyed the front door. Had she locked it? He wrinkled his nose, considering it. Probably, he thought. She was a suspicious bitch. He edged around behind the garage then slunk through the garden looking for the back door to the house. The shouting in the street grew louder and Paul grinned to himself. That old hymn – he had to hand it to Stoat, the man knew how to make an entrance.

Paul wanted to pump his fist in the air and let loose a victory shout, but he made himself stay quiet, concentrating on being stealthy. He could celebrate later, back at home, Robbie in the upstairs room where he belonged. Paul was sure one of the single women from Cornerstone would jump at the chance to help him keep Robbie fed and quiet for the night.

He laughed, he couldn't help it. He nodded his head, ran for the steps up to the back door. He had a good feeling about that door. He didn't think it was going to be locked.

And even if it was, well, wasn't he holding a rock from the garden now? That glass pane wouldn't stand a chance, then it was bang on inside, grab the kid, disappear back into the crowd.

Rowan would never find him.

The only issue was that there was only the coach to drive back to Banwell. His car was at the hire place. But Paul shrugged that problem away. It wasn't important, and he knew, could feel it inside him, that when it came to it, he wouldn't hesitate to drive that big old bus right back down the road, just him and Robbie in it.

The shouting from the road grew louder and Paul nodded, adjusting his plan. He was good at that, he thought. Making adjustments on the fly.

He'd snatch Robbie, go straight to the bus, take him home. The police would be on their way, he reckoned, pretty soon, from the sounds of mayhem in the streets. He didn't want to get caught up in any police action. His plan depended on getting Robbie out of Wellsford.

Something moved in the garden and Paul paused on his creep up the back steps, turning to frown at the pocket of lawn surrounded by garden. He would have sworn he'd seen someone there.

But there was no one, so with one last frowning look, Paul shrugged it off and hefted the rock even as he reached out with his other hand to try the door. It was locked, and a moment later, the rock was launched from his hand, the sound of smashing glass like music to his ears.

Someone touched him on the back of the neck and Paul swivelled so quickly on his feet he almost stumbled and pitched down the steps.

There was no one there.

'Fuck off,' he muttered, trying to ignore the high pitch of his voice. 'I don't fucking believe in Wilde Grove bullshit.'

Back on his feet and then in the door, strangely reluctant to turn his back on the garden but forcing himself to, anyway. And there was Rowan, her face a pale blur in the dimness of the house – why was it so bloody dark inside? The sun was out, wasn't it?

'Paul!'

He straightened and found his grin, smiled what he hoped was wolfishly at her. 'Bitch,' he said congenially. 'Child stealer.'

Rowan's eyes widened even further, and Paul laughed, thinking suddenly that she looked like a horse, with her eyes rolling around in their sockets like that. He looked at Robbie on her hip and made himself nod.

'I've come to take Robbie home,' he said. 'Where he belongs.'

And that was enough talk, he decided. He'd lose the element of surprise if he didn't keep moving. So that was what he did, putting his shoulder down as though he was back in school, playing a bit of rugby.

He sent them all flying, feeling the air whoosh out of Rowan in a great billowing, but he was ready for the tumble and was on his feet again in a moment, reaching for Robbie, grasping the kid around the middle and on his way back down the short hallway and out the door before Rowan could even get back to her feet.

She wasn't even screaming, Paul thought, pinning Robbie under his arm and running across the garden, not looking into the bushes, running too fast for anything to reach out and touch him. He'd knocked the wind right out of her.

Robbie though, now the kid was gearing up to start screaming bloody murder. Paul shook his head. 'Won't make any difference!' he yelled, gaining the street and entering the crowd where everyone was shouting and screaming.

Paul could hardly move for bodies everywhere. Some-one's sign whacked him a good one in the side of the head, and he stumbled, swearing. He'd have to get out of the crowd. Work his way back to the coach a different way.

The crowd was dragging him and Robbie across the road to the church. Paul rode the wave for a moment, eyes on the treeline behind the vicarage.

When he felt the crowd give for a moment, he broke free and ran for the woods.

56

MORGHAN SNATCHED UP HER STAFF ON THE WAY PAST THE summerhouse and slogged her way through the small, sodden meadow to the short path through the trees back to Bridget's Sanctuary. She could hear the song the crowd was singing now, punctuated with shouts and screams that made her blood run cold.

For a moment the memory of a vision rose up in front of her mind, Roman soldiers storming through the Forest House, their blades running red with the blood of priestesses, and behind them the acrid smoke of the Grove burning.

'Pull yourself together,' Catrin hissed. 'The threat is here and now!'

Morghan nodded, made herself run, not heeding Ambrose's shouts behind her. He and Winsome and Kurt would follow, she knew, but she had to get there ahead of the ones coming.

She broke loose from the woods and saw with relief that

threatened to make her legs go weak that the crowd hadn't reached the Sanctuary yet.

Hawk sat upon the stonework above the door. Something fast and black flitted across the sky behind the church.

Morghan's head swam and she stopped where she stood on the green beside the Sanctuary, halfway between the trees and the building.

'What are you doing?' Catrin hissed into her ear.

Morghan shook her head. She didn't know. She only knew that if she tried walking right at this moment, she would fall. The worlds swam around her, mixing, blending into one, the great weaving of the web burning behind her eyes, quivering in the breeze in the clouded sky. She looked at it, watched it, felt Catrin quieten to stand next to her, Ravenna stepping out of the mists of the worlds to join her on the other side.

Just as it had been in her vision of them on the great tor overlooking the coming darkness.

She traced the threads of it, shaking as she did so, seized with the violent feeling that all was coming together, that before the rise, there must be the fall, the casting about the ruins.

Morghan closed her eyes. 'Goddess help us,' she said.

The crowd, high on righteousness and destruction, was coming, placards in their hands, faces red from screaming their hymn about their Godly army, and ahead of them all, one figure, one man who had already seen her.

A capering figure in a green suit.

'Morghan?'

It was Winsome, reaching out to touch her shoulder

before drawing back her hand before it even reached Morghan's shoulder.

'Are you all right?'

Morghan recognised Kurt's voice, the concern, professional and personal in it. She held up her hand to quieten him, then turned and walked to the path that led from the street to the front entrance of Bridget's Sanctuary, her vision wide open, the world wrecked about her.

Must it come to that? Must it all go that far? She stood, and closed her eyes, flood waters rising behind them, the wind screaming over the ruins of the world. Morghan shook her head even as the world of Clover's vision played out behind her eyes.

WINSOME FLUNG A GLANCE AT THE CROWD, AT THE MAN WHO was leading them and was now slowing, grin wide and crazy.

She walked over to Morghan, stood at her side. Listened to the crowd singing their song, and under it, the thumping of her heart. She glanced at Morghan, who didn't look back at her, but stood still on the path, hands loosely clasped on her staff, eyes closed.

Her hair had come loose and flowed down her back, ruffled in the cooling breeze.

Ambrose came and stood next to Winsome. Kurt took Morghan's other side.

Another black shape winged across the sky.

. . .

STOAT HELD UP HIS HAND AND THE CROWD BEHIND HIM FELL silent. He stifled a giggle at how well everyone was doing. At how well he was doing. He wanted to do another little jig, but it wasn't time for that. Instead, he drew himself up straight to find the voice that his mama had loved so well.

Something dark flapped across the top of his vision and he lifted a hand, waved it away, gaze riveted on the dark priestess in front of him.

He'd seen her on the television, of course, even in America, and the endless videos on the internet. This though, this was the first time he'd seen her in person.

He wanted to think she wasn't much. Average height, older, hair completely grey. Nothing to write home about. Nothing to lust over and gasp about.

But he found himself not thinking any of those things, and that was interesting. Instead, he gazed at her, the crowd beginning to shuffle about on its centipede legs behind him. He'd have to say something soon, or they'd do more than shuffle, they'd murmur and mutter and ruin his moment.

But he kept silent for a minute longer, just looking at her as she stood there, eyes closed. Eyes closed! Not even looking at them!

Here he thought, grinning, was a showman, just as he himself was. Someone, he thought, who knew how to command an audience, give a flick of the wrist, a verbal catapult, and have them eating out of your right hand while you had your left in their pocket.

John Stoat sighed happily. He would send her away and then he and his faithful would take back the church, removing all idolatry from it, and praising Jesus from the pulpit once more.

'We've come,' he said, enunciating the words clearly, giving them the necessary gravitas. He swept out a hand to gesture at the crowd behind him. They roared approvingly and his smile widened as Morghan Wilde finally opened her eyes and looked at him.

Eating out of his hand. He gave it a moment then raised his hand again to quieten them.

'We've come to expel you from your false position of power,' Stoat said. 'To expose you as the false idols you are.' He nodded. Expel and expose. Very good word choices. Poetry! He drew breath once more, let it go on a great smile. Turned his back on Morghan Wilde and her flunkies and looked at his great crowd of the faithful.

'Put on the whole armour of God,' he quoted at them. 'That you may be able to stand against the schemes of the devil!'

Then nodded approvingly as they burst into song again.

Crowns and thrones may perish, Kingdoms rise and wane, but the Church of Jesus constant will remain. Gates of hell can never 'gainst that Church prevail. We have Christ's own promise, and that cannot fail.

There was a slight faltering at the end, as heads lifted around him to look up at the sky where Stoat himself was now scowling. He wanted to spit and scream, so great was the fury that rose up in him.

Ravens and their cowardly crow cousins. Of course, he thought. They had pet ravens and crows, kept them for just such occasions as this. Well, he and his people would not be cowed! He would pluck one of those dark devils from the sky if he could, tear its very head from its body and dance upon its tiny, hollow bones!

· · ·

Rowan stood on the footpath, tears streaking down her face. 'Robbie!' she screamed.

How was she going to find him in this mess of people? She stumbled along the street, saw the stall where she and Robbie had been with Lynsey and Marshall earlier, putting all the pretty clothes out on display. She bent and picked a dress up from the ground, dirty with footprints, the fine fabric muddied and torn.

'Robbie!' she screamed, and looked around for some-one, anyone who had seen her boy.

But no one was paying her any attention. She was lost in a sea of strangers. Lynsey and Marshall were nowhere to be seen. She looked frantically about, but couldn't see into the village green, didn't see anyone she knew.

Didn't see Paul.

Something flickered across her vision, and she straight-ened, blinked. Saw it again.

Heard, under the noise and singing from the crowd, a few delicate notes that sounded like the tune from her jewellery box.

'Robbie?' she called, but softly now.

There it was again, the flicker of movement, of someone looking at her, smiling, then turning, long dark hair flying, steps light, like a dancer's.

Rowan followed, ducking under upheld placards, hearing nothing but the blood rushing between her ears and that tinkling tune.

There, across the street, to the right of the vicarage. She

darted behind the crowd and across the road, lifting a hand when a raven flew past, low overhead.

The figure waited for her, translucent and beautiful, then moved on when Rowan was across the street and hurrying down the far side of the vicarage, and disappeared behind the house. Rowan followed, saw the flicker of Mariah's beaming face turned to her again, then she was behind a tree and gone.

Rowan's breath was coming in great panting gulps. She could hear the crowd behind her singing something as she slipped behind the tree and discovered a path there. And behind that swelling chanting, a loud squeal of feedback from the stage in the green. She shook her head, forged on.

Into the darkness of the woods. Her shoes crunched on the path, and she pressed her hands over her belly, feeling her body's protest as she forced herself to run.

THESE WOODS, PAUL THOUGHT, WERE A BLOODY WARREN OF paths. He wanted to loop around and down to the road where the bus was parked, had figured he'd have to go up onto the hills that surrounded Wellsford, then make his way around and back down. Simple.

Yet here he bloody was, lost, for crying out loud.

And Robbie would not stop screaming.

Paul halted a moment and bent over, Robbie still under his arm, wriggling like a bastard and screaming like he was being skinned or something.

'Shut up!' Paul roared with the last of his breath. 'Shut the bloody hell up or I'll feed you to the fucking wolves.'

The woods were thick and dark enough to feel like there would be wolves lurking amongst the trees.

Something flashed in his vision, and he looked up, searching for it.

Under his arm, Robbie fell silent, as though he'd seen it too.

Whatever it was.

Paul straightened, put Robbie on his feet, making sure to keep his hand curled around the kid's neck, just in case he decided to hare off into the woods.

Robbie stared wide-eyed into the shadows. There was someone there; he could see her. He lifted his arm and pointed, smiled at the figure he'd seen before, at night, in his dreams.

'Look,' he said.

Paul's fingers tightened on Robbie's neck as he peered between the trees.

'Who the bloody fuck are you?' he yelled and jumped at the sound of his own voice.

Robbie laughed.

The figure moved, stepped out of the shadows and winked at Robbie, putting her finger to her lips in a shushing movement. Robbie giggled again, stifled it.

'Who are you?' Paul said, taking a step backwards. He didn't like the look of the woman standing looking at them.

She wasn't quite all there. Paul's heart thumped. She was...he shook his head. Swallowed.

Croaked the next words at her. 'Go away.'

She was...something. A spirit.

He didn't believe in those.

Robbie giggled again, and Paul jerked, shoved the boy

away so that Robbie tripped, went down on hands and knees.

'You want him?' he screamed at the ghostly woman staring at him and smiling. 'You bloody have him, then!' He kicked out with his foot and sent Robbie sprawling.

Something came barrelling out of the woods at him then, a great blur, and it was him flying, clear off his feet, smacking into a tree to lie dazed on the ground.

'Keep away from him!' Rowan screamed. 'You leave him alone!'

Paul shook his head, and screwed up his eyes, seeing Rowan, and relief flooded through him. She'd deal with whatever that thing was. The spirit. Rowan would send it on its way.

But it was standing next to his wife, the spirit, the ghost, whatever it was, standing next to Rowan, smiling while Rowan glared at him – at him!

'Get out of here, Paul,' Rowan said, hands clenched with fury as she went over to where Robbie was sitting on the ground and picked him up.

He shook his head. 'Not without him.' He kept his eyes away from the spirit. Refused to look at her.

She couldn't be real, after all. Wilde Grove was just a trick.

'You're not taking Robbie anywhere,' Rowan said. 'Ever.'

Paul opened his mouth to answer, getting to his knees. He felt braver now he'd decided the spirit wasn't real. He hadn't had lunch. He'd just hallucinated, that was all.

He kept his head turned carefully away from where the ghostly woman had been standing.

'Not without the kid,' he repeated.

Rowan was appalled. He couldn't even use Robbie's name. She felt movement in the air near her and knew that it was Mariah stirring.

'You cannot have him,' she said slowly, calmly. Robbie was in her arms now, looking across at Mariah, a wide smile on his face.

Paul staggered to his feet, snarled at her. 'You're useless, Rowan,' he said. 'He's mine. My kid.'

There was a blur of movement then and Paul reared back unable to help the scream that tore from his throat. It was right in front of him – she was right in his face.

'Stop it!' he squealed, and stumbled backwards, a tree branch scraping across his back. He put up an arm to block out the sight of that face, its black eyes only inches away from him. 'Call her off!'

'Get out of here, Paul,' Rowan said, and she held Robbie tighter.

'Call her off!'

Mariah straightened, moved forward a step, hung there in the air, wispy, insubstantial, yet indisputably there.

Paul whimpered, crying, and a dark stain seeped across the front of his jeans. He put a hand to the wet fabric and choked on a sob.

'Fuck off!' he screamed, then turned tail and ran, crashing between the trees and out of sight.

There was a sudden silence in the woods.

'Gone,' Robbie said, breaking it.

Rowan nodded. 'Gone,' she said. Then looked at Mariah, who smiled at her. 'Thank you,' she said. 'Thank you so much.'

Mariah's smile widened and she spread her arms in a

graceful move and for a moment, Rowan and Robbie saw surrounding Mariah a spectacle of shining figures, all of them graceful, richly dressed, beautiful, eyes shining.

'Oh my god,' Rowan murmured.

In her belly, there was a fluttering sensation as the new baby kicked.

And then Mariah was gone, and with her the Fae, their fading brightness leaving Rowan blinking in the dimness of the woods.

She fell to her knees and put Robbie down, keeping one arm around him as she pressed a hand to the butterfly kicks in her belly.

'Oh Robbie,' she said. 'Did you see them?'

57

Morghan lifted her head, watched the ravens flying out from the woods and knew they were part of the great weaving. They were heading for the village green, she thought, and a smile blossomed on her face.

'Macha,' Ravenna said.

Morghan nodded. Erin.

Erin and Stephan, and Clover, and Clarice, and Krista. Lucy, Simon, Martin, Charlie, Lynsey, Marshall. Minnie.

Not just them, either. The people of Wellsford.

The families that had been here for generations, growing up in the magic that was Wellsford as well as Wilde Grove. All of them here together on this day.

As well as the newcomers. Those who would shine their lights on the world even as it descended into ruin. The Beacons.

. . .

Stoat turned his attention back to the woman facing him so brazenly. The Dark Priestess.

'Move aside!' he shouted and raised his arms to shake his fists. He wasn't afraid of ravens, nor any crows, no matter how crafty. He wasn't afraid of anything. He was the vessel of God!

'Move aside and let us take this place back in the name of the one true, living God!'

A cheer from the crowd behind him, but weaker than it ought to have been.

Those damned birds. A cheap stunt!

He focused in on the four in front of him again. He had the upper hand – they hadn't said a word!

'Move aside! This will be God's house once more!'

Morghan smiled at him, spoke finally. 'This is a sanctuary for all those who seek solace for their souls.'

Her voice, though calm, carried clearly. She looked beyond the little man with the misshapen spirit and the dark shadow feeding upon him and addressed the crowd. 'All who live from the heart are welcome.'

A voice called out. 'We live in the love of God!'

Stoat scowled at the interruption, looked at Morghan Wilde, and bared his teeth. How he hated this woman! And the one next to her – he knew who she was, oh yes, he did. She was the priest who had abandoned her own God for this sham. The Reverend Christie had told him all about her, hadn't he? Oh yes, he had.

Sorry, Mama, he thought, but women are not to be trusted in positions of authority.

He wanted to pull and rend the garments from the two women, stomp them into the mud.

'Move aside or we will move you!' he snarled. 'We have righteousness on our side.'

'I will not,' Morghan said, and she took a step forward, planted her staff in the ground and looked past Stoat. 'And you do not.'

He did not interest her.

From the village green came the amplified sound of a drumbeat, slow, steady, portentous. Morghan lifted her gaze to the weaving, felt things moving, shifting into place. Her lips lifted slightly. Whatever was to come, there was always this, the truth of the world. It would not be broken.

A formation of ravens darkened the sky as they flew overhead.

She would not be broken. Her path had begun millennia before and would carry onwards.

Next to Morghan, Catrin smiled. She lifted her hands to the sky, whispered the incantations she had once screamed into the wind on a beach against the Romans.

The clouds thickened, gathered together like a fist. The air whitened with fog.

Catrin's smile widened.

The crowd shifted, buzzing suddenly with unease.

The mist fell to surround them, and a teenaged girl gripped the cross she wore on a thin silver chain around her neck, gaze fixed on the fog that had dropped like a curtain down around them.

She was sure she could see figures moving around in it, and she hid her eyes, tears hot behind her lids.

Morghan shifted her gaze to the crowd as the ravens flew overhead and the mists fell. Out of the whiteness something moved, and a hawk landed on her shoulder.

A shocked murmur ran through the people gathered behind Stoat and they drew closer together, remembering all the stories they'd ever heard about Wellsford.

'Stop it!' the teenaged girl screamed suddenly. 'Stop frightening us!'

Her mother turned and hugged her, cried out. 'Why are you doing this?'

Morghan shook her head. 'I do not do anything. It is you who have come here to Wellsford where the world is deep, while you are not yet ready for it.'

Stoat screamed in frustration. He was losing the crowd, he could feel it, feel their fear as the mist draped over them like a shroud. It was her doing. The She-Wolf, ignoring him, talking over his shoulder. He stomped a foot. Shouted at her, spittle flying.

'You subvert the order the Lord God Himself gave the world.'

Morghan felt the others move to her side once more. Kurt, Winsome, Ambrose.

The crowd behind Stoat shuffled backwards and muttered. She smiled at them.

'We subvert nothing,' she said so that they could all hear, 'but live only in the truth of the world.' She paused, let herself feel pity for the people arrayed against her. 'Be ever hearing, but never understanding; be ever seeing, but never perceiving,' she quoted while beside her Catrin snorted derisively and Ravenna looked on impassively.

'Make the hearts of this people calloused; deafen their ears and close their eyes. Otherwise, they might see with their eyes, hear with their ears, understand with their hearts, and turn and be healed.'

Winsome gasped, recognising the Bible verse from the book of Isiah.

The crowd in front of them twisted and squirmed, bunched together, then threatened to tear apart, lost in the mist.

Morghan watched Stoat as he twitched and jerked about where he stood, mouth opening and closing in impotent howling. She saw him through the eyes of her spirit, and how twisted he was in his form. Grotesque with the spiritual scars of harms done and received. And the attaching entity who fed on him, glutting itself on his madness, its hold on the man was firm.

Morghan sighed at the sight of him and turned her attention to the drumbeat that grew slowly louder. She smiled.

'Come,' she said. 'This way.'

Morghan turned, stepped off the pathway and walked calmly between the graves to the second and oldest of the lychgates in the Sanctuary's stone wall. She stepped under its porch roof and put her hand to the gate, the hawk still upon her shoulder, and pushed it open.

Winsome paused only a moment, then hurried after her, Kurt and Ambrose on her heels.

STOAT WATCHED THEM, EYES WIDE, UNABLE TO FATHOM WHAT had just happened. Behind him the crowd – his people, all 200 or more – shifted on their collective feet and he heard crying from within their number.

'Enough!' he yelled at them, turning to face them with

burning eyes. 'Do not mind the devil but be upright in the Lord's name! We will take the church back now!'

'Who from?' one person yelled, their voice shaky. 'They've left it to us!'

The sobbing increased. 'I want to go home,' the teenager wailed.

Stoat stomped his foot again. 'We will reconsecrate it to Jesus's precious Word.'

For a moment, the people ranged in front of him were silent. The white fog pressed closer to them, threatening to hide themselves from each other.

'It was an Anglican church,' someone called out as they felt the cold touch of the mist upon their skin. 'I say we leave it to them to fix.'

There was a swelling, muttering agreement and the crowd broke apart, turned, siphoned back through the gate onto the street.

Stoat screamed at them. His righteous army, leaving without his order, turning and scrambling out of the grave-yard, back down the street, fleeing – he knew it – to the buses.

He turned back to the church that loomed out of the mist, the white fog that had fallen down from the sky and was drawing itself around him like the cold touch of a dead hand.

And in his ears pounded the steady loud beating of the drum.

Morghan walked swiftly down the old spirit path that

led behind the row of shops to the green, then paused when she heard singing. Winsome stopped just behind her.

'Is that Erin?' she asked, her voice low with wonder. 'She sings beautifully.'

'She doesn't sing of the Antlered Mother,' Ravenna said.

Catrin was smiling. 'No,' she said. 'No, she does not.'

Morghan closed her eyes and listened to the haunting words of the Morrigan's Prayer.

R*OUND THE CIRCLE THREE TIMES THREE*
A worthy channel I will be
And all your power into me
Burning bright and flowing free...

T*HE CROWD SCURRIED DOWN THE NARROW STREET TO WHERE* the entrance to the green was blocked now by two police cars, parked nose to nose across it, while in the distance sirens wailed heralding more cars on the way.

Malcolm put his hand up to stop his flock's forward momentum. The mist was thinner here, as though that woman had conjured it to fall from the sky only in the churchyard. He shuddered at the thought. At least they'd left Stoat behind. Eric had been right. The man was crazy. He'd been capering around in front of them, stomping his feet like a goat.

Bryce and Andrew stepped away from their police cars, shook their heads.

'You'd best be going on back to your buses,' Andrew said

loudly, and lifted his phone to take photos of the crowd, Bryce doing the same.

'What are you doing?' Malcolm asked, alarmed.

'We'll likely be doing you for illegal assembly and destruction of property.' Bryce lifted his shoulders in a shrug. 'We'll need IDs.' He snapped a few more shots.

Malcolm swore under his breath. He'd told Stoat – hadn't he told Stoat – that they'd need a permit to do this?

He looked around, double-checking for the man, but there was still no sight of him. Good, he thought and then shook his head, looking around at the damage they'd done when they'd followed Stoat blindly as he'd overturned the first stalls and tables.

He was suddenly ashamed, and then he was frightened.

The sirens grew nearer. Malcolm turned around to face his fellows, but they were already dispersing, heads down, hurrying to get out of Wellsford, placards dropped to the ground.

Malcolm hesitated a moment longer, looking past the police cars to the band's stage in the green. He shivered again, looking at the younger one – Erin Faith – up there in front of the microphone, eyes closed, singing.

What was she singing? He didn't know, only knew that he was afraid of her. Of the words she was singing in a haunting, otherworldly voice, of the drumbeat behind her that sounded more like a heartbeat.

What had Morghan Wilde said about Wellsford? He shook his head. Wellsford, she'd said, where the world was deep. She was right about one thing, he thought, turning now to look down the street past all the destruction they'd wrought, the food, crafts, clothes trampled over the ground, to where the church was, the mist still hanging over it as though...as though what?

Cursed, Malcolm thought, turning to follow his people back to their buses.

He never wanted to step foot in Wellsford again. Never wanted to go anywhere near its priestesses.

ROWAN SLIPPED OUT OF THE WOODS BEHIND THE VICARAGE and peered through the sudden mist in astonishment. The crowd was gone. There was no one in the churchyard at all. She set Robbie on his feet and looked at him.

'All right?' she asked.

He nodded and beamed up at her.

She lifted her head, hearing police sirens drawing closer. She should go home, perhaps. Out of the way, where it was safer.

But under the wail of sirens there was singing. Someone was on the stage in the green singing. A woman.

Rowan shivered. The tune was haunting and yet it drew her towards it. She felt the pull to go and stand on the green, listen to it properly.

A noise startled her, coming from Bridget's Sanctuary. It was a scream. She started towards it without thinking. Someone needed help.

'Mummy,' Robbie said, tugging on her hand, resisting her forward momentum. 'Lady, look.'

Rowan stopped and looked where Robbie pointed at the gate in the wall.

'Mariah,' she said, looking at the gossamer beauty who beckoned to them then smiled and vanished.

Rowan turned her head to look at the Sanctuary, from which another strangled male cry came. Robbie tugged on her hand.

'C'mon Mummy.'

She nodded. Mariah wouldn't lead her astray. If she wanted them to leave without seeing what was going on in the old church building, then that's what they'd do.

Maybe it wasn't something for her to see.

She hurried through the gate and down the grassy path that led to the green. The sirens cut out and the singing grew louder.

Behind her, Stoat screamed again.

MALCOLM LOOKED AROUND FOR PAUL SUTHERLAND, HANDS clenched as he searched the people swarming onto the three coaches for some sign of the man.

'Damn you,' he muttered. 'Where are you?'

Someone had to drive the bus back to Banwell. Malcolm snagged Roger, who looked none too pleased to be stopped.

'Isn't this a cluster-duck, then,' Roger said and shook his head. The newly arrived police, three cars worth, were parked opposite the buses, the officers making sure everyone got herded back on them.

'Have you seen Paul?' Malcolm asked, hissing the question. He wanted to get on the coach and get the heck home, pretend this day hadn't happened. Eric, he thought. They needed Eric to come home and pull everything back together.

He didn't bother asking if Roger had seen Stoat. He'd

been keeping an eye out for the American, and glad every time someone turned out not to be him.

'Paul?' Roger asked, confused. 'Who's Paul.'

'Sutherland,' Malcolm said. 'He drove the first bus.'

Roger shook his head. 'Nope,' he said.

'Can you drive it?' Malcolm asked, praying for a miracle. Hadn't Roger been a lorry driver before he'd retired?

'Yeah, I can do that,' Roger said. 'If that's what you want.'

Malcolm took a quick look around. The street was almost empty, everyone on the buses now, or left in their own cars. He nodded. 'I don't want to wait. He could be anywhere.'

Roger laughed, then stopped and gave himself a quick shake. 'That singing is spooky,' he said. 'I say we get out of here.'

'Right,' Malcolm said, relieved, then made an effort to save face. 'Live to fight another day.'

Roger looked at him, then away. 'If you say so,' he said.

58

———

MORGHAN STRODE FORWARD INTO THE CENTRE OF THE GREEN as Stephan stepped up beside Erin to sing with her.

Round the circle three times three
A worthy channel I will be
And all your power into me
Burning bright and flowing free...

Erin's voice swelled, grew firm, implacable. Stephan matched it.

I roam the battlefields again
Of warrior cries and bleeding men
And on my wings I carry them
The sacred journey home again.

WINSOME LOOKED AT MORGHAN. 'WHAT ARE THEY SINGING?' she asked, then swept her gaze around the green. Everyone was there – all the members of the Grove, and those who had come to enjoy the Ostara market. Most of them were there too. Winsome recognised many of them from the Stations of the Heart courses and from regular visits to Bridget's Sanctuary.

The young men she'd met there the other day were on the green as well, hats pulled from their heads and hands held clenched against their hearts, gazes fixed on Erin and Stephan.

And everywhere the crows and ravens. Lined up across the roof of the stage, in the trees, on top of The Copper Kettle.

Morghan took a breath before she answered. 'They're singing a prayer to the Great Queen,' she said.

Catrin tipped her head back, breathed deeply. Turned to Ravenna. 'She will be well known to you from across the sea.'

Ravenna bowed her head. 'Hail to the Queen of Life and Death,' she said.

JOHN STOAT FLINCHED AWAY FROM THE SHADOWS IN THE Sanctuary. He'd entered the building when everyone had turned away, cursing them under his breath. Cowards!

He, then, would see it through. He stood in the entrance and scowled. What heathenry was this? The baptismal font uncovered for everyone to come along and dip their toe into!

He shoved at it, wanting to overturn it, but it was heavy, too heavy to budge. He kicked at the pews instead, arranged not in rows as they ought to be, but in hippy dippy circles.

'This place is a farce!' he screamed and headed for the

altar where a candle burnt. Not for long, he vowed, and snuffed it out, then stood back to nod in satisfaction.

Bridget's flame expunged from the world.

Expunged. Another good word!

The candle wick ignited again, and Stoat narrowed his eyes at it. Put his lips over the heavy glass and blew. Smoke wafted upwards. The flame was out properly this time!

He stood back, inhaled, squared his shoulders.

Bridget's flame expunged.

When he opened his eyes, the candle was lit. His smile faded and he shifted on his feet, suddenly uneasy.

'Who's there?' he asked, calling out.

The church was dark, darker than before. Shadows moved around him; the candle burnt yellow and steady.

John Stoat cleared his throat. 'Who's there?'

He whipped his head around. Had something touched him? A shadow?

Shadows couldn't touch you. He screamed as it happened again.

Behind the altar the darkness coalesced, and someone unearthly laughed.

ROWAN HURRIED ONTO THE GREEN THEN STOPPED, STARING with everyone else up at Erin and Stephan singing on the stage. Robbie was silent in her arms, mesmerised by the birds everywhere.

ERIN HAD HER EYES CLOSED, AND KNEW SHE WAS STILL singing, Stephan at her side. She could feel his energy, the way it always entwined with her own anytime they were near one another. She knew she stood on the bandstand in the Wellsford village green, but she was elsewhere too.

Straddling the worlds.

And she stood on the edge of the woods, looking out over a meadow, and as she stood and looked a white horse thundered across the ground and she watched it, saw the crow on its back, saw the woman walking towards her, black-haired, black-eyed, fierce and laughing as she came in her swirling cloak of feathers, a raven upon her shoulder.

Erin swept into a bow, knelt before the Goddess.

'So, it is you who are calling me?' the Morrigan asked, grinning, her lips the red of blood.

'Or,' Erin said, rising. 'It is you who calls me.'

The Morrigan tipped back her head and laughed again. She spun around, feathered cloak billowing.

'Come,' she commanded.

Erin followed and in a rushing of wind or wings, she stood with the Goddess in a village.

'This is Morghan's village,' she gasped, recognising it. The Village of Life and Refuge.

The Morrigan made no answer, simply strode through the cobblestoned streets toward the church where she stopped and lifted her face to the bell tower.

There was movement in the streets, and Erin's eyes widened even as she bent her knee again and lowered her gaze to the stones at her feet.

It was Elen who joined them, she who had once given Erin the gift of diamonds. The treasure of her own self.

Behind Elen, the antlered Goddess, were others, stepping out of the mists, so many of them in so many forms and shapes, that Erin could barely count them to name.

'Now is the time,' the Morrigan said, and the raven on her shoulder stared at Erin. 'Ruin is come upon the world, the tower is falling.' She turned to Erin and smiled.

'But the light shines.'

Erin nodded, looked up at the bell tower, from which shone a light almost too bright to gaze upon.

Elen, of the ways and paths through the wilderness, smiled also, and gestured behind Erin.

Erin turned and found her sight upon the fountain, and as she watched, water flowed strongly and freely from it, sparkling clear.

From the houses around the square, people appeared, drawn closer by the light, by the flow of water, and Erin realised that the village was not deserted, but full of those who had moved there, to the village of belonging, there to make their homes, there to follow the way.

Erin closed her eyes and opened them to the stage once more, her lips still moving with the prayer.

Round the circle three times three
A worthy channel I will be
And all your power into me
Burning bright and flowing free.
I roam the battlefields again
Of warrior cries and bleeding men
And on my wings I carry them
The sacred journey home again...
I hold you gently to my breast
Peacefully and still you rest
Let no more trials be on your quest

Now all your dreams will manifest.
Peacefully resting
Morrigan's blessing
Peacefully resting
Morrigan's blessing.

ON THE GREEN, EVERYONE HAD DRAWN TOGETHER INTO THREE circles, in the middle of which stood Morghan and Winsome, robes fluttering in the breeze of a hundred wing-beats as the birds flew also in circles overhead.

Clarice led the inner circle, arms spread, steps a slow dance, the Morris dancers clicking their sticks together, following her. Krista danced the middle circle round and round the green as Erin and Stephan came to the end of the prayer and began again so that there was no beginning, no end.

Clover and Ambrose gathered up the outer circle as the ravens and crows flew overhead, around and around and around. Kurt leapt onto the stage and took up one of the drums, a double heartbeat, strong, steady, the sound of the world breathing, beating.

On and on and on.

Rowan watched, then looked where Robbie pointed, and saw the shining figure of Mariah step forward into the dance, and from the folds in the world behind her came other figures, bright and shining and beautiful beyond belief.

'Us too, Mummy,' Robbie whispered.

She nodded, and holding him tightly, entered the dance.

.   .   .

THE BIRDS SETTLED UPON THE TREES AND BUILDINGS, THE dance slowed finally and stopped. Erin and Stephan delivered Morrigan's blessing and were quiet.

Stephan stepped down from the stage and walked over to the opposite side of the green. He turned and gazed for a moment at Erin still up on the stage, bowed to her, then called out to the assembled group just as the clouds cleared and the sun broke through to shine upon them.

'We have followed the spirit path,' he said. 'And it has led us here to the green at the centre of things.'

Stephan drew breath, spoke again, lifting his arms.

'We have come here to be together, to face what has been and what is yet to come. To face it in our full, glorious strength, not alone, but with each other, our ancestors, our allies, and our gods.'

ROWAN SHIVERED WITH THE WORDS, LETTING THEM THRILL through her. She gazed around at the three great circles, at the gauzy, otherworld figures who stood with them. She looked at Morghan and Winsome standing in the centre of them all. Two women, two paths, she thought, seeing them. Two paths that converged, carried on together. Rowan squeezed her eyes shut and hugged Robbie to her.

FROM THE STAGE, ERIN SPOKE, SMILING AT STEPHAN, THEN AT them all. Her voice was low and calm, and her spirit was as bright as the light from the bell tower, as clear as the water that flowed from the fountain in the village of life and belonging.

'Hail and welcome,' she said. 'To all who call this earth home, to all in this community, to all who care for the world and everyone in it. Hail and welcome to all the gods we serve, with whom we light this world.'

There was a murmur that ran through the crowd. 'Hail and welcome.'

Erin continued, gazing around the green with suddenly expanded sight, seeing the Fae who had come to dance with them, Mariah laughing in their midst.

'Hail and welcome,' Erin said. 'Hail and welcome to our esteemed Neighbours, with whom we strive to bring the worlds together again after being too long separated.'

She lifted her hands. 'Hail to our ancestors,' she said, seeking Clover out, seeing her for a moment as Rhian, then Clover, then Rhian again, sister priestess, sister of her heart, no matter where she went, what she did.

'Hail to our ancestors, who danced these circles before us, threading the paths between brightness and destruction, and whose wisdom, successes, failings, and tears live on in our hearts, burden and blessing both.'

She brought her hands together, crossed them over her heart, closed her eyes, continued.

'We call peace into this space. We call for peace so that inside this peace we may see the light of the beacon shining bright and hear the flow of the sacred spring through our spirits.'

She fell silent and Stephan took up the call once more.

'In peace may the voice of spirit be heard,' he cried out.

The crowd replied to him. 'In peace may we be heard.'

Stephan smiled, continued. 'May there be peace in the east. May there be peace in the south. May there be peace in the west. May there be peace in the north.'

He paused, drew breath. 'May there be no more division between us. May we walk blessed by the spirits of sea, sky, and soil.' He bowed his head.

MORGHAN, PROUD OF ALL THOSE ABOUT HER, STOOD straighter under the great woven web that criss-crossed the sky above them, then passed her staff to Winsome, who took it and held it steady upon the ground in front of her.

When Morghan spoke, her voice rang out in authority over the assembled community.

'We have been called by the spirits of the North,' she said, and beside her, Winsome felt the world swing around, spinning.

'The Goddess Elen walks with us, opening to us the ways and paths of the spirit.' Morghan lifted her hands and felt the antlers upon her head.

'We have been called by the spirits of the East,' she said. 'The Goddess Brigid lights the way for us, shining brightly.'

She felt the spark of light, of fire within her, and drew it outwards into her cupped palms, where it sparked and flamed for one, bright, glorious moment.

'We have been called by the spirits of the West,' she continued, spreading her arms wide now. 'The Goddess Ceridwen offers us the deep and broad inspiration of her cauldron. We drink of her brew and dream of the world we will make.'

Morghan fixed her eyes on Erin, feeling the web gleam

and glow overhead in its great weaving, each of them a strand upon it, one part of a great and undying whole.

'We have been called by the spirits of the south. We have been called by the Great Queen,' she cried now. 'By the Morrigan who leads us now into battle. She, with her sisters, offers us protection, prophecy, and sovereignty. We will birth the Golden Children under her banner, and the wheel will turn, the weaving will be done.'

She paused, drew breath.

'And the Time of the Great Returning will be upon us.'

ON THE STAGE, KURT BEAT UPON HIS DRUM ONCE MORE, AND on the green, the circles moved once more, step by dancing step around and around, beginning again a dance that had no end.

Erin looked across at Winsome and Morghan, kept her hands pressed to her heart, and spoke one more time.

'May we be the light and flow of truth and depth,' she said.

'May we shine season to season.

'May our light turn the wheel.

'And so shall the worlds be bound together again.'

PROPHECY OF THE WILDWOOD

Five by five the thunderclaps boom,
The seas heave and run ashore
And safe from them the Golden Chil-
    dren are born.
In a rabbit hole they lie,
In a nest on high.
The trees themselves sing their
    lullaby.

AFTERWORD

Thank you all for coming on this journey this far with me – you cannot know how much I appreciate it. I'm planning two more books in this main Wilde Grove series, as you can probably tell, since we definitely haven't got to the end of the story yet! I feel like we're really only getting going.

I want to thank my good friend Sheena Cundy – author, witch, and musician – for allowing me to use her marvellous Morrigans Prayer in the last chapter of this book. Sheena took me on a guided journey not long ago, to meet the Morrigan, and I did, I met the Great Queen, and she looked at me and laughed, telling me I was too busy to be of use to her.

I think she may have changed her mind about this, as her turning up in this book was as much a surprise to me as it likely was to you.

If you would like to learn to sing or chant Morrigans Prayer for yourself, Sheena and I have put together, especially for you, her audio recording of her singing the prayer, along with a card with the text on it. You'll find details on my website at www.katherinegenet.online

May we all be beacons in this world.

Katherine

JOIN THE GROVE

Subscribe to the Wilde Grove mailing list and community to be part of the magic. Find out more at www.katherinegenet. onlinc

ABOUT THE AUTHOR

Katherine has been walking the Pagan path for thirty years, with her first book published in her home country of New Zealand while in her twenties, on the subject of dreams. She spent several years writing and teaching about dream-work and working as a psychic before turning to novel-writing, studying creative writing at university while raising her children and facing chronic illness.

Since then, she has published more than twenty long and short novels. She writes under various pen names in more than one genre.

Now, with the Wilde Grove series, she is writing close to her heart about what she loves best. She is a Spiritworker and polytheistic Pagan.

Katherine lives in the South Island of New Zealand with her wife Valerie. She is a mother and grandmother.